Tracks of the Wind

Tracks of the Wind

Colorado Trilogy - Book Three

L. Faulkner-Corzine

Bible References from The Holy Bible:
King James Version
New King James Version
New Living Bible
Net Bible
New International Version
International Standard Version
Aramaic Bible in Plain English

Tracks of the Wind

"My feet have followed in His tracks;
I have kept to His way
and not turned aside."
Job 23: 11

"The LORD is the one who shaped the mountains,
stirs up the winds,
and reveals His thoughts to mankind.
He turns the light of dawn into darkness
and treads on the heights of the earth.
The LORD God of Heaven's Armies is his name!"
Amos 4:13

Heavenly Father, please bless this book!
May it entertain so readers will turn to the next page.
May it inspire so they will turn to You!

DEDICATION

"Wait on the LORD: be of good courage, and He shall strengthen your heart: wait, I say, on the LORD." Psalm 27:14

The final book in this trilogy is dedicated to Casey and Katie Jones. Their uniquely honorable love story inspired the one found in this novel. This devoted young couple exemplified both courage and faith as they waited on the Lord. Waiting and trusting in God's timing, they fasted from dating, allowing God to bring them to the right person at the right time. It wasn't easy! It meant date nights of playing the guitar for Grandma or watching TV with Mom & Dad. Through it all they remained faithful, for they believed that God would answer their prayers and lead them to their one true companion for life! Now if you ask them…would they do it again? Their answer is…
Oh yes! It was worth the wait!

SPECIAL THANKS

To the man I prayed for since the age of 15, my husband Gary,
who has been my staunch supporter,
wise and constructive critic, greatest advocate
and always my very best friend!

Another heartfelt thank you to my family and friends:
Jan and Kay Knigge, Sandy and Steve Mathis,
Jeff Corzine, Julee Marzella, Franny Kirkland
and to the San Juan Ranch Equine Expert's:
Brenda Harris & most especially Jocelyn Marzella!

You all have been so wonderfully supportive
and encouraging as I struggle along,
attempting to do the work,
I believe God has led me to do.

TABLE OF CONTENTS

Dear Reader,

I hope you will enjoy this final installment in my Colorado Trilogy, <u>Tracks of the Wind</u>. It takes place approximately two decades after the first two books end. Come along for the ride as you meet up again with the characters from both <u>Giant in the Valley</u> and <u>Wings on the Mountain</u>. I've included this character map to help you keep track of who is who. Don't see Lavenia Wrenford? Hmm?

Please don't forget the Discussion Points and Prologue Previews in the back!

If you've enjoyed these books, please share them with friends. Writing a review on Amazon would also be greatly appreciated. I would love to hear your thoughts regarding this trilogy as well as future projects.

Please e-mail your comments to: lfaulknercorzine@gmail.com
You can also visit my website at: http://lfaulknercorzine.com

Thank you and God bless you,
Lynn

PROLOGUE

New York City, NY
1883

"What sorrow awaits you who lie awake at night, thinking up evil plans. You rise at dawn and hurry to carry them out, simply because you have the power to do so." Micah 2:1

The diminutive Irishman, Keefer Flynn, stood in the ornate library, hat in hand, as he waited for his pay to be counted out. It was odd that he'd never noticed it before, but Lavenia Wrenford was showing her age. That or perhaps the rumors were true. She had always been stunningly beautiful. Even as the years passed and her thick dark hair became streaked with silver, it seemed only to make her more alluring and elegant. Now as Keefer read the signs, he was sure the gossips were right. The woman whose posture had always been ramrod straight, now drooped like a withered flower as she bent over her mahogany desk. The skin on her manicured hands was paper thin and spotted. Her long graceful fingers now trembled as she laid each bill on the gilded blotter.

Well now, the rumors must be true—and what a shame it is, Keefer mused. *She's sick all right—maybe even dying.* The realization roused no pity in the man. For Lavenia Wrenford was not the type to receive pity nor to give it. She looked down on her peers, hated her family and had no friends. Still, it was painful to see this once magnificent woman, now only a shadow of her former self. Especially so for Keefer, for Lavenia's demise meant the end of a very long and lucrative arrangement. He considered himself a Purveyor of Information, although some might call him a *snitch*. Regardless of the title, he liked what he did, and because he was good at it, he had a good life. Lavenia was his best client, but he hadn't learned anything of use in quite a while. If she grew impatient or if she were dying, these monthly payments might end abruptly. Deciding he better remind her of his worth, he tapped his hand on her desk and said in his most pleasing Irish lilt, "I'll tell ya true Vinny, I've been workin' mighty hard on this one. Been trailin' that young society touf, day and night. Oh yes, day and night, just like I promised. He's quite the gadabout—hobnobs with the very best of society—and by-gum the very worst—I can assure ya of that! So far he's done plenty his Mama wouldn't approve of—but nothin' we can use—not yet anyway! He acts all proper and genteel in front o' his folks and all them other rich swells. 'Course he does just what he pleases when he thinks no one's a-lookin'. Won't be long before he makes that one big mistake. Then old Keefer will be right there to get the goods on him. Ya can count on me!"

Lavenia sighed as she gazed up, her golden eyes flashing, as a feral look of pleasure spread across her lined and ashen face, "No need to worry Keefer, I haven't lost faith in you. Just keep watching. I have grand plans for that spoiled young man. He's a totally self-absorbed, scheming sort of fellow and I'm told he's becoming more egotistical by the day. A true nouveau riche—new money—no class. Most importantly, his family is closely linked with my daughter Augusta and the Graingers. As you know—for far too long she has escaped my revenge. But when you complete your task, that problem will be remedied. Success will be all the sweeter when it's mine! As you know very well, my dear Mister Flynn, I will never give up!"

Keefer nodded as he picked up the money, folded it and stuffed it into his pocket. "That's a fact Vinny. Ya never give up and neither will I. Sooner or later that gent will make that one big—can't take it back—mistake." Shaking his thumb at himself he grinned, adding, "He'll make it, I'll see it—and he'll do anything we ask him—just to keep the world from knowing about it!"

Lavenia slowly rose from her chair and walked Keefer to the door. "That's right," she sneered. "You be there to see Mister Timothy Barrett Tulane make that mistake. And I know I can count on you to help him make it even bigger—if it's at all possible! Then he will do anything I ask of him, just to save his own skin. Of course, the Tulanes are Augusta's dearest friends. They will go down with the Graingers." A scornful smile spread across her face as she added, "Then and only then, will I be able to—rest in peace!"

Chapter 1
The Mistake

Central Park
New York-1883

"He lies in wait near the villages; from ambush, he murders the innocent. His eyes watch in secret for his victims." Psalm 10:8

"The LORD will repay him for the blood he shed." 1 Kings 2:32

Nineteen-year-old Timothy Barrett Tulane stared down at the still form of his father. The man's black frock coat was in disarray, the front of his starched white shirt spoiled—with powder burns, a bullet wound, and a shocking amount of blood. His stomach lurched at the sight and he cringed at the look of shock frozen on the older man's face.

So, it finally happened. My father the millionaire—is—dead, he whispered. Still he couldn't quite believe it was true. *But now...what am I? A millionaire with a full life ahead of me, filled with power and success? Or a murderer headed for the gallows? Why did I think only of the benefits and not of the consequences?*

Barrett ran a hand through his thick blonde hair and cursed, as the whole ugly scene played out once again in his mind.

That morning had begun like so many others. Father and son out for an early morning canter through Central Park. As usual Lee and Grant, the two elegant, high-stepping thoroughbreds were tacked up and brought to the front gate by Kraus, their groomsman. They had just entered the park and the very first words spoken by Westin Tulane began the argument.

"Nothing like spring time in Central Park, hey Timmy?"

"Father!" the younger man groaned, "have I not been going by the name Barrett since my fifteenth birthday? That was four years ago, you'd think you could remember your own son's name! Timothy...worse yet, Timmy Tulane, sounds like a good name for a ditch digger or a chimney sweep. It's much too common for one of the wealthiest men in New York!   I sign everything, T. Barrett Tulane, now that's a name for a man who commands respect!"

Wes didn't know what to do about his son's growing arrogance, but he and Emily had finally agreed that their egotistical boy had to be reined in.   "Son, I don't mind your going by the name Barrett if you prefer.   You were named for two of the finest men your mother and I have ever known.   If you become in any way like Timothy Grainger or Barrett O'Brien, your mother and I will be proud indeed.   I wish you could understand that it's your actions that earn the respect of others.   It's the presence or lack of integrity that gives a man a good or bad name.   It's how you conduct yourself that will make the difference.   I've known a lot of rich scoundrels in my day and many an honorable ditch digger.   And I might add, that you are simply the son of one of the wealthiest men in New York.   Mister T. Barrett Tulane, no matter how lofty that may sound, is just a boy who has no wealth at all—not yet he doesn't.   We owe our ease of living to Amelia Langstrom-Drew.   Otherwise you would be the son of a café owner in Missouri.   Actually, you probably wouldn't even be alive.   It was Amelia who provided the medical care needed to bring you into this world.   You, most of all, owe it to her memory to manage her estate with wisdom and honor.   That is why your mother and I have insisted that you continue your education."

Barrett gave a loud groan and rolled his eyes, "Yes, yes…of course I am grateful for all Auntie Amelia gave us.   If you'll recall she was the one who always told me that a young man should see the world.   In keeping with her wishes, I think it both wise and honorable for me to go abroad for a year or two. I want to see London and Paris before attending Princeton.   If she were still alive, I'm sure the idea would please our dear benefactress.   After all Father, why have all this money if we never enjoy it?   I'm sure you and mother do enough *good deeds* with the Langstrom money to please the old gal.   Just as it would please her for me to see Europe!"

Wes kicked his chestnut gelding into a canter.   He was ashamed of his spoiled and arrogant son.   Sadly, he had helped to make him that way and now he feared he might have waited too long.   Suddenly, he yanked on the reins and spun his horse around.   "I should have taken a stronger hand with you years ago! We've loved you too much.   Probably because we buried three children be-fore you and three after.   You're ungrateful and self-centered, and that stops—today!   I'm writing you out of my will, and out you'll stay, until you become the right kind of man.   One worthy and responsible enough to inherit a fortune.

You better pray you can prove yourself during the challenge ahead or you'll never be the wealthiest man in New York. Instead, my boy, you could end up the poorest!"

Barrett suddenly grew pale, "What do you mean—the poorest? What do I have to do to *prove* myself and what challenge are you talking about?"

"I've spoken to the Captain of a freighting ship. It sails in three days. You will start as the cook's assistant. Along with peeling onions and potatoes you will empty the slop buckets and swab decks. If you fail to do your work properly…" Wes suddenly grimaced then continued slowly, "I have to warn you son…should you refuse to work or not work hard enough, you will be given no quarter. They administer the lash on sailors who shirk their duties!"

"Hah!" Barrett scoffed, "Mother would never allow that—not to her only child! When word of your doing such a thing to me gets out—our society friends would shame you right out of New York." When Barrett saw his words had no effect on his father, he grew silent for a moment then tried a different tack, "Come now Father, you're being overly dramatic. I graduated at the top of my class at Cutler's Preparatory Institution. After my travels, I can still attend Princeton, if it pleases you. I'm only asking for a twenty-four-month holiday." Giving his father the look of practiced sincerity, which had always worked before, he added, "Now you see this isn't worth getting upset over. I'm a good chap, just a bit high-spirited, that's all! Surely there's no need for me to prove myself. Just think, if I should sail away on some filthy old ship, you two would worry day and night. I'd wager you'd both be sick within a fortnight."

As Westin Tulane listened to his son, he realized that he was already sick—heart sick. Physically he was healthy, a man in his prime although strands of silver tinged his dark hair. This time as he listened to his son's manipulative words, he realized that this is what the boy had always done. Finally, seeing this for what it was, Wes suddenly felt a great deal older than his fifty years. Tears came to his eyes and he clenched his jaw. "My dear boy, may God forgive me. I have allowed you to use and dominate me, your mother and indeed, everyone around you. Your mother and I love you—we always will. But your unscrupulous attitude must be dealt with and soon! As for our society friends, your mother is a back woods girl from Tennessee and I grew up as a poor Missouri boy. We both are vastly aware that our so called social standing comes from 'Langstrom' wealth and nothing else. We could care less what the New York elite think of us. That has always been your concern, not ours! We know

3

you're embarrassed by our country ways and over the years we've tried not to shame you. Because we love you, son, we've always wanted the very best for you. Gave you all the things we never had, thinking you would be as grateful as we were. That was foolish, for it's impossible to appreciate wealth and ease until you've experienced want and hard work. We've tried but failed to teach you about responsibility, honor and integrity. But I vow, if it's the last thing I do, you *will* learn those things!" Wes saw the anger building in his son's face but continued on, "You will board a cargo ship called the Sea Swan in three days. It will return in three months. If in that time, you have earned the Captain and the crews respect then you will be allowed the privilege of attending Princeton University. However, should they report that you are lazy, spoiled and arrogant, then you will sail again, if they'll have you! If not, I'll find another ship. You said a young man should travel and see the world and that's just what you'll do. The education you need right now, Son, is a lesson in humility—and that's my final decision. By the way, your mother is in full agreement!"

Bile rose in Barrett's throat, he couldn't believe what his father was saying. He had never threatened anything like this before. But now, looking into Westin Tulane's stern face he knew that there was no changing his mind. The whole idea of working on a cargo ship alongside rough and grubby sailors disgusted and terrified him. Fear and anger raced through his veins and without thinking, he pulled the revolver from his coat pocket. His hands trembled as he aimed it at his father. "You can't do this to me—I won't let you!"

Sensing the tension around them, the horses became anxious. They sidestepped and pulled on their reins, becoming more and more un-nerved as their riders became more agitated.

"You put that away right now," Wes ordered, "or I'll take you to the woodshed like I should have done a decade ago! Son, don't you see? You want me to change my mind but here you are—proving to me how arrogant and misguided you are. No son with an ounce of respect aims a weapon at his own father! Your Aunt Amelia gave you that revolver and me it's twin to protect us against bandits. Never to be used against each other!" Wes worked at keeping his mount calm as he reined him closer to his son and held out his hand, "Now boy, you give me that gun and we'll forget you ever did anything so foolish."

Barrett defiantly cocked the gun instead, "No! We'll come to some kind of understanding first," he hissed. "We could all be happy if you just let me do what I want! What kind of father dumps his only son on some dirty ship? And you would allow them to beat me if I refused to peel potatoes?" Barrett too was struggling to keep his mount in check and reined it around in a quick circle. His eyes were bright with rage as he kept the pistol pointed at his father. "How do you like it when I threaten you? I wouldn't survive a day on that ship let alone three months. So, I'll put this back in the holster, but only if you promise not to change your will. You want me to go to sea—fine! The SS Servia also sets sail from New York to Liverpool in three days. I'll gladly board that ship! After this—I think we both need some time to forget what's been said and done."

"No son," Wes groaned, "this isn't a day either of us will ever forget. You have just proved that you are headed down a path of self-indulgence and ruination. I'm going to make an honorable man out of you—or die trying!"

Barrett raised an eyebrow and sneered, "Now Father, you really shouldn't tempt me like that," he taunted, as he circled his horse. "You know hardly anyone comes to the park this time of day. The truth is, without you, I wouldn't just be the son of a wealthy man. I would be a wealthy man! You said tomorrow you will cut me out of your will. That means if you died today—tomorrow I could do as I please."

The look of cold-hearted animosity in Barrett's eyes was frightening. Wes didn't want to believe it, but it seemed his son might just pull that trigger! Realizing the danger, Wes spurred his horse and the gelding lunged forward. He grabbed the barrel of the pistol, intending to point it away from them both. Whether Barrett meant to or not, the gun was triggered and both horses reared high, then fell over backwards. Barrett managed to jump free as the pistol flew from his hand. He stood motionless as both horses quickly got to their feet and then disappeared over the bridge. It also seemed as if they carried away the rage that had consumed him only moments earlier. He felt nothing as he stared down at Westin Tulane. His father had always been a simple and kind-hearted man. Now as he stared into his open but unseeing eyes—it was obvious—he was dead.

Just then, Barrett's attention was drawn to the shrill pitch of a policeman's whistle and someone shouting in the distance, 'Was that gunfire? Where did it come from?' Then his attention was drawn to a noise coming from the nearby bushes, as a little man stepped out from them and hurried towards him. It was one of the Central Park grounds keepers that walked the bridle paths, making sure the city dwellers didn't see, or more importantly didn't step on anything…unpleasant. Barrett never took any notice of these men other than to say, 'My horse has left something for you, old boy. Something for you to remember him by.' It took Barrett a moment to realize that this insignificant man was actually speaking to him. In fact, he had taken him by the arm and was shaking him.

"Listen up boy—and listen good," the little man hissed, "unless ya want to hang for murder, ya best do what I say!" He released Barrett then picked up the fallen gun and wrapped the dead man's limp hand around the grip. "I heard him say you both carry the same kind of gun." At that the man leaned over and patted the corpse. When he found the older man's pistol, he handed it to Barrett, "Here put this in yer pocket."

Mind still numb, Barrett mumbled, "No, you don't understand. It was a simple accident. We were just arguing—we always argue!"

"Yeah, I heard every bit of what you said—and what he said too! Then you aimed your gun, cocked it and pulled the trigger! That's what the law calls murder, me bucko!" he snapped as he grabbed Barret by the lapels, "now listen to me, boy! The constable's comin' this way and you'll talk yourself right into a noose if you don't keep your mouth shut."

Barrett vehemently shook his head, "No one would hang me! The Tulanes are important people with power and influence!"

"You're a fool! Even rich people hang for murder, kid. So just keep shakin' your head like that, you're confused, everything happened so fast. Just keep mum and let ole Keefer do the talkin'. I'll get ya out o' this!"

Barrett didn't have to pretend to be confused. He stood over his father's lifeless body, shaking his head while he listened to the stranger give his made up, eye-witness account to the police.

"Yes sir! I seen the whole thing!" Keefer winced, as he wiped his face with a large bandana, "these two gents was havin' themselves a nice ride. Then a man jumps out from them bushes over there. He was wearin' raggedy clothes with a dirty red scarf over his face. He pulled a big o' knife from his boot, grabs the reins of the older man's horse and says, 'I'll slit yer horses throat and then yourn if ya don't throw down yer purses, watches or anything else that's worthy of m' trouble.' This older fella here," Keefer said, pointing down at the slain man, "he told that thief to push off just as he made his horse rear up, then drew that fancy pistol of his, see he's still holdin' it. I figured that sorry robber would turn tail and run but he jumped up and grabbed a holt of the man's gun instead. The horse reared up again but by-gum that bandit hung on and somehow, he turns the pistol around and—boom. The next thing I know this fellow is lying dead on the ground, and his son here, poor boy, he's standing over him in shock. Both horses took off that way, for home I reckon. The bandit though, he ran north, if ya hurry ya might catch him!"

Keefer turned towards Barrett gently patting him on the back then spoke softly to the constable. "Horrible way to lose your father. Tis a sad day when fine upstandin' gentlemen, like these two, can't go for a peaceful ride through Central Park."

Barrett said nothing as policemen and on lookers gathered around. After a while, Keefer pulled the constable aside again and whispered, "The boy has suffered quite a blow. You've got your work to do here, so I'll just be takin' him home and help him break the sad news to his mother."

Chapter 2
The Prayer

Rocky Mountains
Colorado-1883

"How can a young person stay on the path of purity? By living according to your word. I seek you with all my heart; do not let me stray from your commands. I have hidden your word in my heart that I might not sin against you." Psalm 119:9-11

Tanner McKenna rested his hands on the saddle horn and gazed out across the morning mist, breathing in the beauty of his favorite mountain refuge. The pine and aspen trees were stark silhouettes against the blazing red glory that spanned the eastern horizon. "From here it seems as if I could see right into next week," he whispered, "if only I could see into the future and know for sure, which move is the right one." Swinging down from the saddle, he dropped the reins, ground tying his mount. Taking the Bible from his saddle bag he made himself comfortable on his favorite rock. The worn leather opened to Genesis and he read the words out loud, "In the beginning—God," slowly Tanner nodded, "Lord, that sums up just how I feel. I don't want to begin anything unless I'm sure You approve. Don't want to take a step without You! I've got a fork in the road coming up and I need some divine direction! I want to fit life around Your plans, Lord, but I need You to show me the way."

Too restless to sit, Tanner stood and stripped the saddle and bridle from Bonny, his Appaloosa mule. Being born the same summer, they were literally lifelong friends. This was her favorite grazing spot and he knew she would be here when he got back. He gave her an affectionate scratch behind the ears, then picked up his rifle and headed down the mountain trail, one of many that he could have walked blind-folded. But being born to the mountains and their dangers, he kept his eyes open and his wits about him. Coming to a high ledge, he stopped and gazed down onto the valley below. White barked Aspen trees dotted the hillsides. Their leaves a kaleidoscope of changing colors from green to yellow, yellow to amber, amber to crimson. Savoring this breathtaking view, he continued his prayer, "She's out there Lord—somewhere. I know you have that one woman that will be my soulmate, my other half. I want to be where you need me to be so that we can find each other. I know she's part of the plan you have for me." He stopped for a moment to breathe in the crisp pine and sage scented air that was so much a part of this special place. "Lord, I know You made all this perfection for your children to enjoy. And just as surely, I know you made someone special for me and You made me for her! I don't want to do anything that hinders your plan to bring us together. I know you don't mean for everyone to marry but I believe that it is Your plan for me. I believe it because I feel a loneliness for her—more every day. You've blessed me with strong examples of happy marriages, like Ma and Pa and Uncle Quin and Aunt Mariah! Reckon that's partly why I'm so eager for my own marriage to begin. Seems strange to be missing someone I've never met—but I do. She might be right down there in the lowlands or maybe even across the ocean. I know it might not be the right time for you to bring us together. So, until then, I'll keep her close in my prayers. Wherever she is and whatever she's doing today...please Lord, keep her safe, comfort and protect her. If one of us must have a bad day...let me carry that burden for her. Let her day be filled with happiness and joy. Most importantly Lord, help us both to love You with our whole hearts!" Tanner frowned and chewed on his lip for a moment then added sheepishly, "One more thing Lord. I gotta ask ya this. Please keep all those other men—away from *my girl*. There's sure to be others that will see how special she is and fancy spendin' their time with her. Whisper to her heart Lord. Tell her to wait for me—just like I'm waitin' for her!"

Suddenly, he heard the snap of dry timber, and spotted an enormous bull elk trotting down the side of the hill just across from him. "Sam," Tanner grinned, "hello there, old friend."

Samson was far and away the biggest elk on the mountain. He weighed at least a thousand pounds, was over six feet tall at his shoulder, and the span of his antlers was nearly sixty inches across. Tanner's father, Shadrack McKenna, had saved Samson when he'd fallen into a ravine as a newborn calf. Still, the moment her baby was safe, the protective mama had nearly killed Shad as she chased him through the forest! That had been the same summer Tanner was born, and though Samson had never been a pet, the McKennas and their mountain neighbors had spurned the idea of making meat from the handsome bull. Thanks to their benevolence, Samson grew large and powerful, siring more than his share of strong calves. For nearly two decades he had been the great patriarch elk of the Rockies.

Samson and Tanner stared at one another for a long while, a silent measure of respect among two creatures who had been born to the mountains.

"You still look pretty good old man!" Tanner said softly. "This will be our eighteenth summer."

While he was wondering why eighteen was young for him but very old for Samson, a younger bull elk crashed through the brush and bugled his challenge. It was the beginning of the rut and this prancing upstart looked like he might just be the old bull's equal. Filled with confidence, Samson lifted his mighty head and snorted, accepting the challenge. The fight began as the bulls circled each other, curling back their upper lips, grinding their teeth and grunting their mutual disdain. Tanner feared for his old friend as the two bulls suddenly turned and lunged at each other with heads down. The sound of their huge antlers crashing together echoed throughout the mountains. The younger bull was powerful but Samson had technique, again and again he was able to throw the younger bull off balance by the simple twist of his head. Unfortunately, as the battle continued, age coupled with experience wasn't enough to overpower brute strength and youthful stamina. Tanner winced as he watched Samson losing ground.

"Give up Sam," Tanner groaned, "break off and run!" He had seen bull elks fight before, and usually the weaker one would just pull away and head for the hills. But until today, Samson had always been the biggest and the strongest, it just wasn't in him to run away—so he kept on fighting. Soon both bulls were breathing hard while the crack of their antlers clashing together was repeated over and over. Both stubbornly refusing to give up. Had they been in an open field it might have ended differently, but they were on the side of the mountain, head to head with their antlers entwined. Being on the higher ground the younger bull had the advantage. He dug in with his powerful hind legs and drove Samson back, pushing him down the mountain. Just below them was a hundred-yard stretch of crumbling shale. The younger bull made one final lunge and Samson was driven onto the lose rock. Instantly, he lost his footing and began to slide down the mountain. He slid for sixty yards until his left foreleg became wedged in a crevice, and he bellowed in pain as his body was yanked to a stop. Samson was exhausted and in pain but the feeling of being caught this way, terrified him. He fought and thrashed to free himself. Tanner winced when he heard a loud crack. Finally, Samson yanked his leg from the crevice then tumbled and slid to the bottom of the hill.

"Ah Sam," Tanner groaned as he watched the bull struggling to his feet and saw his foreleg dangling at an odd angle, "I'm so sorry boy. A McKenna saved ya once but there's only one thing I can do for ya now. Tears clouded his eyes and he reached for his fifty caliber Sharps. "Can't let ya suffer." Taking a bullet from his pocket he loaded the gun then wiped his eyes with the back of his shirt sleeve. He swung his rifle into place only to see Samson, on his three remaining legs, bolting through the bushes and out of sight. "Why do ya have to make it harder, Sam. I don't want to do this—but I've got to! Oh Lord," he groaned, "help me get to him before a bear or wolf pack brings him down."

An hour later, Tanner's handsome face was grim as he made his way around stacks of cut lumber and uncut logs at the saw mill. It wasn't hard for him to spot his father. He was the biggest man in the yard, standing head and shoulders above the other men, as he stacked long planks onto the back of a freight wagon.

When Shadrack McKenna glanced across the yard, he quickly lost the grin that always came from seeing his only child. The two men looked more like brothers than father and son. Both were exactly six feet, three inches tall with hair as black as coal and eyes as green as the forest. Shad had a bit of silver in his hair, as well as more muscle, but Tanner was quickly catching up to his father on that count.

"What's wrong?" Shad asked when Tanner came close enough to hear over the mill's whirring sawblade.

"It's Samson! What we've feared finally happened. A stronger bull challenged him today and pushed him right down a shale slide. He has a broken foreleg, Pa. I knew what had to be done. But even on three legs—he was too fast for me. I was up on the ridge with Bonny. I couldn't follow him and risk her breaking a leg too. So, I went home to fetch /a pack mule and your rifle. It seems kind o' brutal but it would be a waste not to dress him out. Figured this was something you and me—well—something we needed to do together."

"McKenna—what's the problem?" It was Doherty, the mill owner, who shouted from the tower as he watched over the men. "You know we've gotta get that lumber cut and load the wagons tonight. I promised delivery tomorrow!"

Shadrack squared his shoulders and nodded, "Yes Sir, and it'll get done. Right now, my son needs me to help him with somethin' important. Once we've got it sorted out, we'll come back and finish up here." When Doherty gave him a skeptical look, Shad added, "If me and my boy have to work all night—that order will be ready to roll come mornin'."

Without another thought for Doherty, Shad exchanged knowing glances with Tanner, "All right son," he sighed, as they walked towards the hitching rail, "Samson has always been real special. I know we've both dreaded this day but it's here now and—we know what we've got to do. We may have a lot of hard ridin' ahead. That brute, even on three legs, could do some travelin'," Shad grunted as he mounted Boone, his stout buckskin stallion. "I'll take the lead, son."

Tanner swung up on Bonny, grabbed the pack mule's rope and dallied it around the saddle horn. Soon, they were riding up and down the high-country paths that they knew as well as they did each other.

Shad was relieved when he was the first to spot Samson. The old bull stared straight at him, as if he knew that once again the man was there to help. Shad sucked in a breath, then took the shot.

Tanner rode up next to his father and let out a long sigh, "I was hopin' to spare ya that, Pa. Know you had a fondness for old Samson, since he and I were both born the same year."

Shad rested a hand on his son's shoulder, "And I wanted to spare you."

Tanner couldn't help but smile. His father was the best man he'd ever known. As his gaze settled on the once magnificent animal he shook his head, "Maybe I should have gone ahead and tracked Sam on my own. But when he took off like that, it just seemed like something we were supposed to do together."

"I feel the same, son—ya did the right thing! Ya know the Johnson's live nearby and they've been havin' a hard time of it. We'll take the meat to them, then get back to the mill." Shad sighed, "We've sure got a heap o' work ahead of us."

"Yep, the McKenna men will be sawing logs all night—and for once—I don't mean snorin'!"

Shad smiled, then he became serious, "While we're workin', why don't ya tell me, what's been troublin' ya? Might help to talk it through!"

Tanner shook his head and sighed, "You and Ma—you two have always been able to read me just like Black-eyed Jack reads sign. You know I usually tell you both when I'm prayin' over something important. But this time it's especially hard to tell Ma. She always tears up when I talk of leanin' home!"

Shad winced at the idea of his son leaving and grunted, "Thought it was somethin' like that. So, have ya decided to take Quin up on his offer?"

Tanner's eyebrows went up and he winced. "So, you already know about that— do ya? Been prayin' about it—harder than I ever have. You know I've been doin' a little bit of everything, trying to figure out what God would have me do. I work at the mill part-time, help out at the mission for Uncle Quin, and of course I've been breakin' and sellin' horses." A shy smile crossed the young man's face as he added, "And while I'm doin' those things, I've been keeping a look out for my own 'sweet girl', like Ma's always been to you! There aren't many up here to choose from but I know my girl's somewhere, Pa. Don't want to leave if she's already here or headed this way. Don't want to stay if she's across the country and waitin' for me to come find her!"

Shad smiled in understanding, "Yer still mighty young, son. Could be the one God has fer ya is still in pig-tails and playin' with dolls. Remember yer Mama was just eighteen when we wed! 'Course I had been wantin' and longin' for a bride fer years. But even then, she wasn't quite ready for a husband. I had to be a mighty patient man for a time. As I've told ya before—after one long and lonely winter I was determined to find me a bride. Proposed to a passel of women. It sure hurt when they all turned me down—but thank God, they did! 'Cause I gave up and came home and found that God had yer Mama right here waitin' fer me! 'Course that's kind o' unusual. Have no idea what the Lord has in mind fer you." Shad ran a hand over his face, "Hate to see ya leave, son, but if God's tellin' ya to go then I'm sure not gonna tell ya otherwise. I know yer hankerin' to find a wife but ya got to think on how yer gonna provide fer her and any young'uns that come along. I know yer a prayin' man and yer Ma and me couldn't be prouder of ya! But now tell me son, of all the things that ya've done...what calls to ya?"

"What do you mean, calls to me?"

There was silence as the men picketed the animals where the old elk had fallen. As Shad spread out the canvas to lay the meat on, he explained, "Son, when I come to these mountains, there was good money to be had in trappin', so that's what I did. For the same reason, when Doherty built the sawmill I got a job there. He lets me work as much as I like. It's steady when I need the money but it's not the kind of work that calls to me. On the other hand, when I'm carvin' or buildin' somethin', that's different. I love the smell and the feel of the wood in my hands. It pleases me to carve with a chisel or swing a hammer. That kind of work excites and soothes me at the same time. There's a kind o' thrill when I take a block of wood and release the secrets hidden inside. Or build a table or bed that a family will enjoy for generations. It's work that feeds my soul, Tanner. Yer Mama feels the same way about her drawin's. And that's what yer Ma and I want for you—to have the kind of work that feeds your soul!"

Tanner gazed out across the mountain range, "Wish I could carve like you or look at a view like this and draw it like Ma. I reckon I know what yer talkin' about though. If there's one thing that calls to me, I reckon it's workin' with horses. Feel like I can breathe better when I'm around them. I love the rhythm of ridin' up and down a mountain trail, listening to the scuff of their hooves and the creak of saddle leather. I love workin' with a green colt or filly and teaching them that a partnership with me is a good thing. I like seeing them finally respond to the training. I love it when…" Tanner lowered his head and chuckled, "Yeah Pa, I guess I've always known what calls to me. I want to raise and train horses. I want to be a rancher!"

"Well, yer sure enough the best trainer I've ever known, son. But unless you can do it on a bigger scale than we've been doin' here, it won't be enough to support a family. And a ranch of any size will cost a heap o' money."

"I know Pa, and the best place to start up a ranch is down in the low country. I love these mountains, but if you want a lot of horses, you need to feed them through the winter. We both know that's not easy up here."

Shad stretched his back and groaned, "Nope, don't recall us ever complainin' that winter in the mountains was too easy!"

Tanner chuckled, "Even the folks in the lowlands probably don't complain that winter's too easy, but I still reckon it's easier down there than it is here!"

"Sounds like you've already done some thinkin' on this. How ya plannin' on payin' fer it? Sounds like you'll need more 'n just a couple hundred acres and good land down below won't come cheap."

"That's the hard part—in lots of ways!" Tanner said softly. "Didn't know what to think when Uncle Quin offered me a job. Never thought I'd want to work for a company back east, but he needs someone he can trust. Wants me to be his eyes and ears, make sure his interests are being handled honorably. He even wants me to sail to the orient and bring back a big cargo of spices and other trade goods. Sounds like an adventure, but it's more than that, I'd really be doing somethin' that would help him and I could earn and save quite a bit of money. Enough to pay for a good size piece of land and get a good start."

"How l-long do ya think…" Shad struggled to say the words, "how long do ya think ya'll have to stay away?"

Tanner caught the sadness in his father's voice and muttered, "'Bout three years—no more than that, I hope! If I didn't need the money, Pa, I wouldn't go. But now that I've talked this over with you, I'm realizing that to have the kind of future I want…I need to do this. And Pa—I'd sure appreciated it—if you'd help me tell Ma!"

Chapter 3
High Society

"She obeys no one, she accepts no correction. She does not trust in the LORD, she does not draw near to her God." Zephaniah 3:2

Mosslet Way always seemed magical on the night of the New Year's Eve Ball. Hundreds of burning torches lit the winding lane leading up to the white stone mansion. Guests stepped out of their carriages under a heavenly canopy that could be likened to a cape made for royalty. For the evening boasted a clear velvety black sky adorned with a round, pearlescent moon and an infinity of diamond-like stars. After all, the beauty of a flawless gem must always be displayed in an exquisite setting.

Once inside, the grandeur or perhaps more accurately, the enchantment continued. Standing at the top of the long marble stairway, a distinguished white-haired butler announced each guest. "Mister and Missus Tytus Grainger," he proclaimed in a refined voice, adding somewhat condescendingly, "from the state of—Colorado."

Tytus leaned towards the man, "Best state in the union!" he said with a nod, then laid his gloved hand over Augusta's as they gracefully descended the curved marble steps, leading down to the magnificent ballroom.

Curious eyes lifted and a general hum filled the air as the cream of New York society scrutinized the arrival of *those Westerners* with open curiosity. The gossip regarding their hostess Emily Tulane's special guests, had swung the pendulum of chin-wagging from one extreme to another. One tall-tale was that they were poor, hillbilly relations of Emily's. Come for a handout no doubt. The other, more popular fabrication, was that Grainger was the un-titled second son of a British Viscount who had made his fortune in the West! Regardless of the gossip, not even the harshest critic could deny that Tytus and Augusta Grainger were a striking couple.

At forty-eight, the threads of silver in Ty's dark hair made the already handsome man seem even more elegant and distinguished. Tall and strong, he was dashing in his formal dress clothes, although he refused to wear the dress slippers the tailor at Tuxedo Park insisted on. "I'll wear that tailless coat you called a Tuxedo," he said begrudgingly, "but my western boots will do me just fine—and that's final!"

Augusta had smiled at this, Ty was always Ty, East or West, city or country the man never felt out of place or ill at ease. Augusta wished she had half his confidence. Normally, she didn't care what anyone thought of her, as long as she was acceptable to God and Ty didn't complain. Now, however, as she gazed down at the pale high-society women, she felt like a thistle in a garden of lilies. Augusta's skin was a rosy bronze from spending her days riding horses in the bright Colorado sunshine. Though not fashionable, her sun kissed complexion was flawless and her face was smooth but for the smile lines that flared at the edges of her dark rimmed golden eyes. Augusta forced a serene smile even as she held her husband's arm in a death grip, grasping it a little tighter with each step.

Ty gave her an understanding smile, "Relax sweetheart," he whispered, "you look magnificent!"

Augusta sent him a side-long glance, "You said the same thing when we were herding cattle in that crazy blizzard last year. Please, tell me I look better now than I did then?"

Ty chuckled and shook his head, "Mmmm, I'll never forget that ride. You were a glorious sight in that blizzard, my love. Your hair had come loose and was flowing behind you like flames in the wind and despite the cold your golden eyes were ablaze as well! That was one heck of a storm, but it was no more exciting to me...than you."

When Augusta blushed and lowered her eyes, Ty lifted her hand to his lips and kissed it. "Now my darling, I want you to relax and enjoy yourself. A grand ball can be as enchanting as any fairy tale ever promised!" When they reached the bottom step, Ty stopped and turned to Augusta and said softly, "You are every inch an enchantress and I know that I will not be the only man that you bewitch tonight." With a sly wink he added, "But I'm the only one that counts, right?"

Augusta released a sigh, though she didn't take his flattery to heart. Ty had once again soothed her fears and given her the assurance she needed. Despite her doubts, Ty had been telling the truth. Augusta Colleen O'Brien-Grainger—was a vision! Her elegant gown had been ordered from the House of Worth in France. The ivory satin was overlaid with a dark bronze lace. The two colors perfectly enhancing her dark rimmed golden eyes and glossy mahogany hair. The tightly fitted bodice accented her womanly curves and for a thirty-eight-year-old mother of three, a surprisingly small waist. The gown was sleeveless and gathered at each shoulder with flowerets made from the ivory satin. The cream-colored blossoms accentuated the pearls that encircled her neck and dangled from her ears. Even the combs that held her dark curls in place were encrusted with tiny seed pearls.

As Ty escorted his wife towards Emily Tulane, her long-time friend and the hostess for this grand affair. Augusta couldn't help but reminisce about her friend. Emily had been like a mother to her, and had never ceased to amaze her. They had corresponded for twenty years but until a few weeks ago, they hadn't seen each other in all that while. Before moving to New York, Emily's Tennessee accent was every bit as thick as the meringue she used to put on her famous pies, back when she and Wes owned a café in Missouri. Now, it was obvious how hard she had worked to change herself into someone who would make her benefactress, Amelia Langstrom-Drew, proud. Five years ago, the old woman had died, then two years later Emily's husband Wes had been shot by a bandit in Central Park. These two deaths forced Emily into the role of matriarch of the Langstrom-Tulane estate. Augusta knew that it was for her son's sake that Emily took her new responsibilities so seriously. Just now she was the perfect hostess in an elegant emerald green dress that fit her to perfection. There was almost no trace of her former accent and she moved among these socialites with poise and confidence. Sadly, Augusta had overheard unkind remarks made by the elite of New York. They referred to Emily Tulane as Amelia's adopted hillbilly. Knowing this and watching as Emily graciously welcomed each of her guests only increased Augusta's respect for her friend. Emily's graying red hair was done simply in soft curls held inside a braid that circled her head like a bronze and silver crown.

"Welcome Governor Hill," Emily said with only the slightest twang of her former accent. "I am so very glad you were able to come this evening. I do hope you will enjoy yourself."

As the Governor moved away to be greeted by other guests, a truly joyful smile lit Emily's face as she turned towards the Graingers who were next in line.   Glancing past them and seeing no one else coming down the stairs, Emily felt free to be a bit more herself.   Taking both Ty's and Augusta's hands in hers she whispered, "It's so wonderful to have normal people here tonight! Don't get me wrong, there are a few good ones in New York.   As far as I'm concerned, though, you're scrappin' the bottom of the barrel with most of these so—ci—ety swells!" Looking around Emily asked, "And—where is the beautiful, Miss Tess?"

When Ty and Augusta began to stammer, Emily held up her hand, "Never mind," she bemoaned, "I recognize the fine hand of T. Barrett Tulane.   Has my son, perchance advised her to—make an entrance?" When Augusta shrugged, Emily gave an exaggerated roll of her eyes, "That boy was a gift straight from God, but the apple sure did fall far from the tree!   Still, I don't know what I would have done after Wes was killed, if I hadn't had Tim—I mean Barrett. He's handsome and smart, but I'm afraid the Langstrom fortune has made him a bit—uppity."

Just then the orchestra, began playing a cheerful melody with the bright and lively chords of a spirited waltz.

"Ah, now there it is—'The Voices of Spring' by Johann Strauss!" Tytus beamed, "That's my favorite waltz.   Emily, you don't mind if I steal my wife away for a quick turn around the floor, do you?   Then I hope you will give me the honor of at least one dance?"

Emily grinned, then sounding as if she'd just stepped from the hills of Tennessee, she said, "Why you handsome devil—sure I'll dance with ya—soon as m' duties as hostess are all done, 'cause if I don't stand right on this here spot and..." Emily's words suddenly changed from exaggerated hillbilly to snobbish aristocrat, "and greet each guest properly and with decorum, I assure you that the late Amelia Langstrom-Drew will haunt me to my grave!"

Ty and Augusta both laughed, then speaking in her normal fashion, Emily leaned towards them and whispered, "My favorite waltz is 'Roses from the South'!   They'll be playin' that along towards midnight.   You save that one for me, Tytus Grainger."   Hugging Augusta, she added with a wink, "You remind him for me, darlin.!"   That said, Emily replaced her happy smile with a look of formal serenity as she turned to greet her newly arrived guests.

Ty led Augusta onto the dance floor then nodded towards Emily, "I like that woman," he grunted. Then with a roguish glance, he took Augusta into his arms and waltzed her across the shining marble floor, as if they had the grand room all to themselves. Others stopped to watch them, for they danced together as gracefully as moonlight on water.

Augusta couldn't seem to keep herself from gazing all around as they danced. She knew it was vulgar to gawk, but she was having a terrible time not doing just that! As the son of a wealthy plantation owner, Ty had cut his teeth on this type of opulence. On the other hand, Augusta had grown up cleaning barns and training horses.

The Graingers had been staying with the Tulanes for nearly a month, but Emily had purposely kept her friends from seeing the ballroom until that night. As Augusta swirled around the ostentatious room, she tried to picture the Amelia Langstrom-Drew whom she had known from her childhood. The poor and elderly widow had treated her like a grand-daughter and had taught her how to garden and sew. She had also taught her about all things proper! But she'd barely been able to make ends meet. Then one day, soon after Augusta married her first husband Timothy, Amelia received word that she'd inherited Mosslet Way and the Langstrom fortune. Since Amelia was a childless widow she invited Wes and Emily Tulane to join her, and when she died she left everything to them. It wasn't until this visit that Augusta realized that because of Amelia, the Tulanes were one of the wealthiest families in all of New York, evidenced by this ballroom alone. It was indeed reminiscent of the most elaborate fairytale! The walls of this spacious hexagon shaped room were lined floor to ceiling with mirrors held in place by intricately carved, gold leafed frames. In between each mirror were twenty-foot-tall French doors leading out to the gardens. The mirrors added dazzling illumination to the room as they reflected the thirty electrically lit crystal chandeliers hanging from the curved, forty-foot ceiling.

"Oh Ty..." Augusta whispered, "look up!" Ty chuckled when his wife missed a step as she stared above her. Overhead loomed a sky of azure blue, where dozens of happy cherubs wove colorful ribbons between fluffy white clouds. "Emily said a famous artist painted it when Missus Drew was just a little girl. Can you imagine someone painting a picture that high up? Everything is just amazing!" Then not wanting Ty to think her envious, she added, "Not that

I'd want to live in a place like this. I really do prefer our hacienda." Glancing all around again, she added, "Still, it's all so—breathtaking—don't you think?"

Ty stared down at his beautiful helpmate, lover, partner and wife. After all these years, he still felt that same spark of admiration, love and desire that he had felt the night he proposed. "I can tell you this, my love," he said, his voice husky and low, "after twenty years of being your husband, you are the only thing in this room that can take my breath away!" When Augusta blushed, Ty pulled her closer and whirled her around the room. When she gave a little gasp, he reminded her, "I told you the first time we danced together that I like a rambunctious waltz!"

Augusta lifted her chin, "I didn't mind then—and I don't mind now!"

Just as the music ended, there was a general murmur among the guests as all eyes turned to the top of the staircase leading down into the ballroom. Carswell the head butler announced in his finest voice, Miss Tess Grainger, daughter of Tytus and Augusta Grainger of Colorado."

Ty and Augusta couldn't help but be proud as Tess, with head high and back straight seemed to float down the curved marble stairway. Tall, blonde and beautiful, she was stunning in a dress of deep sapphire blue. Flowers embroidered with metallic gold thread shimmered as they embellished a wide band accentuating her tiny nineteen-inch waist. A matching line of embroidered flowers glistened as they curled down the front of the skirt to the floor where they encircled the gown's small train. Three blue satin folds draped loosely over the snuggly tailored bodice, forming the neckline both front and back. The soft folds were gathered together on her shoulders with wide sapphire blue bows, trimmed in gold. Tess's shining blonde hair was partially atop her head with a few long ringlets falling down her back. Her jewelry, necklace, earrings and bracelet were sapphires set in gold. Everyone seemed intrigued by this young woman from Colorado. She enchanted them all as she glided down the steps, then graced everyone with her one dimple smile, the Grainger trademark.

Tytus squeezed Augusta's hand, his voice was hoarse as he whispered, "It's times like this, I sure hope Timothy can look down from heaven and see our girl. She looks so much like him." A shadow seemed to cross his face as he added, "Can't help but think—what a better father he would have been." Glancing at Augusta he added softly, "maybe a better..."

"Don't you dare say it!" Augusta warned. "Things turned out the way they did and that's that! You and I both loved your brother and he loved both of us. Timothy was the most pragmatic and generous man I've ever known. I can't imagine him being anything but grateful that you and I fell in love and that you have loved and raised his daughter as your own!"

Just then, all the couples on the dance floor parted like the red sea, for now it was T. Barrett Tulane's turn to—make an entrance. There were murmurs all around as the tall, handsome young man dramatically crossed the entire length of the ballroom, to claim Tess for her first dance. He walked with a definite air, although Ty thought it more a swagger.

"Stop that!" Augusta scolded, "you make that exact same face when you smell a skunk. And yes—I know—that boy is a strutting peacock but you must admit, that with them both being, tall, blonde and blue eyed, they make a striking couple." When Ty's expression fell, Augusta patted his arm, "Don't worry, that rogue isn't going to push you off that pedestal she's always had you on. She'll always be, your *Little Bit*."

Ty wasn't so sure as he watched the little girl that had always been his shadow, spinning away in a young man's arms. Worse—a young man, he didn't like. "Think I've had enough dancing for a while," he growled, "let's take a stroll in the garden." Not waiting for an answer Ty took Augusta's hand and pulled her towards one of the many French doors that opened out onto the ornate courtyard and the garden beyond. Augusta's eyes clouded as she stole one more glance at her daughter. Tonight, Tess seemed as bright as the chandeliers. A golden child who belonged neither to the angels or mortals. It did seem true that elegant galas like this were magical, just like the fairytales promised. And if ever, anyone looked like a fairytale princess—it was her little girl—her Tessie May!

⚜

The gardens were just as extravagant as everything else at Mosslet Way. A large, three-tiered marbled fountain was centered in the stone courtyard. Perfectly trimmed, eighteen-inch-high evergreen hedges were carefully planted to form large hollow diamonds. Fanning out around the fountain, these diamond shaped hedges created a sunburst effect with stone walkways zig-zagging in between. Ty and Augusta clasped hands and strolled between the diamonds of greenery. It was December thirty-first, and even though it was uncommonly warm for New York, the night air was cool and Ty slipped his coat off and draped it around Augusta's shoulders. Keeping his arm around her they strolled along, both deep in thought, until they came across something so different from everything else that they had to stop.

"Emily spoke of a fountain that she designed. The others are so formal, this has to be it," Augusta mused. "It draws you to it and makes you smile! Just like Emily herself."

The unusual fountain was designed to look like a simple lily pond, made of green and blue marble and was about twelve feet across. In the center were life sized, bronze statues of a small boy and girl. They were playing in a stream of water that leapt from the mouth of a fat frog, who sat on the side of the pool. As the water rained down on the children's upturned smiling faces, they lifted their small hands, catching the glistening drops of water. Adding a bit of whimsy, a butterfly sat on the girl's shoulder, while a sling-shot and fat round worm peeked out of the boy's back pocket.

As they marveled at this unexpected enchantment in the middle of a formal garden, Ty pulled Augusta back against his chest and wrapped his arms around her. "Remember when that 'belle of the ball' in there was just like that little girl?   Our own little Tessie May—what a sweetheart.   I'll never forget the morning I barged into my office with a chip on my shoulder and a heart of stone.   Alvaro, that wise old scamp, knew what would happen when he put her in there.   She was such a tiny little thing and I frowned down at her, expecting her to cry," Ty chuckled, "but…she just looked up and frowned right back!" He suddenly found it hard to speak, "And then——she smiled.   My hard-old heart melted—and she was my Little Bit from that day on.   Thought I'd burst the first time she called me, Papa!" Augusta hugged his arm as he continued. "Then, just after the twins were born, she said, 'I know you love those boys more than me because they're really yours!'"

Augusta squeezed his hand, "I know that really hurt you."

"I tried to tell her that in a way, I might even love her just a little bit more. She began her life as my niece, then she became my daughter and she would always be my last link with my twin brother.   I love our boys—you know I do—but she's no less special." Tytus wrapped his arms a little tighter around his wife, "You used to call me that grumpy dragon.   I probably still would be if you and Tess hadn't come into my life.   You two softened my heart so I could finally open it to God again."

Augusta turned in his arms and placed her hand on Ty's strong jaw, feeling a hint of stubble under her fingertips. At times like these she saw both Tytus and his twin brother. They were nearly identical in their face and height, but Timothy had been slimmer with blonde hair and blue eyes, like his daughter Tess. Tytus was just the opposite, he had a muscular build with dark brown hair and eyes. All the Graingers including Tess and her brothers shared the family trademark, one impish dimple that creased deeply when they smiled.

Augusta rose up on tip-toe and kissed Ty on the cheek, "You give us too much credit, my love. You were a good man before I set foot on the ranch and long before Tessie smiled at you," giving him a sheepish look, she added, "but you are still—at times—that *grumpy dragon!*"

Just then the strains of one waltz ended while the musicians transitioned smoothly into another, sending their melody out into the garden to mingle with the sounds of the night.

"Dance with me Tytus Grainger!" Augusta whispered, "our Tess is twenty years old—a grown woman now and we've done the best we could. Back home we worried that men courted Tess just to get at your money. Although Barrett is nothing like the two men he was named after, he is well-educated and wealthy. If he is paying court to Tess he must care for her! He certainly doesn't need our money. As for social standing, if anything, she is a social detriment. Even though Tess and Barrett never saw each other until a month ago, they have been corresponding since they were children." When Ty shook his head, Augusta shrugged, "I don't like him any more than you do—but it's Tess's choice—not ours!"

"He's not right for her. We've always prayed that she would marry a Christian man. T. Barrett Tulane is so full of himself there's no room in his life for God," Ty grumbled. "He's not a Christian!"

Tears filled Augusta's eyes, "I know my love..." she sighed, "and it breaks my heart to admit it but...neither is Tess."

In the wee hours of the morning, the last carriage left Mosslet Way. Despite being the proclaimed angel of the New Year's Eve Ball, Tess let out a groan that was anything but angelic, as her mother undid the laces of her corset. "Oh mother—that's heaven!" she moaned as she filled her lungs.

Augusta chuckled as she folded the corset and laid it in the drawer, then helped her daughter slip into a blue satin robe. When Tess sat down at the fancy dressing table, her mother began pulling the pins from her daughter's long curls. "You know, sweetie, you don't have to cinch your corset *that* tight!

A twenty-two-inch waist is just as lovely as a nineteen-inch waist and you might even be able to do this wonderful thing. It's called—breathing!"

Tess was horrified. "Mother—Madame Rousseau praised my waist as being smaller than any of this year's debutantes. She said a figure like mine was the perfect canvas for her divine creations! She was the top dressmaker in Paris and now she's become famous here in New York. No one knows more about fashion and besides, a little bit of misery is worth it. Didn't you see how everyone stared when I made my entrance? Barrett told me over and over how proud he was of me. Said he'd never seen anyone come down those steps with such flair. He's so handsome and dashing. And he told me tonight that together, he and I make the most perfect couple!"

When Augusta bit her lip and sadly shook her head, Tess's radiant smile turned to a frown, "Oh dear, I've upset your sensibilities haven't I, Mother. Please don't spoil this glorious evening with one of your lectures on humility and integrity. I know you're tired, so why don't you just go on to bed. I'll ring for one of my maids."

Augusta bit back her irritation and spoke softly to her daughter's reflection. "I'm not that tired. I've hardly had a moment with you since we got here. I miss you, Tess. Besides I told all three of *your* maids, that you wouldn't be needing them after the ball. Getting you ready wore them out! Right now, I'm sure they're all sound asleep."

"Mother!" Tess huffed, "Emily oversees a huge staff. There are several maids whose only responsibility is the care and comfort of their guests. And three of them have been especially assigned to take care of *me*!"

"Tess!" Augusta chided, then reminded herself that her daughter wasn't a child anymore. Drawing the brush through the mass of golden curls she said gently, "I don't want to lecture you or argue, but sweetheart, did you hear how arrogant you sounded just now? You've been quite demanding since we came to New York." Augusta hesitated than added, "You act almost as if you were... royalty!"

Tess surprised her mother when instead of becoming angry, she looked into the mirror and gave her a patronizing smile. "My dear, humble, Mother," she sighed, as she rose from the chair, crossed the room, then flounced down on the large four poster bed. Lifting her chin, she proclaimed, "I am royalty, and you could be too, if you only realized it! Barrett says that the very rich, like the Graingers and Tulanes, are the closest thing America has to royalty.

More than that, he says we're foolish not to acknowledge it and yes—take every advantage of it!"

Augusta was shocked and saddened, whether it was wise or foolish, she simply had to say something. "Tess, the Tulanes may live like royalty, but if Missus Drew hadn't inherited the Langstrom fortune and then adopted Wes and Emily...Barrett might never have been born! And if he had, he would be cooking steak and onions in a Missouri café right now." Augusta sucked in a calming breath, then continued, "You called me your *humble* mother. That's all I am, Tess. I am a humble rancher's wife and you, my dear Tessie May, are just the daughter of a rancher who has done well. And that, my girl, could easily change. Fortunes are made and lost every day!" Augusta waved her hand around the room, "This suite of rooms, three maids and dancing the night away at a ball, is like a fairytale, I know, but it is temporary. This is not your world. You are not American royalty, nor are you a New York socialite."

Tess was undaunted and her blue eyes sparkled as she smiled up at her mother, "Not yet—but I could be! Yes, I am a rich rancher's...whatever I am... step-daughter...niece? Exactly how I fit into this family has often confused me." She muttered, as she kicked off her slippers then slid her feet under the satin sheets. Leaning back against the huge down-filled pillows, she folded her arms and lifted her chin. "I know you and Papa are uncomfortable with the extravagance of New York. Somehow, I think all this frightens you. Especially when you see that I am so completely at home here. I could quite easily become a New York socialite—American royalty. And if I decide that's what I want— then I shall have it!"

Chapter 4

Upset

<hr>

"Let no man deceive you with vain words: for because of these things comes the wrath of God upon the children of disobedience." Ephesians 5:6

Barrett rolled his eyes and groaned as Kraus, the groomsman, led the tall, thoroughbred stallion out of the barn, wearing a side-saddle. "Tess," he scoffed, "Napoleon is sometimes hard for me to control! I really don't think you can handle him."

Tess smiled, "I can always tell whether I can handle a horse or not." As she rubbed the animal's forehead, she whispered, "You'll be a good boy for me, won't you handsome?"

Barrett was surprised when the powerful animal pressed his great head against Tess's shoulder. Then later he stood perfectly still as Kraus helped her into the saddle.

As they rode down Central Park's bridle path, Barrett didn't mind that Tess was proving him wrong. The lovely young blonde looked as stunningly beautiful sitting atop the powerful stallion as she had while waltzing across the ballroom. She handled the brute with a gentle but firm hand, all the while looking like a queen.

A smug smile spread across Barrett's face as he gazed around at riders and pedestrians alike. Every male within fifty feet had stopped to stare even as their female companions attempted to pull them away. Tess was dressed in a well-tailored, royal blue riding habit. The tiny matching hat, set at a jaunty angle, made her look adorable and alluring at the same time. It was also small enough to allow everyone to see her golden hair shining in the sunlight. Riding next to the center of attention didn't bother Barrett in the least, for all the men were jealous! He glanced around again, laughed, then shook his head, "I can't tell you how very glad I am that you haven't disappointed me, Tess!"

"Well, that's quite a statement," she huffed. "Were you expecting to be disappointed?"

"Absolutely! Your correspondence over the years has been enjoyable, often entertaining, but sometimes a bit too quaint for my taste. You are so terribly fond of the new foals born every year. Your letters are full of horse antics, as if I'd care to hear them. Anyway, I had imagined you being a plain, country girl. I feared you wouldn't fit in, that you would embarrass me." Shaking his head again he added, "Instead you've surprised and pleased me—more than I can say! In fact, you might as well know that every bachelor at the ball asked if you and I had an understanding. If not, they wanted to have a crack at you!"

"A crack at me?" Tess bristled, "that sounds awful!"

"Ah, but that's the way of it, my girl. As I've told you, the rich are very much like royalty. The people who say they are interested in us—only want our money and our way of life! That's why it makes sense to marry our own kind." When Tess seemed put off by that, Barrett cocked his head and said, "Come now, how many times have you written about that farmer that keeps proposing? Be honest Tess, you feel the same as me. You don't want to settle for less—if anything—you want more!"

As she pondered his words, Napoleon sensed her distraction and began to toss his head and side-step impatiently. She gave one quick jerk of her reins, "Settle down!" she commanded, as she placed her right hand on his withers to sooth him. When the horse calmed, she turned back to Barrett, "So—what did you tell the other bachelors? Did you give them leave to... have a crack at me?"

Barrett grinned, "Certainly not—I'm no fool!" When Tess's eyebrows raised and her sapphire eyes seemed full of questions he added imploringly, "I'm hoping that you won't make a liar out of me." He had purposely ridden towards a secluded spot with a park bench and hitching stands for the horses. As he quickly dismounted he said, "Let's sit here for a moment, Tess." Before she could react, Barrett had tied his horse and was reaching up to help her down. The moment they were seated he began, "You've told me that your brothers are to inherit the ranch. I'm sure you must realize, that limits your marriage prospects. As for me, I don't need money and I can't abide any of the fawning New York debutantes I've met. That's a problem because, when my father died I was only given control of fifty percent of his holdings. When I marry, I'll be granted seventy-five percent. Until her death, Mother maintains control of a quarter of the investments and properties. Still, that leaves me the lion's share of the estate. One day it will all be mine to control. So, I've been thinking, it makes perfect sense that you and I should marry, in fact the sooner the better!" When Tess just blinked at him, he quickly continued, "You're an intelligent and beautiful woman. You and I have been corresponding for years and we know each other quite well. We're the same you and me! We're both practical, free spirited thinkers. We may not be in love," he chuckled then added, "perhaps not yet anyway, but I think we are very much—in like! So, my beautiful Tess, why not marry me? Once I have greater control of the estate, there's no limit on the kind of life we can share. I can promise you adventure and excitement beyond your wildest dreams!"

Tess's heart suddenly felt like it might just pound its way right out of her chest.

Is he actually proposing to me? That's why all the debutantes at the ball were sending me such hateful stares. They saw me as competition for the handsome and rich—T. Barrett Tulane. The Ivy sisters call him the catch of the season. It's not like I've never dreamt of this possibility—but it was always just a day dream. Now it doesn't seem real, but it does make sense. Barrett gets what he wants and I don't have to settle for less.

Tess was pulled from her thoughts when Barrett reached into his pocket and pulled out a black velvet box with Tiffany in gilded letters. He opened it to reveal a stunning diamond, surrounded by sapphires, in the newly popular, high pronged setting.

"Tess," he said softly, "after spending this month with you and especially after the ball, I realized that we would make the most perfect couple. The Midnight Star sails for Paris the day after tomorrow. Come with me and I can promise you the most extravagant honeymoon you could ever imagine."

Tess stiffened and gave Barrett a cool, sidelong glance, "My friend Sadie's fiancé insisted on having the honeymoon before the wedding. She woke up the next morning and he was gone!"

"You think I would do that to you?" Barrett chided, then he took both her hands in his. "Of course, absolutely, the wedding comes first—followed by a fabulous honeymoon. Our marriage will secure your lifestyle and give me full control of all Langstrom-Tulane holdings. However, I loathe the idea of the sickening sentiment and the endless etiquette of a formal wedding. Instead, I've always liked the idea of getting married at the Saint-Pierre de Montmartre. It's the oldest church in France. We'll have a simple ceremony with just me and you, and a little old French padre. Then, my darling, we'll sail around the world! We'll consort with the most elegant people and travel to the most exotic places." Barrett took the ring from the box and grinned as he slid it onto her finger, "See, a perfect fit! Say yes, my sweet. Say it and we'll go purchase our tickets right now. In just a few days, we'll be on our way to Paris and then the world!" He pulled her into his arms and kissed her. It was exciting and frightening at the same time. She was drawn to Barrett. He was handsome and he was offering her the world. She stared into his pale blue eyes, then back at the exquisite ring sparkling on her hand. It was a practical plan for her future and the offer of a lifetime. There seemed to be no other direction to go. The night of the ball, she told her mother that if she wanted, she could live like royalty. Finally, she looked at Barrett, and made her choice!

⊰◈⊱

The elegant private car swayed slightly as it rumbled past the rundown tenements of New York City. Augusta staggered a bit as she made her way towards the green velvet settee where Ty sat. His long legs were stretched out, his arms folded as he stared out the window. He grimaced as he watched the ugly truth pass by. Poverty and want were much more common than were the fancy shops, theatres and estates like Mosslet Way. During their stay in New York, they had mostly seen the very wealthy, but there was great hardship and need in this grand city as well.

As the train went around a curve, Augusta lost her balance. Luckily, she was only two feet away from Ty. He caught her around the waist and gently pulled her down beside him, "Best watch your step, darlin', this train car may have all the luxuries of home but it still rides like a bronc sometimes." When Augusta had no witty come back, just put her head on his chest and silently snuggled close, Ty put his arm around her and whispered, "So, is hurricane Tess, finally asleep?"

Nodding, she sighed, "Oh Ty, I've never seen her act like this. Never thought she could or would throw such a tantrum. She's been in hysterics since last night. We were so sure that taking her on this trip was a wonderful idea. I hated leaving Caleb and Joshua behind but they seemed to think that it was a grand adventure. Still, I've worried about them every minute. And now to find that this long trip was just—a horrible mistake."

"Hey now, we don't know that this trip was a mistake—not yet anyway. It may very well have taught Tess some important things. As for the twins, they are fifteen years old for Pete's sake.   Yes, we left our babies all alone," he added dramatically, "all except for Joseph—and Alvaro—and Shep—and twenty ranch hands watching over them day and night."

"Oh, don't tease me Ty.   I know all that but still—we've never been away from the boys this long before.   I've missed them so much, but I've made a point not to say so, because I thought Tess needed this and that it would be such a special time for all of us.   But now?"

"Yeah, kind 'o blew up on us, didn't it love?   I had looked forward to riding in the Tulanes private car for the long journey home.   Seemed like a grand way for us to end our holiday.   Of course, we hadn't expected Barrett's ridiculous proposal or Tess's hysterics.   We might as well have gone home in one of our cattle cars.   That French chef is even preparing her new favorite dish, Lobster Thermidor for dinner tonight.   What a waste!"

Augusta sat up and looked her husband in the eye. "I resent that Mister Grainger," she huffed.   "Just because our daughter is acting like a brat, doesn't mean we shouldn't enjoy ourselves.   It's our holiday too!   The train ride here was exhausting, while this is—" she gazed around at the mahogany furnishings and plush oriental carpets. "This is amazing!   It's elegant, private and wonderfully comfortable.   I don't know how they managed to fit so much luxury into one train car.   Two bedrooms, a parlor and kitchen, complete with a chef!   If I recall, you and I both liked that lobster dish just as much as Tess.   If she chooses to shun us for the rest of the trip then I plan to enjoy having you all to myself!"

Ty smiled and kissed Augusta's forehead, "You really are something, Missus Grainger.   You're still finding that pearl hidden in every hardship— aren't you?   And I love you all the more for it.   Keep at it darling, I need your hopeful perspective on things.   I was about as mad as I've ever been at Mister T. Barrett Tulane last night.   If you and Emily hadn't come in when you did, I fear that boy would have woken up in the hospital and me in jail!"   When Augusta gave him a puzzled look he added, "I really had looked forward to meeting the young man, who had been named after my brother and your father, but he's not worthy to stand in their shadow.   I think the world of Emily, but I didn't like that pompous scoundrel from the start.   He's certainly not the right man for Tess!"   Ty rubbed a hand over his face and groaned, "All I've done with us going home early is buy us some time.   For all of Tessie's weeping and wailing, I haven't stopped their marriage, I fear I've only postponed it." Ty slammed a fist against his open palm.

31

"You know," Augusta sighed, "we've both been so busy making these last-minute preparations that you've never told me exactly what happened." When Ty seemed to draw into himself Augusta reached up and turned his face towards her. "Please tell me. Last night when Emily and I came in from the garden, there were so many raised voices nothing anyone said made sense. The only thing you made clear to me was that we were leaving this morning and that I had better start packing. After that announcement, Tess began crying so hard I couldn't understand her. Then you and Barrett both stormed off in different directions. The truth is, I still don't know exactly what happened last night."

"What happened was that arrogant popinjay wanted to ruin our daughter! If he had just come to me in private and asked me for her hand, or if he'd even wanted a reasonable engagement and a proper wedding..."

Augusta raised her eyebrows, "And if he had...what would you have done?"

Ty ducked his head, "I'd have said NO, of course! But I might have been able to control my temper. It was like he wanted to make me angry." Ty got to his feet just as the train went around another curve and he staggered a bit, then grabbed one of the brass handles bolted into the side of the car.

Staring out the window he spoke through gritted teeth, "I was reading in the library when they just burst into the room. They didn't even want to wait until you and Emily were there to make their big announcement. Tess was waving their tickets in the air, 'We're leaving for Paris on the Midnight Star in two days. Isn't it exciting!' she shouted. "How could she think I'd be pleased by anything so ridiculous?"

"So," Augusta asked, "had they planned to get married today—before they left?"

No—that's what made me so mad. His plan was to cross the ocean together, without a chaperone. He did say he planned for them to marry in some old church. But Augusta, he had to have known that the two of them traveling alone would have ruined Tess's reputation. You should have seen the pompous look on his face. It was the look a cat gives a mouse when he's just toying with it—just before the kill," Ty hissed. "I was about to introduce his arrogant nose to the floor, by way of my fist. Unfortunately, that's when you and Emily walked in and Tess became hysterical."

"I can't imagine what they were thinking? I'd don't blame you for being angry. Even if they had married before leaving it still would have looked bad for Tess. She's naïve about such things but Barrett isn't. He knows very well that he's too entrenched in New York society not to have a formal wedding announcement, a series of engagement parties and then an elaborate wedding. And even if they satisfied all the proprieties, those high-brow socialites would never treat Tess as an equal. This past month they've all pretended to accept her, but I know they're just waiting for her to make a mistake. She thinks they all adore her." Augusta hesitated a moment then turned to Ty, "There's something I hadn't planned on telling anyone. While I was trying on clothes at the dress maker's last week, I heard two women talking about Tess. I peeked out and saw that it was the Ivy sisters, Emily calls them *The Poison Ivy Sisters*. They're the Grand Dames of New York society. Anyway, they said, 'What do you think of Tulane and his little country pet? That foolish girl, she has her sights set on being Tess Tulane. Mark my words, he'll give her a child, but never his name or his wealth.' Then they said, 'That young rogue is shopping for a mistress, not a wife.' Oh Ty, I didn't know what to do. I was afraid that if I'd said what I wanted to say, I'd only make things worse. I'm so glad we're going home today!"

"Mistress? The Ivys actually said, he wanted *me* for a—*a mistress?*"

Ty and Augusta turned towards the sound of Tess's voice. Weary and confused she swayed with the movement of the train as she shuffled from the bedroom end of the private car. Her eyes were red from crying and her blonde curls fell in a mass of tangles over her shoulders. "Barrett wouldn't do that to me Mama. Papa, I know he wouldn't! Still—if that's the gossip the Ivys are spreading, then I guess—it's good that we're going home." Her face crumpled and Tess threw herself into Ty's arms, "I'm sorry Papa, I should have known you were protecting me." Tess stepped from her father's embrace then sat down next to her mother and hugged her as well. "I'm so confused," she groaned, as she swept the curls from her face, "Barrett doesn't like the Ivy sisters but he says they're known for saying what the New York elite are thinking. They're wrong though, he does want to marry me. Still…I guess…I can see the folly of it now." Tess closed her eyes and squeezed her mother's hand. "Right now, I'm sure Emily is explaining all this to Barrett. He's just an impulsive—free thinker—that's all!"

Ty sat down and took his daughter's hand. "If anyone is well versed in the dos and don'ts of society, it is T. Barrett Tulane. An honorable man would never compromise any woman's reputation. Especially if he plans to spend the rest of his life with that woman! And, I might add, every woman is responsible for protecting her own virtue." When Tess stiffened, he added gently, "I'm not chastising you honey, just reminding you that there are always consequences for every decision we make. He was wrong for asking you to do such an inappropriate thing, but you were also wrong to agree. Don't you remember when your friend Sadie ran off with that drifter last year? You were angry at that rogue but you were furious with her for being so naïve!"

"That was entirely different!" Tess insisted, "Sadie barely knew that man, nobody did. You all have known Barrett all his life, he's even named after my Papa Tim and Grandpa Bull!"

"All the more reason for him to treat you with respect, Tess!" Ty grunted. "You have to admit; Barrett's behavior wasn't all that different from Sadie's drifter. Now was it?"

"Papa's right," Augusta added. "Sadie's reputation was ruined and yours would have been too. Colorado gossips are bad enough but they don't hold a candle to those you find in New York! And that's where you two were planning to live, isn't it? You love Sadie but you still couldn't believe her foolishness. That's why we're shocked and concerned that Barrett was able to persuade you so easily."

Tess groaned as she threw her head back and stared up at the paneled ceiling, "You're right and so are the Ivy sisters. I want to be Tess Tulane. I want maids and fancy balls and trips to Paris! If that makes me foolish—so be it. Because regardless of how we left things, I still want to marry Barrett—if he'll still have me. We just need to do it right next time."

Ty and Augusta exchanged concerned glances, wishing they could give their daughter a dose of common sense like when they used to give her a spoonful of castor oil.

Fighting to stay calm Ty struggled for the right words as he gazed out the leaded glass windows of the private car. Then he squeezed Tess's hand. "Sweetheart, I'm not angry. I am mightily confused though. I don't think you are being true to yourself. Being a socialite for a month is exciting, but that's not you!"

"Yes, it is, Papa. Cal and Josh will inherit the ranch. You said, girls marry and go off with their husbands. Well, I found a husband, and I would think you'd be happy. All the young men back home have tried to court me. Sig Rosenquist proposes every time he sees me. He and the others are all decent men I suppose, but I don't want to end up living on some little patch of land, scraping to get by, like Uncle Hitch and Aunt Helen. That's not the kind of life I want. If I can be the wife of a wealthy aristocrat—American royalty like the Tulanes—then what's the matter with that?"

"What about love, Tess?" Ty couldn't keep from raising his voice, "surely we didn't raise you to be this—this shallow. You've lived a privileged life but I thought you were wise enough to know that wealth does not buy happiness nor even contentment!"

"I'm not shallow, Papa! I'm a free thinker!" Tess snapped, then she calmed a bit and added, "actually, I liked the idea of not getting married until we reached Paris. The voyage to France would have given me time to know more about Barrett. He said I didn't disappoint him. I was going to see if he disappointed me. I wasn't going to let him trick me into...you know...and then not marry me! I did learn from Sadie's mistake!"

Augusta shook her head, "We all think we're too smart to be tricked, Tess. Sadly, there are plenty of men who say all the right things to lower a woman's defenses. And if silver tongued persuasion doesn't work—many men will not take NO for an answer!"

The train car was silent for a long while as Tess contemplated her parents words. Then she shocked them when she nodded and said, "All right then, I'll put him to the test. Let me invite him to come to the ranch for a visit." Thinking of Barrett's derogatory words about her love for the horses, she added, "I don't want to miss spring foaling, so I'll ask him to come the first of summer. All the foals should have arrived by then. He can come in time for our annual anniversary and birthday party. I'll get to see him in my own corral, so to speak. What is it you always say, Papa, whenever we buy a new horse? 'Don't make up your mind until you've looked at him from every angle.' Well, that's what I'll do, and I don't mean to be disrespectful but—this is entirely my decision—not yours."

Chapter 5
New Life

"You made all the delicate, inner parts of my body and knit me together in my mother's womb." Psalm 139:13

God took a handful of southerly wind, blew his breath upon it, and created the horse. A *Bedouin Legend*

Tess and Augusta stared out of the darkened parlor windows of the hacienda. They both shivered as glowing veins of lightning danced across the night sky, followed by bursts of earth shaking lightning strikes and loud crackling thunder.

"How do Joseph and Alvaro sleep through this?" Tess shook her head and gave a nervous laugh. "One blessing of being old I guess."

"I don't know about that," Augusta groaned. "The average age of our sick ranch hands in the bunkhouse is about twenty. I just checked on them and they're all so deep in the land of nod, I don't think a cannon could rouse them. Ben and Cody were the first to get sick and should be well soon. But the doctor ordered them to stay in bed at least another night. I'm sure thankful that you and I have already had the chickenpox."

Just then another crash of lightning split the air and Augusta stammered, "I'm also v—very thankful—that—that we aren't the kind of girls to be frightened by a good old—spring storm. Right honey?"

Tess's eyes grew large as another bolt of lightning struck nearby, "Oh y—yes," she cringed as a tremor raced down her spine, "it's—wonderful—that we aren't the types to be a—afraid!"

They gazed out the window a few seconds longer, then looked at each other, and burst into nervous laughter. Truth be told, they were both terrified of storms like this and were struggling to find the courage they needed. They simply had to brave the storm and get to the barn. The dark—cold—dimly lit barn—in the middle of a wickedly wild night. Remembering that her mother had been kidnapped in a storm such as this, Tess tried to think of something that might help. Suddenly she brightened, "Doesn't this remind you a little of the New York Symphony?" she asked, just as a bolt of lightning struck so close it made them both jump.

"Come to think of it, it does," Augusta laughed. "And just like now—we both nearly came out of our skin the first time we heard the snare drums."

"Exactly! So, let's not think of this as a storm at all. That isn't deafening thunder out there, it's just a loud snare drum. The lightning strikes are crashing cymbals. The rain drops on the roof are the quick notes on a piano, and that howling wind...it's just the entire string section...with maybe a few flutes thrown in."

Augusta smiled as she slipped her arm around her daughter's waist, "That's very metaphoric, even poetic of you Tess. But I think your musicians are slowing a bit. Maybe we should make a run for it...before the big finale!"

When Tess nodded, Augusta grabbed the lantern and opened the door, "All right, sweetheart, you take that stack of towels and run like the time that mama pig chased you around the house!"

They both took in a deep breath, then howled and screamed as they burst into the night. They splashed through mud puddles as the rain poured down and lightning crackled all around them. Soon a combination of fear and exhilaration had them laughing so hard they could barely run. When they finally reached the barn, the wind fought them as they struggled to open and then close the doors. Once inside, Tess slammed the heavy latch into place then turned to her mother, "Well," she panted, "if that doesn't make us the two bravest women in the state of Colorado—I don't know what would!" The moment she caught her breath she added, "None of my friends would have done it."

"I—wholeheartedly—agree!" Augusta huffed, "but I think we'll both feel even more courageous...if we get some light in here!"

Tess pushed the wet curls off her forehead, "Good idea," she shuddered as she struck a match and lit each lantern. As light filled the gloomy barn she sighed, "I can already hear Papa scolding us about bringing these mares into the barn to foal. He always gets mad at me when I bring them in, but..."

"But..." Augusta interrupted, as she dried her face on a towel, "this is a bear of a storm. And he certainly would not want us out riding in this mess to check on pregnant mares! So, don't worry about Papa. After all it was his idea to drive the horses to the fort instead of putting them on a railcar. At the time, I thought it was sweet that he wanted the twins to have the experience of a real trail drive. Of course, none of us expected that all the ranch hands he left behind would come down with chickenpox!"

"I know Papa will understand, once it's explained." Tess gave a mock shiver then said, "but I plan to be far away when *you* explain it to the dragon of the Bar 61!"

At that moment, the storm intensified. Lightning struck, the ground shook and the heavens roared. When both women yelped, the five pregnant mares stamped and blew nervously. Augusta sighed as she picked up a lantern, "I fear this is going to be a very long night. Time to go to work, Tess. Let's try to calm them down. You take the mares on the right, I'll take the left."

As they made their way from stall to stall, patting, stroking and speaking softly, Tess looked over at her mother and asked, "What if they all decide to foal at the same time? More to the point, what if they're all in trouble—at the same time? Is there something we can do? Some way to slow them down until we're ready for the next one?"

Augusta couldn't help but grin as she put her hands on her hips and stared at her daughter, "What would you suggest, Tess? Maybe a really big cork?"

The absurd idea made Tess giggle, "I guess not..."

Although it wasn't all that funny, they both kept chuckling at their foolishness. And that, more than anything else, helped them relax. It was a special moment, suddenly they weren't so much, mother and daughter, but two friends working together! It was a good feeling and Augusta stopped for a moment to watch Tess as she spoke to each mare in soothing whispers.

Whether the trip to New York had been wise or a terrible mistake, she and Ty still weren't sure. Tess had been arrogant in the big city, much more humble on the long train ride home, and a bit of both since. But now, watching Tess with these horses filled Augusta with hope. Being around the mares and their foals had never failed to bring out the very best in Tessie May. Augusta couldn't help but wish that their relationship was always like this.

Tess turned towards her just then and asked, "Why are you looking at me like that, Mother?"

"Oh, I was just thinking that there is no one I'd rather have with me tonight than you! These mares trust you and you have good instincts, Tess. Most of the time, mares don't need any assistance, but if they do, with God's help and yours, we'll manage! Your Grandpa O'Brien used to say, 'Don't be surprised

when a brood mare gets a bit pigheaded and notional as her time grows near.'
What he meant was, anything could happen. Just because they *usually* give
birth at night and especially on stormy nights, doesn't mean they won't make
fools of us. We might have braved this storm for nothing. Then again, all five
could go into labor in the next minute. And although we can't see it, there's a
full moon up there too. Just one more thing that could bring on labor. Still,
you just..."

"Never know!" Tess finished for her. "But...I'll wager it's tonight for
all of them. Their bags are full. They aren't drinking. Their water troughs
are nearly as full now as when I filled them this morning. Something else I've
noticed Mother. All through the day they've been restless, even before this
storm hit!"

"You're very observant, Tess." Augusta praised. "Over the years, we've
delivered our fair share of foals. The ranch record is four in one night, but...I
have a feeling we're going to break that record."

Just then a blood-bay mare peeked over the upper half of her stall door
and Tess went to rub her forehead, "Hello Sassafras." Suddenly she gazed around
at the other four mares in their stalls and chuckled, "Mother, I just realized that
these last mares to foal are: Sassafras, Lemon, Honey, Ginger and Cinnamon!
We've had seventy mares to foal this year and they have every name imagin-
able. Some of them don't even have names. It's just the bald face sorrel or that
grumpy chestnut. It's an odd coincidence, don't you think?"

Augusta flashed an impish grin, "Yes! And—I think we should continue
the theme—don't you?"

"I sure do—and I can already hear Papa and the boys holler about it.
But—I think we can *cook up* some appropriate names for the last five foals of
the *season*."

A little after ten o'clock, Lemon, a pale palomino, was the first to have
her foal. Her dark brown filly slipped into the world with apparent ease. On
wobbly long legs, she managed to stand on her first try. Then even before
her mama had time to get up, she was trying to nurse. Tess named the filly,
Cocoa. At midnight, Ginger gave birth to Sugarfoot, a solid dark gray colt with
one white stocking on his right hind leg. He was slower to stand than Cocoa,
but he too was healthy and strong. Thirty minutes later Cinnamon gave birth
to Spice, a speckled little red roan filly with a thin white blaze down her dark
sorrel face. Before little Spice was on her feet, Cinnamon was washing her face

with a persistent, long pink tongue. Augusta chuckled, "That little filly has that, 'oh quit Mama' look the twins used to give us whenever we tried to get the oatmeal off their faces."

Hearing a loud groan coming from the stall just across the aisle, Augusta turned to check on Honey. She was a dark palomino mare, and sure enough, she too looked to be in labor. Both women sighed as they left Cinnamon and Spice to get acquainted, and then stepped into Honey's stall.

Augusta sighed as she slipped her arm around her daughter's shoulder, "Oh Tess, this is the one that's been worrying me all night. Actually, all season! If anything happens to Honey and her baby, it will be my fault. You know, the theory behind our raising Morgan and Arabian crossbreeds was to have the calm strength of the Morgan coupled with the refined beauty and stamina of the Arabian. Papa had heard of another Morab breeder in Kentucky and that's where we got Golden Honey. We bought her from the same horse farm that owned the famous Golddust. She's his great-great granddaughter. I just wish this wasn't her first foal. Papa wanted to breed her to Saber, giving the foal a bit more Arabian blood. It was sentimental and foolish, but I insisted that she be bred to Quest instead. That stallion was my best friend all through childhood and he and I went through so much together." Augusta smiled sadly, "I feared he wasn't going to live much longer and I desperately wanted a foal from both of them. Saber would have been the wiser choice for he would have thrown a smaller foal. Breeding her to Quest was selfish of me. Now—I'm really worried about her!"

Tess squeezed her mother's hand. "It wasn't a selfish decision! We all loved Quest and his dying three months ago just proved that you were right. Besides, Honey is a strong mare! Everything will be all right."

"Yes…God willing." Augusta sighed, then she glanced at Tess, "Sweetheart, will you pray with me?"

When her mother gave her an imploring look, Tess raised her eyebrows and shrugged. "Forgive me for saying so, but I think you and Papa overdo this…praying over every little thing. You know Barrett and his friends are very educated. They don't believe in God, heaven or hell, good or evil, right or wrong. They say everything is here by accident and there's no proof otherwise, so why bother.

Augusta was silent for a few moments, then she nodded, "I'm not surprised that they believe that. But life itself is proof that God exists, Tess. Life coming about by chance, is as unlikely as a cyclone spinning through a lumber yard and accidentally constructing a house along the way. The idea that nothing can make itself into something, defies all logic. Still, it's a very convenient belief. It's human nature not to want to answer to anyone but ourselves. Our baser side doesn't want there to be a God. Doesn't want there to be right or wrong. Especially when doing wrong is easier and sometimes more fun, or so we may think at the time. Rebelling against God's directions began with Adam and Eve. The devil has always encouraged people to hate God, to laugh at all those who dare to follow His will. The goal is to silence Christianity—to kill it. The fact is that God and the devil fight for our souls from the very moment we are born, Tess. When we trust God, He wins. When we turn our backs on Him, the devil wins. Other times people say there is no God because they're mad at Him. They've prayed for something and God said no or they don't understand why something bad has happened. Or perhaps a Christian has let them down. They think they are punishing God by denying Him but all they're doing is cooperating with the devil's plan to turn us away from the truth."

Just then, Honey groaned and Augusta knelt beside her. She put her hand on the mare's large belly and felt the foal move beneath her hand. Then she looked up and said, "Tess, tonight you and I have the privilege of helping bring life into the world. But the creation of that life—is a miracle only God can accomplish!"

Tess sighed as she patiently knelt beside Augusta and squeezed her hand, "All right, Mother, I'll pray with you."

Augusta chuckled self-consciously, knowing that she tended to go on and on because she so desperately wanted Tess to see God for who He was! Sighing, Augusta smiled gently as she took her daughter's hand and bowed her head, "Dear heavenly Father, first we ask your care and protection over Tytus, Caleb and Joshua and the men traveling with them to Fort Leavenworth. And we also ask that you continue to heal and strengthen all the ranch hands that have been sick with chickenpox. We thank you for keeping us safe from the storm and for the three healthy foals born so far, tonight. Only Honey and Sassafras are left and we ask that you help them deliver strong healthy babies and remain healthy and well themselves. Honey is a special worry, Lord, we don't want her to suffer but I think something's wrong. I fear she has an unusually large foal and there's a danger we could lose both of them tonight. Please give Tess and me the wisdom and the physical strength we'll need to do what must be done! Thank you, Lord. In Jesus name, Amen."

Augusta squeezed Tess's hand, "Thank you for being here with me sweetheart and for praying with me. I hate to think how I'd feel if I was alone right now."

Just then the mare lifted her head, then groaned loudly as she laid back down. "You'll be all right, Honey," Augusta soothed as she ran her hands over the mare's belly. "Never have I seen a mare get this large, and by my reckoning she shouldn't even be due for another few weeks. I don't want her to have the foal too soon, but I fear for them both if she gets any bigger!"

Tess pulled the mares tail away from her and shrugged. "Well Mother, for good or bad, this baby is coming tonight. She's bleeding and the sack bubble just came out. It shouldn't be long now."

Just then Tess heard a moan in the next stall and went to check. "Oh no, Mother!" she groaned, "it's Sassafras—she's down too. Leave it to Sassy to disrupt the order of things. They've all done so well at having them one at a time but now—we've definitely got two mares in labor!"

Augusta closed her eyes and she shook her head. *Why is it Ty always seems to be away when things like this happen?* Then she called back to Tess, "We'll manage. At least this is Sassy's third, she should do fine. For now, you watch over her and I'll stay with Honey. And you're right about Miss Sassafras—she's been a hog for attention since the day she was born!"

As if things weren't complicated enough, lightning boomed outside and then it started to hail. Tess and Augusta were hard pressed to keep the mares calm during such a rowdy storm.

When Sassy got up to pace about, Tess hurried back to Honey's stall. She was just in time to see two surprisingly small hooves still inside the birth sack. They appeared for a moment then disappeared just as quickly. Tess glanced at her mother, who was shaking her head and asked, "Mother, you've worried that the foal was too big, but it looks even smaller than the others born tonight! That doesn't make any sense—does it?"

Augusta closed her eyes and groaned, "It makes perfect sense—and your mother is a ring-tailed ninny for not recognizing it. That foal is small, Tess, because there are two of them. Honey is carrying twins! I've been the wife of twins and the mother of twins. When she got so huge—I—of all people—should have thought of this possibility."

"But that's wonderful!" Tess exclaimed, then she realized her mother looked even more concerned. "Is it bad for a mare to have twins?"

"In goats or cattle, it's common and usually works out fine, but…" Augusta sighed as she twisted a lock of Honey's pale mane around her finger, "Horses on the other hand, for all their size and strength, are very delicate creatures. I've only known of one case where the mother and both twins survived. Most of the time at least one of them dies. Sometimes Tess—it's all three!"

Tess stood there glaring at the floor for a few moments, then she spun on her heels and left the stall. Augusta nearly panicked. What would she do if her only help left and didn't come back? Then to her great relief, Tess reappeared, and in her arms were two tarps, more towels and the special cords they kept on hand for difficult births.

Augusta gazed up at Tess, "You look like a woman with a plan. What do you have in mind?"

Tess seemed both uncertain and excited, "Well Mama—I have an idea!"

Augusta's heart swelled, Tess had just called her 'Mama' not 'Mother', as Barrett had insisted on. To Augusta, Mama was the most beautiful word in any language, and she savored the sound of it while Tess explained her plan.

"I realize you know more about this than me, but I thought that we could lay one of these tarps just behind Honey and pull her first foal onto it just as soon as it's born." Tess laid everything down and spread one of the tarps out as she continued, "If the baby is small and weak, this will make it easier for us to drag the foal up to Honey's head so she can be licking on it and bonding with it while…well…" Tess lost a bit of her bravado as she added, "while—YOU—figure out how to get the next one out!"

When Augusta seemed to be thinking this over, Tess continued, "Once we have both foals on their own tarp we can easily move them up towards Honey or out of her way when she tries to stand. It should be easier on them, and, on us too! What do you think?"

"I think it's a very practical idea, Tess!" Augusta praised, "I can't tell you how proud I am of you. And you're right, it might take some time before these babies are able to stand on their own and nurse. The other challenge is that we must get Honey to accept both foals! Being able to move the babies up to their mother and then out of the way…that should really help."

Tess giggled, "I got the idea by remembering our own twins. Remember how the whole house was crazy at first and then we came up with our motto, 'Find the method and you can manage!'"

43

Augusta grinned, "Well, you found the method so—I guess we'll manage!" On a more serious note she added, "The second foal is our biggest challenge. That's the one we're most likely to lose. And when we're most likely to lose Honey, too. At least we know the first one is turned in the right direction. Cows can handle having their calf flipped inside the womb. Some will do that to a mare but I'm against it." Augusta's face was clouded with worry as she rubbed the sweat from the mare's neck with a gunny sack, "Honey is very valuable but more than that, she's one of the sweetest mares we've ever had. She's relying on us and I don't want to let her down. Another thing Tess, my hands aren't as strong as they used to be. That second baby may need to be pulled. Meaning we'll have to tie the cords to its hooves while it's still deep inside the womb. Then it will take every bit of strength we both can muster to get that baby out before it takes its first breath. I'll help you and advise you but…*you'll have to do most of the work!*"

"Oh—Mama—NO!" Tess looked genuinely horrified. "I love Honey and want to help her but…I can't do that. I get queasy even when I see someone else doing something like that. I just couldn't—really—I—I just couldn't do it!"

Augusta met her daughters fear with a knowing gaze and conviction lacing her words, "You will though, Tess. I know you! Maybe even a little better than you know yourself. You are so much more than just a pretty face and fashionable clothes. You are a strong and capable woman. And—though you sometimes try to hide it, you have a very tender heart. I know you're squeamish and afraid. But you would never allow anyone, man or beast, to suffer if there was anything you could do about it."

Tess chewed on her lip and frowned, she had never received such a fine compliment. As she thought about what needed to be done, disgust, panic and courage battled within her until she honestly, didn't know which one would win!

Just three minutes later, the first foal, Rosemary, a delicate little palomino filly slipped into the world without a fuss. All Tess had to do was tear the sack from her muzzle, then pull the foals little body onto the center of the tarp. Honey sat up and stared at the strange little creature in complete wonder. Even though the mare was exhausted, she couldn't seem to take her eyes from her beautiful little filly. When Honey didn't even try to get up, Augusta thanked Tess for thinking of the tarp. Little Rosy, already short for Rosemary, was gently pulled up towards her mama's head. Mother and baby bonded as Honey's pink tongue swept over tiny ear tips, the wide golden forehead and dished face. Her persistent licking went from the filly's wispy, fine mane, all the way down to her curly golden tail.

Both women smiled at the heartwarming scene even as they spread another tarp behind Honey, getting ready for the arrival of baby number two. It wasn't long before the big mare forgot all about her newborn filly as her head fell back against the straw with a loud groan. Rosy was quickly pulled out of the way just as all four of Honey's legs stiffened. Another set of contractions began the work of pushing the second foal from the comfort and warmth it had known, into a world of cold and stormy nights. Honey was trying to do her part but the poor mare was weary and ringing wet with sweat. Augusta wiped her dirty hands on her men's trousers she always wore for foaling, then pushed an unruly curl away from her face with her forearm. "It's always best to let the mare do as much as possible. Right now though, I think Honey's pushed her baby as far as she can. Tess, you are going to have to go after this foal!"

Tess's sapphire eyes grew wide, her face went pale and she chewed on her lip, as a deep frown creased her forehead.

Augusta grabbed her hand, "If your Grandpa Bull was here, he'd say, 'Shake it off, gal. There's work to be done!'"

"Yes," Tess nodded, "shake it off," she repeated as she quickly slipped out of her blouse, then bent and washed her right arm in the bucket of hot soapy water. She grabbed the already washed cords used for pulling stubborn babies from the womb, and with a loud sigh she laid down on the tarp behind the mare, all the while muttering, "I cannot—cannot—cannot—cannot believe—I'm doing this!"

Augusta grinned and bit back a chuckle, "You are doing wonderfully, sweetheart! Now see if you can't get those cords on the front legs. If you can't then the back legs will have to do." Sitting down beside Tess, she added, "But… if you get the cords on the front legs you'll also have to find the foal's head and press it against the legs. If the head gets turned it will block the way out, and we'll lose them both! Once the head and legs are straight, we still must be very careful. We can't just yank the baby out, we have to pull steadily with each contraction, until we're done!"

Tess nodded, suddenly she had a different perspective on this. It wasn't so much disgusting as it was…miraculous. Her full attention was on doing whatever needed to be done to help this mare and foal.

Augusta had never been prouder of her daughter than when Tess grinned up at her, "It's still alive Mama," she cried, "it just kicked me." Then her face was a mask of concentration as she fit the smooth cord around the first hoof adding, "God must have heard your prayer, the baby is facing the right way." Just then Honey's body went rigid with a contraction and Tess howled, "Yeeeoww… Mama…she's breaking my arm!"

"You're all right, sweetheart," Augusta soothed as she rubbed her daughter's back, "I'm sorry, I know it hurts, but you're going to feel the contractions right along with Honey. Try to get the second cord on the other leg as quickly as you can. When that's done and she has another contraction, remember you'll have to guide the foal's head along with the legs while we both pull. Remember, slow and steady."

To Tess it seemed as if hours had passed, but actually it took less than a minute to slide the cord around the second little hoof. The moment the next contraction started, mother and daughter began to pull. They had to prop their feet against Honey's backside and the wall as it took every bit of their strength and leverage to drag the second foal into the world. And what a joy he was to see! He was small but perfectly formed, jet black with a star and strip on his face.

There was a moment of fear when the colt didn't seem to be breathing. Instantly, Tess yanked that little fellow right onto her lap, holding him and rubbing him, while Augusta cleared his nostrils. When he finally sucked in his first breath of air and shook his head they both laughed with relief.

"Just look at him, Tess!" Augusta beamed. "He's a perfect miniature replica of Quest. In keeping with our theme, what do you think of calling him, Sage?"

Tess smiled, "Rosemary and Sage—it sounds good!"

Seeing that Honey was too exhausted to clean her baby, Augusta proceeded to go over him with a clean towel. However, it was vital for the mare to know her second foal, so they dragged Sage forward to be introduced to his mama. Honey's maternal instincts overrode her exhaustion. For a few moments, she managed to sit up and make a few cursory passes over her foal with her long pink tongue. Then she laid back down with a groan.

Augusta studied the mare, pulling from her years of experience. "We aren't out of the woods just yet. Honey is awfully weak and these two foals aren't nearly as strong as the others born tonight. I'm glad we have bottles for times like this. We'll need them for the next few days at least. I'm going to milk Honey and give each foal half of whatever I can get from her. I don't want to waste Honey's nourishing first milk. This will help all three of them." Just then Augusta remembered the other mare. "Oh Tess, we forgot all about Sassafras! Please go check on her while I try to fill these bottles."

Tess had been gone only a few seconds, when Augusta heard her laughter, then she called from the other stall. "Sassafras had her baby, Mama! She didn't need us. They're both up and the little rascal is already nursing. No bottles for this little guy. He's the prettiest dark chestnut I've ever seen, not a speck of white anywhere. In fact, he's such a dark red—" Tess giggled, "well, he's as red as Carlos's favorite new spice! I sometimes wonder if it was a good idea to bring him a full pound of that, cayenne pepper from New York!"

"I know what you mean!" Augusta agreed, but I think you just named the last foal for the year. Cayenne sounds good to me—and it certainly fits tonight's theme!"

⚞⚟

Throughout the night, mother and daughter worked together. It took all of Augusta's experience and all of Tess's stubborn determination to persuade the twin foals to take their bottles. Many hours later they helped them stand and nurse. Exhausted but not able to leave the foals just yet, Augusta curled up for a cat nap on a pile of hay. Although Tess was sleepy, she was too exhilarated from that night's events to rest. Instead, she strolled down the aisle, peeking into each stall for another look at the new arrivals. Cocoa, Sugarfoot, Spice, Rosemary, Sage and Cayenne were beautiful and unique, each in their own way. It had been an awe inspiring and miraculous experience. Six foals from five mares—in one night! Never had she worked so hard—and—never had she felt this good. Best of all, it just seemed right to have another set of twins on the Bar 61. A contented smile spread across her face as she contemplated telling Papa and especially her little brothers about Rosemary and Sage.

Suddenly the long night seemed to catch up with her. Yawning loudly, Tess shuffled towards the barn door, hoping that the morning sun and the sweet scent that always followed a hard rain would revive her. Just as she was reaching for the handle, the door swung open. Blocking the bright morning sun with her hand, she peeked beneath it and saw a pair of highly polished black boots, perfectly pleated gray trousers, a wide black belt, white shirt, burgundy silk vest and dark gray coat. Then finally, she looked up to see blonde hair and blue eyes set in a handsome and familiar face.

"Barrett!" Tess exclaimed, "I thought you wouldn't be here till next week." Smiling she held her arms out and stepped forward. The man's handsome face suddenly contorted, "Oh, no you don't—stop right there!" he commanded, as he placed his hand on her head, literally keeping her at arm's length. Not wanting to prolong even that touch, he immediately took a long step backwards and withdrew his handkerchief from his pocket and wiped his hand, "Tess, what in the world have you been doing? Better yet, don't tell me. I'd rather not know what you're covered in."

Tess wasn't sure what to say or do. Her smile vanished while her hands fluttered about nervously. Finally, she hid them behind her back, feeling ashamed and humiliated. Of course, she knew she was filthy, from head to foot no doubt. Then again, there wasn't anything she could do about it, not at that moment anyway. Only seconds earlier her heart had overflowed with a sense of accomplishment and pride. Now as she saw herself through Barrett's eyes, all those good feelings vanished away.

"Mama and I—uh—" she stammered, "I mean...Mother and I have been up all night. We helped five mares deliver—six foals!" When Barrett failed to be impressed, amused or even curious, her words seemed to stick in her throat, "You—you see, five mares went into labor last night and—and one of the mares had tt-twins!" When he sighed and crossed his arms, she tried harder, "It was a miracle, Barrett. Quite often one or all three die!" When Tess felt tears burning behind her eyes she added softly, "But—all three are doing fine now." Finally, she gave up and lowered her head, "I suppose I must look and smell a little rank... but..." Just then she glanced up and when Barrett raised one eyebrow as if he were awaiting her apology, she lifted her chin and stepped closer! "Do you want to know why I look like this? Because...I laid down on a bloody tarp, reached inside an exhausted mare and literally pulled her second colt from her body—that's why! Probably not what a New York debutante would do—is it? But we very well may have saved the life of a valuable mare and her twin foals." When Barrett blinked and cautiously took another step backwards, Tess advanced, "How dare you arrive earlier than expected, then come in here and turn up your nose. You act as if I should apologize for being dirty in your presence. Well, I'm not going to—Mister T. Barrett Tulane—I'm proud of what we did!"

Augusta, who had been silently listening, was thrilled when she heard Tess giving the pompous city slicker a dressing down. Now, for Emily's sake, she could step in and play the peace-maker.

"Welcome to the Bar 61, Barrett," Augusta smiled pleasantly as she came down the aisle and put her arm around Tess's waist, "of course, it's wonderful that you and your mother were able to come a bit early. We're happy for you to be here. However, as it happens, Tess and I have had quite a night! My husband, sons and half our men are delivering horses to Fort Leavenworth. The rest of our hands, surprisingly enough, are down with chickenpox. That's why we're tired and dirty and yes—maybe even a little cranky! Last night was long and hard, but in many ways, a very typical event on a horse ranch." Augusta gave a slight chuckle as she dusted the hay off her backside. She didn't like Barrett or his highhanded attitude but he was the beloved only son of one of her dearest friends. Also, the Tulanes were invited guests. Hoping to create a more hospitable mood, she motioned towards the stalls and said sweetly, "Come on Barrett, let Tess introduce you to the six little miracles we welcomed into the world last night!"

At that, Barrett held up his hand and shook his head, "Thank you, but no! I doubt that you can show me anything in the recesses of a smelly barn that I would consider—miraculous." He chuckled as he clasped his hands behind his back adding, "Forgive me for being blunt but—rank is the word—for this place and quite frankly—the two of you. I think it best for me to wait with Mother inside your lovely hacienda. We'll look forward to visiting with you both—once you've had a chance to—a—to make yourselves presentable." With that Mister T. Barrett Tulane backed his way out of the barn, turned and walked away.

Chapter 6
Dangerous Game

"Everyone who acknowledges me publicly here on earth, I will also acknowledge before my Father in heaven. But everyone who denies me here on earth, I will also deny before my Father in heaven." Matthew 10:32-33

After Barrett left the barn that morning Tess was hurt, angry and confused. As the insecure but hopeful socialite, she knew she should hurry after her fiancé and apologize. Do whatever it took to make things right. As the proud ranch woman, she wanted to kick the man in the shins then roll him in a mud puddle. It was probably for the best that she didn't have time to do either. Although exhausted, she was also grateful that the twin foals gave her an excuse to avoid the Tulanes. That is, until the doctor came that afternoon and told the men they were well enough to resume their duties and take over for the women. This was not good news for Tess—she still wanted to hide. She even convinced her mother to go in the front door while she snuck into the hacienda through the bathing room window, like she and her brothers used to do after a mud fight.

After a long soak in the tub, Tess quietly slipped back into her room. She hadn't slept in forty-eight hours and all she wanted was to get the tangles out of her hair, then sleep for a month. Sitting at her dressing table she picked up her comb and frowned at her reflection in the mirror. "I look like my head is stuck in a tumbleweed!" She set right to work but her arms were already so tired. When the comb became hopelessly entwined in her rebellious curls. Angry tears threatened as she reached for her scissors to cut it lose, when someone knocked on her door.

"It's Aunt Emily, sweetheart. May I come in?"

While Tess was trying to think of an excuse not to see her, Emily slowly opened the door.

"Please, let me come in." Seeing the comb tangled in Tess's curls, like a rabbit caught in a briar patch, Emily gave her a sympathetic smile. "It may be a different color but your hair is just like your Mama's. It becomes a raven-ous beast after you wash it. I know you're all worn out, why not let me help?" When Tess dropped her hands to her lap in surrender, Emily blew out a sigh, "You and your Mama sure have had a time of it. There's nothing like a chal-lenging day on the heels of a hard night to bring you down. I want to apologize for arriving early. I tried to tell Barrett that surprises often seem like a good idea, but most of the time, they'll swing around and kick ya like a bad-tempered mule!" When Tess's lips twitched, Emily felt better, "Of course there is no excuse for bad manners. If I was half the Mama my Mama was—well let's just say—his hide would be hanging on the barn wall right about now." Emily's face suddenly brightened as she gazed into the mirror and locked eyes with Tess, "But as mad as I am at T. Barrett Tulane, I'm just that proud of YOU!" Seeing Tess's surprise, she added, "That's right, I think you are wonderful, darlin'! You remind me of your Papa Tim. And I know that he is very proud of you." When Tess bit her lip and shook her head, Emily said no more just silently fo-cused on the job at hand. When she was nearly finished, she said softly, "I hope you can forgive Barrett. It's not entirely his fault. You see, Wes and I buried too many babies. His surviving was a miracle. Foolishly, we spoiled him. Of course, Amelia, having no children of her own, was delighted to help. We all knew from the start we could never discipline him. It was Wes's idea to give him a name to live up to—Timothy after your father and Barrett after your grandfather! They were both special but, your Papa Tim wasn't like anyone I'd ever met. He loved God and he loved life! He was born rich in money, but poor in health. His life wasn't easy! Still, he was grateful for every little thing. One of the biggest lessons he taught me was that God hides a pearl inside every challenge. He believed that hardships are often God's way of teaching His children something important." Emily smiled at Tess's reflection in the mirror, "It was your Papa that showed Wes and me, and your Mama, how to become Christians. Unfortunately, my boy is nothing like the men we named him af-ter. Not yet anyway. But you are! I didn't see it when you were in New York. But today, when your mother told me how you saved that mare and her twin foals, it was hard for me to believe that the elegant creature that floated down the steps at Mosslet Way, could be so—selfless—so humble. She also men-tioned that you never miss church and that you sing in the choir. You—sweet Tess—are a very-unique young lady!" When Tess grimaced at the compliment, Emily continued, "The Bible says, 'It's harder for a camel to go through the eye of a needle than for a rich man to enter the kingdom of heaven.'" Shaking her head, she muttered, "That is so true. Wes and I tried to teach our son godly wisdom. But...while God whispers truth, the world shouts pretty lies. People tend to follow whoever speaks the loudest." Emily paused for a moment, a troubled expression clouding her face, "That's why I must ask for your forgiveness. For I was the one shouting pretty lies while you were staying with us."

Tess saw the contrition in Emily's face and was confused by it, "Forgive you? For what—you treated me like a queen!"

"I know I did, darlin'. I didn't see it for what it was at the time. Debutantes buzz around my son like bees on a honey tree. Most of them are shallow and selfish. Just as Barrett is at times." Suddenly Emily smiled, "Then he saw you and it changed everything. He had always enjoyed your letters but when he finally saw how lovely you were—he was impressed! As for me—I wanted to dance a jig when I saw him pursuing you and ignoring the others. I was thrilled at the idea of having you as my daughter-in-law. So, I put you in the best room and gave you three maids to see to your every need. I've prayed so hard for Barrett to meet the right girl and I saw you as a gift straight from God."

"Emily, please..." Tess groaned, "I'm not at all what you think. You owe me no apology. Everyone is always telling me what a saint Timothy Grainger was, but..." frowning, Tess bit her lip then looked up at Emily and blurted out, "I AM NOTHING LIKE MY PAPA TIM! As for my church attendance—I'm healthy and my parents never miss nor would they allow me to. I sing in the choir because I love to sing. I am much more like Timothy Tulane than Timothy Grainger. I might not have grown up in a mansion but compared to our neighbors, we live like kings. And—I have quite deliberately put off embracing my parent's beliefs. I am not a Christian—not yet." Ducking her head, Tess added softly, "The truth is—I want to have some adventures first! Barrett and I have always talked about how both our parents play down their wealth. He and I agree that prosperity should be enjoyed! And for that matter life should be enjoyed—while we're still young! There is so much that we want to see and do. But we don't want to worry whether it's something a proper Christian should do or not. I agreed to run away with your son because it was an exciting idea! Everyone was angry at Barrett, but the truth is, we were both to blame."

Emily sat down across from Tess and sighed, "Well darlin', I truly do appreciate your honesty. But, I'm not apologizing for being kind. What I feel badly about is showing you the benefits without telling you that there's a dark side as well. All that glitters is not gold. If you want to hob-knob with high-society, then prepare to be gossiped about and judged at every turn. Oh, they'll fawn all over you, if you give them what they want. But beware—if you stand in the way of what they want, they will gleefully destroy you." Emily took in a deep breath then blew it out, "It caused me years of heartache before I learned that lesson. And—it's a lesson Barrett refuses to learn. It's all a game to him—a very dangerous one. But it's one that's even more treacherous for a woman. When a man and woman run off together, he's praised for making a conquest, he's teased for being a rogue and a rascal, even as the elite shower him with invitations to their luncheons and balls. It's just the opposite for a woman. Society snobs delight in all their lovely young debutantes. However, if one of them makes a false step, then she's instantly renounced as a fool, a coquette—or worse! Instead of receiving more invitations, like the man, the upper crust will shun her for the rest of her life. The game you're intent on playing with the wealthy elite of this world is very risky, Tess. But the game you and my son are playing with God is far more dangerous. The stakes are eternal life or death. It doesn't matter if you enjoy your wealth or give it away. What does matter, is how you answer the most important question ever posed?"

Tess frowned then asked softly, "What question is that?"

Emily took Tess's hands then asked tenderly, "What if you died tonight and found yourself standing before God and He said, 'My son Jesus died on a cross to forgive your sins so that you might have eternal life in heaven. Did you accept or reject the salvation Jesus died to give you?'"

Tess's face suddenly grew hot even as her heart pounded in her chest. She didn't understand why Emily's words so unnerved her—but they did. "I've got some time—don't you think—before I have to worry? I am young and strong," Tess scoffed, trying to sound amused as she turned and grabbed the brush off the dresser. As she briskly ran it through her now, tangle free hair, she added, "I do plan on making things right with God———someday. I imagine Barrett will too—after we've traveled the world and had a few adventures!"

Emily nodded, "I see, so your plan is to eat, drink and be merry, then pray hard and quick before you die? And…when will that be exactly?" When Tess only shrugged, Emily squeezed her hand, "Your father was twenty-nine and just an hour away from his dream of seeing his brother and living on this ranch. The very last thing he expected was the bullet that killed him. Fortunately, he was ready, but you're not! Becoming a Christian is a decision that must be made before we die. And death comes like a thief in the night." When Tess looked away, Emily sighed, "All right, I know you're tired. Let me share one more thing, then I'll leave you alone. When I first moved to New York, I became friends with a young woman. Because her mother had died when she was young, she was angry with God and wanted nothing to do with him. I tried to explain to her that God is God. He doesn't offer explanations. What He does offer is His love and salvation. One day she said that she was almost ready to accept Christ as her Savior!" Emily looked out the window as her eyes filled with sadness, "I had a terrible feeling that day and I begged her not to wait any longer! She just said, 'Emily, don't push.' So, I said nothing more, just hugged her and we went our separate ways. Children were playing across the street and their ball went wild. I saw it hit my friend on the arm. It didn't hurt her, but she lost her balance. Had she just fallen she would have been fine. Sadly, she struck her head on the sharp corner of a brick building. When I got to her, she was looking up at me. But—she wasn't there anymore. She must have died instantly."

"Aunt Emily," Tess chided, "you are just trying to scare me!"

"No, I am not," Emily insisted, then she blew out a sigh, "well, maybe I am, but you need to know that's how the end often comes, Tess. My friend was happily married, young, healthy, but it was also her day to die. God put me in her life and through me, God gave her one last chance—and she rejected Him! I repeat, you and Barrett are playing a treacherous game with God. And He doesn't play games."

Tess was silent for a while, then she shook her head, "I appreciate your concern, but I don't feel as if I'm playing games, as you say. I'm just sort of asking Him to wait for a while. There are things I want to do without limitations." Tess stared at her hands and frowned, "I don't deserve your earlier compliments. To be honest, I'm not quite sure who Tess Grainger is right now. While I was soaking in the bathtub today, I began wondering what I would have done, had I been alone last night? If Mama hadn't been there, would I have helped that mare and foal or would I have run to my room and hid until they both died?" Tears clouded her eyes as she glanced up at Emily's reflection, "I don't know if the real me is the girl that made a grand entrance at your fancy ball or the one who laid down on a bloody tarp and delivered those foals? Am I both—or neither? Perhaps the more important question is, if I have a choice, who do I want to be? I know this is not what you want to hear, Aunt Emily. But the truth is, I think I'd rather be the first girl and maybe never again, the second."

Tytus Grainger and his twin sons whooped and waved their hats in the air as they raced their horses under the Bar 61 entrance. It was good to be home! They had paid all the ranch hands back in town and had left them there to celebrate another successful drive. The three Grainger men, however, were in a hurry to get home. Ty knew the boys would miss their mother and sister, but he hadn't remembered how homesick he got himself. He couldn't wait to pull Augusta into his arms. He had missed Tess too, and for many reasons, had kept up a constant dialogue of prayer for that sweet and headstrong girl. His next thoughts went to that society fop, Barrett Tulane. He would be arriving soon and Ty dreaded it, because he knew that Tulane wanted to take his little girl away...forever.

As it happened, just as the three were riding into the yard, the last person in the world Tytus wanted to see was the very first person that greeted him, "Welcome home, Sir!" Barrett called out with a smile as he crossed the yard.

Ty's lips twitched as he took Tulane's hand without removing his dirt incrusted gloves. Barrett returned his host's hearty hand shake, "I hope you all had an enjoyable—uh—*journey*." He said as he dusted the dirt from his hand.

Ty leveled a sly glance towards Caleb and Joshua, "Well boys, since this was your first—*journey*—to the Fort, would you describe eating sand with every meal, sleeping on the ground and trying to keep a hundred head of horses together while chasing them through forests, and across swollen rivers—enjoyable?"

Joshua, a dark haired handsome lad of fifteen, took his hat off and slapped it against his thigh, knowing full well that it would raise a small dust cloud, "No Sir, I wouldn't call a trail ride *a journey* and I don't think—*enjoyable*—is quite right either. It was good though and...I'd do it again."

Ty smiled, "Good answer." Then he turned his gaze on Barrett, "It's a long hard ride, but it's filled with the kind of challenges that teach a boy how to be a man! Too bad you couldn't have come with us."

Barrett fought back a retort as the other twin, Caleb, a near perfect match for his brother, rode up to him and said, "Yeah, wish you would have come, too. We'd like to get to know you, Mister Tulane. By the way I'm Caleb and that's my twin brother. It's easy to tell us apart though," he added with a grin, "just remember, Caleb is the one that's smart and handsome, Joshua is the other one!"

Barrett made no response to the boy's jest. He had dreaded this meeting but he forced a smile as he took Caleb's hand, then said as rehearsed, "It's a pleasure to meet the brothers Tess is so fond of and..." turning to Josh, he shook his hand adding, "no need for you two to call me Mister, Barrett will do."

The twins locked eyes with each other and then their father. They didn't need words to speak their thoughts. Ty let out a weary groan as he swung down from the saddle, "Well, Barrett, why don't you come along with us while we tend to our horses then we'll all head up to the hacienda. The boys and I are anxious to see our women folk!"

Barrett wasn't sure what to say. He been there for two days and things were still a little icy between him and the women folk, even his own mother. "I'm afraid you won't find the women in the hacienda. Your ranch hands have all had the chickenpox. Even though the men are finally well enough to work now, Tess and Augusta insist on playing nurse maid to a couple of the foals. I was just heading down to the far barn. Thought I'd have one of your men saddle a horse for me."

Barrett's words caused the twins to stop in their tracks, then stare knowingly at their father. Tytus grinned as he placed his heavy hand on Barrett's shoulder, "We have a tradition on the Bar 61, don't we boys!" When the twins nodded and smirked, Barrett feared what was coming, even more so when Ty's grin broadened, "It started with my father-in-law, Bull O'Brien. He taught it to my brother and me when we were boys. Augusta reminded me of it years later. Bull believed that riding a fine horse is a privilege that must be earned. Before anyone rides one of our horses, they must first show that they can tend to the needs of their mount. That begins with cleaning stalls, grooming, saddling, walking your mount until it's cooled down—that sort of thing."

Barrett's first thought was to tell Grainger that working in a barn was for servants, not for the masters of the house and certainly not for a guest. His second thought was to simply spin on his heels and return to the hacienda. But then he looked into Ty's face, and saw identical expressions on the boys faces as well. The Graingers had thrown down a gauntlet and they all expected him to walk away. He pondered this for a moment, then gave them all a knowing sneer as he silently took the shovel one of the boys handed him.

Ty shook his thumb towards the stall to his right, "This is Leo, think you'll enjoy riding him," he said as the handsome palomino gelding munched on his hay, "but...looks like his stall has already been cleaned. So today you can tend to Saber's stall instead. He's our Arabian stallion," Ty explained. "Even though he's out in his corral, and on the other side of that dutch-door, you still need to be careful!" When Barrett asked why, Ty shrugged and nodded towards Caleb, "Tell him about Saber."

"Well," the boy grinned, "'cause of the smell and dust, you'll want to open the upper half of that outside door. But if you do...you best watch your backside!"

Barrett gritted his teeth, "Because——?"

Not wanting to be left out, Josh answered, "Because Saber doesn't like anybody in his stall, not even to clean it. He pretends he's not watching...but he always is! The minute you forget and bend over with your back to the door, that's when he gets..."

"His pound of flesh!" Ty, Cal and Josh all laughed as they said the words together.

⚞⚟

As Tess walked towards the barn, she was pleased to see Barrett pushing a wheelbarrow. Although they'd gotten off to a rough start, a week had gone by and things were steadily improving—between her and Barrett anyway. How things were going between him and the men of her family, she wasn't so sure. It was a Grainger tradition to challenge a newcomer, especially when they were green horns. She had hoped that Barrett agreeing to clean his horse's stall was a good sign. So far though, asking him to tend to his horse had been their only request. When they liked the guest, the challenges tended to get more creative and amusing. Then finally, her father would say, 'you've done well and the ranch hands will take over now.' That hadn't happened with Barrett and she feared he might never win them over.

Peeking inside the barn, Tess called, "Haven't worked too hard for our morning ride, have you?"

A loud sigh came from the back of the barn, "I'm more than ready!" he answered as he came towards her with Leo and Lucy already groomed and saddled.

They were a stunning pair of dark golden palominos. Their manes and tails were white as were the thin blazes that ran from their forelocks down to their muzzles. They each had four white stockings as well. Other than being male and female they were hard to tell apart. Ty often showed them off as the perfect example of Morab crossbreeds. They had the delicate heads of an Arabian with a more muscular body and calmer disposition of a Morgan horse.

Tess smiled as Barrett led the horses outside. He was wearing a white shirt with the sleeves rolled up and even had a streak of dirt across one cheek. Tess thought she'd never seen him looking more handsome, and she blushed when he leaned down and kissed her, then handed her the reins to her horse.

"Let's get away from here!" he groaned, adding drolly, "far—far—away!" When Tess giggled, Barrett grinned, then swung up into his saddle.

When he reached into the wagon bed and retrieved his hat, Tess hid her grimace and said evenly, "Just follow me, I'm going to take you someplace very special!"

They rode in silence until Tess reined her horse to a stop in the middle of a forest. Gazing up at the canopy of pine boughs that swayed in the wind she said, "Fill your lungs, Barrett. When the wind comes down from the mountains then passes through the pine trees—mmm—it's the sweetest air on earth." She closed her eyes and breathed deeply as a blonde curl fluttered across her face. "Don't just breathe it, Barrett, feel it too. It's like satin ribbons against your skin." When he just rolled his eyes and shook his head, Tess bit her lip then nudged Lucy into a canter.

When they finally reached the top of a hill overlooking a valley, Tess reined in again and pointed to the large mountain looming in the distance. "Barrett Tulane, meet Pike's Peak. This is my favorite view! When my brothers and I were little, Mother used to make up stories of how Pike's Peak was really a huge giant who was just pretending to be asleep. She'd tease us and say that someday he might just decide to get up and walk away! If you use your imagination, the highest part of the peak, above the tree line…that's his lined and craggy face. The ridge on the front is his nose. The lower peaks are shoulders and the foothills are his arms stretching out wide. On clear days like this, the granite mountain against the deep blue sky looks too beautiful to be real, it's just like a painting. I've always loved it here!"

"Oh Tess," Barrett scoffed, "how you do go on. It's not that impressive. Just wait till you see the mountains all over the world!"

"Barrett," Tess huffed, "why not enjoy what you're seeing, while you're seeing it? As it happens, most people find the Rocky Mountains quite impressive!" When

Barrett shrugged again, Tess swung her right leg over the horse's head and slid to the ground. Barrett hated for her to dismount that way and she hid a smile as she turned and tightened the cinch. When the mare nudged her side, Tess hugged her, then rubbed her nose against the mare's cheek, "Lucy, you're a good girl," she praised and breathed deeply. Gazing up at Barrett she squinted in the bright sunlight, "I love the smell of a horse—it's so warm and friendly. I'd bottle it if I could!"

Barrett lifted his eyebrows and cocked his head, "Tess—sweetheart," he sighed, "we really do need to work on your conversational skills. Waxing poetic about mountains having faces and how good a horse smells are uninteresting as well as unsuitable topics. Another thing, you mustn't squint your eyes like that," he chided, "you'll get wrinkles," chuckling to himself he added, "and what man on earth wants a wrinkly bride?"

Tess quickly remounted, then turned to him, "Maybe I'm just the wrong bride for someone as perfect as you!" she sneered, then clucked her tongue. The mare went right into an easy canter but Barrett quickly followed.

When he caught up with her he reached over and reined both their horses to a stop. "Hey now, wait, I'm sorry," he groaned, "didn't mean to hurt your feelings. It hasn't exactly been an easy week for me you know. It's made me a little grumpy and I'm anxious about tonight. I fear the fur is going to fly!" He smiled gently, as he took her hand and kissed it, "But...once we're on our way everything is going to be wonderful—I promise!" Hoping to lighten the mood, he released her hand and lifted his new western hat, "I'm surprised that you haven't said a word about my cowboy clothes. I especially like the hat—don't you?"

It's an embarrassing eyesore, is what she wanted to say but instead she muttered, "It—uh—looks well made." Actually, the hat was fine. It was the hat-band that made her cringe. Usually they were simple strips of leather that went around the crown. Barrett's on the other hand was made from huge silver conchos linked together. Worse still, it reflected the sun like a lighthouse beacon. Tess couldn't believe her brothers hadn't made fun of it by now. At fifteen, Cal and Josh thrived on teasing everyone about everything. The twins had known Barrett for five days now and had barely said a word to him. Just then, Tess remembered that she had heard the boys mumbling something in Spanish whenever they saw him.

Catching herself frowning she turned away from Barrett, *I think they say... cabra something? Cabra cabezón...yes that's it! Now if I can just remember what that means in English.*

The twins often spoke to each other in Spanish. When they were born, Alvaro, their father's longtime friend, who was also their cook, sent for his ten-year-old nephew, Carlos. The boy loved the twins and they adored him. As the twins learned to speak, Carlos made sure they learned each word in both languages. Unfortunately, Spanish hadn't come as easily for Tess. Silently, she struggled to translate the words, as she and Barrett rode single file through a stand of pine trees.

Cabeza means head, and cabezón could mean intelligent. *That would be good! Then again, it could also mean big-headed or arrogant.* *Not good.* *And then cabra means...* Tess groaned and shook her head *Those rascals, they've been calling my fiancé...*

"A BIG-HEADED GOAT?"

"What's that about a big goat?" Barrett asked as his horse trailed a few feet behind hers.

Thinking quickly, she called back, "Oh—Carlos is roasting a—big goat—for the party tonight. It will hurt his feelings if you don't try it! Speaking of the party, we should hurry. I promised Mother we'd help."

Barrett shook his head, "I wish you and your family knew what servants were for, Tess. And I don't mind eating goat, I am adventurous and want you to be too. In a way, I kind of liked that bold Tess I met in the barn that first day. I didn't like the way she looked or smelled, but I did like her boldness!"

Tess wasn't sure how to respond. It was sometimes hard to tell the difference between Barrett's compliments and his insults. She had to assume he liked something about her. After all, he had come all this way to court her.

When the path opened and Barrett came to ride beside her, she snuck a few sidelong glances at the man. *He was so polished in New York.* *I wonder why he seems so different here?* *Probably because being on the ranch makes him a fish out of water.*

Knowing that she should be more understanding with him, she glanced at him again, then found she had to hide her smile. Regrettably, all she could see was that awful hat! The way it reflected the sun, you'd think they were signaling for help. Suddenly she yanked on her reins. "Hold up for a minute Barrett, I really should explain a few things. Everything needs to go well tonight. That's why we both need to help, everyone does, even Papa. Also, many of our neighbors have far less than we do. It's just a country dance, so we dress accordingly. That means—no fancy clothes, no tuxedo and definitely—no hat!"

Barrett cocked his head and sighed, "You're so naïve, Tess. Our goal is not to fit in. This is the night we prove to everyone that you don't belong here anymore!" He frowned, as he appraised her from head to toe. Tess was tempted to warn him about wrinkles, but then he groaned and said, "We are both dressed for ranch life. Your split riding skirt is practical for a little cowgirl, I suppose, but that's not who you are anymore." When Tess frowned, he quickly added, "Remember when we rode through Central Park? You were magnificent. I was the envy of every man and all the women were jealous. We were the talk of New York for days. It will be the same all over Europe. The elite will clamor for us to attend their parties!" Barrett brushed her fingers with a kiss, then added, "I have big plans—but you must follow my lead." Nudging his horse closer, Barrett slipped his hand around Tess's neck and pulled her into his kiss. He all but devoured her lips before pulling away, then whispering, "You will drink in all the pleasures the world has to offer— and I will teach you how!"

Tess's cheeks were on fire and she struggled to catch her breath. When she finally found her voice, she looked down at her clothing and said softly, "It seems there are a lot of things about me, that you want to change."

Barrett sighed and patted her hand, "Tess, quite honestly your country upbringing is a problem, but there's an easy solution! While in Paris, you will spend some time at Madam Sauveterre's Finishing School for Elegant Ladies. There you will learn how to eat, dress, speak, even move in a more elegant way. When we return to New York I'll have no more worries about your country faux pas."

Feeling like a backward hillbilly, Tess asked, "What exactly is a— foe-pa—anyway?"

"It's a French word, my sweet. It means false step," he explained with a patronizing smile. "Tess, you are a true diamond, but one in need of cutting and polishing. Afterwards, there will be no more false steps. So tonight, you will dress as the fiancé of a millionaire should! You will show your family and friends that you were meant for a bigger world—my world."

As they cantered back to the ranch, Tess contemplated what he had said, contemplated her future. While in New York, she had enjoyed being around Barrett. He hadn't been nearly as charming while here on the ranch. It was obvious now that he saw her as inferior. Perhaps she was, but still, he had chosen her over all those elegant city girls. He wasn't asking too much, not really, just that she learn some new things. It was a fair compromise. Impulsively, Tess reined in her horse and spun her around to face Barrett, "I'll do as you say tonight and I'll learn all I can from your finishing school. We will make the perfect couple and enjoy a life filled with adventure and excitement! We won't nibble at life like our parents. We'll grab hold of the world and take our fill!"

Chapter 7

The Party

"Faithful are the wounds of a friend; profuse are the kisses of an enemy." "Better a little with the fear of the Lord than great wealth with turmoil." **Proverbs 27:6 & Proverbs 15:14**

Barrett gazed out the guest cabin window, watching Carlos helping his Uncle Alvaro onto the musician's platform. Once seated, they both began strumming their guitars.

The next thing he saw was his mother, smiling and laughing as she walked arm and arm with Joseph, the old black man. Barrett gritted his teeth and shook his head. *What an insult, I'm not allowed to sleep under the same roof as Tess while that old Mexican and ancient black man are treated like family. Tess and her brothers even call them both, Uncle. My motto has always been and will continue to be, 'The best place for the very old and the very young—is very far from me!'"*

All those not of his social status were also included in that motto. Believing that his own mother was not his equal, he hoped to convince her to move to Colorado, permanently. With her no longer seen about town, the cream of New York society would soon forget his humble parentage and embrace him fully! Barrett was distracted from his thoughts when Carlos began playing a quick and complicated tune. His fingers flew over the neck and strings of the guitar, the notes almost tripping over each other as they built in intensity. Barrett had heard music like this before as he strolled the back alleys near the docks.

Thinking of the darker side of New York reminded him of the letter that had just been delivered. Although he was alone—he gazed around anxiously before he opened it. It was written with a distinctively feminine flair, had no salutation, just began abruptly.

I sent this to the ranch, as proof that I fear nothing and that I have eyes everywhere. I was at the train station when you and your hillbilly mother boarded your private car.

Watched you purchase those ridiculous cowboy clothes in Denver. I shall assume that you are there to complete the task you failed to do last January. However, now you will find that my plan is a bit more final—and more imaginative. You will succeed this time or our mutual friend K.F. will tell all. Oh, yes, my good man—or more accurately—my not so good man. Read the following instructions carefully, for you must carry them out to the smallest detail. Succeed and you will never hear from me again. Fail me and you will hang!

Barrett's heart quickened as he read the instructions that followed. Her plans this time seemed more diabolical than imaginative. Cursing, he folded the letter, put it back into the envelope, then slipped it into his tuxedo's inner pocket. He knew Tess was waiting, but he needed a few moments to think about these new instructions. *That old witch, she's been pulling my strings for three years now. No matter what I do for her...she's never going to stop! I'll never hear the last of her...not until she's dead. However, now that I think of it...these additional changes might just serve my own purposes quite well. I've wanted to marry but just so I can get full control of the estate. Of course, I have never wanted a wife! I've been wondering how to get rid of Tess? Now, it has all been worked out for me. Even better, the news of Tess's disappearance, will bring the mighty Tytus Grainger down to size. Then...I will deal with that old bat and that little spy of hers. I've killed once—I can do it again! Still—everything hinges on Tess going away with me. I was careless this afternoon and upset her! That was foolish, I must make sure she has no doubts about our future together—no doubts at all!*

⌖

Tess forced a smile, trying not to look as ill at ease as she felt. Her gown was a pale blue satin, trimmed with ivory lace. It was lovely, but a thousand times too extravagant for a country dance. And yet, remembering what Barrett had said earlier had persuaded her to put aside the simple gingham dress she'd planned to wear, and put this one on instead. It was her twenty-first birthday, but rather than looking forward to the big party ahead...her mind and heart were in turmoil.

I've always been so confident, so what happens to me when I'm around Barrett. Maybe he was right about that finishing school. After all, he is offering me an extravagant and exciting life. He just wants me to fit in, and I will, once I've learned to eat, dress, speak and—move. He said I just needed to be cut and polished. I wonder if there will be anything left of Tess Grainger, once he's done changing me. Still, if he truly didn't think that there was some part of me that was good enough, he wouldn't have asked me to marry him—would he?

"Best wishes to ya, Tessie May! I'm askin' once more, will ya marry me?"

Tess spun around, but it wasn't Barrett, it was Sig Rosenquist. His proposing had become a tradition, he asked every time he saw her. Though born in America he still spoke with a slight Swedish accent.

"Ah, sweet Tess," he said with a grin. "Come dance with me, then marry me this night. Just like your folks did twenty years ago!"

"Oh Sig..." She groaned, "there are a dozen other girls to dance with and to propose to. You know my fiancé is here tonight and naturally, I've promised the first dance to him."

Sig was a tall, good natured blonde with gentle gray eyes. Undeterred, he bent low and his words tickled Tess's ear as he whispered, "Ja, that might be so, but I'm the man for ya."

Tess frowned and swatted him away like a pesky fly, "You're a very good man, Sig, but not the one for me. You're content to be a simple farmer. I want more from my life...not less!"

The big man straightened then frowned down at her, "So, yus to have more, ya vill go and marry that dude with the fancy hat? Ya don't love him though, do ya? When the preacher asks if ya vill love, honor and cherish that popinjay, vill ya lie?"

"That is none of your business—Mister Rosenquist! So just go—go bother some girl that's willing to settle for a man like you!" The insulting words instantly turned to ash in Tess's mouth, she wanted to take them back but didn't know how.

Hurt flashed across Sig's face, then he clenched his jaw and nodded, "All right, but here's a bit o' free advice, Miss Grainger. When ya truly love someone, ya fear not being good enough for 'em. I'm not good enough for ya, Tess—I know that. But beware o' the man who thinks that yer not good enough for him. Ya may end up settlin' for far less than ya think."

Tess watched Sig walk away knowing that she must apologize, but it would have to wait. Because just then, two of her favorite people in the world were walking towards her with huge smiles on their faces. They were a stunning couple, both tall and blonde.

"Uncle Quin—Aunt Mariah!" she called as she hurried into their open arms. "I was afraid you might not come this year!"

Quin laughed, "Miss your twenty-first birthday? Not likely. Besides, Wings practically runs itself these days. The folks at the mission won't notice that Preacher Long is gone." Smiling down at his wife he tucked her into his side adding, "Now Mariah, on the other hand, will be sorely missed! Even so, we're both here with special presents for a special girl!"

As Mariah placed a beautifully wrapped bundle in her hands. Tess smiled, thinking of how she had always been in awe of her Aunt Mariah, though they were not related. Mariah's hair was a pale blonde and her eyes were deep lavender, like shining amethysts. Most of all she was as sweet as she was beautiful. That thought caused Tess to wonder. People had called her beautiful too, but in her case, was it just skin deep? Shaking off the notion, Tess batted her eyes playfully, "I know I should say, 'Oh, you shouldn't have.' Of course, you know you'd be in terrible trouble if you hadn't!"

Quin laughed, "Yes, we know! You're the birthday ogre. That's why we brought you two presents this year. Since this is a special birthday we thought we better try a little harder."

Tess giggled as she tore off the wrapping to reveal an intricately braided, white and gray horsehair bridle. "Oh my, I've never seen such a handsome bridle. I—I wish I could wear it myself!" she teased. "Really, it's beautiful—thank you!" She gave them both another hug but they were serious about the second gift and they each took one of her hands and began pulling her around the side of the house. Tess was instantly caught up in their excitement. When they rounded the corner, all the guests were there, waiting. Everyone began laughing and making a pathway as Quin and Mariah continued to pull her along. When they finally stopped, Tess couldn't believe her eyes. The Bar 61 produced some of the finest horses in the country, but she'd never seen the equal of the mare that stood before her now. Her delicate head, the width between her large dark eyes, the dished face and narrow muzzle, all pointed to her being at least part Arabian. But her coloring was that of an appaloosa. A breed favored by the Indians. The mare was dark, a bluish charcoal-gray, except for the snow-white blanket that went from the tip of her withers to the top of her hocks, with fist size gray spots dotting the blanket. Her mane and tail were a pale gray, almost a silvery-white, a stark contrast against her dark coat. As for her conformation, she was perfection. Pointing a trembling finger at the mare Tess stared up at Quin and whispered, "M—mine?"

He laughed, "All yours sweetheart! We know how insistent you are about having things that match. We bought that pretty bridle so we just had to find a horse to go with it!"

Tess laughed then threw her arms around the couple again. "I've never seen anything like her! Over the past few years you've mentioned your Arab Appaloosa crossbreeds, but I had no idea they were this beautiful!"

Quin grinned, "Glad you like her, actually Bluejay here was our first foal!" he added proudly, "if you ever came to visit, like we've been begging you to, you might have met my friend, Shadrack McKenna. He has a handsome appaloosa stallion. About five years ago, I purchased an Arabian mare. We call her Zephyr, she's dark gray like her daughter here. It was Shad's son, Tanner, who had the idea to breed their stallion Boone to Zephyr. We breed them every year. They kept the first foal which was Bluejay here, and then we kept the next. Tanner trained her before he moved back East to work for me. He's saving up for foundation stock and for good ranch land where he can raise and train Arab-Appaloosas. Every foal has been beautiful but Bluejay has always seemed special. Mariah and I have always thought that you were the prettiest thing to ever grace the back of a horse. Every time we saw Bluejay here, we couldn't get over the feeling that you two were meant for each other!"

Tess was as touched by his kind words as she was with this amazing gift. She hugged Quin and gave the mare's forehead an affectionate rub while he continued to explain.

"This year's foal was to be mine but Shad took a strong liking to the little stud colt, he needed him to replace their old appaloosa stallion Boone. So, I traded him the colt for Bluejay! I know it might seem odd to give a horse to a horse breeder's daughter but we just believed that this very special animal—was meant to be yours! Of course, you can change her name if you'd like, but watch this first." Quin took the mare's lead rope and led her away at a trot until they disappeared behind the far barn.

Mariah slipped her arm around Tess and said softly, "All right sweetie, just call out, 'Bluejay come!'"

Tess grinned, "I wouldn't dream of changing her name." Then she cupped her hands around her mouth and called to the mare.

Instantly, they heard a soft whinny as the mare stepped out from behind the barn shaking her head. It was obvious that this was a game the mare enjoyed! Without hesitation, Bluejay trotted to her new mistress, then pressed her delicate muzzle into Tess's hand.

"Here," Mariah whispered as she gave Tess a small bunch of carrots, "might as well start spoiling her."

Tess hugged the mare as she fed her the treat then turned with a sighed, "Oh Uncle Quin—Aunt Mariah, you never have to give me another gift as long as I live. She's amazing!" Bluejay nudged her hand for another carrot and Tess laughed, "She's smart too, she'll have me trained in no time!"

Now that the excitement was over, Tess lingered with the mare while the guests strolled back to the party. As she ran her hand across Bluejay's silver mane and white-blanketed, charcoal coat, all she wanted was to toss a saddle on this amazing creature and run away. Sig's words were still ringing in her ears and Barrett had yet to appear. She feared he might be waiting to make a big entrance—she desperately hoped not!

Just then Shep, the ranch foreman, stepped beside her, "Happy Birthday, little darlin'!" he said with a quick one-armed hug, "am I still your favorite cowpoke?"

Tess laughed, "Always and forever!"

"That's my girl, and like I tell ya every year...besides yer mama—me and Joseph were the first to lay eyes on ya. And we've been at your beck and call ever since. So, I reckon you'll trust me to take good care o' this fancy gal for ya!" When Tess grinned and handed him the lead rope, Shep nodded, "All right now, go on and have yourself a good time!"

Shep was a short, stocky man in his mid-thirties, with curly red hair and a ready smile. He patted Tess's cheek then headed to the barn with Bluejay. Suddenly he stopped and turned back to Tess. "Hey, darlin' could I have a word?" When Tess shrugged, he closed the distance between them, "Ya ain't gonna leave us—are ya Tessie? We never have talked of it much but I was on the shady side of death when your Papa Ty found me. I still don't know my real name, how old I was then, or why I was out in the prairie all alone. What I do know is that havin' a family and folks that love ya, is a precious thing, darlin'. Don't take it fer granted." He frowned down at his boots for a while then asked, "Ya ain't gonna forget us and run off with that Tulane dude, are ya?"

Tess's eyes were sad as she handed him her new bridle. "Would you put this with my other tack?" When he cocked his head like an overgrown puppy waiting for a better answer she sighed, "Oh Shep, I only know one thing for certain," she said as she reached out and squeezed his hand, "I'm going to save a dance for you!" Then in her desire to get away, she spun around so quickly that she literally ran right into her best friend, Filippa Rosenquist, nearly knocking her down.

As they helped each other regain their balance, Filly huffed, "Well—my goodness—Tessie May—Happy Birthday!" The petite red-head laughed, adding, "I was hoping to run into you." Rubbing her shoulder she added, "Not quite that hard though, but I am glad to see you!" Then she slapped a hand over her mouth, "Ooops—not supposed to call you *Tessie May* anymore—I know— I'm sorry." Clearing her throat, she straightened and said stiffly. "Happiest of Birthdays, Miss Tess M. Grainger!" When Tess rolled her eyes and made a face, Filly giggled, "I don't know why *you* were in such a rush, but I was hurrying to find you! We're putting together squares for the first dance." Suddenly Filly's face turned the same color as her bright pink dress, "Harvey made me promise him the first dance. We'll be one couple," she beamed, "Preacher and Mariah will be the second, your folks will be the third and we thought you and—um— what's his name—can be the forth. Sig said if 'who's it' doesn't show he'll dance with you!"

"What do you mean if 'who's it' doesn't show?" Tess scoffed as she folded her arms, "his name is Barrett and I'm sure he'll be out in a minute!" Under her breath, she added, "He better be out in a minute."

"Sorry—again," Filly sighed. "Tell ya what, you keep an eye out for— Barrett," she said carefully, "while I go fetch us some punch." Shaking Tess's arm she chided, "Smile—this is going to be the best party you've ever had."

Tess couldn't help but smile, Filly had always been a wonderful friend. They had met exactly twenty years ago, on the day of the Bar 61's very first party. Gazing about at all the smiling faces, she remembered that this event was the highlight of the year not only for her family, but for many of their friends and neighbors. Tess worried her lip as she waited expectantly for Barrett. *Wish he would hurry up. At least with him in a tuxedo, I won't feel so overdressed. Maybe I won't have to explain this gown.*

Filly scowled towards the guest cabin as she came forward and handed Tess her cup. "So, where in the world is…Prince Charming? Is he scared of us rustics?" When Tess gave her a stare that only a good friend could interpret, she laughed, "Oh, don't mind me, drink up, then we need to get in place. I do not want to miss the first dance."

Tess sipped her punch as she glanced up at the platform, "Filly, why are you so anxious? The dance can't begin without music, and only Uncle Alvaro and Carlos are up there. Come to think of it, Hitch and Helen are still back East visiting her sister. There are two empty chairs up there, but I don't know who's going to fill them. Our sweet old McGee said he wasn't well enough to come tonight."

Filly lifted her chin and smiled, "Well, fancy that, I know more about your party than you do! There's brand new talent here tonight, Miss Tess. Oh look, there's one of them now." They watched as a big man jumped up onto the platform, then sat down next to Carlos. "That's the new blacksmith, Beck Hoffman. Have you ever seen such a big, strong man?" Filly blushed as she added, "Beck—I mean Mister Hoffman, also made me promise him a dance! He said everyone would just have to do without him for at least one song. He plays the panpipes."

Tess raised her eyebrows and nodded approvingly, "He's very big and yes, very handsome! I'm glad you have another suitor. I think Harvey takes you for granted. But what in the world are panpipes?"

"I had never heard of them either. It's a wind instrument made up of a row of short hollow pipes in different lengths, they're held together with a thin wire. He blows across the top, kind of like a flute, and just wait till you hear the sound it makes. He came by the school last week and played some hymns for the children. It was sad and strange—but oh—so very pretty! And do you know who else is playing tonight? Gunner!"

"Gunner?" Tess asked, "meaning your little brother—Gunner?"

"The one and only! He's so nervous, he's only twelve after all, but he's been spending a lot of time with Tanner McGee. No one has ever fiddled as well as old McGee but he's taught Gunner a lot! Even if he *is* my little brother, he's really good and I'm proud of him."

Tess rolled her eyes, "Well that little stinker. I'm proud of him too! Even if he did put a mouse in my lunch pail!"

"That was six years ago," Filly chided, "and he was just a little boy... haven't you ever heard of forgive and forget?"

"I forgave him the day he did it. But...ewww," Tess shivered at the memory. "I'll never forget how that thing fell onto my skirt and ran down my leg. That little scamp, he still teases me, he wiggles his eyebrows and pats his pocket, like he might have another mouse in there!"

"He's just funnin' with ya, Tess! As the new teacher, I happen to know your brothers are just as bad. This spring, Caleb laid six, fat white grubs on the chalk rail and hid all my chalk. I picked one up and tried to write a sentence with it...you should have heard those children howl! The whole class was laughing so hard I couldn't get them to stop. Had to dismiss school early that day. What we ought to do, is play a trick on all our brothers!"

Tess laughed, "Oh, I know just the thing, we could..." Tess blew out a sigh and shook her head, "no—I guess we couldn't. I shudder to think what Barrett would say if he saw me playing a school girl trick like—some ill-mannered hooligan!"

Filly suddenly became serious and took hold of Tess's hand, "You are my dearest friend, and I'll always love you. But since you came back from New York, you're—different. I'm afraid this—Barrett—is changing you into someone that—you won't like when he's finished."

Tess stiffened, "Someone *I* won't like or someone *you* won't like?"

Filly stared at Tess a moment, then said softly, "True friends tell each other the truth. You're wealthy Tess, everyone knows it, but you've never flaunted it—until tonight. You look magnificent, but I thought you were going to wear your gingham dress. Are you wearing satin and lace tonight...because 'who's it', told you to?"

"Yes," Tess admitted, "Barrett just wants me to show that..."

"Oh, let me guess," Filly scoffed, "he wants you to show everyone that you're too good for all your friends and your family...and this place. That's it, isn't it?"

"Is it a crime to wear a nice dress for your own birthday party?" Tess groaned. "Barrett and I both want my family, and my friends like you, to realize that I just don't fit here anymore! I want everyone to see for themselves, that my leaving is the right thing to do."

"But it isn't the right thing! I can't believe you're serious about that arrogant dude. Why would you want to leave everything you've always loved?"

"What is the matter with everyone tonight?" Tess muttered as she walked away, hugging herself, as if she were suddenly freezing, "Shep just asked me the same thing. Don't you see, Filly, you've got your teaching but what do I have? I've always wanted to raise and train my own horses. When Papa told me that the ranch would be divided between the boys, I felt like a ship on dry land. He said he'd do right by me, whatever that means, but Barrett is offering me the world, travel, adventure and luxury. It's an amazing opportunity and I'd be a fool to turn it down. Barrett only seems like a dude here because he doesn't belong here. In New York, he's sophisticated and elegant."

Filly cupped Tess's face in her hands, "But you don't love him, Tess, do you?"

Tess pushed away, "No Filippa, I don't love him and I don't care! You know that twenty years ago today, Hitch proposed to Mama. She turned him down and married Papa Ty that very night! A few months later Hitch married Helen."

"And both couples are very happy!" Filly insisted. "Money and luxury aren't a guarantee of a good marriage or even a good life, Tess!"

"Maybe not, but I've seen how Hitch and Helen struggle and scrimp. Mama said she hated Papa Tim, at first. They were married for months before she fell in love with him. And Papa Ty hated Mama when she first came to the ranch, but they fell in love too! If she had married Hitch my life would have been completely different. If that makes me shallow, so be it. I don't want a life filled with struggle, not if I can avoid it. I'll marry Barrett and love will come or it won't but I'll still have a good life!"

"Are you sure about that, Tess? Granny Rose always said there were two kinds of poverty. The poverty of possessions, meaning the lack of things. The other was the poverty of the heart, meaning the lack of love. Granny said, 'For sure and certain, the Rosenquist's were poor in things. But our family was rich in love and without love, all the wealth in the world, is a shallow stream at best.'"

Tess sighed and forced a smile, "That's enough talk, Filippa." There's a good chance that I may not be here tomorrow." When Filly frowned, and started to protest, Tess covered her mouth with her hand, "No more! You are my dearest friend. We may not see each other again, for a very long time. So please, let us both just enjoy this night." Tess laced her arm through Filly's and pulled her towards the others getting ready for the first square dance.

As they passed the gift table, Filly grabbed one of the packages and handed it to Tess, "Here, open my present, you may need it before the evening's over." Tess bit her lip, tears threatened as she hugged the bundle close. "The gift is inside, silly!" Filippa teased. Tess laughed as she quickly tore the paper away to reveal a beautifully crocheted shawl made of white yarn with silver threads running through it. Tess flung her arms around her childhood friend

and held her tight, "You made this didn't you?   It's beautiful and I love it!"
Tess quickly tossed the shawl around her shoulders adding, "it's funny, I've
received three gifts so far tonight and all three have been silver and white...
even Bluejay!"

Filly held her tongue for a moment then in almost a whisper she asked,
"So what about Bluejay?   Will you give her back to Preacher and Mariah?"

"Bluejay?" Tess's heart plummeted, then her mind began spinning, "No—
I can still keep her.   In fact, riding Bluejay through Central Park will create
quite a stir.   I'll wear a dark gray riding habit with white lace.   Before long,
all of New York will be clamoring for a horse like mine.   You know I've always
wanted to breed and train horses.   I don't have to give up on my dream, Filly.
It hadn't occurred to me until just now, but why can't I breed Bluejay to an
Arabian stallion back east?   I'll raise Arab Appaloosa's just like Uncle Quin and
his partner.   You see my friend, I don't have to stop being myself when I marry!
I'll still be me—just me with a little more polish!"

Just then old Cecil Crow stepped up onto the platform wearing his offi-
cial square dance calling hat.   It was dark green with a black crow feather jutting
out one side.   Grinning he clapped his hands, "Well now—find yer partners—
get in yer squares—and be ready to kick up yer heels!"

Tess gazed around nervously, then discovered that Barrett was standing
right beside her.   One look at him and she wanted to faint.   He wasn't wearing the fancy tuxedo or even the shining hat, for that at least she was thankful!
Instead he wore blue jeans with a white shirt, a plain brown belt and a black
string tie.

He looked down at himself and groaned, "Your father brought me these
clothes and—I got the impression that I had better wear them."   Taking both
her hands, he grinned, "You though, my dear, look marvelous!   Suppose I'll
have to allow you to outshine me this time," he teased, then added with a wink,
"but just this once!"

Tess wanted to run back to her room and change, unfortunately, there
wasn't time, for the music began and Cecil started everyone clapping their
hands as he hollered, "All right folks—here we go!"

The usually confident Tess, once again, wasn't sure what to do.   Then
Barrett completely surprised her and everyone else when he laughed, picked her
up and spun her around.   Then Cecil began calling out the dance in a sing-song
cadence with the music:

First you whistle, then you sing
All join hands and make a ring.

Grab that filly and give her a spin
Twice around with your haunches in.

Hand over hand and heel over heel
The faster you go, the better you feel.

Barret fumbled on a few of the steps but laughed it off good naturedly. Before long he picked up the rhythm and timing as well as all the steps. Tess had never seen him like this. He looked genuinely happy as he joked with the men, complimented all the ladies, and teased the children. He didn't look down or talk down to anyone all evening. Tess forgot all about her doubts and confusion and really began to enjoy herself. Barrett was the most handsome and most charming of all the men and she felt so proud that she would soon be his wife. She was sure she was making the right choice. Soon they would be traveling the world, sharing more nights, just like this one. Perhaps—they were even falling in love!

The guests were gone and the hour was late as everyone headed into the hacienda. Tess stopped to stare up at the night sky. Enchanted by the glow of the full moon, a slow smiled spread across her face. *This birthday seemed to have a theme; the fancy bridle, Filippa's beautiful shawl, the magnificent Bluejay and even the night itself seems, to have been created from shades of silver and white! I can only hope that's a good omen. I was worried at first but it turned out to be a lovely party. Now, if only the rest of the evening will go as well!*

Everyone was sleepy as they shuffled into the elegant parlor, with its heavy furniture and thick carpets, and found their places. It was a family tradition to gather there after a party. They'd talk for a while and enjoy a cup of hot chocolate before they all went to bed.

"Well now," Ty said as he sat down next to Augusta and put his arm around her, "that was a fine party but somehow these quiet moments afterwards are always my favorite. Tess, will you pour please?" While Tess served everyone in the room, Ty focused on Barrett, "Well young man, what did you think of your first western square dance?"

After Barrett downed his cocoa in two swallows, then gazed around at everyone, his mother included, all seemed to be wondering the same thing. "Well, I thought it was a perfect party! I have danced the Quadrille before, and it's very similar."

Emily smiled up at him, "Well, I'm proud of ya Son. I don't know when I've seen you so relaxed or have such a good time. As for myself, I loved it!" Emily covered a yawn as she leaned back on the heavily cushioned chair, "as my ole Tennessee Mama would have said, 'Twas a grand time, but it wore me plum down to a frazzle!' Smiling sleepily, she sat up and gazed around the room, "Although I love you all madly—I simply cannot stay awake. So, if you don't mind I think I'll bid you all—good night!"

Barrett cleared his throat and said, "Could you wait a moment, Mother?" He walked over to where Tess was standing and took her hand in his. "We have something important to say, while we're all here together—as a family!"

Augusta's heart seemed to stop, and she slipped her hand into Ty's, then asked, "What is it you want to say?"

Avoiding Ty's penetrating gaze Barret directed his words to Augusta, "First, I want to offer my apologies once more for my impulsive behavior last January. My heart was in the right place even if my brain was not!"

Ty nodded, "I'm glad you see your actions as a mistake."

"Yes sir, we both do," Barrett agreed as he lifted Tess's hand to his chest and held it there. "As you all know we two have corresponded since we were children. When you all came to New York, Tess and I quickly realized that we were good together and that we wanted the same things, like seeing the world and all that life has to offer. I appreciated my parent's nobility in using the Langstrom wealth to do good and Tess admires you all for doing the same. At least for a while though, we want to, well…"

Ty frowned and sat forward in his chair, "You want to enjoy yourselves."

"What's wrong with that, Papa?" Tess scoffed, "we both just want to break free a little. We still want to get married in France, then travel around the world!"

"Hold on there," Emily interrupted, "I'm just now realizing that, you two don't even pretend to love each other—do you?"

Tess stared at the floor, not able to meet Emily's gaze, "We do care for each other and we enjoy each other's company."

Augusta stood and went to the couple. "Then why marry at all? If you both want to travel you can do that separately or perhaps we could all take a trip together!"

Barrett sighed, he'd hoped to be done with this discussion by now, "Please, everyone, Tess and I want to be together, live and travel together! That's why we want to marry!"

"Son," Emily said, "As you know, I have decided to move to Colorado Springs. Why not get married here, so Ty can walk Tess down the aisle and the whole family can be together for the wedding?"

"No offense to anyone—but that's not what we want," Barrett tried to stay calm as he explained, "we wish to be married at Saint-Pierre de Montmartre. It is the oldest church in Paris. It's a place of history where important people are married. I—we want to be part of that history. We aren't typical people and we don't want a typical wedding. We will, however, follow your counsel and travel with a chaperone." Taking his mother's hand, Barrett gave her the smile she could never resist and said, "Mother, Tess and I would be so very pleased if you would come with us! Surely you can put off your move until you return from France? It might be the last chance for us to be with you for quite a long while." Barrett straightened as he turned to Ty, "As I'm sure you know, there are certain times of the year that are the safest for ocean travel. I want Tess and my mother to have a pleasant and safe voyage. Right now, is the best time to sail."

Seeing he was about to lose his daughter, Ty raked his hand through his hair, "Tess, you've always had a rebellious streak when it came to giving your heart to God but what you're doing now is foolish and dangerous! Please, I beg you to consider what God's will is in all this. Marriage is a three-way pledge of love between a man, a woman, and God. It's not an excuse to travel together without gossip. It's about commitment not adventure!"

"Oh Papa, just because we aren't doing things God's way, doesn't make us bad people!"

"Then, what does it make you, Tess?" Josh asked, "we've been raised to honor God. Choosing a life partner is about the most important decision anyone can make. I'm still wet behind the ears and even I know that!"

"Tess," Ty implored, "you're making a mistake. After the newness of this life of adventure wears off, you're going to regret this decision."

Tess squeezed Barrett's hand and her chin quivered as she stared at her family. They all looked alike; dark hair, dark eyes. She was the one that didn't fit. It was a fact that always pierced her heart. Then she looked up at Barrett, he was like her, blonde hair blue eyes, they were a match.

Tess went to her parents and hugged them, "You're both wonderful and I love you!" Then she went to her brothers and hugged them too, "Even though you two drive me crazy sometimes, I love you both so much and I'll miss you!" Tess finally turned towards Emily, "You are the icing on the cake! I think you'll make a wonderful mother-in-law. I'll be forever grateful if you would come with us!" Suddenly, Tess felt completely drained as she gazed around the room once more and sighed, "The very last thing we want is to hurt anyone. Nevertheless, regardless of how you all feel about it, Barrett and I have arranged to return to New York in his private car. Our train will be leaving—tomorrow at noon."

Chapter 8
Deception

"Your trusted friends will set an ambush for you that will take you by surprise." Obadiah 1:7

Emily glanced at Barrett and Tess as they excitedly discussed their travel plans.   Letting out a silent sigh she turned to stare out the window of their private car.   Augusta had told her that the tracks paralleled the ranch's western border, adding that when she stopped seeing the six-wire fence, that she would have finally left Bar 61 land.

My goodness, she mused, *that ranch must be the size of New York!*   It was an exaggeration of course, and that wasn't really what she was thinking about anyway.   Her stomach was tied in knots because everything felt so wrong.   What kind of mother thought her only son wasn't good enough for his chosen bride?   It was ridiculous, but she was happy for Barrett and herself, but sad for Tess and especially for the Graingers.   She could only imagine how miserable Ty, Augusta and the boys must be feeling at this moment.

It had been quiet the melancholy carriage ride from the ranch to the Santa Fe railway station in Colorado Springs.   Ironically, they had traveled south for an hour to board a train heading north!   The next stop would be Denver and then multiple stops before finally arriving at the New Brighton Station in New York.

Oh Lord, I want to be happy about this marriage.   But their notions about life and about you Lord, are as twisted as a curly willow tree!   I'm afraid if I throw a hissy fit, Barrett will just leave me behind and forget about having a chaperone.   I've got to go along with this, for Tess's sake.   It's a big old mess but there ain't...isn't...oh shoot... there ain't a dad-blasted thing I can do about it!   Feeling frustrated and ashamed, Emily squeezed her eyes shut, I'm sorry Lord, please forgive me and help me, help them.   You know I'll do anything you tell me to do!

Unable to sit any longer, Emily left Tess and Barrett in the fancy parlor and went to the sleeping area at the far end of their private car.   Since she and

Tess were sharing one of the two sleeping rooms, she unpacked her things and then Tess's. Then she pondered whether or not to unpack for Barrett. He had not brought his valet, so no doubt, his clothes would be wadded up and shoved into his trunk. The need for something to do, won out over her frustration with her son. "What a mess!" she fumed, as she picked up the dress jacket he ended up not wearing to the party. When she shook it out, an envelope fluttered from the pocket and landed on the floor. "That's odd, it says: 'Marsden & Marsden Attorneys at Law', but that isn't their stationery and they always use one of those fancy new typewriter machines. This address is hand written." Emily felt goosebumps spreading down her arms and she hurried to the door and peeked out. When she heard Barrett's deep voice, still coming from the parlor, she stepped back inside and locked the door. "I really shouldn't read this..." Even so, she picked up the envelope by the corner and gave it a good hard shake. "Well, looky-there, a letter just accidently fell out on the floor. I suppose I should pick it up and put it back in the envelope, "she mused. "Of course, should I happen to catch a word or two, there's no harm in that." Smiling at her own foolishness, she began to read. An instant later her smile faded and tears began to fill her eyes. The letter was not what it appeared to be, it was like a wolf in a sheep's clothing. When she read the words, *'Fail me and you will hang'*, her whole body began to shake.

"Hang? Oh no..." Suddenly Emily couldn't quite catch her breath. She had pretended and denied the truth for over three years. But she knew why her son deserved to be hung. Memories of her dear loving husband, Westin Tulane, tormented her thoughts. He had ridden away that morning so strong and determined. Then the next time she'd seen him, his pale lifeless body was lying in a coffin. This might be the proof that her worst fears were true, and suddenly it felt as if a knife were piercing her heart. She doubled over for a moment but then forced herself to straighten. She couldn't give in to the pain this brought her, there would be time for that later. Now she had to read every word of this atrocious letter. Her eyes flew over the first part but she felt truly sickened as she read the shocking instructions that followed.

When you arrive in Paris, you and Tess must be seen at restaurants and theatres as a doting and affectionate couple. While your mother is still with you, be sure to have Tess write a note on hotel stationery. It must say, 'Didn't want to wake you, have gone out to buy you a surprise! Don't worry I won't be gone long!' Tell her it's for your mother but keep this note as your alibi! After you're married and your mother returns to New

York, take Tess to Madame Sauveterre, at 55 Rue Clapeyron, for her lessons in etiquette. Madame has already been paid and given instructions to deliver her to Hamon Moreau.. He will make sure that silly girl is never seen or heard from again.

 To secure your alibi, I've arranged for a blonde and veiled young woman, wearing Tess's clothes, to accompany you from Madame's house back to the hotel. She will leave your room early the next morning, wearing her veil and pretending to be Tess. When a few hours have passed show the note, written in Tess's own hand, to the hotel manager. Keep it to show the police and to Ty and Augusta when they come searching for their daughter. Naturally, you must play the part of a frantic newlywed husband, searching for his beloved wife.

 As for me...I shall be at the Bar 61 when your distraught telegram arrives. Once I have seen Augusta brought to her knees with worry and grief—then and only then—shall I release you from your debt. When I'm satisfied that Tess is truly gone, Keefer's letter accusing you of murder will be destroyed.

 Should you fail me again, the police will receive that letter and you will surely hang!

 Most sincerely, L.W.

Emily was shocked and sickened by the malicious plans that were intended for Tess. And even more horrified by the fact that her son was actually going through with them! Oh, how she had longed for that boy, begged God to answer her prayers for a child. Now she had to admit that her precious son was a bad seed. He was assisting in the murder of his fiancé just to save himself. And why was he doing such a thing? To keep from being hung for killing his own father. Her heart broke all over again as she thought of Westin Tulane. He had been the finest and best of men and a wonderful husband. They had been happy together, both before and after Amelia Langstrom-Drew had brought them to New York and transformed their lives. The wealth had helped them but it hadn't really changed them. However, by the time their son turned eighteen they feared it might be ruining him. Emily had been in favor of Wes confronting their spoiled boy on that fateful day. A few hours later she'd been told that Wes had been shot and killed. Her very first thought, was that in an arrogant rage, Barrett had shot his own father. Then later, she had chided herself when Keefer Flynn gave his account of how both father and son had been attacked by a bandit. For the past three years, she'd clung to that little man's words, for Barrett was all she had left. Now it was clear that

Keefer had truly seen what really happened that day, and he and this L.W. have been holding it over Barrett's head. Emily could no longer deny the truth, for it had just slapped her in the face! Everything—all of it had been a lie, deception at its worst! She had no idea who L.W. was, but somehow all of this revolved around hurting Augusta. Staring down at the letter once again, her heart seemed to pound in rhythm with the train wheels as they clattered against the tracks. They were speeding Tess to her destruction, and in that moment, she knew what she must do next. It would surely put a noose around her own son's neck but she couldn't dwell on that now. No, now she must find the conductor, then speak to the chef.

The constant swaying of the train caused Emily to stagger as she set the tea tray down before Tess and Barrett. "Hello little darlin's, I brought you two a special treat from the chef! He says that our luncheon will be served a bit late, so he sent us some cocoa and these blackberry scones." Emily smiled as she gave Tess her cup then handed the other to Barrett adding, "I know you like extra cocoa so I doctored yours up a bit."

When the couple stared at each other and then at Emily, she shook her head, "I know, I've been kind of sulky this mornin', maybe even a little mule headed about all of this. But the truth is—I love ya both! It just occurred to me that—if I can't alter your journey—I might as well enjoy the ride!" Lifting her own cup in a toast she said, "May we all end up exactly where we're supposed to be!"

Barrett slanted a puzzled look at her, then shrugged as he finished off his cocoa in three gulps, just as she knew he would. The moment his empty cup was on the tray, Emily stood, "Will you excuse us son? I have a little present for Tess. And you look awfully tired. You can't go anywhere so you might as well get some sleep. We'll be back in a minute." Taking Tess by the arm she pulled her towards the far end of the private car.

Locking his hands behind his head Barrett yawned, "Take your time, ladies. I think I will have a nap. I've barely been able to sleep in that hillbilly guest cabin of the Graingers."

Emily gritted her teeth as she stopped and turned back to her son, "That's why you should sleep all you can, now. We'll leave you alone while you rest and don't be concerned if the train stops for a while. The conductor said we'll be taking on some supplies, but we'll wake you when it's time to eat."

Barrett grunted something and Tess giggled when he started snoring before she and Emily had taken another step.

Knowing full well that her son would stay asleep for many hours, Emily shouted, "Come on, we have to hurry," she urged, as she pulled Tess into their shared sleeping quarters, "darlin' you must believe what I am about to say and do exactly what I tell you!"

The moment those words were spoken, Emily realized that, head-strong Tess would never just do what she said. Especially something this drastic! Feeling desperate, Emily took Tess by the arms and willed her to understand, "You are in terrible danger—you must go home!"

Tess just blew out a sigh, "Emily, I am not going home! We've discussed all this," she scoffed, then folded her arms, "and how am I suddenly in terrible danger?"

Emily took the letter from her bodice and thrust it into Tess's hand, "I found this letter in Barrett's pocket. It's a complete betrayal of my son but you must read it! We have a lot to do and very little time." Emily reached into Tess's trunk, yanked out her riding habit then flung it onto the bed. As she searched for the boots, she explained, "I've already asked the conductor to stop the train before we leave Bar 61 land. He said there's a good spot there to unload your horse. Although he promised to help us, he won't hold the train for long!"

Tess raised her eyebrows, "Stop the train and unload my horse? Emily, a conductor would never agree to do that!"

"They will if you pay them enough!" Emily huffed, "now girl, you read that letter!"

Tess stamped her foot, "NO! I will not! And you shouldn't be reading his letters without his permission! But since you did, if what it says bothers you this much then you should discuss it with Barrett. I'm sure he can explain." Suddenly, Tess gave Emily a skeptical look, "Or did you and my parents write this letter? Is this some sort of trick to keep us from going away together?" Frowning, she put her hand on her hip, "I know my parents are against it but I truly thought you wanted me for a daughter-in-law!"

"Oh, darlin'," Emily sighed, "more than anything I wish you could be my daughter and that you and Barrett could have a long, happy life together. The truth is…I'm just now being honest with myself about my son. Your life is in danger, Tess. Maybe your family's as well. Thank God I found that letter as soon as I did. I think I've known the truth all along, but in my heart, I thought I could will him to be a good man. And that marrying you would inspire him to do better. He's not a good man though, Tess. Still, I never would have thought he'd be willing to destroy you to save himself from being hung!"

"Hung?" Tess gasped.

"Please dear, I beg you to trust me and read that letter. You really need to know what it says!"

Tess sighed skeptically, then allowed her eyes to sweep down the page. She was amused when the author of the letter mentioned the ridiculous cowboy clothes. Then, all too soon the words ceased to be amusing. When Emily asked her to step out of her shoes, she did so without thinking, for her thoughts were completely tangled up in the words. She didn't even protest when Emily unbuttoned the back of her traveling gown and began helping her into a riding habit. As she read on, her mind wanted to deny all of it. Finally, she read out loud the phrases that were the hardest to believe.

Have Tess write a note…it is your alibi!…Take Tess to the Sauveterre's Finishing School for Elegant Ladies, for her lessons in etiquette. Madam will deliver Tess to Hamon Moreau. He will make sure that silly girl is never seen or heard from again."

Tess suddenly felt the stabbing pain of betrayal in her chest as hot tears began blurring the words. Swiping them away she glanced at Emily and read the last words of the letter, out loud, *"When I'm satisfied, that Tess is truly gone, Keefer's letter accusing you of murder will be destroyed. Fail me again and you will surely, hang! Most sincerely, L.W."*

A deep trembling began in Tess's stomach as she looked up and gazed into Emily's heartbroken and tear streaked face. "This isn't some ploy to break us up—is it. You sincerely believe that he intends to escort me to my death—or worse—don't you? Who is this, L.W.? Isn't it possible that this could have been sent by one of Barrett's spurned debutante's? Just a horrible idea of a sick joke?"

"No debutante did this—whoever wrote that letter is pure evil through and through. It sounds like Barrett's just a pawn and this L.W. is blackmailing him to hurt you and your family. Still, we can thank God that I found that letter and that the conductor agreed to help us. It shames me to say it, but it's obvious that Barrett has agreed to sacrifice you to save himself! I've looked the other way and made excuses his whole life. Right now I am being forced to see him for what he is." Sniffing back a sob she urged, "Please hurry now and put your boots on. I gave Barrett some of my extra strong sleeping powders, with any luck he won't wake till we get to New York."

Tess felt like screaming, how had her world spun out of control so quickly? Just a few minutes ago, she and Barrett had been laughing and talking about all their plans. Once they had finally gotten on the train, everything had been wonderful. Now she was being forced to believe that this same man was taking her to her death. It was too much to comprehend and she reached out and took hold of Emily's hand, "How can you be sure we're doing the right thing? My getting off the train like this—it just seems so melodramatic—so drastic—so—crazy."

Emily held the letter up, "Remember what this says, Tess. Darlin', this L.W. is dangerous and so is Barrett! Crazy or not, you have to get yourself away from him. Once he wakes up I might not be able to protect you. And...you must warn your family, especially your Mama!"

Tess nodded, then she surprised Emily when she picked-up her green velvet reticule, and withdrew a small derringer. "I never go anywhere without this—and if you're right—I may need it," she muttered as she slipped it into the right pocket of her riding habit, then put a box of bullets in the left. When the train lurched to a stop, Tess frantically grabbed Emily by the arm, "Wait—this only makes sense if Barrett actually killed someone. As his mother, do you honestly believe he could be guilty of murder?"

Emily nodded sadly, "Yes darlin'—I do—I've been suspicious for three years now. I know who and I know why. But you see, I love that boy with my whole heart and I had convinced myself—that I was mistaken. Then I told myself that even if he had made a terrible mistake, when he was young and foolish, that he was a different person now. And as I said before, I thought if he married you—that you would help him become a better man." Emily grimaced as she gazed down at the letter, "That was foolish and selfish of me. Now, I fear Barrett is as bad as whoever wrote this. If he had any intention of doing right by you, he would have shown this to me or your parents. For Pete's sake, Tess, he would have shown it to you! I know my son very well. I have no doubt that he planned to follow these instructions."

Emily folded the letter and slipped it back into her bodice, "There's one more thing you need to think on. This L.W. had a plan and now it's failed! You can bet they'll try something else. You must get home to safety and warn your parents. All we can do now is trust in God. He's the only one that can make any of this come out right!"

Tess stood there as if her mind and body were frozen. This just couldn't be right. Emily was urging her to hurry but she couldn't move. All she could think of was what a happy evening she and Barrett had shared the night before. How they had danced together in the moonlight. Only a few minutes ago, they'd both been so excited as they made plans for their voyage, wedding and honeymoon. She had even thought that they might be falling in love. Now, was she being wise or foolish to just believe all of this and run away?

"Emily," she groaned, "you still haven't answered my question and I must hear it! You said you knew who and you knew why. So please tell me, who did he murder? And why would he do such a thing?"

Emily squeezed her eyes shut and sighed. When she opened them, she looked directly at Tess and said stoically, "Barrett always hated for anyone to tell him what to do. When he turned sixteen he announced that since we weren't as educated as he was, that we should turn full control of the estate over to him. We refused of course, but he became more and more difficult. Finally, one-day, with my full knowledge and support Wes confronted Barrett about his arrogance. I wasn't there—but I know now what must have happened. Just to have control of fifty percent of the estate, our beloved son, Timothy Barrett Tulane, murdered his own father!"

It was a fearful and strange goodbye. There were no farewell waves or brave smiles. The two women simply stared at each other. Tess sat on her mare while Emily gazed down at her with one hand pressed against the window pane, her face glistening with silent tears.

When the engineer blew the whistle, and the wheels of the train began to groan and whine, Bluejay sidestepped and snorted. Tess reached down and placed a comforting hand on her withers, "It's all right girl," she soothed, then shook her head, "that's a lie if ever there was one. Nothing is all right—and I fear it's only the beginning." Tess patted the mare once again, then reined her south.

"Bluejay," she sighed, "we don't know each other very well but I'm sure thankful you're here with me." She clucked her tongue and the mare broke into an easy canter. A distant rumble caused Tess to glance towards Pike's Peak. Hanging just above the mountain top were churning black clouds. They seemed every bit as dark and monstrous as Barrett Tulane's betrayal. "Sorry girl, looks like we're trying to escape from one storm only to find ourselves in the midst of another. As Emily would say, 'We're in for a real 'toad-strangler!'"

Tess struggled to stay calm as the wind suddenly roared all around her, tugging at her clothes and ripping the pins from her hair. In seconds, the sun was swallowed up by enormous black clouds. They loomed overhead like the unfurled wings of a hungry vulture, just waiting to swoop down on her. Glancing all around, Tess watched as the storm clouds spread across the entire sky, hovering over the mountain range and the valleys beyond. In the distance, she saw jagged lightning bolts, reaching down like sharp talons, clawing at the earth. Suddenly, the rain began pelting her with such force Tess could barely see the path ahead. In seconds her velvet riding habit was drenched and a chill was seeping into her skin. Fortunately, it wasn't much farther to the nearest line shack. Regrettably, the small shelter was located on the western border of the ranch. It was closer to the mountains than the hacienda, but for many reasons, it was the wisest place for her to take shelter.

Emily had thought Tess was safe because she had left the train on Bar 61 land. What she didn't know and Tess hadn't really thought about, was that it was a good long ride from that part of the ranch to the safety of the hacienda. Much too long a ride to make in the middle of a storm! By the time Tess dismounted and led Bluejay into the small barn, the last dying remnants of sunlight were slowly dissolving behind the mountains. Storms had always frightened Tess, so to bolster her courage, she tried to convince herself that what she was going through, was not a hardship; it was instead—an adventure!

"I don't need Barrett nor do I need to travel. The fact that I'm all alone and no one in the world knows where I am right now...is...well...it's exhilarating!"

As if to test her bravado, a brilliant show of lightning streaked across the horizon followed by earth shaking thunder. Tess shivered and Bluejay's eyes grew wide and she tossed her head nervously.

"Easy girl, we aren't going to be afraid of a noisy old storm—are we?" Tess stammered as she stroked the mare's long neck. She might have done a better job of calming her horse if she weren't feeling so terribly vulnerable herself. With every flash of lightning, she imagined a gang of cut-throats and villains watching her through the cracks in the barn walls. When another deafening lightning strike, hit far too close, she shrieked and Bluejay snorted and reared. Tess held out her hand, "We're all right Bluejay, calm down," she soothed. When the mare just snorted at her, Tess blew out a sigh, "I know—I'm just as scared as you are—but all this could be much worse. We've got each other, a roof over our heads, there is grain and hay for you and hopefully, something in the shack for me. This isn't pleasant but we'll be fine..." Tess's teeth began to chatter as she set two buckets outside to catch the rain, then returned to her horse, "P-p-poor Bluejay, you look like a d-d-drowned rat," looking down at herself, she added, "and s-sooo do I!"

Her fingers were so stiff and cold that it was a struggle to unfasten the cinch and jerk the saddle from the mare's wet back. Then, she nearly jumped out of her skin when she lifted a handful of gunny sacks off the pile in the corner and a dozen mice scattered in every direction.

"Eww—eww—eww, I hate m-mice!" she squirmed. After taking a moment to calm herself, she began rubbing Bluejay's coat with the gunny sacks. Once the mare was cooled down and mostly dry, Tess carried the full water buckets inside for Bluejay to drink. Lightning and thunder snapped and roared overhead as she filled the manger with hay and grain. The mare was more frightened than hungry and she pawed the ground and circled her stall.

Tess stayed with her mare until the storm calmed to a steady rain, and Bluejay lowered her head and began munching her hay. Knowing she'd better get dry soon herself or face pneumonia, Tess said goodnight to her mare with a quick pat on her spotted-rump, then stepped into the steady downpour once again.

Of course, it was much easier to ride through a blinding rain in a water soaked riding habit, than it was to walk in it, especially while hopping over mud puddles. It was such a relief when she reached the shack, stepped onto the porch and pushed the door open. It was pitch-dark inside and she shrieked when she walked into a mass of cobwebs, frantically pulling them out of her way. Desperately in need of light, she gingerly tapped her fingertips over the dusty table next to the door. When she felt the box of matches and found the lantern just beside it, she blew out a sigh, "Well, whoever was here last, you have my thanks," then, with trembling hands she struck a match and lit the lantern. A warm welcoming glow spread across the room and she was finally able to take her first peaceful breath since Emily had served her cocoa on the train. Gazing around the small shack she silently nodded her approval. There was an unwritten law of the west regarding line shacks. One which her Papa Ty strongly enforced. Anyone who takes shelter there is honor bound to replenish the supplies for whoever comes next. Especially during the winter, a well-stocked line shack might very well make the difference between life or death.

Tess smiled when she saw that the corner shelf had large glass canning jars filled with coffee, flour and sugar. There were also a dozen tins of beans and a large supply of dry wood beside the stove. As quickly as her shaking hands would allow, she built a fire and stripped down to her petticoats. The small metal bed squeaked loudly as she yanked it away from the wall, then reached down to pry up the loose floor boards. Now she could get comfortable, for her secret cache was why she had chosen this particular shack.

"This is one bit of rebellion for which I make no apologies," she mused, as she lifted the metal box from its hiding place. It held the one thing she needed most right now—warm, dry clothes! She'd been jealous of her brothers' freedom—just because they were boys. So, sometimes she dressed like a non-descript boy herself. Then she'd go places a proper girl dressed in lace and velvet wouldn't dare! The metal box held an old pair of Cal's blue jeans and a faded plaid shirt of Josh's. She had also absconded with two pairs of thick socks, some work boots that one of the boys had outgrown, but fit her perfectly, and some of her own long handled underwear. The last item in the box was a big floppy felt hat—big enough to stuff all her hair into.

By the time Tess had laid out her dry clothes, she was shivering harder than ever. Standing before the stove's open door, she struggled to peel off the rest of the garments proper ladies were forced to wear: two petticoats, knickers, a camisole, a corset, garters and stockings. The room was getting warmer but still her teeth were chattering as she dried herself with flour sacks, much like she'd done for her mare. Finally, she slipped into her boys clothing. It felt luxurious to be warm and dry again. Soon beans and coffee were bubbling on the stove while she finished drying her mass of curls by the fire.

Now that her immediate needs were met, Tess was finally able to think on the problems that faced her. Pacing the room, she stopped at a small shaving mirror on the wall. Peering into it she frowned, "You certainly have been gullible and naïve, Tess. How could you let Barrett trick you so easily? He dangled luxury and adventure before your eyes, like a worm on a hook. And like a hungry trout you swallowed it down! All this time, his plan was to secretly lead you to your death. It was fortunate Emily found that letter." Tess paced the floor again, then she stopped short, "Oh dear—Emily? Should I have made her come with me? No, she has to be safe, I can't think otherwise." Tess shook her head, unable to dwell on the dozens of unknown possibilities. It was dark and musty in the shack and she opened the door and watched the rain cascading off the roof.

"L.W.—you're out there somewhere. You're the real enemy. You're even worse than Barrett. So, who are you and why do you want to hurt us? In the letter you said, you'll be waiting at the ranch. Could you be one of the new hands Shep hired last week?" She glanced at the riding habit she'd hung up to dry, "I can't go home as Tess. I'll hide the side-saddle in the barn and the rest of my clothing I'll stuff into the trunk and put it back under the bed. I'll find the herd and exchange Bluejay for a less flashy mount. Then I'll ride the rest of the way home—bareback—and as a boy!"

The rain seemed to stop for a while, then a few hours later another violent tempest bore down on the already sodden land. The storm grew more and more zealous throughout the night. Bright bursts of lightning struck so close to the shack, Tess swore she could smell scorched earth all around her. The wind whistled through the cracks and the walls swayed and groaned as the rain beat down upon the tin roof. There was no sleeping that night, for along with the angry storm came the torment of another childhood fear. Tess could never forget the frightening tale of how her mother had been kidnapped and had almost been caught in a flash flood while riding down Kettle Creek. The very same waterway she would have to cross on an unfamiliar horse come tomorrow. And by then it probably wouldn't be a lazy little stream, it could be a raging river.

Just before dawn and despite her fears, Tess decided it was time to be on her way. She straightened up the shack and made a mental note to send one of the hands back to restock the place. As eager as she was to get home, the bitter taste of humble pie was already turning her stomach. Her parents had been right all along and she had been naïve, rebellious and foolish! Looking once again into the small mirror, she tucked her long hair into the felt hat and pulled it down tight. The face that stared back at her looked pale and frightened, "Shake it off Tess," she commanded, "you have lots to do!" As she hurried to the barn, she breathed in the crisp morning air and it seemed to bolster her confidence. The feeling lasted until she rounded the corner and found the barn

L. Faulkner-Corzine

door wide open.   Reaching into her pocket, she withdrew her derringer then crept inside.   But no one was there—not even—her horse!

Tess spun on her heels and ran outside, "BLUEJAY!" she called as her eyes searched in every direction.   "BLUEJAY COME!" she pleaded, waited a moment, then called again.   It was no use; her beautiful mare was nowhere to be seen.

Chapter 9

Lost

"I have wandered away like a lost sheep; come and find me..."
Psalm 119:176

Tess raced back to the cabin, found a knife and slid it into her boot, then grabbed a handful of matches. Returning to the barn she quickly hid her side-saddle, slung her bridle over one shoulder, then patted her pockets, assuring herself that she had her derringer and a box of bullets. Stepping outside, she latched the barn door then shook her head scornfully, "What does the Bible say about closing the barn door after the horse has left?"

Thankfully, the rain had stopped in the night, revealing deep tracks in the soft mud. They were just as clear as the story they told. Bluejay had enough of the lowlands—she was heading home. And home for Bluejay was straight back up the mountains!

"What should I do now?" she wondered, "my mare is heading west, while the ranch is in the opposite direction. If I head home on foot, I'll be more vulnerable. That and it will take more than twice as long to get there. But—if I manage to catch up with Bluejay, even if I waste half a day, we could easily make up the lost time."

Before Tess realized it, her feet had made up her mind for she was already heading west, following Bluejay's hoof prints.

An hour later Tess was slipping along the slimy path her horse had taken. Her boots had an extra three inches of mud stuck to the bottom of them and she had yet to spot Bluejay.

"I hate mud..." she grumbled. Looking down at herself, she asked sarcastically, "How are you enjoying your life of luxury so far, Tess?' she sneered, "oh yes, you knew just what you were doing—didn't you? You thought you were going to be American royalty! Instead you've become the Queen of misery and mud!"

For the next two hours, Tess grumbled and whined about her predicament as she followed Bluejay's trail. The sun beat down on the soggy ground, causing steam to float up all around her, making it even more difficult to see the tracks. When they finally ended at the fence, what she saw brought tears to her eyes.

"Oh no! Poor Bluejay, why did you have to run away?"

The top two strands of barbed-wire were broken and stained red. That and the ground on the opposite side told the story of what had happened. The mare had obviously slipped in the mud just as she jumped the fence and gotten tangled-up in the top two wires. As any horse would, she had panicked and fought to get free. Bits of flesh and bloodied hanks of hair from her silver mane and tail were caught on the broken wires. Tess hated to think how badly the mare might be hurt. Still, from the tracks on the other side, it did appear that she had been able to get to her feet and continue on her way.

Biting her lip, Tess scrutinized the path Bluejay had taken, "That's wild country up ahead but I've got to catch up with her. Uncle Quin trusted her into my care and she might be seriously hurt. Then again, I've got to tell my family about L.W." Finally, Tess made up her mind, "If I don't find her by this afternoon, I'll turn around and head to the ranch." More out of frustration than anything, Tess cupped her hands around her mouth and all but screamed, "BLUEJAY COME!"

Her heart nearly stopped when she heard a loud whinny and then, out from a stand of scrub oaks came a familiar bay gelding.

"Scallywag!" she huffed, "as bad as I need a horse right now, why did it have to be you?"

The gelding had a reputation for being moody and unpredictable. If he wanted, he could be an excellent saddle horse. Then again, he might take a notion to buck and spin and toss his rider into next week! He was also a natural jumper. If he didn't like the corral or pasture he was in, he'd simply jump the fence and go wherever he pleased. Tess shook her head as she remembered the story her father told about why he had kept the scoundrel.

"Scallywag has earned his freedom," he had said, "you see, one day my horse went lame and I was a two day walk from the ranch. I turned around and saw Scallywag following us. I knew it was a risk, but I took my tack from the lame horse and put it on ole Scally. When that didn't bother him, I put my foot in the stirrup and just waited for him to cut loose on me. Instead, he rode like a dream horse all the way back to the ranch. I was so pleased with him and happy to get home that night, that I groomed, petted and grained him like a king. The next morning, I headed towards him with an apple in my hand. He snorted at me, pinned his ears back, then sailed over our highest corral fence like it was an ant hill. I didn't see him again for six months. As far as I'm concerned that horse earned my respect that day—and—he earned his freedom!"

Tess held her breath as the gelding came towards her. "Scally," she said softly, "please be in a good mood today. I need to ride you bareback, and my getting hurt would be a very bad thing." Tess sighed when the big bay pressed his muzzle into her hand, "I hope that means you're happy to help."

If it had been any other horse, Tess would have surreptitiously eased the reins around his neck, making sure she'd captured him before she tried to put the bridle on. But this wasn't the kind of horse who tolerated such things. Instead she said softly, "All right Scallywag. If you let me put this bridle on you," she said as she slipped it off her shoulder and held it out for him to see, "it means that you're going to be a gentleman and let me ride you. Okay?" Tess didn't really think the horse understood her words, then again, she'd lived around animals long enough to know that sometimes—things they would just never do—they ended up doing! And just then, for whatever reason, he must have liked the idea for he lowered his head. Tess almost laughed as she slipped the bit into his mouth and pulled the headstall over his ears. He even yawned as she fastened the throat latch, as if this was a daily ritual.

"So far so good," Tess breathed, "of course if Mother were here she'd tell me that God sent you." Forcefully dismissing the thought, she led Scallywag to the part of the fence where Bluejay had broken the top two wires. Struggling to get over the four strands that remained, she wasn't at all sure she could get Scallywag to do the same. Stepping to the side to give him plenty of room, Tess sucked in a deep breath and said, "All right now, come on Scally—jump!" she commanded, as she gently tugged on the reins. Ears forward, the gelding snorted at the smell of blood, then, to Tess's surprise, he sailed over the fence without a care. "Good boy!" she praised as she patted his neck. But that was only her first challenge, the next was getting on the long-legged brute. Leading him to a steep hill she positioned herself on the high side, then managed to jump and scramble her way onto his back. When she was finally aboard and Scallywag didn't seem to mind, Tess let out a grateful sigh and reined him towards the mountain trail, "I appreciate this Scally and hopefully you won't have to put up with me for long."

The sun seemed to follow them as they tracked Bluejay's hoof prints. As each hour passed, they climbed higher and higher into the mountains. Tess cringed when she saw traces of blood on leaves the mare had walked through, and continued to call her name as they rode. The higher they went, the denser the forest, and the thicker the bed of pine needles that covered the ground. For that reason, it was becoming increasingly difficult to follow her tracks. Another problem with riding on the east side of a mountain, was that dusk came early. It was only five o'clock, and yet already part of the sun was hidden behind the highest peaks. The last thing Tess wanted was to stop, but she had no choice. She hated being alone in this wild place. And knowing that she was up here on an unreliable horse only added to her fears. *Scally's done well today but come tomorrow he might just toss me against a tree. What if I get hurt up here? What if a mountain lion finds me? What if...*

Suddenly, Tess realized that she was about to 'what if' herself sick. She sucked in a deep breath and groaned, "Stop it! Remember what Joseph always says, 'Give no thought for the morrow—morrow take care o' itself,'" she quoted.

Feeling a little better, she slid from the gelding's back, determined to make some sort of shelter before night fall. As she searched for firewood and branches, she kept a tight hold on her roguish horse. Scallywag blew and pulled on the reins, reaching for the thin blades of grass that sprouted up in the scant sunlight. Tess lessened her hold but she didn't have any way to hobble him and she dared not take the bridle off. Knowing he was probably as hungry as she was, Tess patiently walked beside the big horse as he foraged for food.

Whenever Scallywag thought Tess wasn't paying attention, he'd rub his head against a tree trunk or even against her—anything to be rid of the bridle. "Stop that!" she chided as she jerked on the reins. Then she softened and leaned into his side, "Oh Scally, please behave. I don't want to be up here anymore than you do. This is such a mess! Why couldn't I have been right about Barrett? I should be on my way to New York and then Paris, without a care in the world." Gazing around her she shivered, "I may very well be in more danger now than if I'd just stayed on the train. I know what Mama would say, that I should be asking for forgiveness and praying for help. But—I can't. I've been avoiding God my whole life. How can I ask Him for help—even now?"

Heaving a sigh, she ruffled the gelding's forelock, then led him towards some fallen branches, "Now it's my turn. I followed you while you ate now you can follow me while I make camp for the night." With Scallywag in tow, she gathered every branch she could carry or drag. The largest ones she leaned against the trunk of a thick pine tree for her shelter. The smaller branches were stacked up to feed the fire and to make a wind break. Pine needles and cones were gathered for kindling. Now all she had to do was start the fire. She'd assumed that was the easy part of making camp. It was soon obvious that she was mistaken about that as well. The first two matches broke and the third fizzled out in two seconds. She was nearly in tears as she struck her eighth out of ten matches. When it stayed lit and soon glorious orange-red flames began licking hungrily at the kindling, she let out a cheer! Her joy and bravado were short lived, however, for as she gazed around, she realized that the sun had deserted her, dragging with it every fragment of light from the sky. She would have been plummeted into utter darkness had she not been able to light the fire. That thought made her desperate to keep it going!

These mountains made Tess feel small and vulnerable as she huddled before the fire with her shelter at her back. As the hours passed, she remembered stories about the creatures that hunted from dusk until dawn. Remembering too, that she was an uninvited trespasser in this wild place. As the night wore on, she listened to the fire crackling, the crickets chirping and to the wind whispering to her as it slid between pine boughs. Later came the screech of an owl, the scream of a mountain lion, and the howl of a wolf. His mate singing her own reply, followed by the rest of the pack harmonizing in their nightly serenade. Tess trembled with every sound, for she knew that she could easily become dinner for any number of nocturnal hunters that prowled in the night.

"I hate being so afraid—so alone!" Tess groaned, then she stared up at the sky, "'Where can I flee from your presence? If I go up to the heavens, you are there; if I make my bed in the depths, you are there. If I rise on the wings of the dawn, if I settle on the far side of the sea, even there your hand will guide me, your right hand will hold me fast.'" Shaking her head, Tess added mockingly, "Psalm 139 verses, 7 through 10! Oh Mama, you and your memory verses. What a fool your little girl turned out to be. I ran away from you and I ran away from God, but somehow, I've brought you both with me!"

When the gelding tried to inch away, Tess groaned and pulled him back to her, "I'm sorry Scallywag. What was I thinking? I should have ridden you straight home. Then I could have sent a couple of ranch hands to track Bluejay. Right now, we both could be safe and warm and eating a real dinner. Don't know what's the matter with me? I can't seem to do anything but make one mistake after another."

Fighting tears, Tess buried her head in her hands. Sensing her sadness, Scallywag murmured softly and nudged her arm as he stood beside her, his head hovering over her lap, his eyes closed. Tess reached up and rubbed his forehead. "You're not really a scallywag—are you boy? I'll tell you who earns that title, Mister T. Barrett Tulane, that's who! All this time, my fiancé was my worst enemy!"

Just then Tess remembered the stories her mother used to tell about being captured by Dewey LeBeau, "Mama will understand how I feel. Her worst enemy turned out to be her very own mother!" Suddenly, Tess recalled something else, "Mama has always warned us about our grandmother, but the boys and I never took it seriously. I think her first name is…Lavenia…but her last name is…Renford. Her initials would be L.R. not L.W." Tess shrugged, as she threw another branch onto the fire. "Wait, her last name is spelled with a W. Could it really be that my own grandmother—is my enemy? Yes, it has to be her—L.W. stands for, Lavenia Wrenford!"

Suddenly, knowing the name of her enemy caused an army of chill bumps to spread down her back, then swarm over the rest of her body. Looking around, it seemed as if the forest had eyes. She built the fire even higher then pulled her derringer from her pocket. Pressing her back against the tree trunk, she gazed up at the gelding and whispered, "Please, Scally you've got to be good a while longer. If my grandmother is behind this, then things are worse than I thought. We don't dare spend any more time searching for Bluejay. Tomorrow, at first light, I need you to take me home!"

Tess had never experienced a longer night. She kept feeding the fire, and gazing up at the moon, but it seemed to be stuck in one spot, "Isn't morning ever going to come?" she moaned. Although Tess was determined to stay awake, she'd barely slept the last two nights and now the smoke from the fire was burning her eyes. Finally, she wrapped the reins around her fist and pulled Scally a little closer, "Now, you listen to me Scallywag, I'm just going to rest my eyes for a little while. So, don't you get the idea that I'm going to sleep…"

It felt like Tess had been running down this same dark and dirty alley for hours. There didn't seem to be any end to it and she was shivering from the cold. When she heard shouts and angry voices, she frantically glanced around then hid behind some filthy rubbish bins. While trying not to make any noise, it came to her that none of this made any sense, she didn't know why she was so scared or even where she was! This alley might be in Denver, New York or even Paris—she didn't know? Still, her instincts told her that she was in danger. When the voices faded, she thought she was safe. Then a hand closed around her arm and jerked her from her hiding place. It was just a thin old woman, but her grip was strong. As Tess looked into the old woman's dark rimmed-golden eyes they seemed familiar somehow, but her expression was one of complete hatred.

"Well now, if it isn't my little Augusta's darling girl," the woman crooned, "I've been waiting for this day—for a very long time." The old woman's face was in shadow, but she held Tess with one hand and with the other she held a knife. Moonlight reflected against the shining blade as it arched through the air, and then...

Tess screamed herself awake. Scrambling to her feet, she fought off the prickly pine boughs that were tangled in her hair and around her arms and legs. Once she freed herself, she gasped for breath as a shiver spread across her shoulders and down her spine.

"It was just a nightmare," she panted, as she rubbed her arms, trying to warm and soothe herself at the same time. The memory of her dream faded as she stirred the dwindling embers of her fire then added the last two branches from her shelter. Her breath came out in cloudy plumes that floated about her face as she moaned, "At least it's finally dawn. OH, I do not like this adventure—not one little bit! I'm cold—and hungry—and I'm scared!" She thought she was just still cloudy-headed, then as she glanced in every direction she realized that she was cocooned in heavy fog. It was smothering the mountains in the exact same way her brothers smothered their biscuits in cream gravy, thoroughly and completely.

Warming her hands over the fire, she then held them to her cold cheeks. It was then she realized that her hands were not supposed to be empty. Spinning around in every direction, her heart sank when she spotted her birthday bridle a few feet away. Peering into the cottony whiteness that surrounded her, she roared as loudly as she could, "SCALLYWAG!"

It was hard to believe, but on top of all her other troubles, Tess found herself afoot again. It was something of a miracle that the impetuous gelding had allowed her to ride him at all. Now, as was his custom, he had simply gone on his way. She'd made camp at the top of a hill. It should have been easy to find her way home, but now there were two sets of hoof prints going down in two opposite directions. One set of prints had to be Bluejay's, the others naturally belonged to Scallywag. The problem was that even though Bluejay wore shoes and Scally didn't, the thick layer of pine needles made it impossible to tell the difference. The fog was growing worse and Tess went from one set of tracks to the other. Scallywag's tracks would lead her safely back to the Bar 61. The other tracks would lead her deeper into the high-country where bears, wolves and mountain lions might already be tracking Bluejay and the scent of blood. The thought came to her, that if a predator couldn't catch up with Bluejay—it might very well settle for a foolish young woman instead. Whether from cold or fear, her trembling refused to stop. She'd never seen fog this thick before. Every direction she looked seemed the same. Now, as she turned around and around, panic began taunting her nerves. It was difficult to think and even more difficult to pinpoint exactly where the sun was hiding.

Struggling to shake off her fears she mumbled, "All I can do is walk towards the brightest part of the sky—that has to be east. I'll keep the sun on my face in the morning, rest when the sun is right above me, then keep the sun on my back till dark. Wasting no more time, she found a sturdy branch to use as a walking stick and started down the hill. Still, the fog was so thick, she was forced to stop and reconsider her direction again and again. Tess knew she was in trouble when she reached the bottom of the hill only to have it turn sharply upwards again.

"No, this isn't right," she whimpered. "The way back should continue to go down. It should have been easy to retrace my steps." Muttering to herself, she began climbing back up the hill. It was much harder going up than it was coming down. In fact, she had to take a different way back to where she'd made camp the night before. When she reached the hill top, she frantically searched for the place she made camp but couldn't find any signs of her cold fire or shelter. She had purposely made note of the kinnikinnick shrub with its tiny pink bell-shaped flowers growing along the path…but now as she looked around she realized that it was growing everywhere!

The fog had finally lifted and she stared up at the canopy of pine trees that towered above her. Never had she felt so small and insignificant. Leaning against a tree she closed her eyes and listened to the hushing sounds the breeze made as it slid through pine branches and aspen leaves. The trees and the mountain itself seemed to be whispering to her, lost...lost...lost.

Nodding her head, she frowned, "Yes indeed, Tessie May," she chided, "you have succeeded in getting yourself well and truly LOST!" Tears sprung to her eyes and suddenly she was finding it hard to breathe. Her legs grew weak and she slumped down on a log and buried her face in her hands, "No one, absolutely no one, not even Emily would think to look for me in these mountains!"

When she heard a rifle being fired, Tess jumped to her feet. Gunfire meant people and people meant help! Actually, this could mean even more trouble, but she had to take the risk. Uncle Quin said sometimes you could roam these mountains for weeks, even months, and never run into another human being. This might be her only chance of getting out of these mountains—alive! Tess knew she'd never find her way home without help, she would also most likely starve or freeze to death. There were no more shots but then came the sound of someone moving through the brush at the bottom of the hill and she hurried that way, calling out, "Hello! I'm lost—can anyone hear me? Please help me!"

To her surprise, she saw a flash of color, not from where she'd heard movement a moment before, but from the hill just across from where she stood. Tess was thrilled to see a woman with amber colored hair and a big man standing next to her.

He held his hand up and shouted in a deep voice, "Stay there, don't try to come down that way. We'll skirt around and come up to you!"

Tess was so relieved as she watched them making their way down the trail. She wanted to laugh and cry, or as Emily would have said, dance a jig! Then she heard something else. It was a guttural, deep-throated growl, followed by the sound of something crashing through the bushes. At the bottom of the hill a dark shadow suddenly broke through the thick brush, no more than thirty feet from where the man and woman were now making their way down the hill. There was a fallen tree between them and she feared they couldn't see the bear.

"LOOK OUT," Tess shouted, as she pointed, "THERE'S A BEAR!" Pulling the derringer from her pocket, she knew full well that shooting the beast with this little gun—would only make him mad! Still, she might frighten or at least distract him. She shot both rounds into the air, then cupped her free hand around her mouth and screamed again. Quickly, she fumbled in her pocket for two more bullets and slipped them into the chamber. When she glanced back down the hill, she couldn't see the bear or the people. Trying to get a better look, she leaned slightly forward and the loose shale she was standing on gave way. Her feet went out from under her, and the sliding rocks carried her down the hill. She grabbed for something to stop her but she was falling too fast. When her foot finally hit a root, instead of stopping her, the momentum flung her body into the air and she ended up tumbling head-over-heels, all the rest of the way down. When at last she came to a stop at the bottom of the hill, she gazed up and saw the bear a dozen feet away.

"Don't move," the man ordered, as he cocked his gun.

Tess couldn't move. She couldn't even breathe. The wind had been knocked out of her, she was fighting to suck in even tiny bits of air. Even as she struggled, she saw that this creature seemed much too large to be real. He was a giant, standing on his hind legs, pawing the air and snorting a warning. For a moment, the bear swayed back and forth, as if considering who was the tastier meal or more likely the easier kill. Tess knew the answer to that and squeezed her eyes shut—waiting for death—praying it would come quickly. Suddenly, the world around her seemed to split apart. There was an ear-shattering explosion and then the forest floor shook. When she finally forced herself to open her eyes, she was nose to nose with the beast. His head was enormous, the size of a bushel basket and his dark eyes seemed to look right through her. Her last thought was that his breath smelled of death. After that...everything went black!

<hr>

Assuming the bear was dead, Copper McKenna turned her full attention to the injured young woman lying next to it. "Hurry Shad!" she cried, "we've got to help her!"

Before she could take another step, her husband grabbed her arm and pushed her behind him!

"YOU STAY RIGHT HERE!" he growled.

Shadrack McKenna had been compared to a bear before, and just then, he sounded and looked like one, too. In three long strides he rushed towards the beast and put two more bullets into him. Shad let out a sigh, "Pretty sure this fella was stone-dead, but it never hurts to make certain. Now, let's see what we can do for this little gal!" In an instant, they were both on their knees, hoping that her injuries weren't too serious.

"Miss...can you hear me?" Copper asked gently as she pressed her handkerchief against the girls bleeding forehead. When there was no response she stared up at Shad and sucked in a deep breath, trying to calm her own nerves.

Finding a strong pulse, Shad released her hand and let out a long sigh, "She's alive and breathin' but I think I'd just as soon she stays unconscious for a while. If I have to set any bones, it'd be a whole lot easier on both of us, if she didn't know about it!" The big man had a tender heart and he dreaded the idea of hurting the little thing. With great care, he checked her arms and legs for breaks and sprains. Finally, he sat back on his heels and sighed, "Well, she got beat up pretty good fallin' that-a-way. Got some scrapes that might need tendin', but nothin's broke, as far as I can tell!"

Copper nodded, "I'm thankful for that but this head wound is deep. Still, God must have plans for this little one. That was an awful fall!"

Shad took off his jacket and gently laid it over the girl, "Yep, God was workin' overtime today. You know, this little gal probably saved our lives! If she hadn't warned us, don't think we'd have seen that bear in time. Her firing those shots and even fallin' down the hill, distracted that old boy. Gave me a chance to take aim." His eyes met Copper's as he added, "Still, ya just don't kill' a bear like that with one shot! The Lord was surely guidin' that bullet, sweet girl. Otherwise that brute would be chewing on all three of us right about now!"

"I've been thinking the same thing, it's a miracle!" Gently brushing some dirt off the girl's face, Copper shrugged, "I thought she was a boy until her hat flew off and all these blonde curls were set free. I sure wish she'd wake up and tell us what hurts. Then tell us what she was doing up here?" Frowning, she lifted her blood-soaked handkerchief, "I can't seem to stop this bleeding." Gazing around, she spotted something, then looked up at Shad, "There's some yarrow just behind you. Would you gather some leaves for me? Dried leaves are better but those green ones might still help."

When he returned with the fern like yarrow leaves, she placed his large hand over the handkerchief on the girl's forehead, "Keep a constant pressure on that, while I fix a better bandage."

There was a tug on Copper's heart as Shad, ever so gently, took her place. Folks on the mountain thought of Shadrack McKenna as a powerful lumberjack, a skilled carpenter, and an artistic wood carver.   He was all of that, but more importantly to Copper, he was also the kindest and the gentlest man in all the world.

A slight smile lifted the corners of her mouth as she reached into Shad's pocket and retrieved his spare handkerchief.   She'd always teased him that, if necessary, she could use it as a tablecloth.   That fact served her well now as she folded it into a triangle, then lengthwise over and over.   The yarrow leaves were bunched together then laid in the center of the bandage.   Holding the leaves in place she picked it up and said, "Now, you need to press just a bit harder for a few seconds, then remove the old bandage, wiping the blood away as you go.   Then, I'll need you to help me put this new one on."   The swap was done quickly.   Shad carefully lifted the girl's head with one hand, and held the new bandage against the wound with the other, while Copper tied it tightly around her head.

When that was done, Shad got to his feet, "Ya know darlin', after a fall like that, we don't dare move her, not for a few days at least."   He paused for a moment allowing his wife to understand the bigger meaning behind his words.   "So, you just keep doin' what ya can for her, while I go fetch Boone.   We've got to get this bear out of here and then I'll make us a shelter."

"Oh Shad!" Copper sighed.   Then she stared down at the girl and shrugged, "You're right of course.   But—couldn't we move the bear, build a shelter, and then you could go back to work?   I could stay with her."   When Shad just sighed and shook his head she knew their worst fears had been realized, "You've worked so hard and now when we're almost finished…to just give up…it's heartbreaking!   Of course, Doherty will be thrilled that we've failed."   Then her shoulders slumped as she added, "We're going to lose everything—aren't we?"

"Nope.   Ya can't lose what don't belong to ya.   Everything we have belongs to God, sweet girl," Shad soothed.   "That bear could have gotten all three of us!   We're all right and I'm believin' that gal's gonna be all right.   Ya know God had us all just where we needed to be today.   As long as we've got each other, we'll be just fine!   You know that don't ya?"

Copper's chin trembled as she nodded her head, "I do!"   Gazing down at the girl, she tenderly tucked Shad's coat more tightly around her and sighed,

"The moment I saw her and heard her cry for help, it suddenly came back to me, how frightened I was when I was lost in these mountains. God led me to your empty cabin and it saved my life. Then a few months later I met you and my whole world was changed forever—for the better! I can't help but wonder— what's in store for us now?" staring down at the poor wounded girl she added, "and—what's in store for her?"

Shad and Copper locked eyes for a while but there was nothing more to say. There was, however, much to do. They couldn't set up camp with a dead bear and an injured girl lying side by side. Every scavenger on the mountain would be attracted by the smell of blood. Shad did the only thing he could. He tied a rope onto the bear's back paws, then with his stallion's reluctant help, he dragged the carcass as far from their camp as possible. Copper followed behind covering the blood trail with dirt. Then while she built a fire over the spot where the bear had died; Shad built a shelter over the girl.

Afterwards, they prayed over the young woman and Copper recited her favorite verse, "And we know that, all that happens to us is working for our good, if we love God and are fitting into His plans.'" Silently she added, *Lord, I trust You, but I have no idea how You can turn the losses of this day—into something that's good.*

Later that night when Copper checked on the girl, the bleeding had stopped, but there were signs of fever. Earlier, she had tried to convince Shad that she and the girl would be fine—alone! Now she was grateful that Shad hadn't listened to her. It was going to take them both to watch over this girl and keep them all safe. Bears, wolves and mountain lions had been unusually aggressive. Shad would never leave them, and she didn't want him too. The risk was just too great. Still, it was a hard pill to swallow. In five days, Ham Doherty would own the home she had always called her 'little bit of heaven'!

Chapter 10
Lavenia

"People may cover their hatred with pleasant words, but they're deceiving you." Proverbs 26:24

It was late afternoon and the last rays of sun cast a soft burnished glow through the wide windows of the hacienda. Just then the familiar afternoon breeze came down from the mountains. The chilled pine scented air felt like a gift, as it swirled into the hot kitchen from the open doors that led to the courtyard. Augusta stilled for a moment, closed her eyes, and gratefully breathed it in. The family had enjoyed an early dinner. Now she and Carlos were frosting the last of three dozen cinnamon rolls for the hearty breakfast they served the family and the ranch hands every morning. After the preparations were made, they had hoped for a quiet evening.

Their wish was short lived, for at that moment Joshua and his twin brother Caleb burst through the kitchen door. Augusta licked the frosting from her thumb as she gave each boy an appraising look. It was that knowing glance that mothers acquire and refine over the years. With long practiced patience she said softly, "Oh dear, what's wrong boys?"

"Everything!" Josh spat the word out for emphasis. "If only Tess had stayed here where she belongs. If she'd just agreed to marry Sig, everything would have been perfect!"

Cal nodded as he grabbed a handful of cookies from the jar on the counter and hissed, "Now, ya know what he's gone and done? Joined the army—that's what! He'll probably get killed and it'll be her fault. She's selfish Mama. She could have been happy with Sig—but no—she had to run off with that rich, eastern dude."

Josh folded his arms across his chest and scowled, "Tessie May Grainger doesn't love anybody but herself. I hate her for leavin' us!"

"And I hate her for saying no to Sig," Cal added.

Augusta wiped her hands on a kitchen towel and went to her sons. "Neither of you mean that," she said in a stern yet soothing voice, "you do not hate Tess!" Linking arms with both boys she added, "We all miss your sister. Then again, we knew the day would come when she would marry and make a home of her own. Naturally, we hoped she wouldn't move so far away—but that was always a possibility. Even when families love each other very much they can't always stay together."

Cal stayed close to his mother while Josh moved across the room and looked out the window, "I know all that but—I thought Tess really loved us. She's being stupid Ma. None of us liked or even trusted that big headed goat but she left with him anyway. Cal and I don't understand why you and Pa let her go!"

Augusta frowned, but she was saved from answering a question she didn't have the answer to when Alvaro stepped into the kitchen. He was leaning heavily on his cane as he said, "Pardon, Senora, I was sitting on the porch enjoying the sunset when I see a man and woman coming this way in a buggy. It is too late for a visit. I think…maybe they have trouble."

Augusta frowned, "I hope not, but you're right. It is an odd hour for someone to come calling. Carlos, would you mind finishing up and putting on some tea? I thought we all might enjoy a cup out in the courtyard." Sighing she added, "I suppose you best bring it into the parlor instead. Whoever they are, the least we can do is offer them some tea, and could you put some of your caramel tarts on the tray as well?"

Leaving Alvaro and Carlos in the kitchen, Augusta and the boys went to the porch to greet their unexpected callers.

Leaning close to his mother, Cal whispered, "Ma, that rig is a rental from the livery in Colorado Springs. Looks like their best one." As the buggy came closer they recognized that it was being driven by Harvey Spunk, the owner of the livery. The elderly woman seated next to him, who was all dressed in black, they didn't recognize.

"Howdy!" Harvey called as he drove right up to the porch. He set the brake and glanced over at the woman who sat beside him, "Well ma'am, we're here now." When she just sat rigidly, staring straight ahead and making no attempt to greet the Graingers, Harvey wasn't sure what to do.

Augusta was just as confused. "Good evening," she said encompassing both the driver and the woman next to him, "not that we mind, but it is an odd hour for callers, is there something wrong or something we can do for you?"

When the old woman just sat there, looking straight ahead and saying nothing, Harvey shrugged, "Well, Miz Grainger. There's nothin' wrong— exactly—I hope." Nodding to the older woman he said, "This here is Missus O'Brien. She sent me a telegram a few days ago, arranging fer me to pick her up from this evenin's train and bring her to the Bar 61. When I met her at the train she looked so tired, I tried to get her to stay at least one night at the Antlers Hotel. But—she said that even though you weren't expecting her, you would take care of her once we got here. She's been feeling poorly the whole way. So, I hope she was right, 'bout you taken care of her and all."

Finally, the old woman turned towards the driver, the brim of her large hat covered her eyes, only the tip of her nose and thin lips could be seen as she spoke in a halting voice, "I feel terribly weak, Mister Spunk. Would you help me inside, then see to my luggage?"

Augusta found this whole thing very perplexing, the old woman was obviously senile. Apparently, she needed someplace to stay and someone to take care of her. How she got it into her head that the Bar 61 and the Grainger family would provide both—she couldn't imagine. Still, Augusta's heart went out to her. At that moment, it really didn't matter who she was or why she was there. She was a sick old woman and was in no condition to travel any more that night. Stepping beside the buggy, Augusta gently took hold of the woman's thin arm, "I'm sorry you're not feeling well. Mister Spunk, will you help me get her inside. Boys, you get her luggage."

As she walked the woman very slowly into the hacienda, Augusta said, "I'm Missus Grainger, my maiden name was O'Brien. My father's name was Barrett, although most people called him Bull! He had no living relatives but perhaps we could be distantly related—you never know."

The old woman kept her head down but Augusta heard her scoff, "Related? Well..." That was all she managed to say before succumbing to a terrible fit of coughing. Soon it was all she could do to stay on her feet, as she wheezed and choked.

Instantly, Augusta took charge, "Mister Spunk, help me get her into the parlor! Cal, run and fetch her a cup of hot tea. Josh, bring her a blanket."

A few minutes later the old woman was seated in the parlor, sipping hot tea while the Graingers waited expectantly for an explanation as to why she was there. Finally, when Ty came into the room with a questioning look on his face, Augusta voiced what they had all been wondering. "Well now, it seems you're feeling better. Perhaps you could explain how is it that you've come to visit us?"

The old woman sat her tea cup in its saucer. Then a strange smile played about her thin lips as she removed her hat and sat it on her lap. She patted her snow-white hair back into place with withered hands, then she leveled a cold, unflinching gaze on her hostess.

As Augusta stared into the woman's dark rimmed, golden eyes, her breath caught in her throat as a chill spread down her arms. She had always been told how unusual, and how beautiful her eyes were; but now as she looked into the same eyes—they did not seem beautiful to her. No, they were just as heartless and cold as she remembered.

A sarcastic sneer crept over the old woman's face, "Un-nerving, isn't it? I look at you and see myself thirty years ago. And now you get to see your-self—as a wasted old woman. Of course we've met," she sneered, "I—am your mother."

The impact of those words left Augusta's heart and stomach lurching. Tytus was nearly as stunned. Then he remembered his brother's death, and how this woman had tried to destroy her own daughter, his beautiful and sweet, Augusta. He crossed the room then glared down at this evil woman who had been responsible for so much pain and heartbreak, "Madame," he growled, "you will return to Colorado Springs immediately. One of my men will drive you. Had we known who you were, you would have never stepped foot in this house."

Her eyes grew wide as she held up a thin finger, "Ah, but you did know, there has been no deception on my part. Mister Spunk told my daughter, quite clearly, that I was Missus O'Brien," she chuckled sarcastically, then added, "but then Augusta has always been a little—slow."

Her snicker soon turned into a crackling cough. This time, however, she quickly regained her composure, but not before everyone in the room saw the traces of red staining her handkerchief. They had seen it before, victims of consumption were flocking to the Rockies. Doctors were prescribing the mountain air as a tonic, even a possible cure.

As she took another sip of tea, Caleb asked, "So, you're our grand-mother?"

"Yes, my name is Lavenia Wrenford-O'Brien. Has your mother never mentioned me?"

"Sure!" Joshua answered, then added with a smirk, "she told us to run if we ever saw you or heard your name!"

A genuine smile changed the old woman's countenance. It was easy to see that at one time she had been quite beautiful. "Oh my!" she sighed, "you must be awfully brave to stand so close to someone as dangerous as me!" Turning to Caleb she added, "You are brave too I see. Neither of you look like you want to run away and hide."

Cal shrugged his shoulders, "We're not scared of you but that doesn't mean we trust you either."

"That's enough boys," Ty grunted, "I want both of you to go out to the bunkhouse and tell Kip to get the carriage ready. We need him to take this woman back to the Springs. He's to stay the night at the hotel and come back in the morning. You two stay out there and help him, make sure there's oil in the lanterns and plenty of blankets in the back of the carriage." When Cal and Josh nodded their heads, but kept staring at their grandmother, Ty snapped his fingers, "Now boys!"

"Yes, sir!" they replied. Both Cal and Josh dared one more look at the infamous old woman, then hurried out the door.

Ty turned to Lavenia, "My brother Timothy is dead because of you! Augusta and I almost died because of you. You should be in prison, not sipping tea in our parlor."

Lavenia was unfazed, "I did nothing to your brother nor to either of you, for that matter. I believe the man responsible for all that was Dewey LeBeau. That scoundrel has been dead for years, hasn't he? Your accusing me is ridiculous—you have no proof." She turned to Augusta, who had still said nothing, "You are my daughter, my only living relative. I suppose you have surmised that I am dying of consumption. My numerous, New York doctors told me to come to Colorado. Of course, they didn't give me that advice until they had drained my purse on useless treatments." Raising her tea cup in mock toast, she sneered, "When they realized they had left me penniless, they said, 'Go west old woman...go west!'"

"So—Lavenia," Augusta asked evenly, for she could not bring herself to call this woman, Mother, "you wished me dead when I was nine years old. Now, you have come here, so that the daughter you despise can take care of you? Isn't that a bit egotistical...even for you? There may be no proof but we all know that you hired Dewey LeBeau to kidnap me. Then he was to take me to work in one of your brothels. He botched his initial attempt and my first husband, Ty's twin-brother, Timothy, was killed trying to protect me! A year later, when Dewey finally took me away, the ranch foreman and Ty came to rescue me, and Dewey nearly killed them both! You've brought about so much misery, just because you hate your own child! I was a part of your life for such a short time, why do you hate me so much?"

Lavenia simply stared at Augusta, then she shrugged her shoulders, "It's a foolish question. Why bring up LeBeau or any of it? It was all a very long time ago. I have a more interesting question for you, Augusta. What kind of person are you?" Glancing up at Ty, she added, "And what kind are you, Tytus Grainger? Over the years, I've kept up with you both. Everyone describes you two as an outstanding Christian couple! I've learned a little bit about what that means. One of the main themes of those who call themselves Christian, is forgiveness and charity! The motto seems to be…love thy neighbor…**even…love thy enemy!**" she added dramatically. She paused for a moment as she stifled a cough. Her hand trembled as she lifted the cup and took another sip of tea, then she gave a self-mocking chuckle, "It should be quite apparent that you won't have to put up with me for long. At this stage of my disease, my doctors said the mountain air might be a comfort… but certainly not a cure. I have no money and you are my only family. If you cast me out, which is exactly what I would do, if our circumstances were reversed, then I shall walk the streets of Colorado Springs crying, "Woe— is—me!"

Ty narrowed his eyes as he listened to this woman in disbelief. He'd heard of people who were born wicked, those who had no redeeming qualities. But he'd always thought that there was some good in everyone. Now, as he stared at Lavenia Wrenford, he knew he was indeed staring at the personification of evil. As this revelation hit him, he was even more thunderstruck when Augusta walked to her mother and held out her hand.

"Come, I'll help you to your room," Lavenia's eyebrows arched, but she said nothing as her daughter helped her stand then added calmly, "we always keep a guest room ready. I'm making no promises about what we will do long term, but for tonight, you may stay here."

"Oh no she's not!" Ty growled, "Augusta, what are you thinking? I'll not have that murderess stay under the same roof with you and the boys. I don't trust her, and neither should you!"

Augusta's expression was forlorn as she locked eyes with her husband. "You're right of course, but the fact remains that—we are Christians. God does say that we have an obligation to honor our parents."

Not wanting her mother to see them argue, she added sweetly but firmly, "Ty, please bring her luggage from the hallway and tell Kip to unharness the carriage. Then ask him to come guard her door through the night."

When Ty stalked off in a huff, Augusta struggled to maintain her composure. As she guided Lavenia down the hallway she added softly, "I know you don't care one way or another, but I forgave you a long time ago." When the old woman scoffed sarcastically, Augusta added, "I don't expect you to understand. You can't appreciate forgiveness until you realize how completely unworthy you are of it. You see, forgiveness is one of God's most extraordinary gifts. He gives it to you freely, but you cannot keep it, unless you willingly share it with others. I didn't deserve God's forgiveness but he gave it to me anyway. That's why many years ago, I forgave you for how you treated me as a child. Even for what you and Dewey LeBeau did to Timothy and then to Tytus and me. And I forgive you for the way you're using me now. I don't do this because of my own generosity. I do this because of God's. Still, you must know this, He does not ask me to trust you. Nor does He ask me or anyone in this house to be a door mat for you to mistreat or belittle. That is why we will put a guard at your door. If you try to harm anyone, family, friend or even foe, then you will no longer be allowed to stay here. We will, however, provide for you until you die. We'll pay for you to stay at a sanatorium in Manitou Springs. It is especially for consumptives. They do their best but it's not a happy place. All the patients stay in two large rooms. One for men and one for women. It's clean and neat but like a cross between a hospital and a prison. If you misbehave here, you will end your days there! And yes, I'm sure you will cry, woe—is—me!"

Lavenia's lips lifted slightly, then she shook her head, "You flatter me, Augusta Colleen," she scoffed, as she ran her hands down her thin frame, "look at me, how could a sickly old lady like me bring harm to anyone?"

Augusta sighed, then said coolly, "I memorized a Bible verse that has always reminded me of you. 'From evil people, come evil deeds.'" Nothing more was said for a while as she helped her mother undress, then put her to bed. Before leaving the room, she added, "Should you wish to look up that verse, there's a Bible on your bedside table. You'll find it in 1st Samuel, chapter 24, verse 13."

Tytus ground his teeth as he waited for Augusta to finish with the old witch. He was furious that his wife had given his brother's murderer a safe haven. When Ty heard the guest room door open and then close, he stepped into the hallway with his arms folded over his chest and a scowl on his face. He was fully prepared for a fight. When Augusta rushed passed him and into their bedroom, he followed her across the room and through the double doors that led outside to their private courtyard. By the time Ty reached her, she had crumpled to the stone floor and was sobbing un-controllably.

Ty's fury vanished as he took her in his arms, "I didn't realize—I'm so very sorry my love," he sighed, "sorry that woman is here and sorry that it didn't occur to me how much seeing her again was hurting you. Talk to me, tell me what you're thinking."

It took a while for Augusta to speak, but finally as Ty led her to a bench beneath the lilac bushes she began to explain, "I know I should have discussed this with you first, but I just couldn't give her that kind of satisfaction. I was always afraid of her and desperate to please her at the same time. All I wanted was for her to like me—to love me! Instead, she always made it clear that I disgusted her. She used to call me a drab little mouse. I had to show her that I was no longer—a mouse! God tells us to honor our father and mother, to take care of them in their old age. He doesn't say honor them if they deserve it or if it's convenient. I think we should do our best to obey God, but He does not say that we should tolerate her cruelty—not towards any of us. He also does not say that we should trust someone like her, and I don't intend to!"

"Augusta, this is going to be so hard on you! Why don't you let me put her up at the Antlers Hotel and I'll hire a nurse? You'll still honor her by taking excellent care of her."

"No—Ty, I don't think that's wise! How does the saying go? 'Keep your friends close and your enemy's closer!' If she has her freedom, then she can hire people to hurt us. No, she'll be less likely to make trouble if she stays here, while we keep a constant watch over her!"

Ty closed his eyes and groaned, "Your instincts are right, as usual. I didn't tell you this before but the day Tess and Barrett left I sent a telegram to the Pinkerton Agency, asking them to have an agent watch over Tess. I'll ride to town tomorrow and send another one to New York...make sure they keep an especially close eye on her!"

Augusta leaned her head on Ty's shoulder, "Thank you! That was wise of you to do that! I don't know if my mother would hurt the children or not. She's always just hated—me! Another possibility is that, God sent my mother here as a last chance for her to make things right before she dies. I know, she's outrageously arrogant and flippant about dying. But what if she's really scared, maybe even feeling guilty."

"That old witch?" Ty scoffed, "I think it's highly unlikely that she will ever change."

"It is *very* unlikely, Ty, but anything is possible with God! Do you remember what I told you about being in the cave with Dewey LeBeau after he captured me? Hitch had shot him in the arm and I knew he would bleed to death if the wound wasn't cauterized. I begged God to tell me what to do. At that very moment, I felt God saying, 'Help him!' Today, when I looked into my mother's eyes, for the first time in twenty-nine years, I asked God the same question…and I got the same answer. I believe He is telling us to help her. He is not, however, telling us to trust her."

Chapter 11
Who Am I?

"Do not remember the sins of my youth and my rebellious ways; according to your love remember me, for you, LORD, are good."
Psalm 25:7

Copper McKenna was somewhat startled by the intensity of her patient's sapphire eyes as they fluttered open for the first time. "Well, hello there," she crooned, "don't be afraid, honey, you're all right. You took quite a fall and you have a deep head wound. I'm sure everything hurts, but nothing is broken."

"W—water...p—please?" Tess croaked. When she'd taken a few sips, she fought to keep her eyes open, "Got to get home!" she whimpered as she tried to sit up. Even that slight of a movement made her head feel like it was coming apart and knives were piercing her body. The pain was too much for her and she slumped back onto the blankets.

Copper gently patted the girls hand, "Take it easy dear. My husband and I will help you get home when you're strong enough. For now, just lie still and tell me what hurts the most?"

Overwhelmed by pain, Tess struggled to speak, "My head hurts...everything hurts. What happened and...who are you?"

"I'm Copper McKenna and my husband Shad is down the trail a bit getting some meat from that big bear you warned us about! Do you remember the bear and that awful fall you took? You're pretty high up in the mountains and it's hard to believe that you came up here all alone and on foot. We looked to see if you had a horse but we couldn't find any signs of one."

Tess tried to make sense of what the red-headed woman was saying but her eyes kept wanting to close and it was difficult to concentrate. Finally, she mumbled, "I don't know. I should have had a horse—shouldn't I?"

Seeing the look of complete bewilderment on the young woman's face, Copper sighed, "Suppose we start with something easy. What's your name, dear?"

"Yes, I can't handle difficult right now," Tess leaned back on the blankets and sighed, "my name is…I'm…um…my name is…it's…" Suddenly she looked up and tears filled her eyes, "I can't think. Surely, I'm not here all alone. Isn't there anyone you can ask? Isn't there anyone that can tell you—who I am?"

Trying not to mirror the confusion and fear in the young woman's face, Copper patted her arm, "Now don't you worry. You've got a nasty head wound and until it's healed you're bound to feel a bit rattled. The good news is that folks tend to heal fast in the mountain air, and you've got Shad and me to take care of you!"

The girl grabbed Copper's arm, "I'm afraid. Afraid to close my eyes. You won't leave me, will you?"

Copper gently squeezed her hand, "We wouldn't dream of it!" she soothed. With that assurance, the girl went limp. A few seconds later her breathing became deep and even.

"I heard some of that," Shad muttered as he strolled into camp, carrying a large hunk of bear meat in one hand and extra wood in the other. As he bent over the fire he asked, "Is it really possible for a person to forget who they are?"

"I've read about it happening, but I've never seen it myself—until now. Obviously, her head wound was much worse than I feared. I've known people to be unconscious for a few days," Copper lamented, "but when they came to, they knew who they were. Still, she woke up and understood what I was saying to her. That's a good sign, it's a start anyway. When she wakes up again, we'll get her to eat something and the healing can begin. Food and sleep, right now that's the best we can do for her."

⚜

Over the next few days Copper and Shad attributed the young woman's recovery to prayer, mountain air and to the fact that youth was in her favor. Physically, she was growing stronger every day. However, who she was, remained a mystery to all three of them.

Finally, on the fourth day, Shad and Copper decided it was safe to break camp and head back to the cabin.

"Good mornin' Miss!" Shad greeted. "Think yer up for a bit of a walk today? We'll take it slow and you can rest as often as ya like. If you'd rather, I could make ya a travois, and Boone can drag you back home Indian style. Now, neither he nor I would mind doin' that for ya, but it'll make for a bumpy ride.

The young woman smiled, "Copper mentioned the travois but I think it would be best for all of us if I just try to walk."

"Good girl!" Shad praised, as he handed her a cup of coffee and a piece of jerked meat. "We'll be leavin' as soon as you've had your breakfast."

It was dusk when they arrived at the McKenna cabin. The clouds above were tinged in scarlet and bronze, making the scene before them look more like a painted picture from a book of fairy tales. Shad put his arm around Copper as the last rays of sun shone down upon their homestead—like a benediction. Copper squeezed Tess's hand, "This is the first view I had of what was to become my home. I was lost and starving in these mountains. I was even younger than you but I had a good mule! One morning we got separated and when I followed her tracks, she led me here, to this enchanting place. My very first thought was that, it was a little bit of heaven! I've called it that ever since."

"Yes," Tess breathed as she gazed at the sight before her, "I can see why."

The homestead had been built in between two opposing hills, with a long stretch of valley just beyond. In the distance was the sound of a rushing river. The cabin was on the left and the sturdy barn and other buildings were on the right. A number of mares with their foals grazed in a small pasture close to the barns. The cabin was actually two cabins that shared a roof with a dog run in between. The honey colored logs were so masterfully joined together they resembled a finely braided whip.

"What a wonderful place!" Tess said reverently as she clutched Copper's hand, "I feel badly that I've kept you away from it. And, oh dear, you have horses and goats and chickens. They must be starving!"

Shad laughed, "Nope, we've been gone a lot lately and we hired a neighbor boy to tend to them. Skip's only twelve but he's reliable. 'Course, right about now he's probably down at the river, fishin'. I'll head down there in a bit and tell him to go on home now. I'll probably have to wake him up, he likes to tie his line to his big toe and take a nap!"

Tess smiled, "Well, I'm glad he was here and your animals didn't suffer because of me. Still, I know it's been a sacrifice for you to take care of me like you have. Hopefully, I'll soon feel like doing more than nap myself! I wish I had some way of repaying you both." Ducking her head self-consciously, she stared down at her boy's shirt and trousers. Even her boots were boy's boots and all of it, worn and faded. Even if she knew who she was, she doubted she would have the wherewithal to repay these good people.

115

Shad and Copper exchanged knowing glances but then Shad grunted, "Nonsense, you don't owe us anything. Just because things seem to be out of our control, don't mean they're out of God's control. There ain't a doubt in my mind that the good Lord brought us together. Now, all we got to do is figure out what He wants us to do next!"

Copper smiled, "Well, I'm thinkin' the next thing He'd want us to do, is get this girl off her feet!" Turning to Shad she added softly, "She's lookin' a bit peaked. Go on and take care of Boone. I'll get her settled and make us a quick vegetable soup."

After supper, Copper surprised Shad with one of his favorite treats, corn cakes with honey and hot coffee.

As was their custom, while Copper washed the dishes, Shad read from the Bible. He began where they had left off in the book of John, chapter three. When he came to verse sixteen, Copper softly repeated the most powerful verse in the Bible along with Shad, "For God so loved the world that he gave His one and only Son, that whoever believes in Him would not die but have eternal life." It was a common practice for the couple to recite special verses together. But what surprised them both was when their guest recited the verse along with them."

"Miss!" Shad grinned, "you know the Bible!"

Tess shrugged, "Well, I know that much at least."

"Let's try some other verses," Copper suggested then said, lots of people memorize, Romans eight verse twenty-eight?" When Tess just shrugged, Copper said, "It goes like this, 'All things God works for the good...'"

"For the good of those who have been called according to His purpose," Tess finished, her blue eyes bright with excitement. "Let's do some more!"

Shad and Copper continued, but Tess only knew a few more scriptures. When she started getting frustrated Shad shook his head, "Now, don't get discouraged just 'cause you can't recite the Bible back to front. I do think we've struck on something that might help ya though. We'll just keep ticklin' your memory and we'll make a game of it."

"That's a fine idea," Copper agreed. "First, let's see how much schooling you've had. Then we'll ask you things that maybe a farmer's or shopkeeper's daughter might know. That should help us learn more about you! Now for your first question, who was George Washington?"

Without hesitation, Tess replied, "The first President."

"That a girl!" Shad nodded, then glanced around the room. Spotting one of his favorite novels, he asked, "Now, do ya happen to know who Moby Dick was?"

Tess pursed her lips, "Was he, the second President? Or was he a general?"

She looked so innocent as she batted her big blue eyes that the McKennas thought she was serious. Then a grin spread across her face as she added, "Either that, or he was a big white whale! A very naughty, big white whale!"

Copper giggled then rolled her eyes, "Oh dear, Shad, I think this girl may have a naughty streak as well. We're going to have to stay on our toes with this one!"

The big man laughed as he shook his finger at her, then the game continued. As the daughter of a school master, Copper was able to think up a number of questions regarding geography, history and mathematics. Tess knew the answers to every question. However, when it came to cooking and housework, it was obvious that she was not as accomplished. Had Shad asked her to help in the barn, they might have learned a great deal more, but Copper insisted that she stay mostly inside until they were certain there were no internal injuries!

As the days went by the McKennas grew quite fond of this blonde haired, blue eyed young woman. Unfortunately, she continued to be as much a mystery to herself as she was to them. After a week of answering hundreds of questions correctly, she was still no closer to remembering anything about her life or who she was. One day after supper, her frustration got the best of her and she jumped up and went to the bookcase in the corner. Randomly she plucked a novel from the shelf and shook it in the air, "I feel like a book that has everything missing but the middle few chapters. You don't know the title, where the characters are from, you haven't the beginning or the end and you don't know why anything is happening!" Feeling embarrassed by her outburst she slumped her shoulders. Carefully putting the book back in its place, she added sadly, "It's of no worth! You might as well throw it away. You rescued part of me, but the part that makes me—me—is still lost! Who am I and why am I up here all alone? There are still no answers. But—do you know what frightens me the most? What if I find out and then I don't like who I am? What then?"

"Miss," Shad said gently, "before you lost your memory, you put yourself in danger to warn us about that bear. We've spent a lot of time with you. Copper and me think that the young woman you are right now, is worth a great deal. Even if ya never put all the pieces back together, yer special to us. Just the way ya are!"

Every day, they continued to play Shad's memory game. One night after their Bible reading, Shad picked up his guitar and he and Copper began singing their favorite hymns. Soon Tess was joining in, she had a beautiful voice and seemed to know every word by heart.

Before Shad could begin another song, Copper patted Tess's hand, "You may not remember your name but we're still learning a lot about you. You've been well educated and I think it's obvious that you've been raised in a Christian home. Maybe if we send letters with your description around to all the nearby churches, someone will know who you are!"

Tess thought about Copper's suggestion for a moment, then shook her head, "No! I don't want just anyone to know where I am...not yet! So far only two things seem to tickle my memory. I feel in my heart that I came up here because of some kind of danger. I don't know if it was danger for me or some-one else. I can't explain it—I just—know it! If you send word about me, we won't know who will respond. It could be a friend or just as easily an enemy. How would we know the difference?"

Copper slipped her arm around Tess, "You're right—and I still believe that God will work this out in His own good time. Now, you said there were two things that tickled your memory, what was the other one?"

Tess bit her lip, this was something very personal and yet it was something she wanted to—no, needed to talk about. "Like you said, it does appear that I was raised in a Christian home. I don't remember but...somehow that seems right. I haven't told you this before because it was something that shamed me. I think it's a memory, maybe not, but it's been tormenting me."

"We hope you know that you can tell Shad and I anything you want," Copper assured her, "nothing will change how we feel about you."

Tess nodded then closed her eyes, "I remember an older man speaking to me. Maybe my father or an uncle perhaps. I can't see his face but I keep hear-ing his warning, he said, 'You've always had a rebellious streak when it came to giving your heart to God but what you're doing now is dangerous!'" Staring down at her clasped hands she added, "In this short while, I've seen your strong faith in God and watched as you've put aside your own lives to take care of a stranger. I don't know who I am but I know what I am not! Regardless of how I might have been raised—I know that I'm not a Christian. If that bear had killed me—I wasn't ready to die." Tess paused for a moment then asked, "Will you two show me how to make things right with God? I'm believing that my memory will come back someday. This may sound strange, but when it does I want the new me to be able to speak truth to the old me! I do want to remember who I was but...I don't want to *be like I was*!" Tess shrugged her shoulders, "That's why it's terribly important for me to make things right with God—now—while He's the only certainty I have."

That very night the young woman who had no idea who she was, gave all she was, wholeheartedly to Jesus Christ. Both Shad and Copper's eyes filled with tears as they listened to her humble prayer.

"Lord, you know who I am, so I'm not going to dwell on that. Right now, it just seems more important that I acknowledge, who **You** are! You are the all-seeing creator, the Messiah, the Savior of all who will believe! I am now one of those who believes. I ask that you come into my heart and make me over, just the way you want me. I ask for Your forgiveness of my old rebellious nature and of all my sins. I pray that you will create in me a new, clean heart, filled with clean thoughts and right desires. And regarding my memory...Lord, I am trusting that You'll let me know who I am, whenever the time seems best. All I ask is that when You restore my memory, please give the new me strength to influence the person I was, not the other way around."

Chapter 12
Buffalo Soldiers

"No longer do I call you slaves, for the slave does not know what his master is doing; but I have called you friends." John 15:15

"I'll race you!" Cal shouted, as he gave his bay gelding his head and the horse shot out in front of Josh's buckskin mare. The boys loved to race and their horses were used to this sport. They jumped over ditches and yucca plants and delighted in leaving each other in the dust! They were almost to the main gate when they both realized there were riders blocking their way. Yanking on their rein's, their mounts came to a sliding stop. They had barely avoided a collision with the six black soldiers that were cantering under the archway, two by two. As the dust they'd brought with them began to settle, Josh ducked his head, "Sorry about that!"

Cal didn't seem to notice or care that they'd nearly crashed into these men, undaunted he called out, "Hey, you're the Buffalo Soldiers—aren't you? Bet you've come to buy remounts?"

The officer in charge was a powerful looking man and the boys figured he was about their father's age, for he too had gray at his temples. He nudged his horse forward and saluted. Then, with a friendly grin he said, "We're buffalo soldiers all right, Captain Zackery, at your service. And this is Lieutenant Abrams, Sergeant Webster, and Privates Jeremy, Hanover and Lark." Each man nodded as their names were spoken.

Hoping to appear older than he was, Josh replied with his own introductions, "It's nice to meet you men. I'm Joshua Grainger and this is my brother Caleb. Soldiers are always welcome on the Bar 61 and we'd be happy to escort you men back to the ranch."

That said, Josh reined his horse beside the Captain while Cal rode beside the Lieutenant.

Both boys were brimming with curiosity, but Josh was the first to ask a question, "Captain Zachery, I've heard you men fight the Comanches in Texas. Are you headed back or is there trouble around here?"

The Captain started to answer but then Caleb ask loudly, "You men all used to be slaves, right? Do you want to fight the Comanches or does the government make you do it?"

Josh frowned as he turned towards his brother, "Cal, that was rude! Don't ask them things like that!"

"I wasn't bein' rude, Josh! Pa never says it's wrong for us to ask questions. So quit acting like you're all grown-up and stop bossin' me around. You're only a minute older than me you know!"

"Hold on now, boys," Captain Zackery held up his hand and everyone stopped. Figuring he'd better take a moment to intervene, he turned to face Caleb, "We aren't offended, it was an honest question. And the answer for me, Webster and Abrams, is yes, we were born slaves but the Yankees freed us and we became soldiers. All three Privates, however, were born as free men. As to your question, Joshua. Yes, we fight the Comanches in Texas. And Caleb, we joined up to fight. The government pays us in beans, saddle sores and seven dollars a month."

Just then Lieutenant Abrams added, "I'd like to add to that, Cal, the government does not make us serve our country. We all volunteered to fight the Comanches. We serve proudly for our race and for our country!"

"Thanks," Cal said, "and I really didn't mean to be rude. My father's family were plantation owners in Georgia. He always hated slavery and when his father died he made sure all of them were freed! He even tried to buy back the ones his father had sold. The owners wouldn't always sell and sometimes he couldn't always find them, but he tried. He tried real hard to do what was right." Cal's voice trailed off, fearing he'd said too much again.

Sensing the boy's embarrassment, Lieutenant Abrams tapped Cal on the arm, "Tell me about these here Morgan-Arabian crosses. Ya call them Morab's don't ya? Are they as fine as I've heard? We could have bought good horses down in Texas but our commanding officer said, 'Nope, you get your remounts from the Bar 61. It'll be worth the ride!'"

Cal grinned, "He was right! The Morabs are my favorite subject. They've got the strength of a Morgan horse and the speed and endurance of the Arabian! I hear Texas gets pure blixy hot but it probably can't compare with the Sahara

Desert. The Morabs really should be perfect for what you need. But if I were a Comanche, I'd fight twice as hard just so I could take your horse if you were ridin' one of ours!"

Josh glared at his brother again and rolled his eyes, "Cal! We're hoping to sell these men our horses not scare them off!"

Caleb turned red, "Oh, well—um—they're real fast too! You men shouldn't have any trouble gettin' away! They'd make really good horses for bank robbers too!"

When the soldiers all laughed, Cal wasn't sure if it made him feel better or worse. He just always said whatever came to mind and then found out later whether he should have said it or not.

The soldiers followed the boys down a long road that curved over rolling hills. Wild flowers bordered both sides and the middle of the lane all along the way. When they finally reached the ranch yard, the men were noticeably impressed. To their left was a large and elegant adobe house adorned with lilac bushes and roses. To their right stood two log barns with numerous corrals and holding pens in between. On a small rise where all the buildings could be seen at a glance, stood a cabin, probably the foreman's house and next to it was a large bunkhouse.

Josh and Caleb seemed not to notice the men's wide-eyed stares as they led the soldiers to a long hitching rail under some shade trees. As they all dismounted, three of the youngest ranch hands hurried from the nearest barn to greet them. Kip, the oldest of the three, called out, "We'll take the horses, boys, and your Pa was askin' about you two." Turning to the tall Captain he grinned, adding, "Looks like you fellas have timed it just about right. The boss thought you might get here today. He just sent some men out to round up about fifty ponies for you to look over. If the herd isn't too far away, they'll be here in three or four hours."

"Thanks Kip," Cal said then turned towards the soldiers, "just come this way men. Our ranch has the best cooks this side of the Mississippi. Between Mama and Carlos, we'll have you all so full, if any of our horses decide to buck you off…you'll probably just bounce!"

Josh punched his brother in the arm, "Cal! Can't you say anything right today? You don't tell a prospective buyer that they're gonna get thrown off the very horses you're tryin' to sell them!"

Cal glared at his brother, "I didn't mean it like that. I was tellin' them that the cookin' was good not that the horses were bad!" He glanced self-consciously at the Captain and then the Lieutenant, "You men knew what I meant—didn't ya?" Then his brows knit together and he kicked at a clod of dirt, "You aren't gonna tell my Pa that I've been puttin' my foot in my mouth—are ya?"

Captain Zackery grinned, "Nope, but I will tell him what fine salesmen he has in you two. We're all mighty anxious to see your horses, but we've been ridin' a long time and when you started talkin' about the good vittles, we didn't really hear much after that!" He looked around at his fellow soldiers, "Isn't that right men?"

When they all grunted and nodded in agreement, Cal sighed, "Good—then just follow me."

Instead of heading straight to the house, he led the soldiers to a small shelter where there was a pump, multiple wash basins, a shelf filled with towels and brushes to rid clothes of trail dust. "Thought you fella's might want to clean-up a bit. I'm not being rude again! You'd all be welcome in the house no matter how dirty ya were. But Josh and I have to wash. It's one of Mama's rules."

When the men laughed, Caleb feared that maybe he had been rude again after all. Ducking his head, his face pinched into a frown. Zachery was quick to dispel his worries as he placed a hand on the boy's shoulder, "This is wonderful Caleb. The truth is, just before we met up with you two, we were wondering how soon and where we could wash off some of this acreage we've been carrying around!"

After a quick wash and brushing off layers of trail dust from their uniforms, the soldiers followed the boys inside. When they were led through the elegant front doors of the hacienda, the Captain wasn't surprised, but it made the rest of the men a bit wary. Even more so when the boys led them straight through to the parlor. For they were treating them like honored guests. Still they had to wonder what their parents would say? The war had been over for twenty years but even the people who fought against slavery still did not believe in equality and this kind of treatment didn't happen very often.

When Tytus heard them arrive, he hurried from the office to greet them. When Josh introduced him to Captain Zackery, Ty couldn't keep from staring at the man, "I know you. We've met before—haven't we?"

The Captain's eyes seemed to flash a warning, then he frowned as he shook Ty's hand and said in a low voice, "Don't believe I've had the pleasure, sir. However, I do have a message from my commanding officer for you regarding your contract with the cavalry. May we speak privately, in your office?"

"Yes—of course," Ty murmured, then turned to the other men, "please make yourselves comfortable. Carlos will be bringing in some refreshments in just a few moments. If you have any questions about our horses, my sons will probably tell you more than you want to know!"

As he led the way to his office, Ty felt an uneasiness he couldn't shake. The Bar 61's contract with the Army was extremely important to the success of the ranch, but he didn't believe this was about the contract. The moment they were inside his office he turned to the Captain, "Is something wrong? I have the feeling that you're not here about my contract or even here to buy horses—are you?"

The Captain glanced down at the floor as he fingered his hat. "The Buffalo Soldiers in your parlor are here to purchase remounts. But I'm not really with them," he said slowly, "I am a Pinkerton agent. I've got a heck of a lot to tell you. Almost don't know where to begin—Mister Ty."

Ty's jaw dropped as he stared at the face before him. He knew that face almost as well as he knew his own. "SAM?" When the man grinned, Ty shook his head and laughed. "Can't believe I didn't recognized you right away!" Stepping closer, he grabbed hold of the man's arm. "Samuel Grainger! We were both teenagers the last time we saw each other. You look so much like your parents, don't know why I didn't see it sooner. You're the image of Joseph and Natty May. I've searched for you for over thirty years. We were told you were dead!"

A slow grin spread across the Captain's face, "I'm alive and kickin' but the name is Sam Zackery now. Haven't gone by Grainger since your Pa sold me." When Ty grimaced, he quickly added, "As it turned out, he did me a big favor that day. He sold me to a Scotsman who took me and a few others north and gave us all our freedom papers. When war broke out, I joined the army and served under General McClellan. Then he and Allan Pinkerton had an idea about recruiting and training ex-slaves like me. Thanks to you, I could read and write and speak like a slave or a well-educated gentleman. I worked as a Pinkerton agent all through the war." He touched his uniform and said, "You're right, I'm not with the army anymore and I'm not here about your contract. As far as anyone else is concerned though, I am a Buffalo Soldier, and that's all I am! I work in New York mostly, but was on another case when you hired the agency to watch over your daughter. As it turned out we were already watching the

Tulane estate. We believe that Barrett Tulane is working with or perhaps being blackmailed by a woman whose been suspected of many crimes, under many different names, but she's never been convicted. We've tracked her here under the name of Lavenia O-Brien although usually she goes by Lavenia Wrenford."

"That old witch," Ty hissed, "yes, she's staying with us now. But what about Tess? Is she safe?"

Sam gritted his teeth and shook his head, "We're not sure. That's why I'm here. We can't find her."

"What do you mean you can't find her?" Ty growled.

"I know that's a hard thing to hear. But I ask you to please stay calm and let me finish what I have to say. We think she may have realized that she was in danger and is hiding somewhere. Right now, I need answers from you. You say Lavenia Wrenford is staying with you—as a house guest?" When Ty nodded, Sam frowned and ran his hand over his face, "This case gets more bizarre by the moment. According to our files, that woman was suspected of hiring Dewey LeBeau to kill your brother Timothy, and of kidnapping your wife! It was never proven but now...this same woman is your house guest?"

"You can't pick your relatives, Sam." Ty muttered, "she's my wife's mother and if there was ever a truly evil woman, it's her! We believe that she's dying of consumption, but that's all we believe about her. That's why we thought it was wise to keep her here. We hoped we could prevent her from hurting us or anyone else. Of course, we don't know what she might have already put into play. Now please, tell me everything you know about Tess!"

Sam rubbed his face as he stepped to one of the two leather chairs across from Ty's large desk, "Come and sit down," he groaned, "I'll tell you all we know. At every turn, nothing about this case has made any sense! As you requested, we had agents watching the train when it arrived in New York. They saw the Tulanes leave their private railway car with a young blonde woman and we naturally assumed that she was Tess. As I said we've already been watching the estate and had a female agent posing as one of the maids. When she went to greet your daughter, Missus Tulane said that Tess was too ill to see anyone. Then for no apparent reason, Barrett fired all the staff, including our agent! It appears that anyone who might have been able to recognize Tess was dismissed. They let everyone of the servants go who had worked in the house or the stables. There were about thirty people in all and many of them had been with the Langstroms and Tulanes for generations. The groundskeeper and the gardeners were the only ones who kept their jobs. We tried to get another agent hired on but they didn't replace a single servant. Of course, we kept an eye on the place, and then two days later, we stopped a young blonde woman who was sneaking out of the house around three in the morning. She was very frightened and told us that the Tulanes had seen her on the train and hired her to pretend to be Barrett's fiancé, not only while in New York, but to travel with them, all the way to Paris! She was to speak as little as possible and never be seen without a veil. Missus Tulane told her that her son had been jilted and didn't want to face the New York gossips. The agreement was that once the ruse was over she would be given five thousand dollars. We asked her why she left and she said that Missus Tulane never went anywhere in the house unless her son was with her and that she always seemed ill at ease. She said that there was just something about them and the whole plan that frightened her, so she ran away. That's all she could tell us."

Ty jumped to his feet, "Why didn't you just break the door down and demand to know where my daughter was?"

"We wanted to, but we couldn't risk them knowing that we suspect anything. It might have made things worse for Tess. We have to proceed very carefully. Right now, we're not sure if Tulane's a victim of Wrenford's or her partner." Seeing Ty's frustration, Sam quickly added, "The day before the girl ran away, Tulane sent a very cryptic telegram to this Lavenia Wrenford while she was staying in Denver. It said, 'Package arrived New York as planned—will confirm when H receives it in Paris.' We think the package he was referring to was Tess. But he was lying. If he had Tess, then why hire a girl to pretend to be her? He might even be hiding Tess to protect her! That might be why he fired all the staff that would know her by sight. We believe he's doing all of this because he needs Lavenia to believe he's in control. Another thing, just before I left New York we found a passenger that was on the same train as the Tulanes private car. The lady went all the way from Colorado Springs to New York. She remembered the train stopping in the middle of an open field. Then she said, when the train started up again, she saw a young blonde woman riding away on a beautiful spotted horse. Could that have been Tess?"

Ty jumped to his feet and ran both hands through his hair, "Yes—that had to be Tess and the horse she took with her. But—I can't imagine a conductor agreeing to stop a train, then help a girl and a horse get off in the middle of a field! And if he did that, why hasn't she contacted us by now?"

126

"That's what we're trying to find out," Sam groaned. "As I said, this case is like a maze of twists and turns. As if there was a conspiracy to keep us from making any headway. The woman that got off that train might have been Tess...or just as easily...another imposter! According to the conductor, Missus Tulane told him that her son's fiancé had a change of heart and wanted to go home. When he found out the young woman was Miss Tess Grainger, and since the train was still crossing Bar 61 land, he agreed to have the engineer stop the train."

"She got off on our land—where?" Ty demanded.

"He said it was near the gate going into the North-West corner of the ranch. Said he even helped her put her side-saddle on her horse before he unloaded it. When the train pulled out he watched her riding south. That's all he knew."

Ty buried his head in his hands, "It's a good long ride from that gate to the hacienda but she could have made it by late that night!" An angry scowl crossed his face, "Where could she be? That was two weeks ago! Last week we even received a telegram that was supposed to have been from Tess. It said that all was well and that she couldn't wait to see Paris! That low-down dog, Tulane, he sent it as if it were from her!" Ty slammed his fist on his desk, "Why didn't the agency inform me about this sooner? My daughter could be anywhere!"

"You're an important man, my superiors believed they could find her. They've had agents looking everywhere. Apparently, they thought it best not to tell you. I wasn't brought in on this case until a few days ago, but I threatened to resign if they didn't let me come here and tell you immediately. We couldn't risk sending a telegram. Now that I'm on this case, I'll do everything I can to find out exactly what's going on here. I promise you, Tytus, we'll find her. You and Timothy were always my friends, never treated me like a slave. This isn't just a case, it's personal to me. I've been praying for all of you, night and day, since I heard Tess was missing. Like Pa used to say, 'Pray every minute—every step!'"

Ty nodded as he blew out a breath, "Yes, he taught us to pray over everything, didn't he?" Suddenly Ty's head snapped up, "Good Lord, I was so stunned to see you and then to hear about Tess," shaking his head, he groaned, "what's the matter with me?"

Sam was confused, "What do you mean?"

"Right this minute we can't do anything for Tess, but I can do something for you! Stay right here Sam—I've got a present for you." Heading for the door Ty smiled over his shoulder, "I'll be right back."

Ty left the room in two strides and found Joseph just where he thought he'd be, talking horses with the Buffalo Soldiers. He was ninety-two, and though his body was slow, his mind was as quick as ever. Ty heard him speaking to the younger men in his deep crackling baritone.

"You sho came to the right place. There just ain't no better horse flesh than what ya can find right chere. Don't spend as much time with my ponies as I used to. Mister Ty's afraid I'll get hurt. Just 'cause I got white hair don't make me old ya know! It's a sad thing but young men don't appreciate old men...until they gets to be...old men! And then it's too late...and ain't that a shame?" The men laughed, as did Joseph who suddenly found Ty gently pulling on his arm.

"Joseph, I need you to come with me, I have a surprise for you." Ty suddenly wondered if seeing Sam would be too much for the old man. "Now, this is going to be a shock to you but it's a good shock, so prepare yourself! Do you think your heart can take it?"

"Hah!" Joseph laughed, "you know this ole heart o' mine can take anythin' that's good! Hope this won't take too long though, I was havin' me a good time with those young fellas!"

Ty was so anxious he wanted to pick Joseph up and carry him, but he slowed his pace to match that of the old man until finally they stood outside his office door. "Joseph," he said gently, "you have taught me about prayer my whole life. 'Don't ever give up—just keep on praying.' That's what you've always said. Well, today my friend, a prayer you've been praying for a very long time has been answered." As Ty swung the door open his voice cracked as he said, "J-just look who the Lord brought to our doorstep today!"

Sam jumped to his feet and stared, then tears filled his eyes even though he didn't quite believe what he was seeing. Then just like that, he was a child again, and he called out, "Pappy?"

Joseph's hand shook as he reached out and clung to Ty's strong arm as he recognized the child he had lost so long ago. "Samuel? Is that you, boy?" he cried as he stood in the doorway, "tis you ain't it. Oh, my boy—my own-boy. O' thank ya Jesus, thank ya!" Joseph choked out the words then threw his head back and laughed as the tears made tracks down his ebony face. Father and son held each other, laughing and crying. Fearing that Joseph was overtaxing himself, Ty said gently, "Come and sit down you two, you've a lot of catching up to do."

Sam helped his father to the settee, he stared at Ty and then back at Joseph, "Pappy, I don't understand how this could be. I searched for you and

Mama. I knew Colonel Grainger sold ya to the Summervilles. I tracked them all the way to California. They said they brought you two with them from Georgia but that you both died on the way."

Ty slammed his fist into his hand, "Savannah Summerville," he hissed, "I didn't think you could be that evil," he groaned. "She was my fiancé, Sam. I finished building the ranch just before the war started. When I sent for her, I also insisted that she bring Joseph and Natty May. Before they set foot on the ranch I demanded that Judge Summerville sign your parent's freedom papers. That angered both the Judge and Savannah. Things between us went downhill from there. We ended our engagement and the Summervilles went on to California. Your mother was happy here, but sadly she just wasn't well. I hope it's a comfort to know that she took her last breath right here on this ranch and as a free woman. She's buried up on the hill, right next to Timothy."

Joseph pulled a large red bandana from his pocket and wiped his eyes and face. He took in a long breath then sighed, "We done a heap o' searching for you too, son. Was told you'd been killed in the war. We're still trying to find yer sister, Dorcas. Do ya know where she is?"

Sam grinned, "I sure do Pappy! She and her husband own a farm in Illinois. You have five grandchildren and fifteen great-grand-children. We'll send her a telegram right away and then you two can exchange long letters!"

Joseph blew his nose loudly then looked upwards, "Thank you Lord! I feared I'd have to be in heaven before I'd find out about m' babies. I am one happy old man today!" Suddenly he became serious and turned towards his son, "Ain't nothing wrong with being a Buffalo Soldier. I'm right proud of those men—but you ain't one of 'em. You've done well son—I see it in the way you carry yoself. I know you didn't come here to see me, 'cause you thought I was dead. So, I reckon you're here on other business—and it ain't buying horses—is it?" The old man stared at his son, then at Ty, then back at his son again, "Now, tell me what's goin' on? If trouble has come, I reckon ya best be telling me what it is so we can get to prayin' about it. Remember boys, when ya gots troubles ya pray every minute, every step!"

Despite the gravity of the situation, old Joseph's observant ways amazed the two younger men, who exchanged glances and shook their heads. Then they filled the old man in on everything. When they were finished, as they had expected, Joseph led them in prayer.

Chapter 13
Summer McKenna

"For I know the plans I have for you, says the Lord. They are plans for good and not for evil, to give you a future and a hope... when you pray I will listen. You will find me when you seek me, if you look for me in earnest." Jeremiah 29:11 & 12

"Dear Lord," Shad began, as he prayed over their evening meal, "Please bless this food and the hands that prepared it. Please be with our young friend here. Help her to recover from her injuries, remember her past and bless her as she becomes who You want her to be in the future. And Lord, we don't know if she has family and friends out lookin' for her or not. But if so, then please whisper to them that she's safe and help us all to find one another. We ask for your guidance and direction, Lord. In Jesus' name, Amen."

Copper added her own Amen, then turned to the young woman, "It's hard to believe but it's been two weeks since we first saw you! Shad and I've been talking and we think you need a name! God blessed us with a wonderful son, but we had hoped to have a girl, too. If we had, we would have named her Summer. You need a name, and when we go to town tomorrow, we thought it would be wise if you're introduced as Shad's niece, Summer McKenna. Would that be all right?"

Tess smiled, "Summer McKenna. Yes, I like it and it makes me feel safer. If you don't mind sharing your name, I would be honored!"

Later that evening, her curiosity was piqued when she saw Shad place a small heart shaped, stringed instrument on his lap. Then he lifted his harmonica to his lips and began to tune it. "That's such a beautiful little thing but... what is it?" she asked.

Shad grinned, "And who wants to know?"

"Summer McKenna, that's who!"

"Well, Summer McKenna, this here is a zither. I had never seen one before but a friend of ours had one that was broken so badly, I pretty much had to build her a new one. Now it seems nearly every time someone sees her zither they ask me to make one for them too." Shad pointed to another one at his feet and said, "These two here make an even dozen. When we go to town tomorrow I'll leave them in the mercantile for sale."

Summer picked up the other zither and helped Shad tune it. She tightened the strings as Shad blew on the harmonica. When both zithers were tuned, Shad stood to get a cloth to wrap them in. Copper was in the kitchen humming her favorite hymn, when suddenly she was aware that Summer was accompanying her on one of the zithers.

Copper stopped singing and she and Shad both stared at her, "You can play a zither?" Copper asked. "That is very strange, they're not a common instrument."

Summer shrugged, "The song was familiar and my fingers just seemed to know what to do. It was like math and reading, I don't remember how I know—I just know."

Shad reached down and took the zither from her, "Well, you got named today, so I reckon we can call this your birthday. He put the zither back into her hands and said, "Happy Birthday, Summer! This here's a present to you from your Uncle Shad and Aunt Copper!"

꽃

As another week passed, all three of them fell into a pleasant family routine. The McKennas became Uncle Shad and Aunt Copper and they treated Summer like a beloved niece. They had missed their son terribly, so having this sweet young woman around helped to fill the emptiness. Although she was content to think of herself as Summer McKenna, she still worried about who she really was. But more than that, she worried that something wasn't right with the McKennas. Occasionally, she caught Shad and Copper exchanging sad looks that told her that there was a problem. Whenever she asked what was wrong or if she had become too much of a burden, their reply was always, 'now don't be silly, it's a blessing having you here!'

Then one day everything became clear. There was a loud knocking at the door and when Summer went to answer it, there was a burly, red-faced man standing there. He looked her over so audaciously she wanted to slap him. Then he puffed himself up, as if she should be impressed, as he introduced himself, "I'm Hamilton Beaumont Doherty, the owner of the Doherty Saw Mill, among many other things," he bragged, "I heard Shad's pretty niece was here and that you'd been hurt and couldn't be moved." At that, he once again allowed his eyes to take a journey up and down her body, then added, "Didn't think you'd be such a looker though! Don't know what your problem was, but as far as I can tell you're fit and feisty now!" When Summer glared at him in disgust but said nothing, he stared down his nose at her and sneered, "I've been patient long enough. I'm here to speak to Shad."

"I'm right here, Ham!" Shad's voice was stern as he and Copper walked from the barn towards the cabin. They were holding hands and looked as if they were walking towards the gallows.

Summer wanted to push this man away and pull Shad and Copper inside and lock the door. "What's wrong?" she asked.

Copper forced a smile, "Listen honey, we've got to attend to some business with Mister Doherty. You mentioned you wanted to go down to the meadow and play your zither today. Why don't you go on ahead? Shad and I'll come find you when we're finished."

Summer stared at Copper and then at Shad. Sometimes she forgot that she really wasn't family, and that their business was none of hers. Still, it seemed wrong to leave them if they were in some kind of trouble.

"Of course, I'll just get my zither and a shawl," she said softly.

Walking towards the meadow, she began pleading with God. *Please Lord, the McKennas are such good people! That awful man, he looks evil, mean and evil. Something bad is happening to them, I just know it! I can't stop it, but You can if You want to. Oh Lord, please want to!*

When she reached her favorite spot, Tess sat down on a small boulder and breathed in the sights and scents of this beautiful meadow. Despite her worries and heavy heart, this place always lifted her spirits. No matter who or what she'd been before now, she was born anew. Her troubles and fears were still very real but even so, she felt as if all the world was fresh and full of hopeful possibilities. Silently she continued to pray for the McKennas even as her fingers began to strum across the strings of the zither. Finally, she began to sing:

Now the shadows slowly lengthen,
Soon the evening time will come;
With Thy grace, O Savior, strengthen,
By Thy help I would go home.

Her thoughts seemed to catch on the very last word—*home*—for what it stood for was such a mystery. Had she escaped from a horrible family or been torn from a happy one? She was so immersed in her musings, and her prayers, that at first she didn't even notice that another voice was singing. It was distant and low, as if the wind itself were harmonizing with her. Then it became more distinct as a man's voice finished the refrain:

Tarry with me, O my Savior,
Tarry with me through the night;
I am lonely, Lord, without Thee,
Tarry with me through the night.

Setting her zither aside, Tess watched as a man rode towards her on a beautiful sorrel stallion with a white blaze down his dished face and four white stockings. The horse caught her attention before she even noticed his rider. It was a magnificent animal, having the exotic and delicate features of an Arabian. She didn't know how she knew that, but he was a glorious sight as he pranced toward her. His coat glistened in the sunlight like a polished bronze statue. When horse and rider came closer, she looked up at the man just as he knuckled his hat back from his face. He had black hair and high cheekbones and a wide, masculine jaw. His tanned skin was a stark contrast to his green eyes and bright smile. *My goodness, the man is as beautiful as his horse,* she thought, then turned away, suppressing a smile. It was silly to think of a man as beautiful. But when she dared another glance, his grin broadened, and she decided that if he wasn't beautiful, then he was at very least—unusually handsome! Summer was surprised by her foolishness and suddenly wondered if she always reacted to men like this? She certainly hoped not and the idea worried her a little. Then again maybe it was just something unique about this one man that so fascinated her. When she felt her cheeks burning, she quickly looked away.

Summer might have felt less self-conscious had she known the man was just as captivated by the picture she made. In fact, this was so like some of his dreams that he feared he might have fallen asleep in the saddle and that this lovely vision wasn't really there at all! He couldn't help but stare as a mountain breeze blew a shining blonde curl across her face and she reached up and tucked it behind her ear. It pleased him when she gazed into his eyes for a long moment, then looked down and blushed. He could feel his heart racing in his chest as a million thoughts spun through his mind. It was almost as if he had written a script and this lovely girl was portraying the fulfillment of his dreams and prayers. He was afraid to speak or even to look away, lest this spell be broken. *Lord, this is her—isn't it? Here she is sitting on my own praying rock! I've always pictured her here but I just assumed it was because this is where I prayed for her. Is this why I'm here? Even before I got Ma's letter, I felt you telling me to get my things in order and come home. I've got to get control of myself but this is so—so much like the way Ma was here when Pa came home. She's so lovely, Lord. She just must be your answer to all my years of praying!*

As the silence between them grew, Summer became even more uncomfortable, but not in the same way as she been with that disgusting Mister Doherty. Still she wished this man would say something and stop staring at her. Finally, she realized that if anyone was going to break this silence, it would have to be her, "Hello..." she murmured shyly. "I suppose neither of us expected to see anyone out here, and its left us both a bit tongue tied—hasn't it?" Tanner nodded, but for the life of him, he couldn't think of anything to say. Summer bit down on her thumb nail, then she looked up at him and asked, "Could it be—that you're staring at me because you think perhaps we've met before? Do you know me?"

"Oh yes!" he blurted out, *in my dreams we've met a thousand times,* he wanted to add. When the girl's eyebrows rose, he chuckled and shook his head, "Actually, no we have never met—but I know we were supposed to—and—you're beautiful!" When the young woman's lovely sapphire eyes grew wary and she leaned away from him, Tanner grimaced. He had dreamt of meeting her nearly all his life, but he had certainly never dreamt that he would act like an addlepated schoolboy when he finally did. He paused a moment then stammered, "I—I meant to say that you sing beautifully. I apologize for intruding like I did, but at first, I thought you were my Aunt Mariah!" There was a tenderness in his voice and in his eyes as he added, "I've been away for a while but Ma usually writes me about any new comers. Are you new to the mountains or are you just visiting?"

"Aunt Mariah?" Summer whispered, as disconnected thoughts and images swept through her mind. She tried to hold onto them, but like steam rising from a boiling kettle, they disappeared before she could make sense of them.

The handsome stranger asked again if she were visiting and she suddenly remembered that she was supposed to be careful around strangers. "I'm—um—I'm Summer McKenna. I live with my Uncle Shad and Aunt

Mariah—I—I mean Aunt Copper. They are having a meeting of some kind so I came out here to give them some privacy."

Tanner narrowed his eyes, and sucked in a breath. Something was wrong, maybe this woman wasn't the answer to his prayers after all. She had seemed so perfect, but she was lying! Neither of his parents had any living relatives. Traveling the world had made Tanner suspicious, certainly less trusting than he had been in his youth. His mother's last letter had troubled him greatly. It was more a note than a letter and it said only:

Please don't worry son, all is well with your Pa and me but God in His wisdom is setting before us a new challenge. From now on send your letters in care of Reverend Quincy Long at the Wings on the Mountain address. We'll write more later. We're in God's good care so please don't worry. We love you, Ma and Pa.

Nothing short of a catastrophe would cause his parents to leave the place they both loved. And yet, here sat a stranger, wearing one of his mother's dresses and calling herself their niece. In his travels, he had met many beautiful women. Some of them were humble and good, but he had also met others who were shallow, mean spirited and conniving.

His face suddenly became stern and he said coolly, "Shad and Copper McKenna have only one relative...me." Tapping his chest, he added, "I'm their son, Tanner. Somethings very wrong here. Summer was the name of the daughter my parents never had. I know you're not Summer McKenna, so who are you? And why are my parents losing their home? Are you the reason?"

"What do you mean they're losing their home?" Summer sprang to her feet, hurt by his accusation but then doubts filled her mind. "That would explain their sad looks and why that Mister Doherty was so arrogant. Oh Lord, that's what their meeting is about!" Glancing up at Tanner she ran to his horse, "Quick, help me up. We have to do something to stop them!"

Tanner was shocked when the woman placed her foot on top of his boot and scrambled onto the back of his saddle. "Hurry!" she shouted, "Hurry!"

They raced across the valley and Tanner reined his horse to a sliding stop in front of the cabin just as Doherty stepped out of the door.

"You have one week to move," Doherty sneered, "if you're not out by then I'll send my men to do the job."

Knowing Shad was doing his best to control his temper, Copper answered for him, "That won't be necessary, Ham! By the end of the week we'll be out and the cabin and barns will be clean."

"The name's Hamilton——not Ham," he grunted, then he turned abruptly and nearly ran into Tanner. Summer had stayed behind to hold his stallion.

"What do you mean...out?" Tanner demanded, then he lowered his voice, "Mister Doherty? Pa? Ma what on earth is going on here?"

"Yer Pa will tell ya." Doherty grunted.

Despite the sadness in his eyes, Shad's smile was genuine, as he placed his hand on Tanner's shoulder, "Can't tell ya how good it is to see ya boy!" Rubbing the back of his neck he added sadly, "Sorry ya had to come home to this though. Sometimes things happen beyond our control and well...this place belongs to Doherty now," his eyes darted towards Summer then back at Tanner as he lowered his voice, "there's no need to discuss it. What's done is done!"

Tanner took his hat from his head and slapped it against his leg, "What do you mean, what's done is done?"

Shad nodded and gazed around at his beloved homestead and shrugged, "Son, all this here is just a stack o' logs put together with a lot of sweat. What's important is our faith and our family. If those things are intact, then we'll be all right!" Shad glanced at Doherty and said, "Good day to ya, Ham. This place is ours for another week. We've never felt the need to lock our door so we don't have a key to leave behind."

As Doherty got on his horse and rode away, Copper and Shad pulled Tanner into their arms and held him close. The three clung to each other a few moments, then Tanner backed away from his parents and looked at them, "I got here as quickly as I could! I sent a telegram to Uncle Quin, hoping that he could help. On my way here, I stopped at the mission and found that they've been gone for two months. My telegram was sitting unopened on his desk."

Shad looked down at Copper and smiled, "Right now, yer Ma and me are thinkin' the same thing. We should say that we hate that you had to come all this way but...we're both so dog-gone happy to see ya, that's really all we can think about!"

Copper even managed to laugh as she put her arm around Tanner's waist, "Oh my sweet boy, you have no idea how much we've missed you!"

Summer stood there by the hitching rail watching——listening. She felt like an unworthy intruder and yet she couldn't turn away from this touching scene. The McKennas were losing what Copper had called her, little bit of heaven. But instead of crying over their loss, they were sincerely filled with joy over the sight of their son! At first, when he said who he was, she hadn't really connected that this was 'the boy' Shad and Copper's spoke of so lovingly. Now all she could think of was his accusation that she was the reason his parents were losing their home. As she studied the man, she saw that Tanner was a young replica of Shadrack McKenna, a man she greatly admired. Like his father, Tanner was big and muscular, his hair was cut shorter than Shad's but it was as black as a raven's wing. When he had turned to watch Doherty leave, she had once again been caught off guard by his penetrating eyes. Copper always said that Shad's eyes were as green as the mountains he loved and Tanner's could be described the same way. He was a very handsome man, but she wondered if he was as good a person as his parents were?

As if in response to her unspoken question, Tanner asked one of his own as he nodded in her direction, "Ma, Pa—I don't mean to be rude but this woman is not your niece, there is no, Summer McKenna. So, who is she?" Lowering his voice, he added, "Is it because of her that you're having to move? Doherty's been trying to buy you out for as long as I can remember. I know what tender hearts you both have. Did she come up here with some sad tale, and you're selling out to help her? If that's what happened, did you stop to think that she might be in league with Ham? Might be playing on your sympathies?"

Copper frowned and put her hands on her hips, "Tanner Angus McKenna, I'm surprised at you. That was certainly not the case and it is unkind of you to say so! Summer came to us quite by accident and not through any kind of deception."

"All right Ma, but I've been out in the world more than you two and I've seen a lot of dishonesty. So, tell me what's going on?"

Copper was about to ask Summer if she would wait outside for a few minutes, but just then that young woman stepped forward with a look of determination on her face, "Yes please, explain this. I want to know too! I've been asking you both what's wrong for weeks now." When Shad frowned and shook his head, she folded her arms and lifted her chin, "I may not know my name, how old I am or much of anything, but I know this has something to do with me. I heard you say, you're moving in a week. Did you plan to take me with you or just leave me here with Doherty? Or did you intend to take me back to the spot where I fell into your lives and leave me there?"

This time Copper frowned at Summer, "You know better than that, young lady. Shad and I have come to think of you like family. We love you and you know it!"

Summer's expression instantly softened, "Yes, I do know it," she said as she took Copper's hand, "I love both of you! And because of that, I deserve to know the truth."

"Well, putting it that way, I suppose you do," Copper sighed. "You can help me fix something to eat while Shad explains."

As the four of them sat at the kitchen table, over sandwiches and coffee, Shad began, "There've always been folks wantin' to buy our homestead. Some say it's the prettiest place in the Rockies. Others like it 'cause of the hot springs. Ham Doherty was the most persistent. I've always said no! Then last year I was working my usual shift at the sawmill when the belt came off the spinner wheel and sliced a hunk off my right leg. Couldn't work for the rest of the winter."

Tanner leaned back in his chair and stared at his father, "Why didn't you tell me? You know I make good money, I could have and should have helped you!"

"You're savin' for your own dreams. And we worked things out with Doherty."

"Pa, I know Doherty, he would never take responsibility for something like that."

Shad heaved a sigh, "He didn't. Instead, he took advantage of the opportunity it presented—and so did I. We made a deal. He'd pay all our expenses until I recovered. Then when I was well I was to cut down approximately eight-hundred trees from a plot of land below the mill, in one-hundred and eighty days! If I got it done, I wouldn't have to repay him a penny and he'd pay me wages for cutting down the trees. Could have worked out just fine for us but... I knew it was a gamble. If I didn't get all the trees cut in the allotted time, then I'd keep the money as full payment for our homestead."

"So, what happened Pa? There's no better lumberjack than you!"

Shad frowned, obviously struggling with how to word the rest of his story. "I had five more days to cut down fifteen trees. Ma had been helpin' me and we were about to get to work when we spotted a bunch of wild turkeys. We'd both been workin' mighty hard and we needed that meat to keep up our strength. After I shot a turkey, we heard Summer callin' to us, sayin' she was lost!" Shad smiled and reached over and squeezed her hand, "Then all of a sudden, there was a bear. She saw him before we did and yelled out a warnin'. If she hadn't I'm sure that bear would have had your Ma and me for supper! This little gal saved our lives!"

"But Pa..." Tanner muttered.

It was then, Summer interrupted, "Tanner, your father is trying very hard not to tell the full story. But I can guess what happened." Her face showed her misery as she turned first to Shad and then to Copper, "This is my fault, isn't it? Because I begged you not to leave me." Lifting her chin, she stared into Tanner's dark green eyes, "I don't remember being lost or warning them about a bear. I don't even remember falling, but I ended up unconscious and hurt. They didn't know how badly for a few days. Those were the days when they could have saved their home but they saved me instead. The McKenna family is losing their 'little bit of heaven' because of a worthless girl who doesn't even know her own name." When she noticed Tanner's confusion, she explained, "Your parents gave me the name, Summer McKenna. Because when I woke up, I didn't know who I was—I still don't." Her eyes were so full of tears they blinded her, but she reached over and grabbed Shad's and Copper's hands, "You've treated me like family even though all this while I've been ruining your lives. Every bit of this is my fault and I can do nothing to make it right. I'm—so very sorry!" she sobbed as she buried her face in her hands and wept.

Shad slipped out of his chair and knelt beside her. As he gently pulled her hands away from her face he said in a soft growl, "Here now—Summer McKenna—you stop this! The only thing Copper and I were thinkin' of that day was gettin' some meat and fellin' trees. If you hadn't called out just when ya did, we'd have run smack into that ornery bear. You callin' to us and even your fallin' that-a-way was what distracted him long enough for me to get off a good shot."

Shad looked over at Tanner with raised eyebrows, "I tell ya that bear was stone-dead after just one shot! And that just don't happen. 'Course, I put a couple more in him, just to make me feel better, but God gets the credit." Turning back to Summer he said gently, "God put us there fer you and—He put you there for us! Now little darlin', what was the first verse you recited along with us? 'All things God works for the good...' How does it go?"

Suddenly, she felt like Summer again. She swallowed and sniffed, then with a trembling voice, she finished the verse, "For the good of those who have been called according to His purpose."

"All things God works for the good," Copper repeated as she looked at Summer and then Tanner, "that means, dear ones, that when things that we don't understand happen, we must not lose heart or become angry with God. Because He in His unlimited power can turn what looks like a disaster into a blessing! He tells us we can trust Him to use these things for good. If—we are seeking to walk in His ways and obey His will, we can have faith that—somehow—all this will work out. Maybe not as we planned but things will work out."

Tanner shook his head, "That's quite a story! I'm so thankful God kept all three of you safe. I guess He has an adventure ahead for Shadrack and Copper McKenna." Then he turned to Summer, "Please forgive me for speaking so harshly to you earlier. Now that I understand more, I thank you for being there for my parents! I'm sorry about your loss of memory. I can't even imagine how difficult that must be for you."

Just then, it dawned on Tanner that her loss of memory complicated things for him, too. Now that he knew his first instincts about this woman were correct, all he wanted to do was to get to know her. To see if they were God's choice for each other. But—if she didn't know who she was, then she couldn't know if she was free. He couldn't even think of courting a woman who might be married or promised to another man. His thoughts were brought back into focus as his mother put her hand on his shoulder.

"Tanner," Copper added softly, "something else that's very special about our sweet Summer—she's a brand-new Christian—a new believer! Her short time with us is a perfect example, of what we've been talking about. Her hardship has already led to a blessing."

Summer smiled, "That's so true! If I hadn't gotten lost, I might never have found God!"

⌁

The following few days were filled with packing and organizing. Naturally there were moments of nostalgic melancholy but also, surprisingly enough—laughter! Tanner had always known his parents were strong Christians. Perhaps because he had spent the past few years among so many nonbelievers, he found their faith in God more amazing than ever. There was a great deal of reminiscing as they retold stories that Tanner had heard all his life but enjoyed hearing again, especially now, for he enjoyed seeing Summer's reactions. Her dark blue eyes were so expressive and her laughter was like music. He was amused at Summer's look of shock when Copper told of how she had held a gun on Shad the first time she'd seen him. Telling him that she had found this cabin and to get off her property. Then Shad told the story of how he had surprised Copper with a gift of chickens and goats. At Copper's insistence, he had reluctantly shared how jealous he had become when the wild old mountain man, Black-Eyed Jack had delivered her surprise. The story Summer found the hardest to believe was when Copper told how she had purposely tried to make Shad angry, just to see if he would hurt her when he lost his temper.

"How could you be afraid of Uncle Shad?" Summer asked, "he's such a gentle man."

Surprisingly, it was Tanner who answered the question, "Ma was an orphan and a bond-servant, Summer. Unfortunately, most of her life she was treated very cruelly—by her father and by others as well. She married Pa because she thought he was a good man and this was a good place to call home. Still, even after they married, she couldn't help wondering if she was really safe. She had assumed that all men hit when they got angry. It was natural for her to fear that he might hurt her, like most everyone else in her life had." Tanner touched his mother's arm, "Have you never shown her your scars, Ma? You should, all young women should know that there are bad men out there. Men that will use their strength as a weapon against the weak." Turning back to Summer he added, "We'll be leaving here in a few days and moving to a mission called Wings on the Mountain. Wings stands for Women In Need of God's Shelter. As the name implies, it's especially for women who have been treated badly or who have no safe place to go. A preacher and his wife built the mission years ago and continue to run it. They can always use help! They're very good friends and although we aren't related I've grown up calling them Uncle and Aunt—just like you call my parents Uncle and Aunt. You don't have to be blood kin to have a special bond."

Shad silently watched the tenderness in his son's eyes as he spoke to Summer and the way her cheeks turned rosy whenever he was near. He thought back twenty some years ago and remembered how Quin had thought of ways for he and Copper to spend time together. Shad concealed a sly smile as he stroked his dark mustache that was now tinged with silver, "Son, I think you had a good idea to take the mares and foals down to Wings before we make the final move. Reckon you could go ahead and do that tomorrow? Once you get them settled I thought you could borrow Quin's wagon and mules. We'll be hard pressed to get everything in just our wagon." When Tanner nodded, Shad glanced towards Summer, "Darlin', he might need some help, would you be willin' to go with him?"

Shad's request surprised Summer, he had never asked her for anything. But if that man wanted her to jump off the mountain, she would have done it. "Of course, I'll help, I can ride!" Summer suddenly cocked her head to one side and chuckled self-consciously, "I don't know why I said that? I wouldn't know if I can ride or not."

"Well," Tanner laughed, "I guess you'll find out tomorrow! Don't worry, you can take Sparrow, she's the mare with the best manners."

"Good! I haven't spent as much time as I'd like with your horses but I think they're beautiful! Sparrow and her filly Swan are my favorites. Just yesterday I found out how much they love to have their ears scratched. Zephyr, on the other hand, wouldn't even let me touch her. And all her handsome little colt wanted to do…was bite!" Turning back to Shad she said, "You mentioned the other day that you traded the first mare from your partnership for this year's foal. You said she was unusually beautiful. Guess I'll get to see her tomorrow, I'm really looking forward to it."

"No darlin', that mare ain't Quin's anymore." Shad ducked his head and glanced at Tanner. The two men had already discussed the fact that Quin had given the mare away but he feared it was still a tender subject. Shad studied the floor, then looked up at his son. "I hope you ain't mad about that, boy. It's just that we tried to breed Bluejay twice now and it never took. Then this spring, Zephyr had that perfect little stud colt. Crockett has the delicate Arabian head and the appaloosa coloring you've been wantin'. 'Twas wise of you to bring that new stallion, Sailor, with you. That stud will be perfect to cover all the appaloosa mares sired by Boone. He'll add a little more Arab confirmation to his foals while they take on the coloring of their mamas! Then in the next few years you can buy more Arabian mares to breed to Crockett. It all seemed to make sense and so when Quin wanted to trade Bluejay for Crockett, it seemed like the right thing to do."

When Tanner shrugged, Shad quickly added, "But son, what really cinched it, was that Quin believed very strongly that it was God's will for him to give her away. The four of us even prayed about it and we all felt the same way."

Tanner squeezed his father's shoulder, "I'm not upset about it Pa, truly! I was shocked when you first told me. Bluejay is a remarkable mare but I'm sure you were right. If the four of you agreed that it was God's will, then it must have been God's will!"

Chapter 14

Trip to Wings

"Flee youthful passions and pursue righteousness, faith, love, and peace, along with those who call on the Lord from a pure heart." 2 Timothy 2:22

Tanner groaned as a sharp hay stem found its way through the blanket and jabbed him in the ribs. Even if they hadn't planned on moving in a week, Tanner still would have chosen to sleep in the barn loft. It was the gentlemanly thing to do. Summer had been staying in what had always been, his room. It was actually a separate little cabin just across from the dog run and the main cabin where his parents slept. There really was no better place for her and he couldn't help but enjoy the idea of her sleeping there. Though he tried not to dwell on it, the thoughts of her long blonde curls and lovely face resting on his pillow and her feminine curves covered by his blankets, were like the buzzing of pesky mosquitos in the night—nearly impossible to ignore! No, he would not think of disturbing her, although her sleeping in his bed was definitely disturbing him!

The wolves were singing and the stars fading as he swung down the ladder from the loft. The two stallions, Boone, whom he'd known all his life, and Sailor, his new Arabian, both murmured their greetings from stalls across the aisle from each other.

"Good morning gentlemen," he crooned, as he forked hay into their mangers. After taking a few minutes to appreciate these special horses, he continued on with the morning chores. The mares and foals were kept in a second barn that had a large corral surrounding it. The two barns were well away from each other, had they not been, the rival stallions probably would have been kicking their stalls down to fight each other. As Tanner made his way to the mares barn, he thought of how good it felt to be back in the high country, as he sucked in a lung full of chilled mountain air. The smile on his lips as he stepped into the large corral, spoke of his tentative pride. These mares and foals were the beginning of his dream. At that moment, Bluejay's younger sister Sparrow, trotted towards him, along with her first foal, Swan. Since Sparrow's sire was Boone, she'd been bred to a neighbor's appaloosa stallion. Still, both Sparrow and Swan were buckskin appaloosas just like Boone, and were eager for Tanner's attention. He rubbed under both their jaws at the same time, until the yearling, Dove, pushed baby Swan out of the way. Dove was Zephyr and Boone's filly from last year. Believing it was her turn, she pressed her soft muzzle against Tanner's arm. The yearling was a leopard appaloosa, white with black spots, and if given half the chance, Dove would have happily crawled onto Tanner's lap. He chuckled as he gave her the attention she craved but a few moments later, Zephyr pushed them all away! As the matriarch of this little herd, when she came forward with ears pinned back, the others obediently hurried away. Zephyr was a strikingly beautiful, pure-bred Arabian mare. Her coat was a dark dapple gray with a silver mane and tail. Although she belonged to Quin, she stayed with the McKennas most of the time. Confident of her rank she pranced forward with Crocket, her newest foal at her side. The feisty little colt had the same eye-catching coloring and confirmation as his full sister, Bluejay. They both were a dark blue-gray with a white blanket across their hips, spattered with dark gray spots and a silvery mane and tail.

Tanner shook his head as he rubbed Zephyr's forehead, "You always make sure your children and grand-children know who is Queen of the Hill, don't ya girl?" He didn't begrudge the spirited mare and colt the attention they sought, and he spoke to them as he petted them both. These few animals were his foundation stock. As he looked them over, he couldn't find fault with any of them. Each one validated the idea of crossbreeding Appaloosas and Arabians. Still, an adventure like this was a gamble. Soon, Lord willing, he would search for acreage in the lowlands and build his ranch. He had saved nearly every penny he'd earned working for Long Orient & Asia Company. He just hoped it would be enough!

Just then Crocket, only a few months old but full of vinegar, clamped his teeth onto Tanner's coat then pressed against him, wanting his back scratched, "Well good morning to you too little man," Tanner greeted. He intended to oblige the colt but when the stinker nipped at his hand, Tanner tapped the little imp lightly on the muzzle with one finger, "No-no-no..." he said firmly, "no biting. Listen here, Crockett my boy, you will learn your manners just like my Pa taught your Pa! I'll be one happy man if you grow up to be as level headed as Boone and as smart as your big sister Bluejay. Also, my feisty little friend, I'll be as proud as a peacock if you grow up and throw foals that look just like you!"

As Tanner moved through the corral to fetch his tack, he patted each animal in turn while the yearling, Dove, followed him around like a love-sick puppy. She watched with attentive eyes as he brushed and saddled her mother, Zephyr. Just then Crockett trotted over and began chasing Dove and Swan around the corral. Tanner couldn't help but laugh. It was so good to be with his horses again, he had missed them. He especially missed Bluejay, but his father had been wise to trade her for Crocket. That little guy had the potential to become a magnificent stallion one day. He would be a perfect replacement for Boone. And since the old stallion had been named after Daniel Boone, it did seem fitting that the new stallion be named after Davy Crockett.

Tanner stopped for a moment to appreciate the first hint of the morning sun. It painted the horizon a fiery red, casting a bronze glow over the cabin and barns. The sight brought a sad tightening in his chest and a lump in his throat. This was a very special place, he had always loved it. And yet, as most people do, he had taken his home for granted, assuming it would always stay in the family. "Ma's little bit of heaven," he whispered into the morning air, "right now, it sure does look like it." He shrugged off the twisting of his heart as he finished saddling Zephyr, then looked around for Sparrow. He grinned when he saw Dove and Swan, their necks entwined, grooming each other's back. Tanner took his hat off and scratched his head as he glanced around, "Now where have Sparrow and Crockett gotten off too?" he wondered. A moment later he found them both when he stepped into the barn and was very surprised to find that Summer was there too. She seemed intent on her work, so he stood there quietly as she proceeded to groom and then saddle Sparrow. Summer was doing everything exactly as he would have. She lifted the blanket over the horse's neck, then slid it slowly over her back, keeping the coat smooth. When Summer picked up the saddle, she pulled the right stirrup and the cinch over the seat before placing it on the mare's back. Then she went to the other side and lowered them rather than letting them fall, so they wouldn't bang against the mare's legs. She made sure nothing was twisted before looping the latigo strap through the ring twice then locking it down with a proper cinch knot. Summer's movements were quick and confident. She would have finished in no time—but for little Crockett. The colt was filled with baby like curiosity and mischief. He did everything possible to get in her way. He nibbled on the latigo straps, then yanked on the stirrup. Summer picked up her pace, realizing that if she didn't hurry, Crockett would probably succeed in pulling the saddle off Sparrow's back before she could cinch it tight. Tanner barely held his laughter in, when the colt reached over and pulled his older sister's tail. Sparrow lifted her back leg, threatening to kick. She was bluffing, but Crockett was too young to know it. However, being the little rogue he was, he instantly stepped away from Sparrow, then bit Summer's—tail—instead!

She yelped and spun around to face the little prankster, "Crockett, you little—stinker!"

Male laughter filled the barn and Summer turned to face Tanner. "It's not funny..." she giggled, embarrassed that she had an audience, "if you were watching, why didn't you warn me?" Rubbing the injured area, she asked, "Just how long have you been standing there?"

Tanner strolled towards her, a smile on his face and a curious look in his eyes, "Long enough to see that you know your way around a horse. Does this mean you've started to remember something?"

Summer touched the saddle, then her eyes swung back to Tanner, "No, I wandered into the barn and Sparrow followed me. I picked up the halter and...I guess I just did the rest without even thinking." Frowning, Tess shrugged, "It's so strange, Tanner. I feel like two people. The old me and the new me. At times like this the old me seems to know what to do—so she just does it! But she stubbornly refuses to give me, even the slightest hint, as to who I am—or was! It feels like there's a stranger inside me—hiding secrets." Summer tried to laugh it off but her words came out as a sob, "Oh, Tanner, I hate this!" Turning her back before he could see her tears, she fumbled for her hankie. "I'm sorry," she sniffed as she rested her head on Sparrow's neck. A moment later she felt Tanner pulling her into his arms. His kindness and warmth felt so comforting, and she melted against him. Her head fit perfectly under his chin, her cheek resting on his shoulder. The barn was a bit chilly and his nearness made her feel warm and safe. They had only spent one week together, and yet, they both felt completely at ease, as if they had always known each other. As Summer regained her composure, she couldn't force herself to leave Tanner's comforting embrace. She still felt so vulnerable. Finally, she whispered, "May I ask you something—very silly?"

"Anything," he answered. And even as he told himself it was time to release her, his rebellious arms tightened instead, then he propped his chin on top of her head, "you can ask me anything. Especially if it's silly."

"Can you tell me what I look like?" she asked softly. Summer pushed away from Tanner just enough to gaze up at him, "I told you it was silly." In fact, she already wished that she hadn't asked, but she lowered her head and explained, "I know nothing about myself, not on the inside or the outside. If you showed me a tintype of me and a woman I had never seen, I couldn't tell you which one was me. Your mother has a hand mirror but it's so pitted and small. It's terrible to be a stranger…especially to yourself."

Tanner tightened his hold, then he realized that he was enjoying her nearness far too much, while she was only seeking his comfort. He cradled her for a second longer, then released her and stepped back, "I'm so sorry, Summer, I can't even imagine what you've been going through." He narrowed his eyes while he studied her, "Well," he began, "I can only tell you what I see. But I should warn you, I've been accused of being honest to a fault."

She quickly straightened, "I'm not asking for compliments or flattery, I just want an honest description."

Crossing his arms, he nodded, "An honest description? Well, the very first time I saw you—you were sitting in the meadow playing your zither and—I thought I might have fallen asleep in the saddle—thought I might be dreaming." He gave a slight chuckle then added, "If you'll remember, I could barely speak. I'm sure that you know your hair is thick and long and curly. It's also the color of sunlight. Your nose is slightly upturned, and your eyes are large and the deepest shade of blue I've ever seen. But they have tiny specks of gold and turquoise in them. The colors remind me of the sandy beaches and clear waters around tropical islands. I can honestly attest to the fact that I've never seen a face that appeals to me more." Ducking his head, he chuckled then added, "And—you are shaped all over like a woman should be shaped. But all that is on the outside, Summer. Yes—you are a beautiful woman. The thing is, I've met other beautiful women but when I got to know some of them, I stopped thinking of them as beautiful." Tanner took her hands in his, "From what my parents say and from what I've come to know of you in this short time, your greatest beauty—is on the inside!"

Tanner tried to remind himself that he didn't really know this girl. And yet the very first time he saw her, his heart seemed to recognize her. Despite these strange circumstances, he truly believed that he'd been praying for this very woman his whole life! The more time he spent with her the more certain he was. It had been difficult not to reach out to her, to touch her cheek, to hold her hand, to know the softness of the golden curls that fell down her back. Just now—they were alone together in the intimacy of the early morning. He had never tasted whiskey or any kind of strong drink, but being this close to her was intoxicating. Her sapphire eyes sparkled with unshed tears as she stared up at him. Her soft pink lips were so very close to his. They remained like that for a long while, then it seemed that without command or consent they each moved closer. Tanner leaned in while Summer rose up to meet him. They hovered just a breath away from each other and then his lips brushed lightly over hers. The kiss was no more than a whisper but even that slight touch felt like lightning passing between them. They both sucked in a breath and then just as the kiss began to deepen, suddenly Tanner stepped away. "I...I'm so sorry," he gasped, "I had absolutely no right to do that! I apologize! We still don't even know if you're..."

Feeling embarrassed and ashamed, Summer lowered her head and took a step backwards, "It's all right, I understand," she said softly, "we don't even know if—I'm a harlot, a thief or an escaped lunatic!"

"Hey, that was not what I was about to say," he chided. Then he let out another frustrated groan and tipped his hat back as his words came out measured and slow, "Once again, I'm probably being way too honest and saying too much. The trouble is, I've never been attracted to a woman like I am to you. But, you're very vulnerable right now. We both need to remember that just because you can't remember your life, doesn't mean you didn't have one. What if the old you, as you say, feels differently about things than the new you? What if you find out that you're happily married or promised to someone you truly love? Where will that leave us? I don't want to do anything we'll regret, nor do I want either of us to end up with a broken heart." Even as Tanner said the words, he knew that just the thought of her belonging to another man was already ripping him apart.

Summer nodded as she slowly stepped further away from him. She had wanted that kiss, that connection to him—but he was right. There was just too much they didn't know. And now she felt more confused and more alone than ever. Just then, little Crockett came trotting up to her, and she was thankful for the distraction. This time he didn't try to bite, instead, he simply leaned against her. Summer smiled as she put her arm around his neck and stroked his fuzzy mane and back.

Tanner watched the interaction between Summer and Crockett. Finally, he said, "you have a good way with horses. They sense your confidence."

Summer leaned down and kissed Crocket's forehead. When she looked up and saw the longing on Tanner's face she blushed, then looked away, asking, "Shouldn't we head out soon?"

The kiss that wasn't quite a kiss seemed to linger between them. They were both self-conscious. Finally, Tanner grunted, "Yeah, I guess we should be on our way." When they both mounted up he added, "By the way, when we get to Wings, Aunt Mariah has a full-length mirror. You'll be able to see for yourself what a lovely young woman you are, from head to toe."

Tanner led the way on Zephyr, knowing that the other mares and foals would follow. Summer rode Sparrow, with little Swan staying right beside her. Later though, as the filly watched Dove cavorting about she hurried to catch up with her half-sister. The moment they rode into an open field it instantly became playtime for all three foals. They had a rough game of tag that knocked little Swan to the ground. It didn't seem to hurt her, for in a flash she was back on her feet and chasing after the others as they ran in circles around the mares, rearing, bucking and kicking!

A few hours later they stopped for lunch by a rushing mountain stream. Tanner quickly hobbled the two mares, giving them freedom to drink or graze but not wonder off. More importantly, this allowed time for the two baby foals a chance to nurse. Although Dove had been weaned a long time ago, she too tried to nurse. Of course, Zephyr would have none of that. She pinned her ears back and snapped at the filly, sending her away.

"Oh, poor baby!" Summer sympathized, as Dove trotted away, opening and closing her mouth, asking for forgiveness.

Tanner chuckled, "She's fine! She doesn't need the milk, she's just jealous of her little brother!" He pointed to Dove as she dropped her head and began grazing with the mares on the deep meadow grass, "See, her mother was just reminding her that she's a big girl now. Of course, you know what will happen next don't you?" he asked. "They've all had some exercise and their bellies are full, so now what do babies do best?"

Summer smiled as one by one each foal dropped to the ground, "They sleep?"

"They—sleep!" Tanner chuckled, then grinned proudly at the three foals who stretched out in the deep meadow grass, their mothers standing guard over them.

"I've enjoyed watching your horses antics today." Summer said as she laid out the picnic lunch Copper had packed for them: fried ham sandwiches with choke-cherry tarts for dessert. Summer stared off into the distance as she absentmindedly sipped water from their canteen, then offered it to Tanner.

"No thank you, I'd rather drink straight from the mountain." He knelt on one knee and allowed the water from the fast-flowing stream to wash his hand. "Whew," he gave a mock shiver, then brought a handful of water to his lips and drank. "This is so cold it burns my hand and hurts my teeth, but it's delicious!" he muttered as he dried his face on the sleeve of his shirt. Then he suddenly became serious as he studied Summer. "You've been awfully quiet. I hope I didn't offend you or hurt your feelings this morning."

"You didn't," she said softly. "I was just wondering, do you and your parents think I might be a run-away saloon girl? That I came to these mountains to find help at the mission?" Summer picked up a blade of grass and tore it into small pieces. "I was dressed in boys clothing, maybe I was in disguise."

Tanner thought for a moment then shrugged, "The possibilities for your being up here—are endless. We will certainly ask Uncle Quin and Aunt Mariah if they were expecting anyone. Don't know if they'll be at the mission today or not. I stopped in to see them on my way home, a week ago, but they were still making their saloon runs. No one knew when they'd return. They always just stay gone for as long as it takes."

Summer was shocked and it showed, "The preacher and his wife—make saloon runs?"

Tanner laughed, "I guess that does sound pretty strange, doesn't it? You see, Uncle Quin and Aunt Mariah make a practice of searching for women in need. Abandoned wives, widows and orphaned girls often have no way of supporting themselves. To keep from starving and to have a roof over their heads, they sometimes end up working in saloons or brothels. For many women, it's their only way to survive or provide for their families. Even if they can cook, sew or teach school they still might not be able to find a job. It becomes an inescapable trap. Once they enter that kind of life, they're often treated like slaves and aren't allowed to leave. That's why Quin and Mariah make their saloon runs a few times a year. They go from town to town, visiting the saloons and offering the girls that work there new lives. Sometimes they have to buy these women from the saloon owners. Uncle Quin has even been known to fight his way out of a saloon, while Aunt Mariah sneaks the women out the back door."

"How long are these women allowed to stay at the mission?" Summer asked, then frowned, "Are they free to go if they don't like it?"

Tanner gave her a kind smile, "Of course, it's not a prison. They're free to leave anytime, but they know that they're welcome to stay as long as they like. Two of the women have lived there since the place was built twenty years ago. They come for many reasons: to hide from danger, to learn a skill, or just to have room and board. Nearly all of them need some kind of healing. Many of them are broken in spirit, body and mind. Wings is a beautiful, peaceful place. Once they feel up to it, they can take classes in cooking and sewing or even learn to read and write. The mission tries to provide whatever is needed. Mostly, they learn that God loves them. If they have children or younger siblings or even parents that are depending on them, they can bring them too! It's a pretty impressive place."

"I'm scared Tanner," Summer winced, "what if I'm one of those broken women, plagued with terrible memories. Maybe it would be best if I never remembered. I'm afraid of what I might learn about myself. What if you don't like or approve of the person I really am?"

Tanner put his hand over hers, "It doesn't matter who you were. It only matters who you choose to be now!"

Summer shook her head, "But what if we find out I'm a terrible person? For all we know I might have been in league with that awful Mister Doherty. What if I was out in the woods as part of some sort of evil plan and just got hurt by mistake?"

Tanner stifled a laugh, "Ham Doherty is a rounder—that's fer sure. But not even that scoundrel is clever enough to make the turkey Pa was hunting run straight towards you, or have you fall down a hill right in front of a bear. Pa said he shot that brute a second before it would have killed you! No ma'am, any way you slice it, your meeting my parents that day was planned all right. But like Pa said, God gets the credit!" Tanner suddenly took on a serious note as his voice became soft and low, "I can't help but think that it was meant for you to meet my parents and it was meant for me to come home when I did, so that we could meet each other."

"I wish that was so," Summer sighed, "I wish you came home just to find me. Just like your father came home all those years ago and found your mother in the cabin he had built for her." Her next words were little more than a whisper, "It was a miracle for them, but it would be foolish for us to expect that same miracle for us."

Tanner knew they had probably shared too much about their feelings. They both needed to proceed with care. Standing, he said, "What we should expect now is that God will reveal His will for us in His own good time." He held out his hand to her and helped her to her feet. "Come on, the foals are awake now, we best be getting to Wings." That said, Tanner moved towards the meadow. He took the hobbles off the mares, put their bridles back on, then tightened the cinches. Soon they were heading towards the mission again. They rode for a while in silence. Tanner was consumed with what he and Summer had shared that day, but also with what he and his parents had discussed the night before. They too wondered what God's plan was in all of this? God had led Summer to the mountains for a reason, perhaps for many reasons. She had saved Shad's and Copper's lives. She had also become a Christian. Still, they felt sure that the scope of God's plan was greater still! Perhaps even that she was the answer to Tanner's prayers for a wife? Losing their home might be God testing them, but they didn't think for a minute that was all it was.

As they rode closer to the mission Tanner couldn't help but occasionally glance back to check on Summer. There was so much he liked about her. Forcing his eyes back on the path ahead, he breathed yet another prayer. *Lord, my heart wants to believe that I have finally found my mate. I look at her and feel so many things I haven't felt before. We can't take another step until she remembers who she is! I know I should distance myself, but she needs a friend. I can't just turn my back on her. I'm falling hard, Lord. When she prayed over our noon meal, it was a new believer's prayer, halting and shy and...the sweetest thing I've ever heard. After coming home for the first time in three years and finding this wonderful young woman playing a zither and singing hymns, in the same meadow where I've prayed for a wife...I just can't stop myself from believing that she's the one!*

As they came to an open meadow Tanner gazed up at the sky. We should make it in less than an hour if we pick up our pace a little. He clucked his tongue and Zephyr stretched out into a long trot and the others matched her gate. They were able to ride abreast now and Tanner glanced over at Summer, "You have a light hand on the reins and you sit that saddle like it's your second home! It's as if your seat is glued there." When he saw the color rise in Summer's cheeks he felt his own face grow warm. Softly, he muttered, "I didn't mean to embarrass you. I just happen to know for a fact that Sparrow has a trot that could shake your back teeth lose. You are an experienced horsewoman, Summer. Not just someone who's ridden before!"

Summer's expression was doubtful, "What if I know how to ride because I'm a notorious horse thief?"

Tanner laughed, "Summer McKenna, I like you! So, should you turn out to be a horse thief. I'll give you two days' head start before I turn you in!"

"Better make it three, I have the feeling that whoever I am, I get lost easily!" Summer tried to say it with a straight face but she giggled. "Outlaw or not, I think you're right about me and horses. Being around them so much today *has* made me remember things. At least I think they're memories. I seem to recall chasing a large herd of horses across a field of wild flowers, holding a tiny foal in my arms like a baby, and riding a horse through a terrible storm with rain and lightning."

"That's wonderful Summer, anything else?"

Her face suddenly grew pale and she frowned as she turned towards Tanner, "Fear! I remember being afraid. Terrified that someone wanted to hurt me!"

"Hurt you? How," Tanner frowned, "do you remember any details, names or faces?"

"No—" she shrugged then sighed in frustration, "and...I could just as easily be remembering a nightmare rather than something that really happened."

Tanner didn't know what to say. He wanted to take her in his arms and kiss away all her fears—to sooth and protect her. Instead he drew rein, and raising his voice a bit he said, "We're almost there, can you hear it?"

"What is that?" she asked. "I hear something, that's for sure."

Just then the mares began to nicker and some horses down the hill answered back. Tanner grinned at Summer, "We're almost to Wings." They rode around a bend in the path and Tanner smiled when he heard her gasp.

"Oh my...Tanner," she breathed, "I don't know if I've ever seen anything more glorious or not! But I can't imagine how anything could be."

Summer breathed in the pristine beauty before her. A snow-white cascade of water gushed over the jagged rocks high above them. It fell at least fifty feet, thinning into a silvery veil as it splashed into the pool below. Encircling the area were a dozen white barked aspen trees, their bright green leaves trembling in the breeze.

Tanner spoke louder to be heard above the falls, "This was Uncle Quin's and Aunt Mariah's favorite place when they were first married. They built the mission just a short walk from here—it's just down this trail. They wanted to leave the falls and this little haven surrounding it, untouched and unspoiled. It's a very special place!"

Tanner's expression was filled with kindness, as he added, "Some people think Wings on the Mountain is a strange name for a mission. I think it's perfect, because with a little help those who come here are able to spread their wings and build new lives. Right now, you're needing a little help. I know you've been nervous about meeting new people but these folks are just friends you haven't met yet. I promise!"

As they rode into the yard, two women were holding the corral gate open for the mares and foals. Once all the horses were inside, Bee, a stout older woman with a long gray braid down her back, latched the gate, then grinned up at Tanner, "Howdy, you handsome thing, you! We watched ya riding down from the falls. Land sakes, you McKennas sure have an eye for good horse flesh! Prettiest critters I've ever seen!"

Tanner smiled, "Thanks Bee, good to see you again! Yeah, we thought we best bring the mares and their foals today. The pass gets pretty narrow in places and we didn't want to worry about these little ones getting in the way of the wagons." Then he waved his arm at Summer adding, "And Bee, this is Summer, she's a special friend of my parents and mine too! And Summer, this is Bee, she keeps this place going whenever Quin and Mariah are gone." Just then Tanner remembered the other woman. She was half the size of Bee and hardly ever spoke. It was always easy to forget that Kora was even there. Chiding himself for the oversight, he quickly introduced Summer to Kora, then added, "Wings just wouldn't be the same without these two special ladies."

Kora ducked her head while Bee giggled like a schoolgirl at the compliment. As Tanner and Summer dismounted, he turned back to Bee, "By the way, Pa wanted me to ask if we could borrow your wagon and mules for our move?"

"Why sure!" Bee answered as she slapped him on the back, "You know you and yer folks are always welcome to anything we got. And I know you, Tanner, you like to take care of your own critters but you two just leave them with us." With that settled, Bee hurried over and shook Summer's hand,

"Lookin' forward to getting' to know ya Miss. What do ya think of these fancy horses? Sure do like the look o' that little stud colt. He's a dandy if ever I saw one!"

They all laughed when Crockett reared in the air and spun around as if he were showing them all, just how right she was. "Yep," Bee scoffed, "that one is plum full of vinegar. Reckon, I'd do some prancin' too, if I was as purty as him!"

Tanner grinned, as he released his reins, "Thanks Bee! Are Uncle Quin and Aunt Mariah back?"

"No sir, but we got a telegram though! Said they'd be home by tomorrow evenin'. Jack's inside, why don't you two go on in and say howdy! That old man has been hankerin' to bend someone's ear and none of us have had time to listen." Bee turned to Summer with a sly grin, "Now, you watch out for Jack, young lady, he's a terrible flirt!"

Summer nodded shyly, vaguely recalling Shad's stories about a man called Black-eyed Jack. As she handed Sparrow's reins to Kora, her heart went out to the shy little woman. "Thank you, Kora," she said as she leaned close, "watch out for Crockett. He's not only pretty, he's pretty sneaky. He likes to bite when you aren't looking." Summer nodded her head while she patted the spot that was still sore from that morning. "If you know what I mean?" she added with a giggle.

Kora pressed her lips together, then turned away, but not before Summer saw her hide a smile.

Tanner took Summer's arm as they climbed the porch steps. Bending down he whispered, "See, you've already made a friend." He turned to watch Bee and Kora lead their mares into the barn. "My mother comes and visits here as often as she can. She told me that Kora came to the gold mines with her father. He died when she was just thirteen, and his partner wanted to marry her. When she refused, he chained her inside their mine and kept her there for two years. Quin heard about it when he was first building this mission. He rescued her and she's lived here ever since. Mother says she's painfully shy. You may have been the first to get a smile out of her."

Summer glanced back towards the corral, "Poor thing. Do all the women here have stories like that?"

Tanner shrugged, "Everyone's story is special to them, Summer, and that's how the folks here treat each other.

Summer couldn't help but wonder about her own story as they entered the large parlor. There was a strange old man sitting by the window. The skin around one eye was black while his hair, mustache and beard where all snowy white. His beard was so long it flowed down his chest and across his lap, like cotton batting. If she had to guess, she would say he was at least a hundred years old.

"Good to see you, Jack," Tanner greeted. "I want you to meet Summer, she's been staying with Ma and Pa. She helped me bring the mares and foals down from our place." Turning back to her he added, "Summer, this is Black-Eyed Jack, one of my family's oldest and dearest friends." A knowing look covered Tanner's face as he said, "Tell her about yourself, Jack."

The old man squinted his eyes and grinned a broad toothless grin, "Pleased to make yer acquaintance, Miss Summer." Jack's voice was gravelly and low as he reached out and took Summer's hand, then kissed it, "The boy was speakin' true when he said I was his family's—oldest—friend. Fact is, I'm so old these here Rocky Mountains was just foothills when I got here."

Summer bit her lip as she glanced at Tanner, not knowing if it would offend the man if she laughed or offend him more if she didn't. At any rate, she was fascinated, even drawn to this peculiar little man, as he continued to describe himself.

"Yes, ma'am in my day," he said, with a bright twinkle in his eyes, "I was the best shot, the worst liar, and the most humble man in all the Rockies. I've sailed from Maine to Spain, and I've trailed a million buffalo from Mexico to the North Pole. I've fought armies and Injuns and bandits. Been a cowpoke, a miner, a trapper, an outlaw and a lawman. But m' years at this here mission have been m' best! Before long though, these old bones will fade back into the dust from whence they sprung. Then my home will be in heaven!"

Tanner's face grew tender as he listened to the words he'd heard a thousand times before, "You're a legend all over these mountains, Jack. God still has work for you. Uncle Quin, Aunt Mariah and these women, still need you, and so do all the McKennas!"

Although Jack humbly waved away the compliment, he had truly made a difference here among these wounded women. Quin and Mariah had initially invited Jack to help at the mission, because he was old and needed a place to stay. Still, they were concerned that the women coming to the mission might be afraid of the old mountain man. After all, few men had as rough an exterior as Black-Eyed Jack. He was a scary looking man. The skin around one eye was completely blackened from a load of buckshot exploding in his face, and these women came for the healing of wounds inflicted by evil and frightening men! And yet, somehow, with his kind ways, funny stories and eccentric personality, he became a source of comfort to these wary and hurting women.   Copper, Tanner's mother, had also been abused, and she had reacted the same way to Jack. He had been good for her. And over the years he had shown countless others that there was such a thing as a gentle man with gentle ways!

"Jack," Tanner asked, "after we get moved in, will you tell Summer about the time you saved Pa and Uncle Quin's life? And the story of how the three of you saved Ma and Aunt Mariah from the Highlander gang? None of us would be here today, if it weren't for you Jack!"

Summer sat forward, "I would love to hear those stories! Uncle Shad and Aunt Copper saved my life about a month ago. If you hadn't saved them…then they couldn't have saved me. So, that makes me grateful to you, as well!"

Jack was patting Summer's hand when Bee and Kora came into the parlor, along with two other women. "This here is Opal and Donetta," Bee grinned as she made introductions all around. The two women smiled sincerely when they met Summer, but their response to Tanner was far less cordial. It was obvious that they were uneasy in the presence of a man they did not know.

Understanding their fears, Bee soothed the tension in the room when she pounded Tanner on the back, "No need to fret over this fine young man, girls. I've known him since he was knee-high to a short chicken. He's Shadrack McKenna's son and cut from the same cloth as his pa, Preacher and Jack here." Moving to stand near the old man she said, "Was you about to tell that story of going down the up-tilted hill?" Grinning at Summer she added, "That's my favorite and I've been hankerin' to hear that'n again! Wait 'til he gets to the part where Remy the mule and the albino jump off a cliff and saved Mariah and…"

Jack laughed, "Now Bee, these young'uns got to get back up the mountain. They're burnin' day light. Ain't gonna be here long enough to hear m' story, so don't go stealin' m' thunder. I'm the onliest one that can tell that story, and it takes time to tell it proper!"

Bee shook her head and sighed, "Well, I reckon that's true. No one can tell a story like you Jack!" Then she leaned towards Summer, "Jack should be on the stage, he takes these pauses for…oh what's it called?"

"Dramatic effect!" Jack grunted, then he sent a mock frown her way and shook his finger, "Don't be given away all m' secrets Bee, or I'll send ya to your room! Or I'll go to mine, one or t'other."

Tanner frowned and stared at the floor, "We sure hate that we're moving you out of your home Jack. It's very generous of you!"

The old man ran a wrinkled hand down his long beard and grinned, "Now son, I would move into a hollow log fer you and yer folks. But the truth is, I already moved from m' cabin two months before we heard about Doherty and his low-down ways. Ya may not have noticed, but I've been gettin' a bit long in the tooth. Mariah said, she wasn't sleepin' nights fer worryin' about me. So, to put her at ease, I moved in here, where she can keep an eye on me. Yer Pa and Quin built me that cabin across from this here lodge, so I'd have a place to grow old. Reckon it's as much the McKennas as it is mine. And there's plenty of room here in the lodge for Miss Summer! Son, you ought t' know the good Lord ain't never taken by surprise. He knew all about this ten thousand times ten thousand years ago!" Jack turned just then and looked into Tanner's eyes adding, "In my ninety and one years I've learnt not to fuss when something's blockin m' way." He looked over at Summer and grinned, "Now, you two head on back and you can be assured that we're prayin' fer ya. And remember, God knows best and His plans are always better than anything we can dream up. Ya can count on that!"

Chapter 15

Face Off

"Who will rise up for me against the wicked? Who will take a stand for me against evildoers?" Psalms 94:16

Tytus stormed out of his office, leaving Sam and Joseph to catch up on a lifetime of lost years. His jaw clenched and his fist tightened as he headed down the hallway and into the open courtyard in the center of the hacienda. He knew he would find Lavenia there, propped up on multiple pillows, reclining on a long couch. She'd been living at the Bar 61 for a few weeks now and seemed to be improving. He hoped she was feeling especially well today, for he had questions and she was going to give him answers! Dropping to one knee beside her couch, Ty took the old woman by her thin shoulders and pulled her up to a full sitting position. "What have you done to our daughter?" he demanded. "Tess is missing, and there is no doubt in my mind...that you are behind it!"

Lavenia gasped at waking in such a way, but then her lips turned into an amused sneer. "You and Augusta have me watched day and night. How pray tell, could I do anything to anyone?" Pursing her lips and lowering her brows she added, "And you don't have a daughter. Tess is your niece—isn't she?"

Ty pushed the woman back onto her pillows and stood, "After you killed my brother, I became her father in every way that matters. I'll do whatever it takes to find her! I've always loved her and she knows it."

"I doubt it," Lavenia scoffed, "perhaps before your precious sons were born, you might have had a fondness for her. I'm sure that changed when you had your male heirs. It's a shame you didn't remember how badly it made you feel when your mother rejected you. It's too late to make amends now. All the tongues in town are wagging about Tess, and how her running off will end badly. And my goodness, if she's gone missing in France, finding her will be next to impossible."

"Wait? How do you know she was headed to France and why do you assume she went missing there?" Ty probed. "We don't know where she is as yet, but she went missing somewhere between here and New York."

Lavenia was genuinely confused for a moment, frowning she struggled for an answer until finally she stammered, "Well, I—I heard it from the gossips of course! It seems the high and mighty Graingers are not as well liked or respected as you think. While I was having my things removed from the train and hiring a buggy and driver, I spoke to a number of people. When they heard I was coming to the Bar 61, they were only too eager to spread gossip about the arrogant and spoiled young couple. How they were heading to France and ruination no doubt."

"I would be very surprised if anyone spoke maliciously about our family. The people in town are our friends!" Ty once again knelt beside the couch and looked the old woman in the eye, "You're slipping Lavenia, I can see it in your eyes, your expression. You were expecting her to go missing in France. But now, you don't know where she is—do you? Still, I know you're behind this. Just as you were behind what happened to Timothy and Augusta years ago. Tell me what you've done and who you've hired! Help us find her before anything bad happens and I promise you can stay here until you die! If you'd rather I'll pay for a room at the Antlers hotel with a private nurse. But I swear woman—if you refuse to help us, you'll spend the rest of your days in that sanitarium Augusta told you about—and you'll be moving there today!"

Lavenia twisted on her couch, something had gone wrong but she would never back down. Her lungs seemed to constrict as she realized that Tulane's last telegram had been a lie! She tried to breathe calmly as she fingered her lace shawl, trying to calculate her next move. "How can I possibly prove that I don't know what—you—are—talking about?" Lavenia choked out the last sentence but then the act of breathing became her only concern. At first, Ty thought it was an act to divert his attention. Then he realized her face had lost its color and her lips were turning blue. She was in serious distress.

As it happened, Carlos had just opened the door for Doctor Trumble when they heard the strangled sounds coming from the courtyard. As Augusta hurried past him, the doctor grabbed her arm and held her there as he called out his orders, "Carlos, fill every pot and pan you have with water and put them on the stove to boil—I have special herbs we'll add to it! Then bring a large sheet into the kitchen. Augusta," he added, as he handed her a brown bottle, "this

160

is Hore-hound juice. Mix a cap full of this with hot strong tea and add a little honey. I'll bring her into the kitchen."

Trumble could hear the old woman struggling for air as he ran to the courtyard. As he carefully picked her up, he turned to Ty, "Don't just stand there man, bring her couch into the kitchen!" Ty made no objection to the doctor's command, for he was terrified Lavenia would die before telling him all she knew about Tess! The couch was pushed near the stove and draped with a sheet to make an impromptu tent. Lavenia was as white as the sheet herself, but finally her breathing became less labored. Still, her thin hands trembled as she drank her tea and struggled to inhale the steam that rose from all the boiling kettles.

It was a long and difficult night. At three in the morning the doctor and Ty both insisted that Augusta go to bed. Ty finally joined her while the doctor slept bent over the kitchen table. When he awoke, he was surprised to find Lavenia sitting next to him, writing a note on a tablet of paper. "Woman," he grunted, "what in the world are you doing?"

"Good morning...Doctor," she whispered. Although her breathing was much improved, her words came out in raspy gasps, "It's...good of you...to stay. If I were still a...wealthy woman, I'd reward you...but...alas."

The doctor groaned as he yawned and stretched his sore muscles, "Madame, none of us thought you'd live to see another day! A live patient is the best reward a doctor can receive. As for any compensation, the Graingers are always more than generous." He rubbed his eyes and stared at the old woman, "My new prescription for you is to look out that window. It's a beautiful morning. It snowed overnight and with the summer sun shining on the mountains all covered in white...they almost look as if they're lit from within. Mornings like this always fill me with hope." Glancing back at the sickly woman he added, "I would have been pleased just to see you breathing this morning. The fact that you're sitting here doing your correspondence after such a difficult night, is miraculous. Are you truly that much improved or is it urgent business that drives you?"

Lavenia's lips lifted slightly as she finished writing, then looked up at the doctor, "I was frightened last night—and I don't frighten easily. I don't need to gaze out that window, what I need is a favor." When the doctor nodded, she took a labored breath then continued, "You see Tytus and Augusta have been terribly good to me! More than I deserve, but I'm beholding to them for every little thing. Being dependent on your children is quite a hardship for an independent woman. I need to send a telegram to a friend in New York. Tytus would happily do this for me, but my pride is feeling a bit bruised these days. I've already asked so much. Plus, it's regarding a surprise for them. Using the last of my funds I have arranged for a few gifts for my family. The first of which has been delayed. So, you see it's awkward for me to ask any of them for help. However, I do have a friend in New York who can make inquiries. As far as the cost of the telegram, I should have just enough to cover it! I would be ever so grateful if you would discretely take this to the telegraph office. Call it part of the confidentiality between doctor and patient. This favor would be the best medicine you could give me. I've tried to make it as brief as possible. What do you think?"

Taking his glasses off, the doctor wiped them with his handkerchief, then cleared his throat and began to read:

"To Mister Keefer Flynn
Grand Hotel, Room 505
New York City, New York"

Statue lost on way to destination...stop...deal with TBT...stop...collect bookends as planned...stop...must find statue and deliver it and bookends to Salvador...stop...LW Bar 61...stop."

Doctor Trumble chuckled as he folded the note and placed it in his pocket. "Telegraph messages always sound so cryptic, don't they? Suppose when you're paying by the word that's the way to do it. Don't worry about the cost. The telegraph operator pays for my services with free messages." When Lavenia sighed and a smile spread across her face, the doctor chuckled as he patted his pocket, "I see this favor must indeed be good medicine, and I will treat it as such." As he headed for the door he added, "Carlos will be coming in to start breakfast soon. Have him brew up some more of my special Hore-hound tea. Then get some rest. I'll check back with you tomorrow!"

Lavenia wanted to laugh as she watched the doctor walk away. *How strange life can be. I feared I might die, but it all worked to my advantage. That fool Tytus, demanding that I help him find Tess. Instead, he has no idea how much he has helped me! Doctor Trumble too! How fortuitous of him to make a house call, just when*

I needed a doctor as well as a discrete messenger boy.   I don't know how Tulane could have failed again—I made it all so easy!   Of course, there are at least two possibilities.   Tess realized she was in danger and ran, or Tulane had to deal with her before she could.   He better have dealt with her.   But if he did, then why send that telegram, lying about them boarding the ship to France?   How dare he try to deceive me!   I'll never get Tess to France now and it was such a glorious plan.   I had so hoped that Grainger would spend his fortune traveling all over Europe, trying to find that little chit.   Then Augusta would go mad with grief.   Still, she is missing.   It was pleasing to see Ty so frantic and I'm sure Augusta is beside herself.   If Tess is alive, things could get complicated, but that little bit of fluff is no match for me or Keefer!   He will find her.   Thankfully I can easily include Tess in the plans I've already put in place for the boys.

Salvador will have two strong backs to work in the mines in Mexico, and I'm sure a man like him, will think of something interesting. . .to do with Tess!

Chapter 16

Awakening

"You need to persevere so that when you have done the will of God, you will receive what He has promised." Hebrews 10:36

It wasn't easy and they didn't expect it to be. Sometimes a cabin is just a pile of logs and chinking but then sometimes—it's like a member of the family. The McKennas homestead had been built with love and care. It had been nurtured along like one of their young foals. Now to just leave it in the hands of a man like Doherty, felt wrong in so many ways. They couldn't just walk away from their beloved homestead. So, they said a parting prayer over it, asking that the next family would find happiness there and that they would honor God as they made their home in this enchanting place.

As Summer and the McKennas said good-bye they were trusting God for whatever lay ahead, even as they left so much behind: Maudy McKenna's grave, the petrified stump where Shad and Copper had been married. The place where Tanner had been born and where they had all been so very happy! They were open to what God had next, and were all being very brave about leaving their 'little bit of heaven'...still...it hurt!

The two wagons were heavily loaded and hitched to Quin's stout draft mules. Copper drove one wagon and Shad the other with Boone tethered behind. Tanner helped Summer onto Bonny since she was so tall, then he swung up onto his stallion, Sailor. Bonny was an appaloosa mule and every bit as sweet and mischievous as her mother Remy had always been. It pleased the McKennas to see that Summer loved the mule just as Copper had loved Remy. Although they all were trying to keep their emotions at bay, Copper and Summer both began to weep as they took one last glance at the pretty little homestead. Then when Bonny brayed out her own loud farewell lament, Tanner and Shad began to laugh and soon the women couldn't help but join in. That laughter was just what they all needed. But for Tanner, what gave him strength was having Summer riding beside him. He had spent nearly every moment for the past week with her and be it wise or foolish, he was falling in love. He knew sometimes people were mistaken about love. He didn't see how that could happen to him, after all he'd prayed for years and searched the world for the one who would be his match. Now, he truly believed that Summer was that woman. He felt so sure, until he reminded himself that he was falling for someone he knew nothing about.

Dusky shadows of late afternoon welcomed the McKennas as they drove their wagon into the mission's yard. Instantly, a swarm of women and even a few children surrounded them and went straight to work. By the time Tanner and Summer had put their mounts away, nearly everything had been carried into Black-Eyed Jack's cabin across from the lodge. The old man having already moved was another sign of God's providence.

Jack, of course, was especially anxious to greet his friends and waved from his chair on the porch grinning broadly, his gravelly voice calling out, "'Bout time you young'uns got here! Sorry fer yer troubles but I reckon the good Lord knows what's best." With a sly wink he added, "'Sides, I'm always good medicine fer you two, especially my sweet little Copper!"

Shad laughed and shook his fist, "Jack, you old rascal," he teased, "ain't you ever gonna stop flirtin' with my woman?"

"Why sure..." Jack grunted, "when I'm six feet under—not a minute before!"

Copper hurried up the porch steps and hugged the old man whom only she called by his first name, "Siah, you dear thing," she cooed, "you are absolutely right—seeing you is always good medicine!"

Feeling a gentle tug on her arm, Copper turned into her best friend's embrace. Mariah hugged her tightly as she whispered, "You all are as welcome here as springtime. I hope you know that!"

Tears filled both women's eyes, then they smiled and recited their slightly paraphrased favorite scripture, "When faith is tested...endurance grows." Mariah put her arm around Copper's shoulder, "I'm sure it's a comfort to have Tanner home." Shading her eyes, she watched him leading his horse towards the barn with a young woman walking beside him, "Who is she? Has Tanner finally found that wife he's been praying for?"

Copper shrugged and shook her head, "I certainly wouldn't mind if she was...but...oh, Mariah everything is so complicated." Before Copper could explain, they saw Quin step from the barn and nearly ran into the young woman they were discussing. To Mariah and Copper's surprise, he broke into a huge grin, picked the girl up and swung her around.

"Well now sweetheart," he laughed, "have you finally come for a good long visit? Mariah," he called, "come and see who's here!" Quin's jovial mood altered the moment he set her down for she jumped away from him and clung to Tanner's arm.

Quin stared down at her, feeling very confused, "Sorry darlin', didn't mean to startle you. The last we heard you were headed to France to get married. What happened?"

"Married?" Tanner groaned. That one word seemed to suck all the air out of his lungs. Summer looked nearly as thunderstruck as she clung to his arm.

Just then, Mariah recognized who the girl was. She ran across the yard and threw her arms around her. "Tess! You sweet thing, we're so happy to see you. Even if it has only been—what—a month since your birthday?"

When Tess just stared at them as if they were strangers, Mariah and Quin exchanged concerned glances, then they both asked, "Tess, what's wrong?"

Shad stepped up and said softly, "Now everyone, just give her a minute. Darlin' girl, are ya rememberin' anything?"

Summer nodded, then her eyes narrowed as she stared at Quin and then Mariah. Pictures flickered in her mind. Childhood tea parties with this woman and the man teasing her and making her laugh. Finally, she placed one hand on Quin's stubbly jaw and the other on Mariah's soft cheek, "Uncle Quin…Aunt Mariah." Tears slipped down her cheeks as she stared up at them, "I don't exactly know why—but—I do remember you!"

Shad slipped his arm around her shoulder and said softly, "Summer, how is that you know Quin and Mariah?"

Shaking her head, she muttered, "I'm not sure." Holding her hand out to Mariah she said, "You sing beautifully, and you play a heart shaped zither. And—you gave me one—for my tenth birthday!" Then instantly, she turned to Shad, "That's how I could just pick it up and play it so quickly. Oh, Uncle Shad," she cried, "you must have made my zither. You made it for *me*—years ago!"

This was obviously a miracle and though Tanner tried to be happy, all he could think of was that—she was to be married. Possibly, she already was! Finally, he muttered, "Listen, why don't you all go inside and talk this out. I'll put the wagons away and help Bee and Kora tend to the mules."

Shad and Copper saw the pain in their son's eyes and of course they felt it too. That morning this girl had been their own sweet Summer McKenna. Now in an instant she had become a stranger to them.

As everyone gathered in the lodge, Shad quickly explained how he and Copper had met the young woman they called Summer. How she had warned them about the bear, taken a terrible fall, then awoke without her memory.

"Tess darling," Mariah asked, "as you remembered Quin and I...did you remember anything or anyone else?"

Tess shrugged, "Only bits and pieces. If you could see into my mind it would look like a crazy quilt. There are fragments of pictures in my head, but they don't quite fit together." Giving Mariah an apologetic look she added softly, "I don't remember everything about you, just random things. That's more that I can say for myself, I don't remember anything about me! The only thing I seem to be sure of, is that I was or am in danger. Does that make sense to you? Or why I would come up here alone and dressed like a boy?"

Understanding her distress, Quin knelt down beside her and took her hand, "I know of no danger, but it would be wise to proceed with caution. You came up here for some reason. Now let me tell you about Tessie May Grainger. First, you prefer being called Tess. We all just celebrated your twenty-first birthday last month. You are the much-loved daughter of Tytus and Augusta Grainger, owners of a large ranch called the Bar 61. Caleb and Joshua are your fifteen-year-old twin brothers, whom you adore, when they aren't irritating you. You're parents are like Shad and Copper. Both couples are strong Christians, the salt of the earth. In fact, the McKennas and the Graingers are the finest people we know! Your family is also one of the richest in Colorado and you were engaged to T. Barrett Tulane, one of the richest men in New York, maybe the country. The only reason I bring that up is because the wealthy always have enemies. We've always known you to be a strong-willed girl, and so we weren't too surprised when the day after your birthday party you agreed to go to New York with Barrett and his mother. The three of you were to travel on to Paris for your wedding." Quin paused for a moment and rubbed his hand across his jaw, "As for why you came to the mountains, what you were afraid of, or why you were dressed like a boy? I have no idea! It does suggest that something very serious is happening. I promise to do all I can to find out what it is and to protect you and your family!"

"And so will I," Tanner added as he stepped into the room. He hadn't been able to stay away any longer and had entered the lodge in time to hear that Tess, was the daughter and the fiancé of wealthy men. He knew there were women who valued wealth over love, but the look on Tess's face told him that she wasn't pleased by this news. Just then she looked up at him and their eyes locked. They both seemed to be asking the same question. What now?

Quin noted the silent dialogue between the young couple, then said, "Perhaps if we keep on telling you about yourself, it will help you remember. Until you do, we have no way of knowing why you came up here and what kind of danger you're facing. First of all, you are intelligent, independent and accomplished. You are also an exceptional horse woman. There are soldiers all over this country, riding mounts you've helped train and sell."

When Tess only sighed and nodded, Tanner interrupted, "She does ride like she was born to the saddle, and she mentioned remembering being with horses. But Uncle Quin," he said gently, "Summer...I mean Tess, seems a bit overwhelmed by all that she's just learned. What with the move and all, it's been quite a day. I think it might be wise for her to rest this evening and try again in the morning."

Mariah smiled as she went to Tanner and slipped her arm around his waist, "That is sound advice!" Turning to Tess, who did indeed look like a lost lamb, she said in her soft southern accent, "Sweetheart, we don't mean to push you. There's only one thing we want you to know right now, whether you remember it or not. We all love you and will do anything to help you!"

Tess smiled up at Mariah, then at Tanner, her relief was obvious. However, when no one could think of anything to say she became self-conscious and got to her feet. Wandering around the parlor, she touched one thing and then another until she stared up at the drawing that hung above the fireplace. It was a beautifully framed charcoal portrayal of a younger Mariah, sitting on the floor in front of the McKennas fireplace. She recognized Shad's carved mantelpiece and the heart shaped zither on Mariah's lap. Then she reached up and lightly touch the artist's name in the lower right corner, C. Delaney-McKenna. "Aunt Copper, this is beautiful!" she praised.

Copper shrugged, "I had a beautiful subject."

Mariah rolled her eyes, "It was done by a talented artist! Copper is too modest. Her work should be shown in the finest galleries!"

Suddenly, Tess clutched the mantelpiece and shut her eyes tight. Instantly, Copper and Mariah went to her side asking what was wrong.

Tess shook her head and groaned, "I'm fine it's just that memories are flashing in my mind, they make me dizzy." Looking up again at the drawing, she said, "I'm remembering four other sketches, they're so much like this one, but they're above a different fireplace." Tess stared at Copper, "Is it possible that you could have done them? Three of them are of various ranch scenes with horses and cowboys, but I remember one standing out as special somehow." Squeezing her eyes tight, she continued to describe what she remembered about the forth drawing, "It was actually two sketches on the same page. The upper half is of a handsome black man and a beautiful horse, they were both in their prime. It's just of their head and shoulders as they face the sunrise. The lower half of the drawing is the same except the man and horse are much older. They're facing in the opposite direction, towards the setting sun." Tess turned to Copper and asked, "Do you remember ever doing any pictures like that?"

Copper put her hand to her throat, "Oh my—I surely do remember them. It was when I was riding all alone towards the mountains. I had no grain for my mule, Remy. Then I came across a large ranch called the Bar 61. I saw nothing but men living there at the time and I was afraid to show myself. I'm still ashamed of it, but I snuck into the barn in the middle of the night and stole a bag of grain. I left those four drawings as payment. At the time, I thought it was the safest and wisest thing for me to do!"

Quin shook his head, "I've always admired those drawings for years but never noticed the signature." Then he took Tess's hand, "Honey, you are remembering the framed artwork in your father's library. They've been there all your life!"

Shaking her head, Copper let out a long sigh, "This is beyond strange to me! The lives of our three families seem to have been crisscrossing for years." Turning to Tess she added, "My dear sweet girl, my mind is spinning like a top. I can only imagine how you must be feeling right now. You started this day as Summer McKenna and you're ending it as, Tess Grainger. It's obvious we were all meant to know each other. Still, Tanner was right, you have, in fact we all have dealt with enough for one day!"

Mariah nodded, "Yes, we'll all feel better after a good night's sleep."

Tess awoke the following morning knowing exactly what she needed to do. "There's no time to waste. I have to go home right away!" she announced over breakfast. "I have a family that is probably worried about me and might be in danger. I must go to them! I still don't know who Tess Grainger is, or what frightened her, but I must warn my family and let them know that I'm safe." Tess lifted her chin then added, "That said—I refuse to further impose on any of you. All I ask is that someone draw me a map and point me towards home. I must leave right away!"

Tanner hid his smile as he reached for her hand then stopped and rested it on the table instead, "you're right about going home. And Uncle Quin described you as being independent, but I think you need a horse as well as a map, or are you planning to walk?

Tess narrowed her eyes at Tanner then gave Quin a sheepish look, "I would also appreciate the loan of a horse!"

"I am coming with you, I have to know that you get there safely," Tanner growled, sounding very much like his father.

When Tess stiffened and the young couple locked eyes in a slight battle of wills, Shad, Copper, Quin and Mariah exchanged knowing glances. The four of them had been good friends for a very long time and there was a silent dialogue taking place between them. They all felt very protective of this girl. It was also obvious that not only Tess but quite possibly her entire family was in trouble. They needed no discussion, they knew what had to be done. It was Shad who stood and then spoke for all of them. "We'll all go son! If there's trouble ahead, it may very well take all of us to sort it out."

Mariah leaned over and hugged Tess adding, "It is certainly no coincidence that the McKennas found you or that they brought you to us! We'll just trust God to give us wisdom and direction!"

Tears filled Tess's eyes but she shook her head, "I've already cost the McKennas their family home. If there is danger I refuse to risk any of your lives," looking at Tanner she added, "and that's final!"

Copper smiled as she reached across the table and took Tess's hand, "That's commendable of you sweetheart but can't you feel it? God is in this. Many years ago, when I needed help, God led me to your ranch. You grew up looking at my pictures. When you needed help, God led you up to these mountains and straight into our path. Don't forget, that bear might have killed Shad and me both had you not been there to warn us! And now you've learned that the Longs, our very special friends, are also your parents' very special friends. None of this is a fluke, Tess. It couldn't be! Now...who is that handsome couple over there? I heard you myself, you call them Uncle Quin and Aunt Mariah." Pointing to her husband she asked, "And that good lookin' mountain man over there. What do you call him?"

Tess gave a tremulous smile then answered softly, "Uncle Shad..."

"And—who am I?" When tears filled Tess's eyes and her chin began to quiver, Copper answered for her. "I'll tell you who I am. I'm your very own red-headed Aunt Copper! None of us are blood kin, but we've all adopted each other just the same. One more thing you need to understand—we stick together! If one of us has trouble, then we all do. So, we're all gonna saddle up, head down the mountain and sort this out!"

Shad winked at Tess as she gazed at everyone in wonder, "Darlin'," his deep voice rumbled, "when ya can't get the words out, a smile and nod will do."

While everyone went to pack a few things for the trip down the mountain, Tess decided to wait for them outside on the large veranda. The sun was just lighting the path leading down from the waterfall when she saw a strange looking couple leading a beautiful appaloosa mare towards her. The woman was an Indian but the man was as white as the clouds floating overhead. However, it was the mare that suddenly started her mind whirling. It was like thumbing through pictures in a book. She remembered Uncle Quin's smile and Aunt Mariah's laughter and she remembered hugging...this mare.

"Bluejay?" She whispered.

Just then, Quin joined Tess on the porch. He broke into a big smile and called out a greeting, "Ladd! Little Fawn! How are you?"

Tess watched in silence as he hurried down the porch steps with a laughing Mariah coming right behind him. Ladd was Mariah's brother and the Indian woman beside him was his wife. They were a handsome, but unusual couple. The man was an albino, his skin and hair were both a snowy white, even his eyes were pale. In contrast, his wife, Little Fawn, had hair as blue-black as a raven's wing and her skin shone like bronze in the morning sun.

"Hello Ladd, Little Fawn," Tanner greeted as he trotted down the steps then asked, "how is it that you have Bluejay? Thought she'd been given to some flatlanders."

Quin groaned and shook his head, "Of course, she's another piece to this puzzle. I can't believe I forgot about Bluejay! That's how Tess got all the way up here." Then he turned to his brother and sister-in-law, "Thank you for bringing her to us. We'd sure like to know how you found her. First though, you both look wonderful, especially, you Little Fawn. Looks like the newest member of the family will be arriving soon."

The woman nodded, "Yes, our little one will come before the leaves change color. It is good to know that our brother and sister are home again." Then she turned to Tanner and smiled, "It is good that you have come back. The mountains have missed you and..." Fawn looked up and grinned when she saw Shad stepping out of the house, "Hello McKenna!"

"Little Fawn!" Shad grinned as he jumped off the porch. "So good to see you," he said as he reached his hand out to her husband, "Ladd, it's good to see you too!"

"McKenna," Ladd greeted. "Found your mare when I was out hunting. She was cut up pretty bad, but Little Fawn can heal anything." He added proudly.

Fawn smiled up at her husband, then ran her hand over the scar spreading across the mare's chest, "Her wounds were deep but my medicine was good." Then she turned to Shad, "We brought her back to you, McKenna, but found that dog, Doherty instead. He said your home was now his. Perhaps today you will wish to trade for her? We will give you the hides of six wolves and one grizzly bear." Fawn's dark eyes were bright as she laid her hand over the place where her child grew. "Bluejay will make a fine horse for our son!"

Quin scratched his jaw while Shad rubbed the back of his neck. Neither man was sure how to deal with this. Just then Tess stepped forward and stood before Ladd and Little Fawn, "Hello, my name is Tess. I'm the flatlander," she added with a glance at Tanner. "Uncle Quin gave this mare to me." As she patted the mare, hazy memories darted in and out of her mind, "I was also injured and I lost my memory. But looking at Bluejay—is helping me remember."

Tanner stepped to her side, "Like what Summer? I mean Tess—what do you remember?"

"Bluejay and I were caught in a terrible storm. We took shelter for the night. I stayed in a shack and there was a small barn for her. When I awoke the next morning, the barn door was open and Bluejay was gone. I tracked her to a broken and bloody barbwire fence." Tess shook her head as she stared at the scar on Bluejay's chest, "I was so afraid she would bleed to death before I could find her." Smiling at Little Fawn she said, "Your medicine is very good, indeed!" Tess seemed to think for a moment then she asked, "Uncle Quin, what do you think of allowing the mare to choose?" When he smiled in agreement, she turned back to Little Fawn. "We'll both walk the same distance away from her. If the mare comes to you, then you will keep her—without trade—she is yours for saving her life. If she comes to me, then I will keep her. But for using your good medicine to make her well, I will send you twenty pounds each of coffee, flour and sugar. What do you say to that?"

Little Fawn looked up at Ladd and when he nodded his head she did the same.

"Good," Tess sighed, then explained, "I will walk to this side of the house. You go to the other. The mare will choose."

Little Fawn didn't exactly smile but there was a sparkle in her dark eyes for she liked games of chance. She was also pleased that either way, they would not walk away empty handed.

Both women went to their opposite positions and Quin led Bluejay an equal distance between them. Then he tossed the lead rope over the mare's neck and stepped away.

Little Fawn called first, speaking in her native tongue. Bluejay took a few steps but then she stopped. Tess paused a moment then called softly, "Bluejay—come!" Again, the mare took a few steps forward but she didn't favor either woman. Then, they both called at the same time. Bluejay shook her head, then trotted the rest of the way to Tess and nuzzled her hand.

Little Fawn shrugged then walked over to Tess, "She has chosen you, but the next time the sky grows angry, you must stay with her."

Ladd and Little Fawn remained only a few more minutes for he was still a wanted man. He and his wife lived a life of self-imposed confinement in a secret valley.

Mariah watched sadly as her dear brother and his wife lifted their hands in farewell and walked away. Seeing the look of confusion on Tess's face, Mariah dabbed at her eyes then explained, "It's a long story and I'll tell you about it someday. Their visits are always short and they never say much. Still, it's a blessing to know they both have given their hearts to Christ and that they are both happy. That's all that really matters—isn't it?"

As Tess rode Bluejay down the mountain, she seemed to remember a little more with every mile. And yet so many things remained in the shadows, like the faces of her family.

"You're frowning again, Summer—I mean Tess!" Tanner corrected, then asked, "tell me what you're thinking?"

"I wish I knew," she groaned, "some memories seem too crazy. Would the conductor of a train stop it in the middle of a pasture and help me unload Bluejay from a freight car? Could that have really happened? If it did, why would he do such a thing?"

"Well, I agree it is unusual, but it makes sense if he thought you staying on the train wasn't safe. At least we know you weren't chased into the mountains, you were just following your horse." Tanner's smile became tender, "It's reminiscent of my mother tracking her mule to my father's homestead." He reached out and squeezed Tess's hand, "Sometimes God goes to a lot of trouble to bring two people together." He stared at her beautiful eyes then his gaze wondered to her soft lips. Just then he wanted to kiss her more than he wanted to breathe. Somehow, he held himself in check. He didn't have the right, not now anyway, maybe he never would.

They rode the final mile into Colorado Springs in the moonlight and Quin paid for them all to stay at the Antlers Hotel that night. By noon the next day they were standing at the impressive entrance to the ranch. The archway was centered between two towering hogbacks and a split rail fence. Bar 61 Ranch, was carved into an enormous black log, the lettering painted in white, which sat atop large log and stone columns. Beyond the entrance was a winding lane adorned with wild flowers all along the way with the majestic span of the mountains in the background. Just this entrance spoke of power and money and Tanner couldn't help but think again of Tess's wealthy father and fiancé.

Just as everyone was about to ride under the sign, Tanner suddenly drew rein and called everyone to a halt, "Wait!" he called out. "This doesn't feel right. For all we know, we might be delivering Tess right back into the hands of her enemies. Let me ride in alone. I'll ask to speak to the boss about a job as a wrangler. Let me see if it's safe first."

Shad smiled, "That's good thinkin' son."

Quin nodded his agreement then added, "Yes, but don't ask for a job or you'll wind up talking to Shep. He's the ranch foreman, a red-headed, good natured fellow. Instead, ask to speak to Tytus Grainger about buying a remuda for a cattle drive."

Tanner frowned, "How will I know if I'm speaking to the right man and not an imposter"

"No wonder I hired you!" Quin praised. "Tytus is about my age, he's as tall as me with dark, silver tipped hair and one dimple on his right cheek."

Tanner cocked his head and smiled at Tess, "So, that's where you got that adorable dimple."

When Tess blushed, then looked away, Tanner silently rebuked himself. He had always tried to be an honorable man.   It wasn't exactly honorable to flirt with a woman who was engaged.   Then again…being engaged and being married were a world apart.   Feeling the heat spreading up from his neck, he cleared his throat and pointed to the hog backs. "Uncle Quin, is there an easy way up to the top of one of those things?   You all would be a lot safer up there and Pa could keep a look out with his spyglass."

Copper nudged her horse forward, "Actually, son, that spy glass belongs to me!" Then she pointed to the hogback on the right, "Of the two—that one has the best view of the ranch and there's an easy pathway to the top.   I can lead the way."

Shad braced one hand on his thigh and stared at Copper, "Missus McKenna, how would you be knowin' a thing like that?"

"You're forgetting that I spent a few days here, twenty or so years ago. Up there was just one of my many lookouts.   I found a closer spot when I did my drawings." Copper reached over and squeezed Tess's hand, "If we hadn't known it before we know it now.   God works in mysterious ways!"   Glancing back at Tanner she said softly, "Now son—you be careful—for all we know you might be riding right into a hornet's nest." That said, she moved out at a trot with the others following behind.

⊱⊰

Tanner didn't know what he had expected, still, he was surprised as he rode into the ranch yard. Nestled between large elm trees and lilac bushes was an elegant hacienda.   It had thick adobe walls with dark wood trim and a wide wraparound porch.   A path of flagstones circled the entire house, making a clean dry walkway that continued on to the barns and other out buildings.   It reminded him of the beautifully landscaped villas he had seen in Spain. Tanner couldn't help but think of Tess.   Once her memory returned, could she be happy with anything less than the opulence he saw now? Then he remembered that the fiancé she had chosen was a wealthy New Yorker. The woman he knew was unassuming but what was the real Tess like?

"Howdy!" A red-headed man pulled Tanner from his thoughts as he stepped from the barn asking, "what brings ya to the Bar 61?"

Tanner reined his horse in and glanced down at the man, "I'm assuming that your Shep, the ranch foreman?" Giving the man an easy grin he added, "I'm Tanner McKenna. According to Quincy Long, the Bar 61 has the best horses and the best man to deal with is Tytus Grainger. He also gave me a personal message for Mister Grainger. I'd like to speak to him, if I may?"

The two men shook hands, then Shep glanced warily at the hacienda. Finally, he muttered, "The boss is—busy right now—but I can help ya. I've been the foreman goin' on fifteen years. Pull your saddle, we'll give ya a fresh mount then we can ride out and look over the herd. How many head are ya needin'?"

Tanner was afraid this would happen. Stepping down from his horse he lowered his voice, "Sir, the message I have from Quin is something Mister Grainger will want to hear. In fact, it might be best if you brought him out here to me."

Shep studied the young man in front of him, then his eyes swept over the surrounding hills, wondering if this stranger had come alone. Just then he saw a flash of light on the top of the nearest hogback, Shep drew his pistol and aimed it at Tanner's stomach. "Drop your gun belt," he ordered. "You're not here for horses. Is this about Tess? Do you have her?"

"Take it easy," Tanner urged, as he unbuckled his holster and let it fall. "I have a message for Mister and Missus Grainger, but I'm not talking to anyone else. Just ask them to come out here."

Shep gazed around again then spat on the ground, "How do I know you don't have a compadre out there with a Sharps, just waitin' to shoot the boss?" Shep narrowed his eyes and chewed on his lip, trying to decide how best to handle this. Finally, he grunted, "Nope you're gonna walk into his office with my gun in your back. But yer not goin' in unannounced. Caleb...Joshua!" Shep called, "come out here will ya?" Before the boys arrived, Shep hissed through gritted teeth, "Don't say anything about Tess in front of the boys. And know this, if she's hurt—you're a dead man!"

"Hey, what's goin' on?" Cal asked, "Why ya holdin' a gun on him, Shep?"

Josh was right behind his brother, adding, "You aren't gonna shoot him—are ya?"

Tanner kept his hands spread and grimaced, "Nobody's gonna get shot! Your foreman and I are just having a misunderstanding. I want to buy some Bar 61 horses and I refuse to talk to anyone but Tytus Grainger himself!"

Josh kicked at the dirt, "That's not a good idea mister, Pa's pretty crotchety right now. Best you deal with Shep or come back another day."

"That's right," Cal added, "sometimes Ma calls our Pa a fire breathing dragon, and that's what he's been lately. I'd sure deal with Shep if I were you, he'll give ya a good deal."

Tanner looked straight into Shep's eyes, never wavering, never blinking, "Trust me, Mister Grainger will want to hear my message from the boys' Uncle Quin!"

"Uncle Quin, huh?" Shep chewed on his lip and shook his head, finally he nodded, "We'll see what we see. All right boys, no wild cuttin' up by either of ya. Yer Pa's usually in the library this time o' day. Don't go story tellin'—just say, 'Pa, Shep's bringing in a man who has news. And boys," Shep wasn't sure how to word what he needed to say next. Finally, he added, "Then find yer grandmother. Tell her nothin'—and I mean **nothin'**! Keep her company and keep her away from the courtyard and the library. Ya understand me, boys?"

"Sure we do, you want us to keep her from eavesdroppin'," Josh mumbled as he turned towards the house. "Then I sure hope somebody will tell us what's goin' on around here."

Caleb stopped his brother, then turned to Shep and asked, "If we keep our Grandmother busy—will you teach us how to make a whip like yours? Make it and show us how to snap it, like you?"

Shep was more family than foreman to the boys, and gave them a look they understood perfectly, "You two do exactly what I said or I'll show you how I snap my whip—on yer backsides! Ya catch m' drift?"

Cal and Josh both nodded then took off at a run for the hacienda.

Five minutes later Tanner stepped through the library door and met Tytus Grainger. The big man's expression looked as lethal as the double barrel shot gun he held in his hand. Standing beside him was a lovely, dark-haired woman, Tess's mother no doubt. Tanner's heart went out to her. She looked like she hadn't slept in a month. Her eyes were red-rimmed and she looked pale and thin. Tanner glanced back at Shep and said, "The message I have for you is private."

Grainger stepped back and said, "Shep come in and close the door." Then he turned to the stranger, "What's your message?"

Tanner gathered his thoughts for a moment then plunged ahead, "Mister and Missus Grainger, your daughter is fine! She's with my parents as well as her Uncle Quin and Aunt Mariah!"

The news caused Augusta's knees to buckle. She would have sunk to the floor had Tytus not grabbed her and held her tight. Of course, he was just as shaken but wanted answers, "Where are they?" he demanded, "Explain what you know and how? And who are you?"

"My name is Tanner McKenna. Please bear with me while I try to explain what we know so far. My parents live up in the mountains. About a month ago, they came across your daughter. She was lost and alone. It's a long story, but she fell down a hill and was injured."

"Oh no!" Augusta gasped. "How badly was she hurt?"

"My parents have devoted themselves to taking care of her. Physically, she seems fully recovered," Tanner paused then added, "except that—she's lost her memory! She didn't know her name or even how she'd come to be in the mountains. Then a few days ago, we took her to Uncle Quin and Aunt Mariah's mission, Wings on the Mountain. The Longs are my family's dearest friends and apparently, yours as well. Of course, they knew her, and seeing them seemed to ignite her first sparks of memory. She remembers very little about herself and knows nothing of her family, other than what Uncle Quin and Aunt Mariah have told her. Still, when she found out about you all, she insisted that we bring her here. She believes she's in danger and fears that her family might be as well."

"Who was she running from?" Ty asked. "Why did she get off that train? And how do we know we can trust anything you say?"

"Sir, I wish I could tell you more but Tess has only just begun to remember anything." Tanner walked to the fireplace then gazed up in wonder. "As for trusting me? I don't know what's going on here but we all believe that God is surely at work in all this. The Longs, McKennas and Graingers are somehow linked together."

"How so?" Augusta asked as she dabbed at her eyes with her handkerchief.

Tanner pointed to the drawings above the mantelpiece, "My mother drew these as payment for a sack of grain."

"What are you talking about?" Ty scoffed, "I've had those before I met my wife and long before you were born!"

"Just a little over a year before I was born, sir. When Tess saw my mother's drawing of Aunt Mariah, she remembered these. You see, God led my mother to this ranch when she needed help. Two decades later, your daughter needed help and God led her to my family's homestead. Now, we all believe that God has sent us here to help the Graingers. This is not a coincidence, it's God at work!"

Augusta gazed up at the young man, "I certainly hope He's at work—for none of this makes any sense to me. We put her on an eastbound train, how did she wind up in the mountains? And if she thought she was in danger, why didn't she come straight home?"

Tanner shrugged, "She did finally remember that her horse ran away and she followed it. But I'm afraid we still have more questions than answers. Tess only remembers bits and pieces. That's why I couldn't risk bringing her here until I knew more." Realizing how possessive he sounded, Tanner ran a hand through his hair adding, "I mean—we all—were concerned. Thought we better make sure it was safe here, before we brought her home. Can you think of any enemies that might wish her or your family harm? If you're sure it's safe, then of course I'll bring her home!"

"No, you must not bring her here," Augusta huffed, as she twisted the handkerchief in her hands, "it isn't safe." Locking eyes with her husband she quickly got to her feet, "Ty, let's get our horses saddled. We'll ride out with him. I want to see our girl—right now!"

While they were saddling the horses, Tanner asked, "Why is it not safe here? We all want to help but we need to know what we're up against."

As they led their horses outside, Augusta swiped away a tear then mounted up. "I'm ashamed to say it but my mother is our enemy. Her name is Lavenia Wrenford."

Tanner frowned, "The danger to Tess…is her own grandmother?"

Augusta turned to Ty as she spoke through gritted teeth, "That's the real reason she's here, you know. She must have planned something dreadful for Tess. Naturally, she wanted to be here, so she could enjoy our misery. We mustn't let her know that Tess has been found and is safe. We can't let her know, Ty! She has to think that she's finally having her revenge."

Chapter 17
Truth & Lies

"The truth teller speaks what is right, but the false witness speaks what is deceitful." Proverbs 12:17

Shad frowned as he squinted into the spyglass, then collapsed it and handed it back to Copper, "Don't know if it's a good sign or bad? Looks like the Graingers are riding back with Tanner. Must not be safe for us to come to the ranch."

"What if I don't recognize them?" Tess groaned. "What if they're just riding out here to tell me that I was a rebellious daughter and they never want to see me again? What if they sent me away in the first place?" Tess covered her face with her hands and moaned, "Maybe I should have just sent a message for them to be careful and stayed in the mountains."

Mariah put her hand on Tess's shoulder, "Listen to me, sweetheart! I know your parents very well and they love you even more than the Longs and McKennas do." Mariah gazed off in the distance then chuckled, "They just spotted you and spurred their horses into a dead run. Looks like they can't wait another minute to see you!"

When Tess just sat there frowning, Shad rode to the opposite side of her, then reached over and patted the girl on the back. "Reckon I know Summer McKenna a little better than I know Tess Grainger but...neither one is a coward. So, I say let's head on down and meet those good folks...alright?"

Ty and Augusta were about twenty yards from the Bar 61 entrance when they saw Tess cantering towards them from the hogback. They hurried towards her but when she reached the entrance she suddenly reined Bluejay to a stop. She looked as if she were afraid to set foot on the ranch. Ty covered the distance between them in a flash, then bolted from the saddle and cried out, "Little Bit!" Tears of relief clouded his eyes as he reached up and held his arms out to her.

Tess stared down at Ty and then at Augusta who was hurrying towards her as well. Hearing Ty's pet name for her had been the perfect words to trigger sparks of memory. She stared at him and then at her mother as tears slipped down her cheeks, "Papa? Mama? Oh, thank God—I know you! I don't know much else but I know you."

Ty slipped her from the saddle and she melted into her father's arms. He held her close while Augusta hugged them both.

Cradled in her parents embrace, Tess stammered as she wept, "I was so afraid that y-you wouldn't want me. Afraid that I w-wouldn't know you. I still don't know myself!"

Tytus tightened his hold, "Everything is going to be all right," he soothed. "We know you! You're our precious girl. You were lost to us and now, thank God, you're found! That's all that matters. We prayed that God would bring you home and He has. Now, we'll just trust Him to work out the details."

While the Graingers were getting reacquainted, Tanner quietly told the others what had happened at the ranch, "Missus Grainger said the strangest thing. When I asked if they had any enemies, she said yes and that it was Tess's grandmother. It sounded like the grandmother devised some plan to hurt Tess. Then she came to live with them just so she could watch them fall apart with worry and grief. Does that make any sense?"

Mariah and Quin both nodded. "Yes!" they said in unison then Quin added, "She's responsible for kidnapping Augusta and killing Tess's father!"

"Tess's father?" Tanner frowned as he stared at the man holding Tess, so Quin lowered his voice and explained, "Her real father was Timothy Grainger. He was Ty's twin brother and Augusta's first husband. The brothers were separated as boys when they were about ten years old. Ty stayed with his father in Georgia and Tim went to Boston to live with his mother. That's how I met Tim, our families went to church together. Anyway, he and Augusta were married and came by wagon train to live with Ty on the ranch. They were just a few hours from this very spot when they were attacked. Timothy was killed trying to protect his wife and unborn baby. A few weeks later, Tess was born. The following year, Ty married Augusta. It's definitely a story worth telling but one for another day."

Feeling an inner warning that had never failed him, Tanner glanced around and called out, "Listen everyone, I don't' think it's safe or wise for us all to stay here in the open much longer. We're too exposed!"

"I was thinking the same thing," Ty grunted, "The Stubborn Scotsman is the closest ranch and McGee is like a grandfather to our children. He would protect them with his life and so would his men. Quin, would you take her there." He leaned close and kissed Tess on the forehead then said, "Sweetheart, until we figure out exactly what's going on here and who all is involved, we need to pretend that you're still missing." Then he turned to Augusta.

"I know," she nodded, "we need to get back to the boys and pretend that we're as miserable as ever." Augusta closed her eyes and blew out a long sigh, "My mother is very shrewd, she knows I've been sick with worry. If she even suspects that Tess is safe then she'll try to hurt the boys. I don't know how— she never sees anyone but the doctor. Still, we don't dare trust her." Augusta pulled Tess into her arms for an almost fierce hug as she whispered, "I love you! Stay safe baby girl, I couldn't bear to lose you again!" She turned away and there stood the strangers that had saved her daughter's life and brought her back to them. "Oh...I'm so sorry we've all but ignored you, and we owe you our deepest gratitude!"

Sensing a kindred spirit, Copper stepped forward and took Augusta's hand, "You owe us nothing! We've come to love your daughter like our own. She's been such a joy. We can only imagine how terribly painful all this has been for you."

While the women were speaking, Ty turned to Shad, "Thank you for saving her life and for bringing her home!"

Shad nodded but his expression showed that something was still worrying him. "Truth is, she saved us first. Then I reckon we returned the favor, but God gets the credit!" Glancing back at Copper, Shad rubbed his jaw. "We've grown real fond o' that little gal and just had to see her safely home. The trouble is, she's not safe yet, is she?" He studied the ground for a moment then added, "To tell ya the truth, Tytus, we don't quite know what to do?"

Sounding nearly frantic, Tess took both Shad's and Copper's hands, "I do. Please don't leave me! I'm not ready to lose you." Then she turned to her parents, "I hope you can understand...I love them too. In my mind, this past month has been my entire life, and they've been my family. I was afraid to meet you. But Uncle Quin and Aunt Mariah said that my parents were like Shad and Copper, the salt of the earth. Now as I'm beginning to remember, I know they're right! God has truly blessed me. Would it be too selfish to have the McKennas come with me to this other ranch?"

Augusta hugged her daughter, "If the McKennas don't mind, I know they'd be welcome! Old McGee could never deny you anything and he loves having company." Addressing the McKennas, she added, "He has a huge house and delights in filling it up with guests. He never married and with no children of his own, he's adopted all of his neighbors—young and old." Just then Augusta reached out and took Copper's hand, "Before you agree to stay, I must warn you that it could be dangerous! Although we have no idea who all is involved in this scheme to hurt us, we do know the instigator of this. My first husband, Tess's father was killed trying to protect me from this same person. If you stay, you may all be risking your lives!"

"Missus Grainger," Shad murmured, "we McKennas believe that we are to see this through. We won't rest until we know that Tess and your family are safe!"

Augusta smiled, "I can see why Quin and Mariah value your friendship. Tanner said something earlier that I can't forget. He said that you and the Longs believed that God meant for our three families to sort this out together. God has already used you mightily to protect our daughter. The truth is we would very much appreciate your staying. But should you ever feel God telling you to return to the mountains we would certainly not hold that against you!"

Quin watched everyone mount their horses while he mulled over the idea that the doctor might be helping the old woman, even without knowing it. Just before Ty and Augusta rode away, Quin stopped them. "Wait everyone, I just had an idea. Tomorrow is Sunday. Ty, you and Augusta bring the boys to church as usual. We'll ask McGee to invite them to spend the week on his ranch. That way all three of your children will be in the same place and will be guarded every minute. More specifically, Lavenia won't know where they are!" Turning to his wife, he added, "Mariah, will you show everyone the way to the Scotsman Ranch? I think I better ride to town and see what that doctor knows."

⚜

When they arrived at McGee's ranch and knocked on the door, they were greeted by the stubborn Scotsman himself. He was a very old man, bent over from years of hard work and walked with a slow shuffling gate. The twinkle in his eyes though, showed that the man was still young at heart. "I dinnae ken what brings ye to me door, but yerr all as welcome as can be." His greeting was filled with rolled r's as was the way of the Scots, and though his hearing was a bit off, his eyes were as keen as ever. His grin quickly turned to a frown when the usually smiling Mariah stepped through his door looking worried and he saw Tess's red rimmed eyes. He took their hands and sighed, "Och, now what could be wrong with me bonny lassies?"

Mariah hugged the old man, "Oh, dear McGee, it seems the Graingers are in trouble. We don't know exactly how or why—but they are! Tess might know what this is about but she was injured and has lost her memory." She held her hand out to the McKennas, "Forgive my manners. Tanner McGee, let me introduce you to three of our dearest friends! This is Shadrack and Copper McKenna and their son. And he, coincidentally, is also named Tanner! By God's providence, they were the ones who found Tess when she was lost in the mountains, and by another miracle they brought her to us!" Squeezing Tess's hand, she added, "When she saw us, her memory began coming back, but she still has a long way to go."

The old man nodded as he listened to Mariah's explanation. His expression was kindness itself as he held his hand out to Tanner, "I'm verra pleased to know ye." His shaggy eyebrows rose as he added, "I've never met another Tanner! Almost forgot that's m' name. Everyone just calls me, Ole McGee." As he shook Shad's hand he added, "McKenna is a fine Scottish name! My dearest childhood friend was a McKenna. We grew up together and together we crossed the sea." McGee frowned adding softly, "And then…"

When the old man seemed suddenly lost in his own thoughts, Mariah reminded him why they were there. "Until more is known about this danger, the Bar 61 isn't safe. Quin has gone to town to see if he can learn anything. For a while at least, we all need to stay here, if you don't mind? Ty also asked, when you see them tomorrow at church if you could invite the boys to come stay with you as well? I know this many of us is a huge imposition but…."

"Och, lass, ye offend me with such talk. Yer all—every one of ye—is as welcome as a warm hearth on a cold night!" Then he smiled down at Tess and asked softly, "Do ye remember me lass?"

Tess bit her lip and stared up at him, "May I touch your face?"

"Darlin' ye can yank m' whiskers off if it helps! When ye were a wee bairn, ye use to pull m' beard till m' eyes watered."

Placing her hand on his cheek she frowned, "That wasn't very nice of me, was it?" Tess's bright blue eyes studied McGee's lined and craggy face while her fingers slid over his soft white beard, then she smiled, "It was a game wasn't it? I'd pull your beard…but then…I would kiss your cheek to make it better… didn't I!"

"Aye, that ye did!" McGee laughed. "That's m' sweet bonny Tess. We've been friends a verra long time! Would break m' old heart for ye to forget me."

McGee had one arm around Tess and put the other around Mariah as he nodded to a raven haired young woman waiting in the hallway. "Freya, will ye show these good folks to the kitchen. N'doubt, Cook heard them arrive and has already got a wee feast waitin'." The three women followed the young maid out the door, but the old man caught Shad by the arm and motioned for Tanner to come closer, "I'll have a word with m' foreman. Men will be standin' guard this and every night 'til all fears are allayed."

"Thank you, sir!" Shad said with a grin as he shook McGee's hand. "That's just what I wanted to hear."

The following morning, the guests all rose early. The women went to the kitchen to see if they could help Freya and Cook. Shad and Tanner went to tend to their mounts and see if they could be of any help to the ranch hands. Afterwards Shad went for a short walk around the grounds. When he returned to the house he found old McGee looking spry at the head of the table, waiting for his breakfast with Tanner sitting next to him. Shad took a seat just as his son was explaining, "Pa named me after a friend who save my grandmother's life. My Pa always said Maudy McKenna was the sweetest woman in the world and asking that her grandson be named Tanner was just about her only request. So, I was named Tanner after my grandparent's best friend and Angus after my grandfather."

"Maudy and Angus ye say?" McGee asked, then he surprised Tanner when he quickly grabbed his arm. "Was her name Maudy Duncan before she married Angus? Did they live in Tennessee?"

"Yes!" Shad and Tanner answered together, then Shad asked, "Sir, did ya know my folks?"

McGee couldn't speak for a while, he lowered his head and rubbed his face with his weathered hands and groaned. Shad and Tanner weren't sure what to make of the man's reaction. Finally, McGee looked up and stared at Shad and then Tanner as if he was only now truly seeing them, "Aye, and may God be praised this day! I can see them, in both of ye! Are they...are the two of them gone, then?"

Shad nodded sadly, "Pa died when I was twelve. Ma died about twenty-seven years ago. I brought her up to the mountains so we could have a fresh start, away from the war—away from everything. She seemed to be so full of life but then about the time I finished the cabin she took a fever and..." Shad looked away, "Ma was quite a woman!"

"Aye, she was the bonniest and the wisest lass I ever knew. There was nae a lad that could look at the fair Maudy Duncan and nae fall in love!"

Tanner smiled, "Including you, Mister McGee?"

The old man nodded and his eyes took on a faraway look, "Aye, especially me!" Then he turned to Tanner, "Listen here laddie. Take m' advice, dinnae be stickin' yer toe in the dirt when ye see the woman o' yer dreams. Tell her yer feelings and be quick about it! Or ye might just lose her—forever!"

"Ma told me you saved her life. What happened?" Shad asked. "She promised to tell me the story one day—but—she never did."

McGee frowned, "Och, I've never shared that story, nae to a livin' soul." Then he looked at Tanner and then Shad, "Reckon, ye should ken, so I'll tell it from the start! Angus and me, we grew up together—like brothers we were. Grew up hungry and cold! One day we decided to leave the highlands, cross the ocean and make our fortunes! 'Twas an excitin' voyage but when we got to the big cities—we hated them. Folks told us the west weren't so crowded. We wandered about finding work here and there until we finally got as far as Tennessee. 'Twas Autumn and och, the trees were ablaze with colors, the like we'd never seen, pinks and reds, oranges and yellows. We thought the place was grand indeed and, a sign fer sure, that we were home at last. There were other Scots there, too, and we made friends and found work. Angus and me, we thought alike about most things. Lookin' back, 'twas nae surprisin' that we both fell in love with the same lass! Angus could do anything he set his mind to, and do it well. He set up a blacksmith shop but he could build a house or make a violin with the skill of a true craftsman!"

"What kind of work did you find, Mister McGee?" Shad asked, eager to finally hear all about this man who held such high esteem in his family.

"Nae Mister, laddie, just McGee," the old man grunted, then continued, "'twas a wee mountain village and they needed a minister. I loved the Bible and could out talk a magpie...so all the folks agreed that I could be their preacher. It puffed me up, I'll tell ye. On top o' the world was I. All I needed was—a wife! I arrogantly thought that as the town's spiritual leader, any lass I chose would say yes, and that would be that!" McGee shook his head and chuckled at his own foolishness. "So, one fine Sunday, after services, I asked Maudy to stay behind.   Once we were alone, I said, 'I've been watchin' ye Maudy Duncan, yer a kind and godly lassie, and right bonny, too.   You'd make a fine pastor's wife and I am in love with ye.   Old Judge Hanson has agreed to marry us next Sunday—now isn't that grand!"   When Shad and Tanner's eye-brows went up in surprise, McGee scoffed at himself, "Aye, I see ye both are wiser than me!"

Shad grimaced, "I can well imagine what my Ma said to that!"

"Och aye, that lass was full of vinegar—that one!   She said, 'So ye ken I'd make a bonny wife do ye?   And what kind of husband would ye make me, Reverend McGee?   Ye ken verra well what God says about marriage?   A husband should cherish his wife as Christ cherishes the church.   A man should court a lass and prove that he's her friend and champion.'"   McGee shook his head, "Then she really lowered the boom when she added, 'Ye barely speak to me, have spent n' time with me a'tall.   And yet, in just seven days ye think I'd pledge me life to ye?'"   The old man leaned back in his chair and let out a sigh as if she had just spoken those words.   "Right she was of course, but I'll nae forget how bonny she looked as she spun on her heels and walked out that door."

"So," Shad asked slowly, "when did she agree to marry Pa?"

"'Twas the very next day!" McGee sighed.   "Angus met me at our favorite fishin' hole.   I could tell Maudy had nae told him a thing.   He was so happy as he shared his good news that he'd been quietly courtin' Maudy for the past ten months and that she'd agreed to marry him.   Neither of us ken that the other was in love.   I'd ne'er seen him so happy and was glad he had nae heard o' m' foolishness.   Still, performing that weddin' was the hardest thing I've ever done. Alas, the truth was, I loved 'em both!"

"Still a mighty hard thing to do I reckon," Shad said softly, "how did it happen that you saved Ma's life?   Where was Pa?"

McGee frowned, "They'd been wed 'bout six months when Angus was hired to shoe all the horses in another village.   He asked me to check in on Maudy while he was away.   When I got to their cabin I heard raised voices. Seems the town bully had also fancied her.   The man was short of temper and long on drink.   He was demandin' that she leave Angus.   When she told him he was daft, he swore he'd kill her.   I looked through the window and saw she was tryin' to fight him off.   Don't exactly know what happened after that.   Never in me life have I felt such a blindin' rage.   I knew that scoundrel had hurt people before, but that day, he was hurtin' Maudy. While she was screamin' he was laughin'! Pure evil he was. I ended his life that day—and in a way—mine as well."

Shad put his hand on McGee's shoulder, "Ma said she surely would have died, had it not been for you! I heard her prayin', many a time, askin' the Lord to bless and watch over Tanner McGee," he assured the old man, then asked, "So, what happened to you after that?"

"The judge and the town elders met with Maudy. She stood up for me and said the man had told her that if he could nae have her, no one would. She was certain he meant to kill her. The leaders of the town and elders of our church declared me innocent." McGee looked at Shad then Tanner and sadly shook his head, "I was nae though. I was glad I killed that reprobate. Glad that precious Maudy would nae fear that man again—nor would any other lass. Some called me a hero for purging the land o' such evil. Others judged me, reminding me that I had just preached a sermon on the Ten Commandments. 'What about the one that says, thou shall not kill?' they asked. 'Does God nae hold preachers accountable?' I felt like a hypocrite, so I gave up preachin' altogether. I knew that it was best for me to leave. I wandered for years, herdin' cattle and playin' me fiddle. Finally, I settled here and took up ranchin'. I've had a good life but the only woman I've ever loved…was Maudy!"

Quin left the doctor's office shaking his head and in no doubt that Augusta's mother was indeed conniving and shrewd. She had quite impressively manipulated the gullible doctor into secretly doing her bidding. Quin stopped to look at his watch, the evening train had just arrived from Denver. When he saw Barrett Tulane stepping from his fancy private car, his first instinct was to call out to him, but something made him step behind a wagon and watch instead. Barrett made his way to a bench where he sat down next to a little man wearing a grey suit and matching derby hat. After exchanging a few words, Barrett got up and walked away. The man in the derby hat waited a while, then stood and headed in the opposite direction. Quin was torn, who should he follow? Feeling like a child playing catch the bandit, he decided to follow Barrett, who rented a horse at the livery then stopped at the telegraph office. He was there only a few minutes then he was back on his rented horse and leaving town, heading in the direction of the Bar 61. Once Barrett was out of sight, Quin started for the telegraph office. He stopped when a tall black man dressed in a well-tailored gray suit burst out the door, then sprinted across the street towards the train station. At first, he seemed to be heading for the ticket window. However, when he recognized a man stepping out of the passenger car of the recently arrived train, he went to speak to him instead. The two men talked excitedly for a time as Quin nonchalantly strolled a little closer, pretending he was looking for something he'd dropped. He couldn't hear their conversation but they nearly ran him over when they spun around and hurried back to the ticket window. They purchased two tickets to Denver, and were told it would be leaving within the hour. This scene sparked Quin's curiosity as he entered the telegraph office. He could only hope he would soon find some answers to the questions that were troubling him. After that it was crucial that he catch up with Barrett Tulane.

"Hello Click!" Quin greeted the telegraph operator as he hurried towards the man's desk. "I need your help and there's no time to explain, except to say that it's a matter of life and death. I must know what that blonde man's message said. And who was that black man that just ran out of here?" When the telegraph operator folded his arms and pursed his lips, Quin scowled down at him. "I realized this is against company rules, but you know you can trust me. You may very well know something that might save a life!"

"Life or death, again?" Click asked. "That's just what that Pinkerton agent said!"

"Pinkerton agent?" Quin wondered about that, as he took his hat off and slapped it against his leg, "What in the world is going on? Listen Click, there's no time to spare, you must tell me everything you know about the last two men that were in here!"

"Well," Click pondered, "that blonde feller's message was a little odd." Picking up the paper Click read, 'Complications here…stop…sweep house… stop…continue as planned…stop…TBT…stop.' He paid me then ran out the door. Thought I was alone after he left, but then that Pinkerton agent came storming up here from the back room. He showed me his badge and told me I had better cooperate or be considered an accomplice to murder. He read this here telegram and it seemed to really upset him. He shoved me aside and tapped out his own message. Must have been in some kind of code or something…'cause it didn't make no sense to me. The second he was finished he ran out o' here like his boots was on fire! Now, Preacher Long…why don't you do some explainin', 'cause I'd like to know what's going on?"

"Can't take the time now, Click. I'll explain everything later." Quin grunted as he sprinted to his horse. Pushing his mount as hard as he dared, he managed to catch up with Barrett about two miles outside of town. "Barrett," he called, "hold up, we'll ride in together. I noticed you just as you were heading out of town." Quin thought that the man seemed ill at ease, but then he would be, if he was behind all this. Or to be fair, he would be unsettled if his fiancé had gone missing. Deciding to plunge into the fray he asked, "I know something has happened to Tess. What do you know about it? Do you know where she is?"

Barrett's expression turned into a look of disgust, "I had assumed that she was safely at the ranch—but now—I have no idea where she is! My beautiful fiancé's life has been put in danger all because of my mother's foolishness. She's so upset and ashamed for what she did that she refused to come back with me." Barrett suddenly scowled at Quin, "I didn't dare send word to the Graingers— so who told you she was missing?"

"That's not important…tell me what you know!" Quin demanded.

Barrett was skeptical. He had no idea how the preacher could have heard anything about Tess. Still, he was going to have to convince Tytus that he and Tess were both victims. He might as well practice on Quin. "It's a long story," he began. "For the past few years a man has been blackmailing me. Actually, it was for something my father did, but I've been trying to protect his good name and I didn't want Mother to be hurt by it. When I was here last time, I received a letter from the blackmailer. In it were instructions saying that I would finally be free of this burden once and for all. The demand this time was to deliver Tess to a place in Paris and leave her there."

"Deliver her to Paris?" Quin growled. "And then what was to happen to her?"

Barrett ran his hand over his face. "I'd rather not to think of what they'd planned. I do know it was some sort of vendetta against the Grainger family." Seeing Quin's anger rising, he held up his hand and quickly added, "Of course, I had no intention of putting her in danger, but I had to make them think that I would! If I had refused they simply would have found another way. The best way to keep Tess safe was for me to pretend to go along with their plan. They are always watching me. However, I believed that once I got her to Mosslet Way, she'd be safe there. Unfortunately, my mother saw the letter from the blackmailer, she drugged me, then asked the conductor to put Tess and her horse off the train before it left Bar 61 land. I have no idea what could have happened, Tess should have gone straight home! When I realized what Mother had done, I found a young blonde woman on the train and hired her to pretend to be Tess. She left the train with us and even stayed at Mosslet Way. She acted the part for a few days, then for whatever reason she ran away. A few days ago, I received another letter from the blackmailer. It was a cryptic message but basically it said that they knew Tess wasn't in New York nor at the Bar 61. They said to find her before they did or they would kill us all. I came here immediately!"

Quin took his hat off, wiped his brow on his sleeve, then resettled it, "Tess had the right to know her life was in danger and so did Ty and Augusta!" he growled. "At the very least you should have told Tytus! He has close connections with the military. The hacienda was built like a fort to ward off Indian attacks. The ranch would have been the safest place for both of you."

Barrett yanked his horse to a stop and turned on Quin, "It was my job to keep my woman safe…not her father's!" When Quin said nothing, Barrett calmed a bit, "All this happened because my own mother and my fiancé wouldn't give me the benefit of the doubt. The truth is I'm furious with them both. How could they believe I would do such a thing?"

After that, the two men rode in silence. When they reached the yard, Tytus stepped from the barn and Quin spurred his horse forward while calling out, "Don't get your hopes up Ty, he doesn't know where Tess is either. He's here to help us find her!"

Ty's face became an unreadable mask. He stared at Quin, understanding his warning, then he narrowed his eyes at Barrett, "My daughter was under your protection. I entrusted her into your care and now you don't even know if she's alive or dead!" Ty grabbed Barrett, yanked him from the saddle and tossed him to the ground, "Explain yourself before I break that smug nose of yours!"

When Quin saw Ty's right-hand curling into a fist, he stepped in front of him. "Easy Ty, Barrett's as worried as we are and he has some information we didn't have before. It could be useful. We all want the same thing and that's to find Tess and make sure she stays safe."

"That's right!" Barrett agreed as he got to his feet and brushed the dirt off his suit, "I hate that Tess is in danger but this was all my mother's fault, not mine. Let's go inside and we can talk this over."

The men followed Ty as he stormed into the library then turned to Quin, "Augusta will want to hear this. Stay here, I'll be right back."

When Ty returned to the library, he was accompanied not only by Augusta but to Barrett's annoyance, Joseph and Alvaro hobbled into the room as well.

Giving the two older men a disdainful glance, Barrett sneered, "I think this talk should include family only."

Ty had just started to sit down behind his large desk, but then he straightened to his full height. The room seemed to shrink around him as his voice rumbled, "The only person in this room that's not family...is you. But since we need to hear what you have to say, you may remain."

Barrett's eyes flashed then he shrugged, "My apologies—I meant no offense," he grunted. It was obvious that Ty viewed him with suspicion and distain. In fact, Grainger was watching him in the same way a cat watches a rat. With an inward sigh, Barrett retold what he had shared with Quin. Using as few words as possible, he put himself in the best light and his mother in the worst, "I could have kept Tess safe—had my mother not interfered. I didn't want to frighten her or Tess, so I chose not to informed them. I admit now that was a mistake. When I found out Tess had left the train, I was not immediately concerned. It was a spontaneous decision and there was no way my enemies could have known about it. I believed she was safe here on the ranch and I could use it to my advantage. In a way, if she was missing, she was safe. We may not know where she is but then neither do our enemies!"

Augusta shook her head, "Why didn't you or Emily send us a telegram to make sure Tess had arrived home safely? Instead you lied! You sent a fake message, as if it were from Tess, saying that you were all having a grand time and would soon be leaving for Paris. All these weeks we thought her happy and well, when we should have been searching for her! How can you expect us to believe anything you say?"

Barrett ran a hand through his blonde hair as he paced the floor, "Don't you see I had to pretend that Tess was with me. I even hired a young blonde woman to leave the train wearing Tess's clothes and come back to Mosslet Way with us. I had to make everyone believe that I was following the plan. If I had sent a telegram asking if she had made her way back to the ranch, our enemies would have found out immediately and gone after her. I could only assume that she had found her way home and that she was all right! Then when I received yet another note from the blackmailer, saying they knew Tess was missing...I knew I had to come here immediately and I did. As I said, the only good news is that they don't know where she is either!"

Lavenia smiled, her grandsons had been especially busy all day and no one had asked them to keep her from listening. She had to be careful not to give herself away as she stood beside the French doors that opened from the library into the courtyard. It was such a hot day, no one had thought to close the doors. Their carelessness had allowed her to hear every word, and it was all she could do not to laugh with the pleasure of it.

My goodness, I've got them squirming like worms on a hook. It almost makes me feel young and powerful again! Tulane's fear of hanging has certainly honed his skills as a liar. It's almost a pity to hang such a kindred spirit. He's quite nearly as wicked as—I am! Of course the plan has always been to destroy him, his quaint little mother and most especially...all five of the Graingers. My revenge is very close. I may just live to see it after all!

Lavenia spent the rest of the evening in her room. Then late that night she made her way to the parlor. During her short stay, she'd become familiar with the habits of all those residing at the hacienda. The two old men went to their rooms just after supper. Augusta and Tytus retired around nine o'clock. Her twin grandsons, however, often spent their evenings in the parlor. Something was amiss, though. Tomorrow was Sunday and she'd heard Caleb ask his mother what he should pack. She feared Augusta was sending the boys away. She needed to arrange a surprise for her grandsons and this might be her last chance to speak to them. Most nights they enjoyed a game of chess and then they would read until quite late. It was nearly midnight when Lavenia made her way towards the parlor, knowing that she would find them there—alone!

"Well now, good evening my handsome grandsons!" she cooed as she entered the room. "You are two fine boys to spend your time broadening your minds like this. I do hope I'm not disturbing you."

"No ma'am," Joshua answered as he stood to his feet.

"Is there something you need, Grandmother?" Caleb asked as he reluctantly stood as well. He glanced at Josh then added, "We're surprised to see you up so late."

Lavenia lifted one brow and smiled her sweetest smile, "You boys are very perceptive. I realized that the moment I met you both! The truth is I have a mission for you two. A secret mission!"

"Hmmm, I don't know about that. Our parents wouldn't want us to keep secrets," Josh's face turned red as he muttered, "don't mean to be rude, but especially not your secrets."

"At least let's hear her out, Josh," Cal argued, "All right, Grandmother, what secret mission are you talking about?"

Lavenia lowered her eyes to the floor, "I'm sure you both are well aware that I have not been a good mother to my daughter. You are no doubt equally aware of how much she loved her Papa! Barrett O'Brien or Bull as everyone but me called him, was a truly fine man." A tear slid down her cheek as she added, "Although my daughter didn't know it, I too attended his funeral. Augusta was so distraught, I couldn't bring myself to speak to her. You boys may not understand but I just had to have something of his. I'm ashamed to say, I stole his saddle." Sighing she dabbed a hankie to her cheek then added, "I took it while the entire town was paying their respects. It was a selfish and mean thing to do. Augusta used to ride in front of her Papa on that saddle. I know it would mean a great deal for her to have it. A friend of mine has been keeping it for me and I've arranged for him to bring it to Colorado Springs. He said that if someone could meet him at the train station, he will give them the saddle. His name is Keefer Flynn. He's a fragile little man who always wears a gray-derby hat. His train is arriving at five o'clock this Tuesday morning. Keefer assured me that train is always delayed at the station a few hours before continuing on to Pueblo. We must get the saddle then, for if we don't, Keefer said he would have to sell it! Please, won't you help me boys? I know that you are planning to stay with one of your neighbors for a while. Surely you two are clever enough to slip out of their house, retrieve the saddle and be back before you're even missed. It's very important for your mother to have this one gift from me—before I die." Lavenia's lips trembled as she added, "Please, help me make right at least one thing that I've done wrong. I can count on you two, can't I?" She reached out and took each boy by the hand, "You know, your grandfather was a man of integrity and honor, he would have been so very proud of you both."

That said, Lavenia turned away from the boys and lifted a hankie to her eyes.

Josh stared at his brother then shrugged. "You can count on us Grandmother," Josh replied, "we'll take care of it!"

"Yeah, I suppose we could do that," Cal added, "Mama would love to have that saddle. But that's not enough. You should apologize for all the terrible things you've said and done to her!"

Lavenia stiffened, then she gathered her composure while she brushed an invisible tear from her cheek. As she turned, she made sure the boys saw her sorrowful expression, "You boys can't begin to know how I feel about my broken relationship with your mother. I'm hoping the saddle will give me the courage to say all that I've longed to say...before I die."

Chapter 18
Trouble

"Better a poor man whose walk is blameless than a rich man whose ways are perverse." Proverbs 28:6

Everyone was seated at McGee's spacious dining table. Tess's eyes swept over all these special people until her gaze finally settled on Tanner, "I don't really want to—but I should see this Barrett Tulane. I must talk to him! Don't you see?"

Ty and Augusta exchanged concerned glances. They'd been thankful they had the excuse to bring the boys back to McGee's after church. They needed to see Tess again and to tell her about Barrett's arrival, but they really did not want her to see him.

"I'm not doubting your words, and I understand your concerns about telling Barrett or my grandmother that I'm alive and well. But if I could just remember more what happened, that might answer all our questions. Quite honestly, what you have told me sounds like an exaggerated melodrama." Tess held up her fingers as she counted off the strange events one by one, "First of all, that I was engaged to a man, whom I admittedly did not love!" She made sure not to look at Tanner as she said this. Did she only imagine it, or had she heard his sigh of relief? It was good news but it confirmed her fears that she had been a shallow young woman, and it shamed her. Shaking off the thought, Tess held up a second finger as she continued, "I boarded the train with this man and his mother, eager to be on my way to Paris and my wedding! Ant then in less than two hours, my fiancés own mother is suddenly convinced that her son means to harm me." Tess shook her head, "The last thing she does is drug him and bribe the conductor to stop the train and let me and my horse off." As I said, I'm not doubting you but it all sounds so ridiculous! I think if I can just look into Barrett Tulane's face, perhaps I can shed some light on this. I only wish his mother was here too. Then I might be able to link all this together."

"Sis," Josh groaned, "think you've taken enough chances with that big headed-goat!"

Tess sighed, she was sandwiched between Cal and Josh. It had taken her a few moments to recognize her dear little brothers but once she had, the boys had not wanted to leave her side. Tess smiled, and in a playful, sisterly gesture she patted Joshua's cheek with her right hand and Caleb's with her left. "I never would have thought a mere bump on the head could make me forget you two!" Her hands dropped to her lap and her expression became stern as she gazed at the others sitting around the table, "But I had to look into all of your faces. I even had to pull sweet McGee's white beard before I truly remembered him!" Sighing she added, "I can tell that none of you like this Barrett Tulane and that you're trying to protect me. Nevertheless...I still must see him! He claims to have been misunderstood and that is a possibility—isn't it?"

Tanner knew this was none of his business but the desire to protect her was too strong to keep silent, "It is a possibility that he was misunderstood," he said with a shrug, "but it is also possible that his mother understood her son, only too well. Mothers know their children." Tanner looked across the table at Copper and saw her loving concern, "Just like my mother knows me and your mother knows you. Barrett admits that his own mother told you to get off the train. Tess, she did that because she believed that her son was capable of hurting you—maybe even killing you!"

Nodding, Tess gave Tanner a grateful smile, "I know you are just trying to be my friend. But I must try to be fair with this man. I have to—because I am finally seeing more clearly what I have been like!" Tess looked down self-consciously and sighed, "There are some things I need to say to all of you. Except for the McKennas, you all have known the girl I was before. While I was staying with Uncle Shad and Aunt Copper they saw that I had memorized Bible verses and hymns. It made sense that I must have been raised in a Christian home. Still, I knew in my heart that whoever I was...I was not a Christian. The more I was around them, the more I realized that I needed to give my heart to God, submit to His will. I needed to make things right and do it before my memory came back. That was very important, because I wanted the new me to be able to speak truth to the old me! Thanks to God's grace and the McKennas, I am now finally—a Christian! And because of that decision, more than anything, I want to do what is right—in God's eyes."

Augusta quietly stood, tears filled her eyes as she went to her daughter and put her arms around her. "Oh, my sweet girl, we are all so grateful to God for that and so very proud of you too, for making that decision! So tell us, what do you believe God is telling you to do?"

"Oh Mama! I want to start by asking you and Papa to forgive me! I still don't remember why I agreed to elope to Paris or why I agree to call New York my permanent home. Right now, I can't imagine why I would want that kind of life. However, I can imagine how that must have hurt all of you!" Her eyes turned to Tytus, "Papa, I'm just now remembering that you've always talked about the day you would walk me down the aisle. And more importantly, that you've always wanted your children to marry Christians and have a godly, prayed over wedding. Uncle Quin, I am sure you assumed you would perform the ceremony. I must have known how my eloping would have upset all of you." Looking at Joshua and then to Caleb she added, "I haven't been much of a role model for you two. I don't understand why I didn't care. I care now though and—I'm so very sorry!" Suddenly her eyes met Tanner's and she felt a urgent need to talk with him, alone, "Tanner, I—I would like to speak to you about something... could you take a walk with me?" Glancing around uncomfortably at the others, she added, "If you all will please excuse us, we won't be gone long."

Surprised by the sudden request, Tanner stammered, "Um—well— certainly!" he said as he stood, hurried around the table and helped Tess from her chair.

As they walked towards the barn Tess shook her head self-consciously, "I'm sorry, I didn't realize how bold that sounded until we walked out of the room together. I hope I didn't embarrass you too much. You see, I really care about all those people in there. It's almost as if I have six parents now, instead of two. But you—you are my only friend."

That wasn't exactly what Tanner had hoped to hear. He didn't realize that he was frowning until Tess winced and asked, "You are my friend, aren't you?"

Forcing a smile Tanner tugged on one of her blonde curls and winked, "Of course, you silly girl. You already know that...I am at very least...your friend."

Tess stared into Tanner's dark green eyes that looked almost black in their intensity and repeated softly, "At very least." She looked away and smiled to herself as she continued, "I know you pretty well. Your parents have told me nearly everything about you. From their description, I had assumed that instead of a hat, you probably wore a halo!" When Tanner cringed, Tess laughed.

"They are rightfully very proud of you!   But that isn't what I want to talk to you about."

"Good," Tanner grunted, then asked gently, "so, what do you want to talk about?"

"Well, one day they told me that they asked you, if any young woman had caught your fancy and if there was anything you wanted them to be praying with you about?"

"They asked that in nearly every letter.   What did they tell you?"

"They told me that at first you had been trying to court nearly every woman you met, wondering if she was the one.   But then one day, you felt God telling you to stop doing His job.   Instead, you believed He was telling you to be still, to wait and to prepare.   Because when the time was right…He would let you find her.   And in the meantime, you should concentrate on being the kind of man she deserved.   A better man—a more godly man."

Tess had bashfully kept her eyes downcast as she repeated what his parents had told her.   When Tanner suddenly stopped walking, she stopped as well and glanced up at him.   He was staring at her with such warmth in his expression that she couldn't move—couldn't even look away.

The two stared at each other for a long while, then Tanner asked, "Are you saying you want to make yourself ready for God to lead you to your husband?"   When Tess blushed crimson and seemed embarrassed by his question, he asked gently, "What did you want to talk to me about, Tess?"

"Well, what you told them impressed me so much that I want to follow your example.   I–I want to do what you did!   I want to be a very different girl from the one who left her family and boarded that train.   I want to learn how to listen to God.   To follow His lead in…everything…every decision…everything I do.   I'm pretty sure that I've never been that kind of person before, but I want to be that way now.   Daily it seems I am remembering a little more about myself.   I see a picture of a girl whose main focus was on what pleased herself.   Not on what pleased anyone else, especially not God.   I wish I didn't have to, but I must meet this Barrett.   If I was running from him, I must know why.   If he would harm me, then he would harm someone else and must be stopped.   On the other hand, if he's innocent and was simply misunderstood, then we need to clear him of these terrible accusations.   Maybe he's just spoiled and selfish like I was—maybe he'll see a change in me and want to change as well!"

"And—if he does, Tess, will you want to go away with him?"

Shaking her head, she shrugged, "I can't imagine why I would. Even if I remembered him, I'm not the same person that got on that train. Mama told me that he was very self-centered and that we didn't love each other, didn't even want to love each other. I left with him because he represented freedom and adventure. Sounds like we were a match," she scoffed sarcastically, "but certainly, not one made in heaven. That's not the life I want now—not anymore!"

"I'm glad to hear that," Tanner sighed, suddenly feeling better than he had since he'd heard about her rich suitor. He wondered if he should tell her that he'd promised God that he wouldn't even think of courting a woman, until he returned to Colorado. In fact, the very day he met Tess was the day he had planned to end his fast. Deciding that now was not the time to share this, he said, "Actually, Tess, it seems that you are already trying hard to live your life in a way that honors Christ. What I've been doing the past few years is what I called a courting fast. Basically, I just stepped back from the world a little. I avoided social entanglements so I could concentrate on what God was saying to me. Is that what you're wanting to do?"

"Exactly! I don't want to distract myself from what God wants to teach me. I need to concentrate on who I am as His child. I know we need to do that all our lives. But as far as the courting fast is concerned, I feel that I should keep to that, at least until Christmas. I asked you to come out here so I could tell you that, and to ask if you would help me? Keep me in your prayers, maybe share verses that helped you to grow as a Christian!"

"I would be honored to help you in any way, Tess. You're quite a girl."

The following night, McGee, Copper, Mariah, Augusta and the twins all sat around the dining room table at the Scotsman Ranch, waiting for T. Barrett Tulane to arrive for dinner. When he knocked on the door he was greeted by young Freya, who instantly ushered him into the parlor where Tess stood by the fireplace. She had insisted on meeting this man—alone. Although she wasn't aware of it, Shad and Tanner stood outside the window while Tytus and Quin both planned to guard the door once Barrett was inside.

As the man sauntered into the parlor, Tess appraised him very carefully. He was tall and quite handsome, with pale blue eyes and a straight nose, but the expression on his face troubled her. There were flutters in her stomach and her heart pounded in her chest, but not in the same way as when she was with Tanner. Perhaps she was judging him unfairly but her first impression was that he seemed arrogant. Tess suddenly looked away when she realized that she was scowling at the man. As if she'd stumbled across a snake, and wasn't quite sure if it was a garden snake or—a rattler!

Barrett stood in the doorway, waiting for Tess to say something. When she remained silent, he entered the room and closed the doors behind him.

However, when he came forward reaching for her with his customary air of confidence she held up her hand. "Please stop," she demanded, "I'm sure you've been told that I have lost my memory. I've heard of you but—I don't remember you." When she felt no sparks of recognition, she asked, "Let me hear your voice. In fact, I would like very much for you to tell me your side of this very strange story."

Barrett grinned broadly, "First of all, it's just so good to see that you're safe and well! Perhaps I've lost my memory too, for I don't recall you being so amazingly beautiful. In fact, I see something special in your face. There's a maturity and even a serenity that wasn't there before. I've missed you terribly, Tess. I've worried myself sick over you!" Barrett moved closer as he briefly told Tess about the letter. How his mother had misunderstood and misjudged him.

"Yes, Uncle Quin told me about that letter. Maybe it would help if I read it!"

"It might have," he grunted. "Unfortunately, Mother destroyed it."

Tess nodded, "I suppose what I really need to know is...why didn't you tell me or anyone else about it? And then, when you woke up from the sleeping powder and found that I was not on the train, what did you do?"

"I was furious!" he hissed. But when he saw Tess's eyebrows raise, he put his head down and added sadly, "Mostly though, I was disappointed and hurt that you could think so poorly of me. After all, we've known each other since we were children!"

"Since I can't read the letter now, I must assume that it put you in a very bad light, otherwise, I would not have gotten off the train as I did. And your actions the past few weeks have certainly done you no service. You should have warned me that I was in danger. Warned my family! So again, I'm asking, what did you do?

Barrett frowned, it was unlike Tess to confront him like this. He thought by now she would be apologizing for not believing in him. This wasn't the same girl he had known in New York or even the same one who had agreed to leave her family and travel to Paris. In fact, he could tell that now, the girl had become a woman, and he feared a strong one at that. Barrett suddenly wasn't so sure that he wanted Tess to remember him. He would hang if he didn't follow the instructions Keefer had given him from L.W. Rubbing his jaw, he stammered, "I—I was frantic of course. But don't you see, if I'd sent you a telegram or had come back here, I would have drawn unwanted attention to you." Barrett ran a hand through his hair, "I did all I could!"

"What you did Mister Tulane, seems to me like nothing at all! I've been told that you are a wealthy man. If you couldn't come back yourself, then why didn't you hire someone to return here and make sure I was safe? To alert my family so they could help me if I was in danger. To warn my family that they might be in danger themselves. I understand that we didn't love each other but I would assume that you'd feel some responsibility for the wellbeing of your fiancé as well as her family."

"I told you I had my reasons. What I should have done is beside the point!" Barrett snapped, "and when you got off the train you should have come straight home." When he saw a flash of wariness in Tess's eyes, he quickly reminded himself that he must not lose his temper. Finally, he sighed and hung his head, "I'm not putting any blame on you. My point is that sometimes, even when we're trying to do the right thing, we decide poorly. You'll never know how much I've wished that I had handled things differently. Please Tess, tell me that you'll forgive me. Do you remember anything about me?"

Her sapphire eyes grew dark as she stared at him a long while, then she shrugged, "I remember...a large fancy room and everyone dancing. Were you there?"

Now it was Barrett's turn to study the woman before him, "Are you toying with me? Of course I was there. You're remembering our annual New Year's Eve Ball at Mosslet Way. You wore a dazzling sapphire dress, trimmed in gold. You and I danced nearly every dance together." Barrett closed the distance between them. Standing before her he ran his hands up and down her arms. She tried to move away but he held her there, "Please Tess," he urged, "we've always been good together. We used to mock people who talked of love. I never believed in it—or maybe I didn't want to admit it. But after I lost you, I realized that I had indeed fallen in love. I don't care what we told each other before, I love you! I will die if I lose you again. Tess—I beg of you to believe that I never would have hurt you. I want only to take care of you. We were going to have a wonderful life together—don't turn your back on it."

Tess wasn't sure what to believe. The expression on his handsome face when he first entered the room was egotistical and haughty, but now at least he seemed less sure of himself and perhaps, more sincere. Feeling confused, she moved away saying, "I think it might help if I met your mother. I seem to be remembering things that have to do with you, but for some reason I'm not remembering...you!"

Barrett's jaw jerked as he turned away and stared out the window. He wondered if the clever Miss Grainger actually did remember. Was she punishing him because he hadn't come looking for her, or had she somehow found out the truth? No, if the Graingers knew the truth they would have him in jail now, they would not have invited him to dinner. He used to be able to intimidate Tess, but something about her behavior warned him not to attempt that now. He might not get what he wanted. In fact any attempt to manipulate her now, might just backfire.

Finally, he turned and faced her, "Tess, please forgive me. I know I didn't manage any of this very well. As far as sending someone I could trust... in my world, it's hard to know if you can trust anyone. That's why, when you and my mother...the two women I love and care for more than anyone in the world, thought I might be dangerous..." Barrett rubbed his eyes with his hand and his voice cracked, "it—it was quite a blow. I'm so sorry that you thought you couldn't trust me. I think you've saved all the letters I've written you over the years. Perhaps if you read them again...you'll remember what great friends we've been—all our lives!"

His words had their desired outcome. Tess felt guilty, "I can see how all this has left you in a difficult position as well." Sighing she added, "Actually, I have read your letters, all of them. We seemed to have enjoyed a very long friendship over the years." She stared at the man and knew that if she touched his face she might very well remember. But the thought of touching him, handsome as he was, distressed her. And then her thoughts went to Tanner and his finely chiseled features. What would it be like to place her hand against his jaw. He shaved every morning but by evening, his beard made a dark shadow against his skin. She couldn't keep from remembering their almost kiss. The barest touch of his lips against hers, and then it was over. And yet she couldn't seem to stop thinking of how it had shaken her and how often she had relived that one unguarded moment. Tess gave an imperceptible shrug. Like everything else, any possible future with Tanner was in God's hands. Still, the sweet memories of him filled her mind. *We're friends...at the very least!*

"That's a very beguiling expression you're wearing, Tess," Barrett murmured seductively as he stepped closer, "I think if you let me kiss you, it would help. You used to enjoy my kisses very much. Or are you already beginning to remember?"

Tess shivered and frowned as she stepped away from him, "No, I'm not— I'm not remembering anything yet. But I do forgive you, everyone makes mistakes. Right now, I think we should concentrate on doing whatever is necessary to stop the person whose intent on hurting you and my family. They used you to target me, but that's only because in hurting one of us they would hurt us all! Papa said you've admitted to being blackmailed, and that's how this all began. So, for your sake and ours, I think we all need to work together to find a way to stop them!"

⚜

The moon was full and the stars were still shimmering in the night sky when Joshua and Caleb slipped out of the room they shared at McGee's. Josh, usually the more level headed of the two brothers, couldn't contain his excitement over doing something so daring. As he closed the bedroom door he grinned at his brother, "We've never done anything like this before. It's a pretty big adventure, huh? That fella better have Grandpa Bull's saddle. I'd sure hate it if we did all this for nothin'!"

"Hush!" Cal hissed, as the two boys crept down McGee's long hallway. "Ya want to wake everyone? Carry your boots till we get outside."

The boys crept down the steps and through the house. Silently, they watched out the back window as Slim and Zack made their hourly walk around the house, then headed off towards the barn.

"Ok Josh, it's safe to step outside now. We'll put our boots on, then run like Billy-Bejeebbers for the east pasture." They were out of breath and grinning wildly at each other when they finally reached their hobbled horses without being seen. Seconds later their mounts were bridled and the boys were on their way, riding bareback, for it would have been too easy to spot the missing saddles from the tack room. Also...they could put their Grandpa Bull's saddle on one of the horses.

"So far so good," Cal whispered, "we're leavin' in plenty of time to get to town. With any luck at all, we'll be back before anyone wakes up. Just like Grandmother said."

Adventure aside, Josh's conscience was beginning to bother him, "I still kind of think we should have told Uncle Quin, or even old McGee." When they came to the main road to town, he stared behind them, "Just don't have a good feeling about this. We still could have kept it a surprise for Ma. Sure hope this doesn't end up with us taking a trip to the woodshed."

"Quit worryin' Josh! We had to get Grandpa Bull's saddle—didn't we? Besides if we handle this just right, maybe Pa won't treat us like a couple of kids anymore, like we're still wet behind the ears. We'll be sixteen soon and that's pretty much a man in my way of thinkin'. After this, Pa will start treatin' us with more respect!"

"Maybe, but if we *don't* handle this just right, Pa will skin our hides and tack 'em to the barn wall. We'll be lucky if we live long enough to see sixteen! Besides, what if this Keefer is an outlaw like Dewey LeBeau?"

"Aw, come on Josh, Grandmother said Keefer was a fragile little man who wears a derby hat. Sounds like a bona fide dude to me. He doesn't stand a chance against the two of us. You remembered your derringer didn't ya." When Josh nodded, Cal patted his pocket. "And I've got mine! If that Keefer fellow tries anything...he'll soon learn he's no match for the Grainger brothers!"

The boys were just approaching town when a rider trotted towards them. The moon was lighting their way, but they heard him long before they saw the small man in the derby hat.

"A fine mornin' to ya gents!" came the jaunty greeting, tinged with a friendly Irish lilt. "Needed a bit of fresh air before boardin' that stuffy train again. Thought I'd bring the saddle out here to meet you lads." He kept his words low in keeping with the early time of day, "The name's Keefer and you men must be the Graingers, no doubt!"

Cal and Josh puffed up a bit when the stranger called them men right off. The fact that they were having a secret meeting in the dark of night was exhilarating. They were both feeling quite grown-up and self-assured, as they reined their mounts to a stop, "Yep, we're the Graingers," Josh said with a nod.

"Yeah, and we're in a big hurry," Cal added, "so, if ya don't mind we need to be getting Grandpa Bull's saddle and head on back to the Scotsman before we're missed!"

"You gents are wise beyond your years." Keefer praised, then he lowered his brow in concern, "But...I heard your lovely sister was injured recently, you know I met her in New York, and what a lovely thing she is. I certainly hope she's feeling better?"

"Yeah, she still doesn't remember everything yet but…"

"Hush Cal!" Josh hissed. "Listen Mister, we just need to get that saddle."

"Of course, that's what we're here for—ain't it! In fact, since you're in such a hurry, I'll be handin' it over to ya, here and now. I don't mind ridin' bareback!"

"That would be good of you sir," Josh sighed when the little man slipped from the saddle.

The boys were gazing about impatiently when Keefer suddenly drew his pistol and aimed it at Josh and then at Cal.

"Excuse me lads, but there's a little more to all this than what yer granny told ya. So far, ya've followed her directions real good. Now ya'll do exactly *what I tell ya* and we'll get along just fine! Also gents, I happen to know that yer in the habit of carrying derringers. I'll be taking them now—if ya please. Pull them from yer pockets, slowly now, drop 'em on the ground, then back your horses just a bit. I'll be more than happy to pick 'em up!"

"Listen Mister, we just want the saddle," Josh insisted, "we didn't come out here with any money!"

"Josh, he doesn't want money," Cal hissed, then looked around as if he might try to run.

Keefer cocked his gun, "Listen up boys. This is the way of it…if one of ya decides to draw m' fire by runnin'…just know that I'll shoot the other one. And don't be thinkin' ya can get back in time to warn yer sister. Another man will be bringing her—ya'll be seeing her soon enough. Now drop those little pea shooters—or I'll put a bullet in one of ya just to make ya both behave."

"But then, why are we here?" Josh asked as his derringer dropped to the ground, "if you don't have Grandpa Bull's saddle, then why?"

"There never was a saddle, Josh," Cal spat the words out, as his own gun fell next to his brother's. "Grandmother lied! She lied just like Mama always told us she would—and we fell for it. Like two boys—still wet behind the ears."

"Ya mustn't be too hard on yerselves lads," Keefer grunted as he picked up both guns and shoved them inside his belt. "That woman is a wizard when it comes to spinning yarns. Men far more jaded than you two have believed her lies." Then Keefer surprised them when he turned to his own horse, grabbed the horn and sprang into the saddle.

Cal shook his head then whispered, "He may wear a derby but he's not fragile and he's no dude, Josh. Don't' try anything yet. We need to meet up with Tess first, then we'll figure something out."

"Then we'll try to get away—right!" Josh asked.

"That's enough whispering," Keefer growled, his Irish lilt no longer held the friendly air it had before. Now his words sounded coldhearted as he gave his first order, "Follow that trail east, and don't be tryin' anythin'. Remember, I won't shoot the one who acts up right away...I'll shoot the other brother first instead. So, unless ya want to be killin' yer own kin, ya best not cause me any trouble."

Chapter 19

Missing

"Don't be so surprised! Indeed, the time is coming when all the dead in their graves will hear the voice of God's Son, and they will rise again. Those who have done good will rise to experience eternal life, and those who have continued in evil will rise to experience judgment." John 5:28-29

Soft morning sunlight caressed Tess's cheek as she strolled along the upstairs corridor of the spacious ranch house. It had pleased McGee to have all five of the second story guest rooms built on the west side of his house, so every visitor could enjoy their own glorious view of the Rocky Mountains. One long hallway connected the bedrooms, running the entire length of the eastern side of the house. Tess breathed in the pine scented breeze as it curled through the many open windows. White curtains billowed out, all along the way like the sails of a ship. The gauzy fabric floated all about her as she stopped and gazed out one of the windows. The sights and sounds tickled her memory. Suddenly she was recalling what mornings were like on a busy ranch. Horses whinnied, cows bawled, chickens clucked and roosters crowed. All that, while the ranch hands whistled and called to one another as they went about their chores. Tasks that would fill their day from sunup to sundown.

As she descended the long stairway, it dawned on her how quiet the house was in comparison to all that was happening outside. Surprisingly quiet when you considered all the guests that were staying there. As she wandered into the kitchen, it was no longer the scent of pine that greeted her but the promise of fresh coffee.

"Good mornin' Miss," Freya greeted as she filled a cup with a dark rich brew, topped it off with cream, then handed it to Tess, looks like yer needin' this. I'll have your breakfast in a blink."

"Bless you!" Tess sighed as she cradled the steaming cup in her hands, then gazed around the room. "Where is everyone? Seems awfully quiet this morning."

"Aye, tis a strange day to be sure. I fear it began with tragedy. 'Twas over at the Larsens, mother and babe both died in childbirth last eve. She left a husband and six other wee bairns. The doctor stopped by quite early this mornin'. He asked Reverend and Missus Long if they could go and help with the family. Missus McKenna went too. Mister McKenna and his son are out helping with chores. I dinnae ken why, but I've nae seen hide nor hair of the lads, this day. They must have stayed up verra late, indeed. Most of the time, sun up finds them in the kitchen, searchin' for crumbs from last night's dinner." Freya smiled and shook her head, "Always make them a pre-breakfast just to keep the poor lads from starving, 'fore the main breakfast begins."

Tess rolled her eyes, "Those stinkers…I hope they show proper appreciation for your kindness."

Freya blushed as she quickly added, "Och, I dinnae mind a bit. They're good lads!"

Tess nodded but then she began to worry, "I still don't remember a lot of things but I don't think it's like them to sleep late!" Leaving her cup on the table, she stood and hurried up the stairs. When there was no answer to her knock, she opened the door and found them both still in bed. "What is the matter with you two? Are you both sick or just being lazy?" When the boys didn't stir, she sighed, then sat down on the side of the bed. "Is living at McGee's spoiling you? You should be out helping the hands with the chores. Come on…my brothers…wake up…wake-up!" she chanted as she playfully yanked the covers away, only to reveal a bed full of rolled up blankets and pillows. "Oh no! Caleb, Joshua, what kind of mischief have you gotten yourselves into, now?"

Tess ran down the stairs and out to the barn. Soon the entire ranch was in chaos. It was quickly discovered that the boys had taken their derringers and their horses but had left their saddles in the tack room. There was no note and none of it made any sense.

Dallas, the ranch foreman, took some of the hands and began tracking the stray boys towards town. Shad quickly rode to the Bar 61 to make sure they hadn't gone there and if not, to deliver the unsettling news to Ty and Augusta that their twins were missing! Tanner stayed behind, in fact, he refused to leave Tess's side.

The chaos that began on the Scotsman Ranch only escalated when it reached the Bar 61. Barrett had stayed the night in town but had arrived there early that morning. He was just stepping from the courtyard when he overheard that the boys were missing. He shouted over his shoulder as he hurried towards the door, "I'll ride to the Scotsman." When Ty gave him a skeptical frown, Barrett opened his jacket to reveal a pistol then said, "I can watch over Tess while you find your boys!"

"No wait!" Augusta snapped, then softened her voice, "I want to go with you."

Barrett glared down at her, "You're my mother's best friend, it's ridiculous for you not to trust me! If it makes you feel better, I'm sure I won't be alone with your daughter. Old McGee will be there and if I don't miss my guess, Tess's faithful hound-dog, Tanner, will not be far from her side. Right now you need to concentrate on finding your sons!"

Just then Shad placed a gentle hand on Augusta's shoulder, "Tess is like a daughter to me and Copper, I'll ride back to the Scotsman with this fella. We'll make sure nothin' happens to that sweet girl."

Augusta was thankful for Shad, he was still a stranger but somehow she knew she could trust him! She had only enough time to nod her thanks to the man, before Tytus grabbed her by the hand, "Come with me, now," he demanded as he pulled her towards the courtyard, "you have to convince your mother to tell us what she's done! I don't know how but she's behind this."

As they burst into the courtyard, they saw Lavenia sitting on the side of her couch. She was downing the contents of one cobalt blue bottle and held another in her free hand. She tossed the first bottle away, chanced a quick, almost amused, glance at Augusta, then lifted the other to her lips and drank.

Augusta screamed, "No Mama!" Hurrying across the courtyard she slapped the second bottle from Lavenia's hand.

The old woman raised her eyebrows and laughed, "No Mama!" she mocked, "what's the matter, don't you want your sweet Mama to die? Too bad...." she added in a sing-song voice. "It's known as Tincture of Opium or Laudanum. I got more than enough of it down to do the job."

"But why? Now that you're finally getting to see me suffer—just as you've always wanted—why kill yourself now?"

"I have my reasons," Lavenia sighed, "it became apparent today that this was necessary in order to accomplish my goals." When Augusta seemed even more confused she added, "I also prefer to die on the day, and in the way of my own choosing. But the final and most compelling reason is simply that it's one thing to prolong your suffering Augusta, it's quite another to prolong my own!"

"Woman!" Ty growled, "I don't care why you're trying to kill yourself. But you will tell us what you have done with our sons and you will tell us now!"

The only description for Lavenia's smile was cold-blooded. But then her words were colder still, "I wish I could tell you! In fact, I'd like very much to brag a little, for my plan is quite clever. Of course, I won't, for you see I intend for you both to spend the rest of your lives asking that same question. What did she do with our children? You see my dying today, is just another twist of the knife. Once I'm gone there's no chance of coercing me into telling you anything!" Turning to Augusta she lifted her chin proudly, "I can tell you this though, I learned a great deal from your besting Dewey LeBeau. You are stronger than I had imagined and it's difficult to hurt a strong person. Caring for people is your greatest flaw, Augusta. So, I used it to my advantage. The best way to hurt you—was to hurt someone you loved. So, voilà, my revenge is to take away—all three—of your beloved children! You may as well start mourning them now. They are, even as we speak, being taken far away. You will never find them, never know their fate. It will haunt you both to your graves!"

Nothing had ever frightened Tytus Grainger as much as Lavenia's words frightened him just then. In desperation, he grabbed her shoulder's and lifted her from her couch. "Woman, you will tell me where my children are! You will tell me NOW!" he demanded.

"No Tytus," Augusta sighed, "that will do no good, put her down." When Ty settled the old woman back onto her couch, Augusta knelt beside her. "Mother, if your life is about to end, then this is your very last chance to make amends. Don't you fear what awaits you? You are about to spend your first moments in hell, followed by an eternity of punishment!"

Lavenia's golden eyes were growing heavy and her voice became soft, "Why should I fear hell? If there is such a place, all my friends and associates are there. I am sure of it!" she added with a weak flourish of her hand. She even managed a sarcastic smile, "Now, I would be happy to sell, *your soul*, Augusta... if it would *save mine*. I don't suppose it works that way though, does it?"

Augusta shook her head, "I give up. I had so hoped to find something redeemable in you. What have I done to make you hate me so?" When Lavenia simply shrugged, Augusta knew her words were a waste of air. Sighing, she glanced up at Ty, "All we can do is have faith in God as well as in our children. The plan she hatched with Dewey LeBeau was foolish and ineffectual. It wasn't hard to get the best of him. And I'll wager our children's intellect and resourcefulness against the kind of hooligan she would hire! Our boys are probably on their way home or to McGee's right now. And she said she'd take all three of our children but we know Tess is safe—we know that!"

A soft groan came from Lavenia's pale lips, "Oh bother—how you do go on! I had hoped I would be dead by now. I know you're just trying to get my goat, but you are wrong!" Lavenia suddenly succumbed to a fit of coughing. When she could speak again, she reached over and clutched the fabric of her daughter's dress, "Now, my weak little mouse," she asked scornfully, "what was it you said earlier? That you know Tess is safe. Are you truly sure about that? You say that I'm about to spend my first moments in hell." She sneered up at Ty and then to Augusta, "Hell can be a state of mind as well as a place. Know this—you will never see ANY of your children again. So, you see, in a way, I'm taking you to hell, right along with me!"

Augusta had always believed her mother to be evil but the woman's pure hatred was worse than she'd imagined.. "Lavenia!" she cried as she knelt beside her and shook her mother's arm. "Hell is not a joke. It's a real place of punishment! I have no doubt that many of your acquaintances are there. I know Dewey LeBeau awaits you, though he was certainly not your friend. Please, ask for forgiveness and ask Christ into your heart. For as long as you have breath it's not too late for sincere repentance. And I plead with you, do one honorable thing before you die. Tell us where we can find our children before it's too late. Save yourself and your own grandchildren! Please!" Augusta sobbed.

The look Lavenia bestowed upon her daughter just then was one of malignant triumph. "I see you as the worst *mistake of my life!* And the day you were born was the worst *day of my life!* Now—finally—I've broken you. This is what I've waited all these years for—to see you brought to your knees...grief-stricken and miserable! Yes, revenge is sweet." Then she gazed up at Tytus, "I've never believed in God, but if there is one, only He could save your children now. You two are such fools, believing in the grace and goodness of an all-seeing God. I'm dying just as I've always lived...on my own terms. There is no God and I'm not afraid!" Suddenly, her eyes grew large, as if something horrific had just entered the courtyard. Ty and Augusta glanced all around but saw nothing. Even so, Lavenia jerked and raised her hands as if fighting off an unseen assailant. "NO!" She shrieked. An instant later her scream stopped and her body went limp.

Ty and Augusta were shaken, for they had never witnessed anything like this before. They knew beyond a shadow of a doubt where the soul of Lavenia

Wrenford-O'Brien now resided. Even as they watched her golden eyes glaze over, the expression on her once beautiful face was now frozen in fear.

Barrett Tulane raced his horse to the front of McGee's large house, jumped off, tossed his reins over the hitching rail, then hurried into the house without knocking. "McKenna!" he shouted, "McKenna, where are you?"

When both Tanner and Tess stepped from the parlor, Barrett gave the man a look of disgust then turned to Tess with concern, "Your brothers didn't go home. We have no idea where they are!" Looking back at Tanner he added, "I'm sorry to tell you this, old boy, but your father's in a bad way too! Since nearly everyone in the territory is out searching for the twins, he and I rode back here together to help guard Tess. Just as we were about to ride through the entrance to this ranch, someone shot your father's horse out from under him. He was able to get to cover, then he yelled for me to ride on and tell you to come back and bring help. You'll need to round up some of the hands and head back. I'll stay with Tess."

Tanner scrutinized Barrett as he ran a hand through his hair then looked at Tess and groaned, "I can't just leave you. All the ranch hands are out looking for the boys and McGee's gone to bed with a fever. Freya gave him some medicine, he probably won't wake up for the rest of the day." Locking eyes with Tess, he rubbed the back of his neck and sighed, "I don't know what to do. I've got to find a way to help Pa, but I don't feel right about leaving you—I can't leave you!"

"You must," Tess insisted, "neither of us could bare it if anything happened to him. You must go! I won't be alone, Barrett will stay with me, I'll be safe!"

Barrett placed a hand on Tanner's shoulder, "She's right of course. I saw my own father shot before my eyes. I wouldn't want you to lose your father, you must help him and there's no time to waste! I'll watch over Tess. She is my fiancé after all—I'll guard her with my life!"

Tanner shook his head, trying to think what he should do, then Tess took his hand, "Don't worry about me. Just please—hurry and be careful!"

Tanner gave her a quick nod, then ran from the house. From the parlor window Tess watched as he sprinted towards the barn. A few moments later he was mounted up and spurring his stallion, Sailor, into a dead run.

As she watched him ride away she whispered, "Father in heaven, bless and protect him. Please Lord don't let anyone get hurt today. Bring everyone home safe!"

"Since when have you been the praying kind, Tess?" Barrett mocked as he slipped behind her and locked his hands tightly around her waist.

"Let go of me this instant!" she huffed, as she tried to claw his hands open and push him away, "You promised to protect me not attack me!"

"Now, that's not entirely true. If you'll remember, I did not say that I would *protect you,* my sweet. I said I'd watch over you and guard you—and I will—like a wolf guards his prey from other predators. But that isn't the same thing as protect at all, now is it?" He chuckled as he pressed her close with one hand and slipped his free hand into her dress pocket. "Ah, there it is! I knew you'd have your little derringer. You really shouldn't have told me that you and your brothers always carry these little toys everywhere you go. I made sure to warn my associate. I have no doubt that he has your brothers well in hand by now. I know you've been worried about those boys, so if you behave yourself I'll take you to them!"

Tess spun around, intent on slapping Barrett, but he caught her hand. When he smiled and pointed the gun at her, Tess narrowed her eyes, "So, your Mother didn't misunderstand that letter at all—did she? You were going to deliver me to Paris and leave me there—to die or worse!" Suddenly Tess feared for Emily, "Where is your mother? What have you done with her?"

Barrett shrugged, "Well, let's just say she's gone away, and now I have full control of the estate!" he patted her cheek, adding, "as for you, I had intended for us both to have had some fun, before—well—before you went away too. It's such a nuisance when plans change—isn't it?"

Tess was stunned and suddenly wondered how she or anyone had ever thought this man appealing in any way. "How can you be so cruel?" she asked.

A look of cold indifference contorted his face. "I find it very easy," he sneered. "You see, T. Barrett Tulane is my first—well—actually my only priority. I am one of the fortunate few who have never been plagued by a conscience. Of course, that can be a liability. Feeling no remorse can make you careless at times. For instance, when I killed my father a few years ago, I was very relieved that he was gone. Unfortunately, an underling of your grandmother's, Keefer Flynn, saw me do it. Barrett smiled at the look of shock he saw in Tess's eyes as he ran a finger down her cheek adding, "I was naïve back then, I allowed Flynn and your grandmother to blackmail me. But now I know better. It is strange don't you think, how our two families are linked together. I turned the table on your little granny this morning, and it felt wonderful. I gave her two bottles of Laudanum before coming here. Told her that if she didn't drink it, I would return you and the boys to your parents! It was a bluff but it worked!"

Tess gazed into Barrett's wild eyes, suddenly wondering if he was not only mean but mad as well? Finally, she shook her head, "Why not rescue us? You'd be acclaimed as a hero all across the country!"

"Don't be absurd," he laughed, "that would please your father too much! Of course, your grandmother—quite literally—would rather die than to have you three rescued. I was watching her sipping from the first bottle when I heard Shad burst into the parlor. He was so worried about the boys. Naturally, I volunteered to come here straight away so I could watch over you—then capture you! It worked out even better than I thought it would." He gave a loud sigh adding, "Can't tell you how good it feels to finally have everything falling into place. All it took to be rid of my nemesis was an ultimatum and a farewell gift. And now I have you again. Yes, everything is going according to plan."

"But if this was all my grandmother's idea and she's gone now, then you're free of her threats! Just tell me where the boys are and you can ride away. You must know that all this could end as badly for you as you as it will for us. You don't have to finish what she started!"

"Ah, my sweet," he mocked, "it pains me that my own fiancé knows me so little. Your dear grandmother might have been the instigator of all this. But I continue on for my own reasons. I thought you knew how much I liked a challenge!"

Barrett stepped closer to Tess, with one hand he pressed the gun to her stomach, while his other hand slipped around her neck and pulled her into his kiss. She struggled until he finally released her. Glaring at him only made him grin. His expression was terrifying, she'd never imagined that he could be like this.

Scoffing he added, "Obviously, it's not you that challenges me, Tess. You see the powerful Tytus Grainger and I have been playing cat and mouse. When you agreed to elope with me—I won! When you left with him last January to come home—he won. Then when you left the ranch to come with me to Paris—I thought I had won the final match. But now, here we are again and Tytus Grainger thinks he has the upper hand, that he's the cat, that he's winning! But I'm going to prove to him that T. Barrett Tulane is not a man to be taken lightly. You didn't really think I'd let him get away with it, did you? Treating a man of my standing like hired help! He enjoyed humiliating me, insisting I clean barns and mix with the local riff-raff. But all the while, I was playing a part, luring you both into my trap. Now, the tables have turned. Your father will spend every penny he has, frantically searching for his children. In a month or so, he will hear that I've returned to New York. He will come to me for answers—threatening me at first—then he will beg me to help him. Of course, I will tell him simply that, I was a victim too, that we were put on four separate ships in Galveston. I escaped when it reached the New York harbor, but have no way of knowing where you and your brothers went. Naturally, your father won't believe me—but he'll find no proof otherwise. The entire Grainger fortune will be dispersed all over the world while he searches for his brats. Meanwhile, I will play the part of a man bereft over the loss of both his mother and fiancé! Next year's debutantes will fawn over me as never before!

"My Papa will find the proof of your deception and he will see you hang!"

"No, he won't, Tess, because my wealth and power will be growing while his dwindles away. As I said, I was young and foolish to give in to blackmail— I'll never do it again. I don't liked people telling me what to do, so I just remove those who stand in my way. First my father, then mother and today the infamous L.W.! All it took was a bullet, a telegram and two little blue bottles— and now all three are gone!" Barrett raised his chin adding, "And should your father become too much of a nuisance he'll be dealt with too. I'm the wealthiest man in New York, perhaps the nation! I can do anything Tess, no one can touch me, not even your God!"

Tess shrank back from Barrett; his egotism was horrifying. Then memories of their time spent together began filling her thoughts. He had forced his kiss on her and though she'd tried to fight him off, the contact had triggered an onslaught of remembrances. What stood out most was his puffed-up condescension. And now, he had arrogantly challenged God! Shaking her head, she groaned, "Listen, do whatever you like with me but the boys are so young, just let them go...please!"

"You were a lot more interesting when you were selfish, Tess," he scoffed. "In fact, your love for your brothers it wildly annoying." He took Tess's chin in his hands and glared down his nose at her. "For once, I'm glad that you wore your quaint little riding skirt. Now let's get saddled up and we can be on our way." With that said, Barrett grabbed her arm and dragged her to the barn.

⚔

Tanner sat on the highest ridge overlooking the entrance to the Stubborn Scotsman ranch. Staring through the brass spy glass he methodically quartered the expanse of pastures, trees and foothills—in every direction. The spot where Barrett said his father had been ambushed was void of any kind of tracks. There was no evidence that anything had happened there. He blew out a frustrated groan, "If Pa's horse was shot out from under him, where is it? You don't just move a thousand-pound horse in a few minutes—and why would you bother?"

If there were other men and horses in the area, his stallion would have been alerted to their presence. But the animal was only interested in nibbling the leaves off a nearby bush. Tanner suddenly felt the hairs on the back of his neck prickle and he turned the glass back towards the ranch. He spotted a feathery dust trail heading east, away from McGee's barn. He followed the trail with his glass and saw two riders. Bluejay's coat made her as unmistakable as did the golden hair of her rider. "What—I don't believe it. He took her out for a ride—that fool!" he hissed. "He can't protect Tess out in the open like that." Then he adjusted the glass and saw that Barrett was leading Bluejay and although it was too far to see clearly, it looked like Tess's hands might be tied to the saddle horn. "He tricked me. I knew I shouldn't leave her," he groaned. "That scoundrel is the enemy after all. Father in heaven, I fear for Pa, Tess and the boys. They're all in trouble! Please God, protect them and tell me what to do? Lord…I need help!"

As Tanner was riding down the hill he saw two men on horseback following a buggy driven by a woman. Spurring his mount, he caught up with them just as they rode under the Stubborn Scotsman archway. One man was a tall black man, the other, Tanner recognized as McGee's foreman.

"Dallas," he called, "wait, I need to speak with you," not knowing who the man and woman with him were, he added, "in private, please." They trotted a few paces away, and keeping his voice low Tanner said, "I've done something stupid and things have gotten worse! Barrett has taken Tess. I just saw them through my spy glass. He was leading her horse and they were heading east. I have a feeling he may be meeting up with whoever has the boys."

Dallas frowned, "Of all the—why did you leave her alone with him?"

Tanner shook his head and groaned, "Tulane came storming in and told me that he and Pa had been ambushed, right here at the ranch entrance. He said that Pa's horse got shot out from under him, but he managed to get to cover

217

then he told Barrett to come for me and bring help. All the ranch hands were gone and I knew Tulane would be of no use in a gun fight. I knew something was wrong when I got out here. There's no dead horse, no blood, no spent cartridges, no sign of other riders or of my father. Then I saw Barrett leading Tess away. That scoundrel is in league with the enemy, everything he's said has been a lie!" Tanner sucked in a breath, panic wouldn't do any of them any good but he was feeling desperate. "I have to go after Tess, but if Barrett sees me, I'm afraid of what he might do. And...I've got to find my father! He may be somewhere around here bleeding to death! I need help but nearly everyone is scattered to the winds looking for the boys."

"Mister, help is only part of what you need!" It was a powerful and distinguished looking black man who spoke as he rode closer, adding, "We need a plan—and the good Lord himself—to help us carry it out. You were wise not to ride after Tulane. If he sees you, he might decide to kill those boys and the girl too!" Holding his hand out to Tanner he said, "Samuel Zackery, Pinkerton agent. Sorry for eavesdropping—but it's part of the job."

Tanner gave a sigh of relief, "I've heard of the Pinkerton National Detective Agency. Your agents are well respected back East. I'm glad you're here!" After introducing himself, Tanner nodded to the woman in the buggy, "And who is that?"

"Come over here," Sam motioned as he led the men back to Emily, "this is Missus Tulane—Barrett's mother." When Tanner frowned at her warily, Sam quickly added, "It's all right, she can be trusted. Her son has been keeping her a prisoner in her own home since they returned to New York. The day Barrett arrived in town, he telegraphed the order to have her killed. Fortunately, another agent had already found a way into the mansion and rescued her. I went to meet her in Denver and we both just came in on this morning's train. When we heard the Grainger boys were missing, she feared her son might be to blame and insisted on coming out here. She says she'll do anything to help and I believe her."

Emily pulled the veil from her head, "Forgive me gentlemen, but I've been listening too, and if Tess is with my son, she is in terrible danger! I'm ashamed to say it but—I know now that he's capable of anything. I've pretended and made excuses for him for far too long. The truth is, my son is ruthless and smart. He has only one weakness that I know of; he views nearly everything as a game. Tess and the boys are safe until the thrill of hiding them is no longer a challenge. If he recognizes anyone as a potential rescuer—he will—end the game." Emily's chin quivered as she stared at the ground, then added sadly, "You see, if he can't win, then he'll make sure that no one does." Looking up at the Pinkerton agent she added, "You're right, we need a plan and for God to help us carry it out!"

Tanner groaned, "Yes and we need more than just the four of us, but finding help won't be easy. Nearly everyone, ranch hands and townsfolk alike, are all out looking for the boys."

At the sound of approaching hoof beats, they all turned to see three riders coming towards them. They needed an army but seven was better than four. Tytus and Augusta were in the lead and to Tanner's great relief, his father rode between them, a blood-stained bandage on his head.

Seeing his son's concern, Shad quickly explained that Barrett had cold-cocked him in the Bar 61 barn. The Graingers had found him, and now except for a bit of a headache, he was fine! Tanner ground his teeth for a moment. When he'd finally gotten his anger under control, he quickly explained to his father and the Graingers what else Barrett had done. Then he turned to Ty and Augusta, "I'm so sorry, it's because of my foolishness that Tess is now in danger as well as the boys."

Sam placed his large hand on Tanner's shoulder, "Don't be too hard on yourself, Tulane is a master of deceit. Now everyone, try to think of any places that the ranch hands and townsfolk don't know about or might have been abandoned!" Dallas sighed, "I told all our hands to scout North and South," he grunted, "they've split up in twos from Denver to Pueblo."

Tytus nodded his thanks to Dallas, "That's good—all my men are concentrating on the stage and railway lines." Then he turned to Sam, "Abandoned places—huh?"

Augusta frowned for a moment, then she cried out, "Yes! I think I know where they might be!" When all eyes turned to her she explained, "While we were riding here I looked over to make sure Shad was all right and I saw something odd. It might not mean anything but there was a wispy, yellowish dust coming from the east, near the old Trading Post."

Dallas frowned and scratched his chin, "Never knew there was a Trading Post out that-a-way. But with all the men out looking for the boys, a wisp of dust, that don't tell us much."

"Actually, if it had a yellow cast to it, it tells us a lot!" Ty smiled as he grabbed Augusta's hand. "Thank God for your tender heart and sharp eyes!" Turning to the others he explained, "You see there used to be a Trading Post due east from here but now it's mostly hidden behind scrub oak. It was abandoned twenty years ago when a freight wagon took shelter there and was blown over in a bad storm. It was filled with salt and sulfur. The whole load seeped into the ground and tainted the well water. The owner gave up right then and moved away. I always know if someone has ridden through that area because of the swirls of fine yellowish dust. It's just east of the Scotsman ranch and that's the direction Tanner saw Barrett leading Tess. We've all assumed they'd run either north or south, heading to Denver or Pueblo. Now that I think on it... the Trading Post would be a perfect place to meet up. And there'd be fewer chances of running into anyone along the way. Especially if they simply continued East towards Kansas."

All right, that's probably where they are—what are we waiting for—let's go!" Augusta huffed, as she reined her horse around, then saw that everyone was just staring at her. Glaring at Ty, she chided, "They've got our children, we've got to hurry!"

"No, Augusta, not yet," Emily pleaded, "I know it's killing you to have your children in danger. But we must plan this out very carefully. Remember who you're dealing with—he mustn't for a moment think he's losing this game!"

Sam locked eyes with Augusta, "We all have to try to stay calm and I hope you will trust me. I have a great deal of experience with this sort of thing." Then he turned towards Tytus, "Tell me everything you can remember about that Trading Post, especially, if there is a secret way out? That wouldn't be unusual, they often had some kind if hidey-hole or escape route, in case of robbers or Indian attacks!" While Ty was thinking, Sam turned to Emily and Augusta, "I just thought of another man that can help us. And ladies—I hope you're both good actresses, because what I need you to do is..."

⚜

Tess stared down at the ropes that were cutting into her wrists. *This just can't be happening. After getting off the train and all that followed, how did I allow this haughty dude to get the upper hand? My memories, especially concerning Barrett and even his mother are coming into focus. I even remember what that awful letter said, that I would never be seen or heard from again. Is that the fate that awaits not only me but Joshua and Caleb as well? Oh Lord, I have no idea what to do but nothing is impossible for You.* When Barrett reined to a stop she called out, "Isn't there anything I can do to change your mind?" Tess heard his scornful chuckle before he turned to face her, "You do have a problem, don't you, my sweet. You have nothing to bargain with, your father's money means nothing to me and you and your brothers mean even less!" he sneered. "McKenna, your newest conquest, sure left you in a hurry today—didn't he? Thought he might give me a fight. His father went down easy too!"

Tess's heart plummeted, "You—killed—Shad?"

"I'm not sure. As it turned out, both McKennas were a disappointment, I had expected more from them. Don't know why, they're nothing but a couple of hillbillies. I have heard some Pinkerton agents are on my trail—perhaps they'll be more of a challenge!" His eyes became oddly bright as he added, "Still, I'm betting people will die today, my darling. Want to make a wager on who it will be?"

Tess was too stunned to make a response. Just then the weathered old door to the Trading Post scraped across the wooden porch and Keefer stepped outside. "Ah well, wonder of wonders, ya managed to get the girl!" he chuckled as he lifted his derby hat in mock salute, "her brothers are inside." Pointing to a stand of scrub oaks, he grunted, "You go fetch our horses, they're tied up in those bushes over yonder while I get the boys. We best shake a leg, Salvador ain't the kind of man to be kept waitin'." He stopped and gazed up at Tess, enjoying a long appreciative perusal, then said, "I was feeling sorry fer Sal, havin' to deal with those brothers of yours, but now that you've joined us, I envy him the task."

Tess frowned, "Are my brothers all right?"

"I've not laid a hand on them—not yet anyway. They foolishly came to meet me ridin' bareback. They'll be mighty sore by the time they reach Mexico but that's their worry—not mine!" Assuming Barrett was getting the horses, he stepped closer, "Would ya be wantin' to stretch yer legs a bit pretty girl? We've a long ride ahead of us and we won't be worryin' about yer comfort once we're on our way."

Tess wasn't sure what to do, the only thought that came to her was that maybe she could get this little man on her side. She gazed down at him and nodded, "Yes, thank you. I need to use the necessary and if that well has water in it, I could sure use a drink." As he reached up to untie her, she asked, "Are you really taking us all the way to Mexico?"

Barrett suddenly rode his horse between Keefer and Tess, "I'll take care of the lady," he grumbled. "You get the horses." Then he grabbed Tess's chin, and covered her mouth with his. She wanted to get out of his reach, but with her hands still tied to the saddle horn, she couldn't move far enough away. Thinking of only one thing to do, she lifted her booted foot from the stirrup, planted it against Barrett's side and shoved him away as hard as she could. Fury shot from his eyes and he raised his arm to slap her, but when she dodged his blow and nearly fell from the saddle, he laughed instead.

"You little minx," he snorted, "don't try to be friends with Keefer. He has no friends. And don't make me mad, Tess," his gaze included the little man in the derby hat, adding, "or you either Keefer. Neither one of you are in my league!"

A pistol suddenly appeared in Keefer's hand, he cocked it as smoothly as a whisper and pointed it in Barrett's face, "I hope to shout I'm not in your— league—bucko! I begrudgingly take orders from Vinnie. But I'll take none from the likes of you. I'll be givin' the orders from now on. So—lad, go fetch the horses—and be quick about it!"

Barrett glared down at the cocked pistol for a moment, then grumbled a curse and rode away. As she watched him go, Tess muttered under her breath, "Big headed goat!" When Keefer chuckled as he put his pistol away, she added, "That's the title my brothers gave him. Those boys saw him for what he was— better than I ever did!"

"Well now, that could be, but know this you pretty thing," Keefer said as he stepped closer. "That big headed goat was right. I ain't yer friend and never will be. I answer only to Vinnie and what she's ordered, will be done. There'll be no reprieve, not for you nor none o' yer kin."

"What is to become of me and my brothers?" Tess asked. "What has my grandmother planned for us?"

Flynn tipped his hat to the side and grinned as he began to untie her hands, "Tis quite a plan she's concocted for you three! We're to ride for an hour East then go South till we meet Salvador, he's a Mexican trader. When Tulane bungled yer trip to Paris...twice over...Vinnie somehow managed to shift the plan a bit. The trader was always to take the boys but now he'll take you too!"

"And—what is the plan for—for me and the boys?' Tess stammered.

"That Vinny, she's a clever one! She had me tell Salvador to bring some decoys. He's bringing two lads but then I told him to bring a blonde girl along too—just in case we found ya. While he takes you and the twins south to Mexico, I'll head West with the other three, then disappear! The folks out looking for ya won't know which trail is true and which is false! Meanwhile,

Barrett heads for Galveston, he'll leave a few more false trails then board a ship to New York. Yer right, he is a big-headed fool...thinks his story is so good he can go back to his estate and fancy life! Wants to hide in plain sight and tweak yer father's nose. Says Vinny never got caught and neither will he, and if he does, he's too rich to be hung." Keefer scoffed then shook his head, "Vinnie never got caught 'cause she never did her own dirty work. Tulane ain't in Vinny's league, that's for sure. She's forgotten more about trickery and deceit than a whelp like Tulane could learn in a hundred years!"

Tess, considered telling his little man that Barrett may have already killed her grandmother? Deciding against it, she gave a loud sigh as she swung down from her saddle, then asked, "What kind of grandmother wants to hurt her own family?"

Keefer shrugged, "Don't know and don't care. But ya best hurry and get yerself a drink of water and use the privy." Just before she could walk away Keefer grabbed her arm so roughly she winced, "Wait now, ya need to know what I told yer brothers. Give me any trouble—any trouble a'tall, and I'll shoot one o' them before I shoot you. Ya understand me?"

Tess glared at him as she yanked her arm free, "Perfectly!"

As she slowly walked towards the well, her eyes were on the dilapidated building where her brothers were being held. She dared not do anything to help them, assuming she could think of something. Of course, now just when she needed to be clever, her mind was as empty as... Just then she scowled down into the well, picked up a rock and dropped it. When she heard a dry thud instead of a splash, she finished her thought. Her mind was as empty as this well. When she turned to glare at Keefer, she found him right behind her. He grinned as he handed her a canteen. Tess was careful to wipe it clean before she took a few sips.

Just then she heard the squeak of harness chains. Her gaze followed the sound up the hill and she saw two women driving a buggy towards them. Tess nearly choked when she realized that one of the women was her own mother. Her dress was torn and covered in dirt and there was a large bruise on her cheek. Tess's heart plummeted as a trembling began in the pit of her stomach. It became worse when she saw the rough looking black man riding beside the buggy. He was powerfully built, and looked like he was strong enough and mean enough to break any other man in two. He was dressed all in browns, from his leather chaps and vest, to the large slouch hat on his head. He looked like he wanted to blend in where ever he went. Nothing on him or his horse reflected light, unlike Barrett, there were no shining conchos and even the buckles on his bridle and the shanks on his bit had been blackened. He wore a double brace of pistols and a huge knife was in a scabbard tied to his belt. If ever someone looked like an outlaw—this was the man! She'd been afraid of Keefer and Barrett, but the leviathan who was riding towards them now, would laugh at puny men like them. Tess's hopes of being rescued seemed to vanish before her eyes! Now they had Mama and her children—all the Graingers but Papa—and her heart couldn't bear to think of where he might be.

"Well now," Keefer sneered, "if it ain't the grand lady herself. Looks like she's brought along the daughter she's always hated and...a body guard no less! I wondered if she could stay away this time. Especially when the final card was being played. She's come to savor her revenge, I warrant."

"Oh no!" Tess groaned. "That other woman—is that my grandmother?"

Keefer chuckled at Tess's fear, then his attention was drawn to the buggy. Augusta had jumped out and tried to run. Her hands were tied and she stumbled as she ran. It was a futile attempt, for an instant later, the black man spurred his horse and to Tess's horror he threw a rope around her mother's shoulders. He said something to the woman in the buggy, then led Augusta down the hill as if she were a dog on a leash. Meanwhile her grandmother sat in the buggy like a general overseeing a battle.

Tess tried to run to her mother, but Keefer grabbed her arm, "O' no, pretty girl, you stay here with me. And don't try to be a heroine in this little melodrama, 'cause if you do, I'll shoot one of your brothers and then your mama. And ya won't be likin' what I do with you after that!"

When Barrett saw that Lavenia was in the buggy, he silently shielded himself between the boy's horses. He whispered a string of curses as he tried to make sense of what was happening. *L.W. must stand for lying witch. So, she didn't drink those vials of Laudanum after all. She's probably not even sick. That black man, he's a hired gun or bounty hunter—I'm sure of it. She's probably paying him a bonus to kill me, or they'll sell me as a slave in Mexico along with the Graingers!*

As the fierce looking man on the horse led Augusta into the yard he called out, "Boss lady wants to change things a bit, wants to talk to both of ya!

Still holding Tess's arm, Keefer stepped forward and lifted his chin in the air, "I take orders from no one but Vinnie—and well she knows it!"

The big man glared down at Keefer, "If I wanted to give ya an order—that's just what I'd do," the stranger growled, his voice deep and harsh. Just then

Augusta tried to move closer to Tess and he frowned and yanked on the rope, forcing her to take two steps back as he added, "But for now, Miz Wrenford's givin' the orders, and she ain't comin' down here, her lungs can't abide the fine dust. Said you wouldn't take to a change in plan, *unless she told ya herself*," he sneered. "So, my orders are to guard her—dear family, while you and Tulane find out what she wants to do next. She won't tell me nothin', I'm just her hired gun."

Just then Barret felt a fury growing inside him. *If Augusta is here, all battered and bruised, then where is her bully of a husband?* He stepped out from behind his horse, "And who do you think you are? More importantly..." he hissed as his face turned into a scowl, "where is Tytus Grainger?"

Straightening in the saddle the man glared down his nose at Barrett, as if he were something to be scraped off his boot, "I've had lots o' names," he mumbled, "some folks call me Blade."

Keefer let out a slow whistle, "Best mind yer manners, Tulane. I've seen this man before! Yer no match for the likes o' him. He's as deadly with that big knife he carries, as a good gunslinger is with a pistol, and he's faster than most with them too! As fer the whereabouts o' Tytus Grainger? I'm thinkin' if Blade has his woman, then that man is dead or on his way there. That right, mister?"

Blade didn't even spare another glance for Barrett. Instead his dark eyes centered on Keefer, as one side of his mouth gave a slight uptick, then he grunted, "What do you think?"

Barrett ignored Tess's gasp at the news of her father's death, for he was trembling with rage over hearing it himself. He had never wanted anything as badly as he wanted to best Tytus Grainger. His eyes grew wild as he glared up at Blade, "Grainger was mine to deal with—he was mine!" He stood there for a long while as he fought to regain his self-control. Finally, he turned to Keefer, "All right, I'll go see what the old lady wants."

Keefer shook his head and spat on the ground, "Listen here boy! If I'll be takin' no orders from a man like Blade, you can be sure I'll take none from an arrogant cur like you. Ya can stay here or go with me but I'll be hearin' what Vinnie has to say—first hand."

Barrett couldn't allow Keefer to speak to Lavenia. She'd tell the little snitch how he had given her two bottles of Laudanum and told her to take it or he'd rescue the children himself. Then he glanced at Blade. Would she have told him about it? Probably not, that wasn't her way, but he could guess at the old witch's change of plan. Blade was probably there to help Keefer hand him over to Salvador, along with Tess and the boys. The more he thought about it the more it sounded like something that would delight and amuse the old bat. The stakes he was playing had suddenly gotten much too high. Barrett chewed on his lip as he glanced around, thinking of how he could use Tess as a shield and make a run for it. Suddenly, they heard a loud crash coming from inside the trading post.

"Those confounded lads!" Keefer bellowed, as he drew his gun, ran across the yard then jumped onto the porch. The moment he burst through the door, it slammed shut behind him. Then came the raucous sounds of landed punches, cursing and furniture breaking. It was quite a hullabaloo coming from that Trading Post. It made a Saturday night brawl sound like a tea party in comparison. Then suddenly, two shots were fired and everything fell silent.

It sounded like the guns had been triggered at the exact same moment. One was the loud boom that came from the hogleg, Keefer had pulled before running inside. The other, both Tess and Augusta recognized as the sound of Ty's modified colt revolver. Tess sent a questioning glance at her mother. Augusta's slight nod confirmed that yes, her father was inside the trading post. Still, their hearts plummeted for they each knew that it was very likely that someone in there was wounded or dead!

When no other sounds came from the building Augusta became desperate to know what had just happened. The past month of worry mixed with her mother's brow-beatings had worn her down and she couldn't help but fear the worst. This was just too much like the day Timothy had been killed. She had never been the type for rash behavior, but just then, she was unable to think if her next actions were wise or foolish. She released her hold on the ropes that made it look like her hands were tied, then shrugged the lariat off her shoulders. Glancing back at Tess she ordered, "You stay here!" Then she lifted her skirts and ran towards the trading post.

"No—don't go in there!" Blade bellowed as he spurred his horse forward trying to block her path. Nearly mad with worry, Augusta dodged around his horse and hurried past him.

Barrett grinned, this was just the confusion he had hoped for, he leapt into his saddle and before Tess knew what was happening, he grabbed her and tossed her across his lap. "Fight me and I'll break your neck!" he warned as he sunk his spurs into his horse's sides. As they rode away, he shot a volley of bullets into the air, spooking all the other horses. Seconds later, Tess could see only the prairie grasses becoming a golden blur as they streaked across the pasture at a dead run!

Tytus ran out of the trading post and nearly knocked Augusta to the ground. Overwhelmed by panic and rage, he brought his gun up to aim at Barrett's back, even though he knew he couldn't risk the shot. His arm fell and he holstered his gun just as Blade galloped past him. Spinning around, he desperately searched for a mount but all the horses had scattered. Then in the distance, he saw the appaloosa mare trotting up the hill and called out, "Bluejay come!" Although the mare stopped. she was no longer as trusting as before. It took long minutes and a patience he certainly didn't feel as he coaxed her closer. When Ty finally swung into the saddle, he locked eyes with Augusta, "We'll get her! You and Emily stay with the boys. And keep your guns close and your wits about you! Barrett may have had other accomplices."

At the sound of pounding hoof beats just behind him Barrett glanced back to see Blade riding hard. "Well now—things are finally getting a little lively, Tess!" he shouted. "I think that bounty hunter might just be after both of us. Think we'll live, darling? I'm still wagering that I'll live longer than you." he laughed.

Chancing another quick glance back, Barrett not only saw the bounty hunter right behind him, but in the far distance he saw Tytus Grainger as well! *So, Grainger is alive, is he? I had hoped to out-wit that man, but since that's no longer possible... I can still bring him down! All I need to do is lessen the odds against me. Otherwise there's no way I can win this!* Looking back over his shoulder he pulled his pistol and fired at Blade, cursing when the shot went wild. His heart hammered inside his chest as he pulled the trigger over and over until he'd emptied his gun. Not one bullet had even gotten close, and when he saw Blade grinning, he nearly threw the gun at him. Instead, he forced himself to holster it, then let loose a string of curses as he spurred the gelding. There were two very lethal men behind him, both wanting his blood, and he had foolishly wasted his bullets. There were plenty more in his saddlebag, but he'd have to get to cover and stall them until he could reload. He had always liked a challenge but he was quickly losing control of this one. Barrett's eyes grew wild as he shouted. "At least that bounty hunter and your father are making things interesting, Tess. That's more than you've ever done."

Though he feigned confidence, nothing was going as Barrett had intended. The gelding was struggling to keep on running with two riders on his back.

Barrett spurred his horse with every stride, all the while watching for just the right moment to throw Tess from the saddle. They weren't shooting at him because of her. She was his protection but he needed to be rid of her added weight. Barrett grinned when he spotted a narrow path between two large boulders about a hundred yards ahead. He would shove Tess from the saddle just before he got to them. When the men stopped to see about her, he could take cover behind the boulders and reload his gun. Once he was in position, Tess, along with her rescuers would make easy targets. Leaning over her body, Barrett yelled, "We'll soon be parting company sweetheart, I'm ending our engagement. Sorry about Paris," he laughed, even as he buried his spurs deeper into the gelding's sides. The poor animal squealed in pain then lunged forward. His hooves thundered under Tess's ears, the sound of his loud wheezing gasps for air were matching every stride.

ᐳᐸ

Tanner sat on the hill watching everything through his spyglass. All the while praying harder than he had ever prayed. Anything could happen down there! The plan began with Augusta and Blade creating a diversion. It was intended to draw Barrett's and any of his cohort's attention, away from the trading post. This would allow Ty to sneak inside through the back tunnel, rescue the boys and stay with them. What happened next depended entirely on Barrett. Augusta had made certain that her mother had nothing that could harm her family. Lavenia had no Laudanum in her possession, of that she was sure. The only person that could have given it to her was Barrett and he had been seen leaving the courtyard that morning. The question was, had she asked him for it, perhaps in one of her telegrams? Or had he brought it and insisted that she take it, possibly turning some kind of blackmail back onto Lavenia? Still, this charade they were acting out allowed for both possibilities. If she had asked for the Laudanum, then Barrett would not object to riding up to see her with Keefer. In that scenario, Blade would get the drop on them while Augusta rushed Tess into the safety of the trading post. On the other hand, if Barrett had somehow coerced Lavenia into taking the Laudanum—but then she didn't take it—he might be afraid to face her. Especially with a man like Blade there to back up any orders she might give. They all believed that if Barrett became afraid for himself—he would run!

The entire plan teetered on turning Barrett's focus away from hurting Tess and the boys and onto saving himself! After all, what was the challenge in hiding children from their parents when the mother was one of your captives and the father was presumed dead? At that point, they all hoped that he'd forget about the Graingers, and focus on his own escape!

The second part of their plan was to block his way in every direction. Emily, wearing Lavenia's favorite dress with the matching oversized hat, bravely sat in the buggy on the trail leading South. Even though she might be facing her own son, she had insisted on being armed with a pistol and a rifle. Still, with her looking like Lavenia, they hoped Barrett would avoid her at all costs. Dallas blocked the West trail, but they doubted Barrett would go that way, due to the dozens of people out searching for the boys from Pueblo to Denver. Shad took the North trail, while Tanner positioned himself on a hill just East of the Trading Post. That was the most likely route of escape and that's why he'd insisted on being there. The first plan was to capture them all at the trading post. But if things went awry, they all believed stopping him would fall to one or both of the McKennas.

Tanner had not taken his eyes from the scene as he saw it play out before him. At first everyone was calm, and he'd blown out a nervous breath even as he remembered the Pinkerton agent's warning, "Stay on your toes for even the best of plans can fall apart!" Suddenly, that's just what happened, and Tanner clenched his jaw and his knuckles turned white as he gripped the spyglass. It was indescribable agony to watch helplessly as that cur Barrett, tossed Tess over the saddle and raced away. All he could do was pray for her safety, even as they rode within rifle range. He didn't dare shoot, he could do nothing but grind his teeth in rage. He had never felt such a fury burning within him. He lifted his hat, wiped the sweat from his brow with his sleeve and groaned as he resettled it.

"That horse is getting awfully tired. If it goes down hard, it could very well kill Tess! Maybe if I shoot into the ground, far enough in front of him but not too far, it will slow him down. Then it'll be up to that agent to get to her in time." Tanner breathed a prayer, as he lifted his rifle and aimed ahead of the racing horse. Sweat trickled into his eyes and he quickly cleared it away with his shirt sleeve. Once again, he aimed, added a bit more space for good measure, then slowly squeezed the trigger.

Barrett cursed as a small explosion of dirt burst about ten feet in front of his hard-running horse. The gelding jerked and shortened his stride. A second later came the report of a rifle. Barrett couldn't allow the animal to slow, he was desperate to get behind those boulders. They were his only chance to reload and make a fight! Suddenly, he was riding through clouds of dirt as one explosion after another, burst in front of him. Each time his horse slowed a bit. Still, Barret beat and spurred his mount, forcing him to keep going.

Although Tess still couldn't remember falling down a mountain, she decided that this had to be worse. She was being bounced, battered and bruised everywhere. And yet, she knew if the horse lost his footing just now, all three of them would be injured, if not killed. She had to stop this horse but her side was jammed against the saddle horn and she was being tossed about like laundry in the wind. If she could just grab hold of one rein, she might be able to at least slow the gelding. It was a risky move, for if she pulled too hard, she would be the cause of the horse flipping. Then there would be a tangle of thrashing legs and hooves, not to mention the probability of a thousand-pound horse landing on top of them. Knowing the dangers, she cautiously made a number of failed attempts. At long last, she managed to catch one rein in her right hand. As gently as possible, she pulled straight back, released it slightly then pulled again. Barrett cursed as he tried to wrestle the rein from her hand. The horse was exhausted but also frightened and confused. He slowed to a canter then a trot. When Barrett continued to beat and spur him, the poor animal became frantic! He crow-hopped and side-stepped until finally he rose up on his hind legs. Barrett was so intent on gaining control of the horse that he didn't even notice when Blade caught up with them. Terrified, the horse reared higher and higher, he twisted in the air, then fell over backwards. Just as he did, Blade reached out and snatched Tess from the horse's back, moments before his body slammed to the ground!

Tess felt herself being half carried, half dragged away. Her eyes grew wide with fear as she looked up into the dark face of the bounty hunter. Blade gave her a stern looking over, then simply sat her on the ground, facing away from where Barrett and the horse had fallen, then he hurried away. She didn't know why Barrett had run but she did know that he had emptied his gun at this man. Hunching over she waited for the fight that was bound to ensue, but heard only the wheezing of the horse's lungs as he sucked in great gulps of air. Turning stiffly, she watched as the horse got to his feet, then gasped when she saw Barrett. He was lying in the sand; his body twisted in a crumpled heap.

"Don't look Miss," Blade warned, "at least this was quicker than hanging. And now he won't be hurtin' anyone ever again."

Tess was surprise by the sound of the man's deep voice. Something about it seemed familiar—almost comforting. Still, she said nothing. Although he had made no threats or demands, she wasn't sure what he meant to do with her. Glancing over her shoulder she watched as he laid Barrett's body out in a more dignified pose. Then he took the slicker from his saddle and draped it over the still form.

After studying this man for a while, Tess finally spoke, "Thank you! I might be lying there too if you hadn't saved me from that fall. But now I'm suddenly wondering if you are a bounty hunter? I think it's more likely that you're a sheriff or marshal. Somehow, I don't think you're in league with my grandmother—are you?"

He smiled and Tess was surprised how his countenance changed. He didn't seem frightening at all anymore.

"No ma'am, I only pretended to work for your grandma," he stated emphatically. "Most of the time, I'm Samuel Zackery—Pinkerton agent. To be completely honest though, my work causes me to be many people. Sometimes, *I am* a Bounty Hunter called, Blade."

When Tess's eyes grew wide, his expression became tender, "I wish we could have met under less traumatic circumstances but I can't stand here and not tell you one more thing. I was born Samuel Grainger. And you, Tessie May, are named in part after my Mama, Nattie May!"

Tess shook her head in wonder as she studied the man before her, "Your smile—your voice—you're Joseph's son! Of all people to come to my rescue. We all prayed that our dear Joseph would find you someday. But…we thought you were dead."

Sam gave a slight chuckle, "Well, I'm happy to be alive and happy to be of help today. But it wasn't just me that came to your rescue." Pointing to the spot where Tanner had been shooting, he added, "If it weren't for that young man up there and his quick thinkin' and good shootin', I fear I might not have reached you in time." Glancing around he added, "'Course it wasn't just him and me, all of your rescuers will be here in a minute!"

Suddenly they were surrounded by the sound of running horses, coming from every direction. Tess turned to see her papa sliding to a stop on Bluejay, and in the distance came Caleb and Joshua riding their horses bareback. From the North came Shad, thundering towards her. Then her heart jumped, when she saw Tanner on his powerful stallion, Sailor. They were sliding down an impossibly steep hill one minute, then racing towards her the next. Tess's chin began to quiver when she saw her own sweet mama driving the buggy and instantly recognized that the woman sitting next to her, wasn't her grandmother at all, but Emily Tulane! Even Barrett's own mother had come to help. Tess bit her lip, she loved them all—and—she owed them so much!

It wasn't long before all five of the Graingers were tangled together, in an embrace of laughter and tears of relief. When Tess felt a gentle touch on her shoulder, she turned around and was instantly swept into Tanner's arms. He knew he had no right to intrude or to be so bold, but he just couldn't hold himself back a moment longer.

"Tess!" he groaned, "thank God you're safe!" Taking a moment, his eyes raced over her, searching for any signs of injury. "You just got over falling down a mountain and now this. You look all right—are you—all right? Truly?" he asked. "You had quite a ride!"

Tytus and Augusta exchanged glances as the young couple seemed to forget that anyone else was there.

Shad gazed at the slicker that covered the wealthy young aristocrat, T. Barrett Tulane. "It's such a shame, but it was bound to end this way. He had so much and could have done so much good with all he had. He's already reapin' what he's sown. Ain't nothin' we can do for him now."

Tess glanced again at the still form of the man who had planned to marry her and then leave her to a horrible fate. What seemed worse to her was that he had agreed to hurt her two young brothers as well. She hurried over and hugged Caleb and Joshua, and it was at that very moment, Tessie May Grainger finally remembered everything! Memories of her parents placing two babies in her arms and allowing her to rock them both for the first time. Then came other memories: laughter and songs around Christmas trees, her Papa putting her on her first pony, working beside her mother breaking in a new colt. Until that moment, bits and pieces of her memories had stubbornly remained in the shadows. But now, as she looked around and saw all the people that meant the most to her, everything came flooding back. And now, she was even more grateful that they were all safe.

The joyful reunion suddenly became somber when Tess saw Emily standing silently, gazing down at the still form of her dead son. Now it made sense why Blade, or more accurately, Sam, had thoughtfully laid the body out. It was to make, in some small measure, a mother's pain a bit less traumatic. Tess's heart went out to the poor woman. Emily had willingly played the part of the evil Lavenia Wrenford, so as to thwart her own son. Tess skirted around Barrett's body as she hurried towards her, "Oh Emily…I'm so sorry!" she cried. Glancing back at her brothers she asked sadly, "That other man—is he dead too?" When her brothers nodded, she covered her face with her hands. "Two men are dead because of me!"

"No, Sis—it was their fault!" Josh hissed.

"They chose their path," Cal added

"You both sound just like Papa, but I'm ashamed of the path *I chose*. If I hadn't been so willful. Cared only for my own desires for adventure and…" Tears spilled down her cheeks as she choked out, "I nearly got you boys killed. Nearly got us all killed! This all started with my arrogance while we were in New York. I put every one of you, everyone I love in danger!"

Tanner was suddenly at her side, gently taking her hand, "Please believe me Tess, I know the kind of men they were. It really didn't matter what you chose. It was your grandmother's and Barrett's plan to hurt you and your brothers, one way or another. Regardless of what you did or did not do, they would have kept on until they succeeded."

Emily squeezed Tess's hand, "Darlin' your grandmother wanted to destroy your family. But for Barrett's part in all of this…if anyone is to blame it's me. I always knew something wasn't quite right with that boy. Sadly, when Wes died, Barrett was all I had. So, I listened to what my heart was telling me, when I should have listened to my head. That mistake nearly cost my life as well as yours and the boys. He would have had his own mother killed for full control of the estate!" Emily's chin quivered and she shook her head, adding, "That and maybe to stop me from embarrassing him. I'd be dead now but for the Pinkertons. My son only loved two things, himself and besting someone in a challenge. When you listened to your father and left New York, then later when you got off the train like that…it intrigued him. It was a challenge. You having the courage to do those two things…quite probably bought us the time we needed to figure this out. When the final danger arrived, God brought us all together. He knew we needed Him and we needed each other—we couldn't do it alone!"

Just then Tanner put his arm around Tess's shoulders, "Now you can relax and let things get back to normal. And then maybe…you and I can…."

Tess shook her head and stepped away, "Remember what we talked about? I still feel the same way…about the courting fast! I'm finally remembering

Tess Grainger and God has some serious work to do on that girl. There are things she needs to learn and to make right! I need to find my own rock in the meadow—just like you did. I need to spend some time there, reading the word and listening to God. I still feel very strongly that I should take this time—at least until Christmas!"

Tanner nodded solemnly, "I'm very proud of you Tess. I can respect and honor that." He bent down and took her face in his hands and kissed her fore-head. After giving her a very chaste hug, he turned away. She wasn't sure but she thought she heard him whisper, "Just...don't forget me."

Chapter 20

Christmas with McGee

"Blessed is the man who remains steadfast under trial, for when he has stood the test he will receive the crown of life, which God has promised to those who love him." James 1:12

Emily smiled as she stepped into the beautifully decorated parlor of Tanner McGee's spacious home.   Evergreen boughs, garlands and wreaths all tied with red ribbons adorned the stair railings, doorways and mantelpieces.   The entire house smelled of roasted turkey, pine, cinnamon and cloves. Spotting McGee she impulsively hurried across the room, then bent over and kissed him on the cheek, "That's for using your chair!   You can get around a lot better now, can't you?"

The old man chuckled, "Aye, ye were right.   Tis a grand contraption! Shouldna' been so stubborn but that's m' way.   Why d' ye think I named m' ranch the Stubborn Scotsman?   Tis nae easy admittin' that I'm so old I can barely walk."   Running a swollen arthritic hand over the smooth mahogany arm rest, he added, "Ah, but what fine craftsmanship, it is.   I ken ya sent all the way to London for it—and I'm thankin' ye.   Tis far better than canes and crutches, I can tell ya that.   Yer as considerate, as ye are bonny, sweet lass."

Hands on her hips, Emily gave the man a sidelong glance, "And here I always thought it was the Irish that were full of blarney.   Now I know it's the Scots instead!   As for the chair—I was happy to do it."   Gazing around the room again she added, "You certainly know how to throw a fine Christmas party.   And you're cuttin' quite a handsome figure in yer McGee plaid tonight."

"Aye, I'm mighty fit for a dying man.   You've heard, n' doubt, that this Christmas party is also me wake!"   When Emily frowned, the old man grinned, "Now don't be vexed with me lassie.   A wake is where family and friends come from far and wide to celebrate the life of someone who ain't even there. What foolishness!   If I'm to be the center of attention—think I'll enjoy it a lot more—if I'm still breathin'—don't you!   Tonight, I want to celebrate our

Savior's birth, share happy memories and enjoy it all with the folks I've come to love like kin. Havin' yer wake while yer still alive makes all the sense in the world. Why miss out on the only fun part o' dyin'?"

"Tanner McGee," Emily chuckled, "you certainly are one of a kind—and more's the pity!"

⁓⧉⁓

Tess gazed around the room and sighed as the musicians began to tune up for the first dance. She was wearing a green dress that she'd worn before. It was pretty but definitely not ostentatious. Her curly blonde hair fell long and loose down her back with the sides pinned up and adorned with sprigs of holly.

Suddenly, Sig Rosenquist stepped in front of her, "Happy Christmas, Tessie May. Ya look like the Christmas angel again this year!"

"Thank you, Sig, and a Happy Christmas to you too," she said softly as she reached up and tapped the brass buttons on his coat, "you are looking very handsome in your uniform. Speaking of looking like an angel though, have you by chance noticed how lovely Sadie is tonight? Did you know that girl would save all her dances for you—if you'd just ask?"

Sig was a ruggedly handsome young man with reddish blonde hair and keen hazel eyes. He glanced at Sadie as she poured Emily and McGee a cup of punch. "Ja, well maybe she would." He shrugged then frowned at the floor as he seemed to study the shine on his boots. "I've always thought Sadie was a sweet girl, sure." Sig ran a hand over his face not wanting anyone to hear, "but you know...with that trouble she got into last year, I...OUCH!" he cried when Tess pinched his arm.

"Sigvar Rosenquist. Should Sadie be punished forever, just for trusting the wrong person? You know very well that she's been sweet on you since she was a little girl. The only reason she listened to that man's lies was because she'd given up on you ever noticing her. Sadie is loyal, kind and good! And...there has always been a tenderness in your eyes when you look at her. The trouble is that our mothers are best friends, and your sister and I are best friends. The women in your family have told you over and over that I'm the girl for you but—you know in your heart—they're wrong! Filly loves Sadie, too. She should have chosen her for you—not me! Oh Sig, I don't want to hurt your feelings because I'll always love you—but as a sister. Don't waste any more time on me. Sadie sincerely cares for you. If you would just think on it a while…you'd realize that you two would be perfect together." Giving Sig a playful shove, Tess added, "Now go ask that girl to dance before some other man recognizes what a treasure she is!"

Sig gave Tess a lop-sided grin then walked towards Sadie. A few other men had indeed gathered around to talk to the pretty brunette. However, when Sig stepped towards her with a bashful grin on his face, Sadie forgot there was anyone else in the room. Sig didn't say a word, he simply took the cup of punch from her hands and gave it to one of her admirers. Never taking his eyes from her, he pulled her into his arms and danced her away.

Just then Filly Rosenquist came to stand next to Tess and whispered, "I heard what you said." Then she turned to watch her brother and her dear friend Sadie seem to float around the room, never taking their eyes from each other. "Oh dear, how could I have been so blind?" Sighing, Filly put her arm around Tess's waist, "Alright, I admit that you are the better matchmaker! They do look perfect together—don't they?"

"They look content because they belong together," Tess added as she linked arms with her friend, "we'll always be sisters of the heart, Filly! But you and Sadie will make the very best sisters-in-law."

When Beck Hoffman, the blushing blacksmith, came and asked Filippa for a dance it was Copper who took the place next to Tess. "Merry Christmas Summer!" Copper laughed. "I can't help it. I fear we'll always think of you as our own sweet Summer. Hope you don't mind if Shad and I slip every now and again?"

Tess smiled, "I don't mind if you always call me Summer. In fact, I think the best part of Tess Grainger is Summer McKenna. You're family now, just like Uncle Quin and Aunt Mariah. Though the time I've known you has been brief, you McKennas have been the instruments God used to save my life both physically and spiritually. All three of you will always…always be dear to me!" Tess couldn't stop herself from gazing around the room, "Since you all have been staying with McGee these past few months, I assumed I would have seen Tanner by now. He isn't nervous about having the right clothes for the occasion, is he? I mean we all just come in what we can." When Copper's lips trembled and tears filled her eyes, Tess panicked, "What's wrong? He isn't sick or hurt, is he?"

"No…nothing like that. It's just that he thought he'd purchased the last good available ranch land in the district and yesterday, inexplicably the deal fell through. I hate it but he's decided to go back to Boston and work for Quin's company a few more years. He's realizing that he needs more money than he originally thought." Copper rung her hands, "It frightens me to think of him going out to sea again, but he makes twice as much money on a voyage and he's determined to buy his ranch as soon as possible." With downcast eyes she added, "He believes he has to have his ranch first—before he can settle down. Please pray for him Tess, I've never seen him so torn. He doesn't want to leave, but he feels that he must!" Glancing at the small watch pinned to her shoulder she frowned, "McGee asked him to go to town earlier, I thought for sure, he'd be back by now!"

"Excuse me, Miss Tess, may I have this dance?" The deep voice came from one of the Bar 61's newest wranglers. Tess's hand went to her throat. It would be impolite to refuse him but she had turned down every form of courting for the past few months. Her fast from all such encounters was to end tonight. But...there was only one man she wanted to dance with and he wasn't there!

Understanding came to Copper and so did an idea, "Tess, honey, would you mind if I stole this young man? Just for one dance!" Copper smiled up at the obviously startled cowboy and said, "I hate to intrude but...I need a favor. You see, I love dancing with my husband, but he tends to be a little stubborn. At least, until he sees someone else dancing with me. So, if you would spin me around the room for a while...well...I think that might just get my man up on those big logs he calls feet!"

The cowboy took his disappointment with good nature. He bowed before Copper and gave Tess one last longing glance before saying, "It would be my pleasure, ma'am."

"Good answer, cowboy!" Copper teased as they stepped into a lively polka.

Tess felt the sting of tears and suddenly she knew she couldn't hold them back much longer. Over and over she kept hearing the words, Tanner's leaving—Tanner's leaving, as she made her way to the front door. For months she had focused on her prayer life and studying her Bible. Daily, she had asked God to direct her path and help her mature in her faith. She had declined every invitation to social gatherings and turned away a number of suitors. Each day she asked God for direction. And in those times, thoughts of Tanner stole quietly into her mind, and she believed that *he was* God's will for her. Now, this sudden news of his leaving confused and overwhelmed her. Throwing her winter cloak about her shoulders she was desperate to get outside before she broke into sobs—but a man was blocking her way. He was bent over like a boulder with his back to her. Tess bit down on her lip, waiting impatiently, as the man wiped the snow from his polished boots. He wore a well-tailored black suit. It wasn't extravagant like the ones Barrett Tulane was partial to, and she liked this one much better. She was surprised she even noticed this but then the man stood to his full height. She couldn't help but notice that the jacket accentuated his broad shoulders and lean muscle. Just then he turned towards her and removed his hat. Tess gasped when she saw the black hair, green eyes and handsome face of Tanner McKenna. Why had she worried that he might feel out of place or not having anything to wear. Obviously, she'd forgotten that he'd been a business man in the big city of Boston. He was a confident man, the type who would always be himself and yet still be able to fit into any setting. Be it a Boston office, a mountain hunt, training horses, sailing across the ocean or attending a Christmas ball. She couldn't stop staring, nor could she imagine a more appealing man. And although they hadn't seen each other for nearly six months, she had listened with keen interest anytime his name was mentioned. She'd heard of how he'd helped Emily fix up her new house in Colorado Springs. Helped McGee organize his account books. He had even taken Caleb and Joshua hunting up in the mountains. But as she requested, he had not called on her. He had respected her desire for solitude. But now they were finally face to face, and this wonderful, honorable man—was about to tell her that he was leaving!

Tanner stared down at her, as if he were memorizing her face. "Tess! I can't tell you how I've looked forward to seeing you!" His voice was low, his words meant for her alone, as he stepped a bit closer and took hold of her hand, "You are as enchanting as ever." His eyes were drinking her in but then Tess saw the sadness in them too. "I want to speak to you if I may but...." He slapped the large envelope against his leg, then added, "McGee said these papers were urgent. Once I've given these to him, can we talk? Maybe go someplace quiet and just talk?"

Tess stared down, focusing on their entwined hands, "I already know what you're going to say. You're leaving—aren't you."

"It's not what I want, Tess. I've been doing a lot of praying and fasting myself. You have no idea how hard I've prayed and searched for another way. But everything I've tried has fallen through. Please," Tanner glanced uneasily towards the parlor, then added, "I want to explain everything, but first I have to…"

"Son!" Shad sighed as he stepped into the foyer, "sure glad you're back. McGee's not feeling well and he's been awfully anxious to see you." Pointing to the papers in Tanner's hand he grunted, "You best be getting those to McGee. Maybe then we can get him to settle down!"

Still holding tight to Tess's hand for he couldn't bear to release her, Tanner pulled her with him as together they hurried to McGee's side. The old man had worn himself out, making the most of the evening. He'd grown tired of his wheelchair, and they found him lying on the sofa by the fireplace. Freya had covered him with his McGee plaid and propped him up on multiple pillows so he could still be a part of the festivities. Although his face was pale, he grinned as the young couple approached him. "There's me fine laddie and me bonny lassie too! I think the world of ye both."

McGee clasped Tanner's arm with such desperation it worried the younger man. "Are you all right sir?"

"Aye, fer a dying man I'm fit as a fiddle." he teased, but Tanner didn't like the glassy look in the old man's eyes. "Dinnae be lookin' so serious—for tis joy ye bring me—pure joy! Now lad, will ya fetch Pastor Long? I want him to do the readin'—that is if I cannae do it. In fact, I'd like everyone to gather round." When Quin stepped forward, McGee handed him the envelope Tanner had brought from town. "Open it for me, dear Preacher. I shall begin, but if me strength fails then will ye take over?"

Quin's expression was tender as he nodded to his old friend, then opened the envelope and withdrew the papers, "McGee," he questioned, "this is your Last Will and Testament. Surely you don't want to read this now?"

"Aye, but I do! Dinnae wish to make light of me Savior's birthday party but tis also me wake. I'm enjoyin' it so far and I want all here to know me wishes. We'll continue with the party shortly, but for now, I ask ye all to be listenin'!"

Quin helped McGee put on his spectacles and handed him the papers. The evening suddenly took on a somber note as the old man cleared his throat, then began to read his final wishes.

"Now dear friends, I want ye to remember what I've been tellin' ye fer decades, that I'm an oldish sort of fella. Passin' from this life to be with me

Lord is a grand blessin' indeed and not a thing to be mourned! So, I'm askin' ye to remember this:

All songs end with one last note.
All glorious sunsets slip into the hem of darkness.
All night skies fade with the dawn.
All petals fall from browning stems.
And—all flesh and bone must one day turn to dust.

Aye, all of that is true but truer still is the promise the Savior gave to me and all those who give their hearts to Him. That our souls live on forever under the sweet shade of His enduring love! And what a grand thing it is!

So now I say to one and all, I Tanner Aloysius McGee, being of sound mind and aging body do bequeath me earthly belongings in the following fashion:

To Cook, Dallas and Freya, I leave two hundred dollars each and to each of the ranch hands I leave a gold-eagle as thanks for yer hard work and loyalty. Tis me prayer and belief that the new owners will choose to keep all you good people here at the ranch fer as long as it pleases ye."

Whispered murmurs flew about the room, "New owners?" It was widely known that McGee had no heirs. And for years folks had speculated about what would become of the Stubborn Scotsman Ranch.

Quin cleared his throat and when the room grew silent again, the old man nodded his thanks then continued, "To the Grainger lads, who have always brought me great joy. I leave to Caleb me fiddle and to Joshua me mandolin. Ye both have done well to learn the wee bits I could teach ye. Also, in the library there is a box of book fer each of ye. Heed an old man's advice, love God first, then people! And yet, dear lads, don't forget to cherish learning and music as well. But keep them in that order lads…in that order!"

The boys were touched to be remembered and blushed as everyone laughed at McGee's additional advice. When Quin looked around the room again, then back at McGee, indicating that there was more, everyone grew still and listened, "To dear Shadrack and Copper McKenna who quickly became like a son and a daughter. I leave ye me first wee cabin near the lake and waterfall. It was as close as I could get to replacing yer little bit of heaven. And now, as to who will inherit the Stubborn Scotsman. As dear Cook would say, 'I'm fixin' to do some meddlin'. Tanner Angus McKenna, I loved yer grandfather like a brother. Had things been different though, you might have been me own grandson. Although I have nae known ye for long, I've been prayin' fer your family a verra long time. You and your Pa are fine men and I'm right proud of ye both! I look forward to getting' to heaven and tellin' Maudy and Angus how God worked mightily and brought us all together. Mayhap they're even now lookin' down and laughin' with joy! For it was pure joy for me the day God and my sweet Tessie May brought the McKennas down that mountain and answered an old man's prayers. I have praised and thanked my most generous God every day since. Just in case ye haven't figured out just how mightily God has been at work...well...this is where the meddlin' comes in. Tessie May Grainger, my sweet bonny lassie, ye have a gift with horses and I've seen that same gift in Tanner McKenna. It's clear to all and mayhap even to ye two, that ye were meant for a double harness. Meant to be life-long partners and helpmates! And so, I am leaving the Stubborn Scotsman to ye both. The bank has the deed already signed over to ye. And may God bless ye and keep ye safe always and forever!"

Tanner and Tess were still holding hands as they stared at the old man in disbelief, then their eyes locked on each other.

McGee sat up a bit and clucked his tongue, "I dinnae ken what else to do fer ye, Laddie!" he fussed, "must I propose fer ye, and kiss the bonny lassie too?"

There was low chuckling around the room as Tanner grinned and turned Tess to face him. Never taking his eyes from her he said, "No sir, I think I can do this on my own. Tess," he said softly, "from the first moment I saw you, I believed that you were God's answer to all my prayers. Then when everything I tried fell through, I feared that I must have been mistaken, not about you, but perhaps about the timing. I haven't been very subtle, I think you've known all along how I feel about you. These past six months, I've honored your desire to spend time alone with God. To seek His direction. So what has He been telling you?"

Tess placed her hand on Tanner's cheek, her eyes bright as she said softly, "That I should love God with my whole heart and that I should love you now and forever. I've wanted to be with you from the very start too! And it really doesn't matter, rich or poor, ranch or not. My dream now is only for us to be together, loving each other and serving God. However, and wherever He leads. I just want us to be together, no matter what!"

Tanner grinned, "I've wanted to ask you this when I first heard you singing in the meadow. My darling Tess, will you marry me? And marry me soon?"

Happy tears filled her eyes as she whispered, "Oh yes, Tanner, very soon!"

It wasn't the intimate moment either of them had dreamt of but just then it seemed as if a private curtain had been drawn around them. Tanner took Tess's face in his hands, leaned down and kissed her with all the longing and love he possessed! And Tess kissed him back in the exact same way!

Chapter 21

Wedding

"So we fasted and petitioned our God about this, and he answered our prayer." Ezra 8:23

"Now glory be to God who by His mighty power at work within us is able to do far more than we would ever dare to ask or even dream of—infinitely beyond our highest prayers, desires, thoughts or hopes." Ephesians 3:20

It was the last day of the year, and the beautiful church in Colorado Springs was bubbling over with excited guests and well-wishers. Tytus glanced into the sanctuary and nodded his approval. Everything looked beautiful. The front doors, foyer, sanctuary and hallways were still decorated for Christmas. Tess had requested that everything be kept the same for the wedding and the church staff had been happy to oblige. It was both elegant and festive. Every door, stained glass window and pew were adorned with wreaths made of holly and evergreen boughs bound with gold and white ribbons.

Ty made his way down the aisle, then stepped into the small room next to the front foyer of the church. He knew Tess would be waiting there, but when he saw her, there just were no words for how he felt. She was standing before an arched window as golden rays of sunlight shone all around her, like a benediction from on high. Just then she glanced over at him and smiled. Ty knew he would never forget how very blue her eyes seemed just then, or the way her golden curls fell over one shoulder. He knew this precious memory would be added to a thousand others. His mind went back to the little pixie who could outride most of the ranch hands by the time she was ten. To that sweet, strong willed girl, who had always been able to wrap him around her finger. Still, he knew he would hold today's memories especially close to his heart, just as he did the memory of her as a curly-headed cherub. Then too, she had been bathed in rays of sunlight. But on that day, she was trying to pluck the dust fairies from mid-flight as they swirled beyond her grasp. Today she was reaching out for her future. Both times she had smiled at him and stolen his heart.

These were typical thoughts for a father perhaps, but anyone with eyes would have described Tess as an enchanting vision that day. She was wearing the same gown her mother wore when she married her father Timothy Grainger. It was a deep, almost bronze shade of ivory satin, with a high collar at the nape of her neck and lapels tapering down, ending in a 'V' at her small waist. A delicate netting spread across her bodice making the dress both alluring and modest. The skirt was gathered in a series of soft folds on either side, held with tiny clusters of satin orange blossoms. Yards of Venetian lace made up her veil and was held in place by an exquisitely delicate wreath. Her necklace and earrings were the same pearls her Papa Tim had bought for her mother over twenty-two years earlier.

Gazing in wonder, Ty groaned, "Ah, Little Bit, my sweet girl. You... look like...like every bride should!" He was finding it nearly impossible to get the words past the lump in his throat, "I look at you and I see all the people I've loved most in this world. I see you, my dear Little Bit, but I also see Tim, your father and my brother, and I see your beautiful Mama. Tess, you've matured into an amazing woman—a godly woman. Timothy would be so proud of his girl today. Just as I am! I've never felt him so much with us...as I have today."

"Yes, I know what you mean," Tess sighed, as she brushed her hands down her gown. "As I put on Mama's dress and veil, I couldn't help but think about how she and Papa Tim married the day after they met. And then for him to die so suddenly, so tragically. I can't imagine how Mama must have suffered that first year. Then you two fell in love! I've always thought your love story was almost...unbelievable. That is until I experienced my own love story. It was nothing short of a miracle the way I met the McKennas and how Tanner came into my life...our lives!"

"He's a fine young man, Tess. It's not easy giving you away but knowing that you have a man like him...well...it helps a lot."

Tess laughed, "We will also be your closest neighbors, Papa."

Ty grinned, "That helps too!"

Throwing her arms around him, she sighed, "I love you and Mama so much, and I am so very much in love with Tanner! I'm very blessed. I marvel at how God changed the course of my life. And how He worked through and around Grandma Lavenia's treachery. She meant to destroy us, but God turned it all about for good…didn't He? Had we not gone through all of this, I might never have become a Christian. Sweet McGee might not have found the McKennas. Tanner could be back in Boston or sailing around the world right now. If I hadn't lived through all the events of this year, I'd find it impossible to believe. And today, I'm going to become Missus Tanner McKenna." Tess suddenly sighed and looked out the window, "Speaking of which, I can't imagine what's keeping Shad and Copper? McGee looked well last night but they planned to get him here early so he could rest a bit before the ceremony." Turning back to Ty she sighed, "I'm getting a little worried. McGee always insists on being early and the McKennas would never be late for their own son's wedding. Not unless something was wrong!"

Just then one of the ushers knocked on the door and he said in a loud whisper, "Missus McKenna says everyone is in place. If you're ready we can begin now!"

Tess laughed, "I'm definitely ready!"

A few moments later the organist began the wedding march and the doors to the sanctuary were opened. Tess's heart quickened the moment she saw Tanner. His smile just then, seemed brighter than the sun that was shining through the windows. He had been praying for this day for a dozen years and his joy was so evident that everyone in the church found themselves smiling with him. His loving gaze was for Tess alone though, and it drew her to him. She hastened her step, but Ty held her back, whispering, "Slow down Little Bit. From the look on that man's face, he's not going anywhere, not unless you're with him."

When they reached the end of the aisle Tess rose up on tip-toe and kissed her father's cheek. This had not been rehearsed and Ty clenched his jaw as his vision grew hazy. It was a small gesture, but it meant the world to him. He gave Tess's hand one last gentle squeeze, then released her into Tanner's strong grasp and stepped away. The coupled smiled at each other as their fingers instantly entwined. Just then Tanner let out such a sigh of relief that everyone in the church heard it. Those who knew his story understood…but everyone laughed.

Though he refrained from doing so, Quin wanted to sigh long and loud himself. He'd never looked so forward to performing a wedding as he had this one! But just now he stood before them not as their, Uncle Quin, but as Reverend Long. He smiled at them both then said, "We've come to celebrate

246

the joining of two very special hearts! A wedding should be the happiest of times but it is also a sober and solemn occasion. A time where two people dedicate themselves to a lifelong commitment. A three way commitment of a man and woman bound together in Christ." Quin led them through their wedding vows and when he finally announced that they were husband and wife, Tanner could not wait for Preacher Long to say his next line.

"Can I kiss her now, Uncle Quin?" he asked.

The whole church laughed and Quin grinned, "Son, you've been praying for this day a long time, you just haul off and give your bride a kiss she'll always remember!"

And that is exactly what Tanner did! A cheer when up from all the guests and then they applauded! What a wonderful way to begin the new year!

Later everyone gathered together for an elegant dinner and reception held at the Antlers Hotel. It was a wonderful evening but after the cake was cut, and Filippa had caught Tess's bouquet, it was time for the celebration to come to an end. Just then Shad gave Tanner and Tess a questioning look. When they nodded their approval, he tapped his knife against his water glass to get everyone's attention, then his voice boomed, "FOLKS! I have somethin' I'd like to say. This is a very special day and it's been evident to the ones who know these two best, that God has been working in their lives in mighty ways! As it happened Copper and I witnessed something else today that showed forth the mighty ways of God! I hesitated to speak of it here and now, but the newly married Mister and Misses McKenna have asked me to share it with you all tonight. We all have known Tanner McGee as a wise, talented and generous man. Our own son was named after him because he and my father grew up together as dear friends. Later he even saved my mother's life. It was a miraculous answer to prayer, that we were able to meet up with Tanner McGee after so many decades apart. McGee loved people and he loved God. His powerful faith was evident throughout his life and I might add—even more profoundly—at his death." Shad paused as the guests took in his words, "Yes, our dear friend Tanner McGee, went home to be with Jesus just this mornin'. Now you all are probably thinkin' this ain't the kind of news to be shared on such a happy occasion. But the fact is, McGee's home going was one of the most joyful events Copper and I have ever witnessed. We went to McGee's room this mornin' to help him prepare for the weddin' but found him pale and weak. He couldn't even lift his head from the pillow. Even so, he greeted us with a smile and these words, (just then Shad mimicked the Scottish accent of his parents, sounding very much like McGee himself), 'Tis the bonniest mornin' of me life!" he said, "A grand thing it is, to be waitin' fer the angels of heaven to come and fetch ye home. Will nae be long before I see me Savior Jesus Christ! Aye, and you tell that lad and sweet lassie, that old McGee will be sharin' in their joy. Tell them how happy I am and how vexed I'll be if there be tears on this grand day. I would nae miss their weddin' fer the world, but I ken the Lord has a better seat in mind.'"

Shad stopped and shook his head, "As you can imagine, his words tired him out and he fell into a deep sleep. Copper and I sat on either side of him, each holding a hand while Freya, Cook and Dallas, stood around the bed. It wasn't long before his breathing grew more and more shallow and we expected each breath to be his last. What happened next, none of us had ever seen before, nor will we ever forget. As I said, McGee, had lost every ounce of his strength and was just barely breathing. Then his eyes flew open and I tell ya, that man sat straight up in bed, with no help at all, and never in my life have I seen such true joy on anyone's face. It was a radiance I don't reckon could be described this side of heaven! Of course, we all knew that he was seeing wonders that we could only imagine. Before his words came out as a raspy whisper, but at that moment, his voice was as strong as a man of twenty, and he said, 'Aye, I've been waiting fer ye, Lord. Tis so grand—all so verra grand! Thank ye Jesus!'"

A reverent silence fell over everyone as they contemplated the special old man's miraculous home going.

Then Shad continued, "Those were the last words of our friend, Tanner McGee. As suddenly as he sat up, his body fell just as quickly back onto the pillows. We found no pulse nor did he draw another breath. We all loved McGee, and we'll all miss him. But it seems like blasphemy to be sad right now! For we know for certain that our dear friend just stepped away from us and straight into the arms of Jesus." Shad stopped, marveling at what he'd experienced and allowing the others time to ponder this for themselves. "Sometimes friends, it's far too easy to take God's power and love for granted. We often downplay our faith in God as well as our belief in both heaven and hell. Jesus said it himself: 'Blessed are they that have not seen, and yet have believed.' Still, like today, I have known times where we are given a glimpse of God at work. To watch Him actively answering our prayers." Shad laid his hand on Tanner's shoulder, "Son, your mother and I have seen God at work in you. It has humbled us to watch your faithfulness as you have prayed for God to reveal His will for your life and to guide you to your helpmate. To hear your prayers for God to watch over your wife, whoever she was, wherever she might be, and to bring you together when the time was right." Shad glanced up to include all the guests, "Some of you may think this wedding was a bit rushed. Tanner proposed on Christmas Eve, and here their wedding is on New Year's Eve! But what you may not know is that God's been doin' the courtin' for them! He has been at work preparing these two for each other, for quite some time now." Just then Shad took Tess's hand, "Did you know that Tanner often went to pray on one certain spot on the side of the mountain? I went with him to pray a few times and he always kneeled beside a special rock facing east." A grin came over Shad's face, "Straight as the crow flies from Tanner's favorite spot—lies a ranch called—the Bar 61. Tanner didn't know it, but God was pointing his prayers to cover his bride all those years before you two met. The way God has brought ya both together, the way yer faith has grown so quickly Tess—it's all a mighty testament to God's abundant grace. And also, the way Copper and I loved you like a daughter, even before you met our boy. Now today, the way old McGee went home so God could give him the perfect seat for yer weddin'. This is one of those rare and special times when God has allowed us to see Him at work." Tanner and Tess smiled at each other and locked hands as Shad continued, "Now that you two have finally found each other and have said your vows, keep all these miracles close to your hearts. Never forget all that's happened, allow these memories to strengthen you both in the years to come!"

EPILOGUE

Thirteen years & seven months later...

Bar 61-Colorado
July 4, 1900

"Through the power of the Holy Spirit who lives within us, carefully guard the precious truth that has been entrusted to you."
2 Timothy 1:14

Even before dawn split the horizon there was a flurry of preparations. The ranch was always a busy and noisy place, much more so on the day of a party! This party, however, was singularly unique, it was July fourth, nineteen-hundred. As the guests arrived and the day wore on, no one could remember a happier or more perfect day. It was gloriously sunny, without being too hot. As if ordered just for the occasion, a constant breeze slipped down from the mountains. Like invisible pine scented feathers, it lazily floated over everyone as it cooled the red cheeks of children at play, and lifted the spirits of all those it brushed against.

As evening drew near, five weary but contented women rested under the shade of the hacienda's wrap around porch. Tess sat on the steps near her mother, while Augusta sat in a line of rocking chairs amongst her dearest friends, Emily Tulane and Mariah Long on one side and Copper McKenna on the other. Copper of course was Tess's mother-in-law but she was also her closest friend. It had been a long, wonderful day and the best part of it was yet to come. Of course, they had all unanimously agreed that the annual fourth of July festivities at the Bar 61, had to be bigger and better than ever. It was, after all, the very first Independence Day, in a brand-new century! All their children and grand-children, along with their neighbor's children and grand-children were there. Everyone playing games and stuffing themselves with barbequed beef cooked over a pit.

Not to mention the decadent array of trimmings. There were rolls and cornbread, potato salad, casseroles, pies, cakes, watermelon and everyone's favorite treat, hand-cranked ice cream. It was the usual fare for a typical fourth of July feast, plus a little more!

Augusta fanned herself with the red, white and blue paper fans the children had made especially for that day. "Every time we give a party, my mind always takes me back to that very first one," she mused. "Crazy and miraculous from start to finish. I wasn't even nineteen, and I still can't believe I challenged the dragon of the Bar 61, to an arm wrestling match of all things!" Shaking her head, she added, "Of course, he let me win…and I think that surprised him…as much as it did everyone else! We were barely speaking to each other at the time. It shocked all of us, when he agreed to host that first party." Augusta's expression was full of memories as she added, "So much happened and everything changed so drastically between those two events."

Tess laughed, "I should say so! An arm wrestling match, followed by a kidnapping, then the first party at the ranch, ending with the host and hostess getting married. And just think of all the parties that have followed." Tess suddenly frowned and tugged on her mother's skirt, "By the way, Mama, you know I love hearing that story. But could you wait a few years before telling it to your granddaughter? Colleen may only be five years old but she's already a force to be reckoned with, and she doesn't need either of her grannies giving her ideas. She's half her brothers' age and half their size, but that doesn't seem to slow her down. Not one little bit!"

"Goodness, but Colleen is a darlin' little imp…isn't she?" Copper laughed, "but I can assure you that neither of us grandmothers encourage her antics. Although, I guess I should take some of the blame. She did inherit my red hair and you know what they say about us red heads."

"Copper McKenna, you are not foolin' us! You love that she's got your red hair and don't you deny it!" Mariah teased.

Then Emily added, "That's right and she's also got the McKennas green eyes. But she has Augusta's nose and the Grainger dimple!"

Tess giggled, "You all make my daughter sound like a patchwork quilt." Then she looked up at Mariah, "Colleen loves it when your Abigail comes to visit. You're a wonderful mother to her, and you've given her such a happy home."

Mariah's lavender eyes lit with a contented glow, "Thank you, Tess, Quin and I love her so much. It doesn't seem like it's been four years since we adopted her. We'd given up on ever being parents, and feared we were too old to take on a year-old baby. It's been wonderful though. Of course, we had God's help and with all the extra hands at Wings, we've managed very well. In fact—I've been just bursting to tell you all our news but there's been so much going on today."

"What?" everyone asked at the same time.

"Well," she grinned, "it seems God is—blessing us again! Tomorrow mornin' we're headed to Denver to adopt another child!"

Happy gasps spread around this circle of special friends, followed by a dozen questions, "How did you hear about this child? How old is it? Is it a boy or girl?"

Mariah laughed, as her face shown with excitement, "Well, give me a minute and I'll tell what I know. A dear friend of ours had his granddaughter living with him. It's an all too familiar story. Her husband liked to drink and afterwards he always became mean and abusive. He's in jail now. We had offered to bring her up to Wings but sadly she died in childbirth. Neighbors are helping him with the baby, but it's only a temporary solution. He sent a telegram asking if we would adopt the baby but he didn't say if it was a girl or boy! We're just like every other parent, just getting what God thinks is best. Of course, it's very sad about the mother, and it doesn't look like the father will be getting out of jail any time soon. Still, their little one will have a wonderful big sister in Abigail. And Quin and I have plenty of love for another child! So, the next time you see the Longs we'll be a family of four."

Instantly there was a tangle of hugs and happy tears. As things settled down, Tess spoke for all of them, "Well, that's a blessed little baby to have you and Uncle Quin as Mama and Papa! You know, we're getting to be a pretty big bunch when we all get together. Tanner and I have our three, Caleb and Joshua each have their three. Counting this new baby…that's twenty-three! We are definitely a growing family!"

"What's all this about a growing family?" Quin teased. His handsome face wore a broad grin as he took the porch steps two at a time. He gave Mariah a quick wink then added, "Well, I see you ladies have your hankies out. I can only assume that you've heard our news!"

Quin barely had time to say the words when suddenly, he was the one receiving hugs and the hankies were employed all over again. Finally, Quin held up his hand, "Now, you mustn't distract me, I'm here on a mission. We men have everything ready for our evening festivities to begin." Offering an arm to both Mariah and Tess, he grinned at the other three women, adding, "Just follow me—dear ladies!"

The bronze-colored sun was slipping behind the mountain as everyone headed towards an open field beside a large pond. Blankets and benches had been set out facing the water. Shooting the fireworks over the pond kept the risk of fire down, plus the reflection in the water doubled their splendor! Beside the pond stood a makeshift stage, created from a long hay wagon decorated with bunting of red, white and blue.

It had been a wonderful day, and yet sunset against the mountains always seemed to take on a dreamlike quality, as the sun silently began slipping away. Above them floated thin striated clouds, every one awash in vibrant colors painted across the sky, in pink and peach and cranberry. In the midst of this glorious sunset, everyone found their places. Benches were saved for the elders in the group while the younger ones sat together on blankets. Sparks of excitement and expectation vibrated through the air, for they were all eager to enjoy this final time of celebration!

Tess's heart quickened as it always did when she spotted Tanner walking across the field. He was as handsome as ever, still tanned and powerfully built from time spent in the sun training his horses. When he purposely caught her eye, and received her nod of encouragement, he seemed noticeably relieved.

He gave her a quick wink just before he jumped up onto the wagon bed, cleared his throat and grinned, "Happy Fourth of July everyone!" His deep voice seemed to encompass the meadow, and when the crowd responded in kind, he continued, "This annual Independence Day celebration has always been one of my favorite days of the year. I don't say it often enough, but it's been a true blessing to be raised in a God honoring family. But I am twice blessed, for I also married into such a family. In both my families, regardless of the occasion, we always make sure to give God a chance to have a voice in the celebration. As is our tradition, we'll sing a few of our favorite hymns and hear from God's word. After that, we'll enjoy some fireworks and square dancing. Now you're probably wondering why my Pa or Tytus or Uncle Quin aren't standing here right now?" Tanner ducked his head and shrugged, "This year those good men informed me that since we're entering a new century, they were passing the torch to me!" he grinned self-consciously, then glanced at Cal and Josh, "for this year anyway. So, as our old friend Tanner McGee used to say, 'It is time to bid farewell to the day and call up the moon and the stars.'" He nodded once again to Caleb and Joshua who were also sitting up on the wagon. Cal picked up his violin and Josh his mandolin. The first song was the same ancient Scottish ballad that old McGee always played first. The melody was so sweet and so beautiful, it seemed to overshadow the entire valley and for a time every man and beast went still. When the last note fell silent it was followed by a reverent pause. Then Cal and Josh began playing a medley of lively patriotic hymns with everyone singing the songs by heart. When the music stopped, Tanner stood up to share his message.

"Independence Day, Nineteen Hundred, it doesn't seem possible but here we are, in a new century with many changes ahead. This is the verse I believe God wants me to share with you on this special day," Tanner opened his Bible and read from second Chronicles, chapter seven, verse fourteen. 'If my people, who are called by my name, will humble themselves and pray, and seek my face, and turn from their wicked ways, then I will hear from heaven, and I will forgive their sin and will heal their land.'" Tanner closed the Bible and gazed out at all the people he loved most in the world, "Our great Father in Heaven asks us to pray, and if we do, He promises to hear from heaven! When this nation fought for independence, we fought for freedom. Freedom from tyranny and oppression but also to gain the freedom to worship and pray to our God as we choose. I fear that we take these precious rights for granted. And at times we may even wonder, does prayer really make a difference? YES, I can attest to the fact that in my own life, I have learned that prayer changes things! In first James, chapter five, verse 14 it says 'This is the confidence we have in approaching God: that if we ask anything according to his will, he hears us.' Furthermore, I know that God *always* answers." Tanner looked down at his own three young ones. Gabe was twelve, Luke was ten and little Colleen was five. They were sitting on the blanket, cuddled close to Tess. He grinned at them, then added, "I prayed for my wife, my sweet Tess, for so many years. God didn't say no...but for a long time he said...not yet! Just like we as parents must say yes, no or not yet to our own children. My life is a testament to answered prayer. My Pa and Ma have such a wonderful marriage. I grew up watching them working together and loving each other and I longed for that kind of relationship for myself. It was my sweet red-headed mama that gave me the best advice. 'Son,' she said, 'it's never too soon to pray. So, start now, pray for her, pray for her family, pray that she'll love God with her whole heart. Ask Him to watch over her and keep her safe. In the meantime, you be sure to ask *God* to prepare *you as well,* to be the best man you can be.'" So, I began praying for Tess and the Graingers when I was ten years old. Of course, I didn't know their names or where they lived. But God knew! You see I had a mountain lookout, my favorite place to pray and it looked down onto this very valley. Turns out, I was sending my prayers right over this ranch. Just a coincidence? No, I believe God was quietly at work, directing a young boy's prayers!" Tanner locked eyes with Tess again, "God moved mightily in Tess's life as well. She went through quite a time of testing and she came through it a strong godly woman. Had she not gone through that trial, we wouldn't have been right for each other. Our marriage, of thirteen years, is a tribute to the fact that God does indeed answer prayer. The way God led Tess to me and the way He answered both our prayers for a horse ranch was—nothing short of miraculous! But folks, God is God and He chooses to answer our prayers in His own way and in His own good time. It took a dozen years for God to answer my prayers for Tess. Tanner McGee prayed for decades to find us McKennas. God wasn't being cruel to make him wait. The timing just had to be right. What I'm trying to share with you is, that leading up to these events are the tracks of faithful prayers lifted to God and His response to them! I know among you all there are some strong prayer warriors. It's not hard to spot a prayer warrior, just look for the tracks they leave behind." Tanner grinned, "Ah, I see you're all wondering about that. Growing up in the mountains, my Pa taught me a lot about tracking." Tanner locked eyes with his father, "Pa, I remember you saying, 'Everything leaves tracks, even the wind.' I thought you were teasing me, but you explained that long after the wind stops you can tell which direction it blew. Just look at the snow drifts or the way a tree is bent by a prevailing wind." He paused for a few moments then smiled, "I think you're wondering—what's my point? Well, it seems to me that prayer and the wind are alike. You can't see either one, but you can see their influence on the things they touch. They both leave tracks! Lives and circumstances are changed because of prayer. And yes, sometimes it takes a heap of praying before you see any changes at all. But I say, don't give up! Sometimes God works through prayer to change—things. Sometimes, the act of praying, is meant only to change *us!* Time spent with God is never wasted. Today I want to encourage each of you to take God's command to pray seriously. Pray for yourselves, your families, your friends, and pray for our country!"

Grinning broadly, he said, "Now, as we light the fireworks to celebrate God's grace over this great nation and over us, let us be committed to pray. Let us leave tracks others can follow and be encouraged by. Knowing that your prayers will make a difference, lift them up to God and they will be like the... *Tracks of the Wind!*"

THE END

The greatest man in history, had no servants, yet they
called him Master.
Had no degree, yet they called him Teacher.
Had no medicines, yet they called him Healer.
He had no army, yet kings feared Him.
He won no military battles, yet He conquered the world.
He committed no crime, yet they crucified Him.
He was buried in a tomb, yet He lives today.
Author Unknown

His name is Jesus.

**My prayer is that in the pages of this book you have
come to know Him.**

Now, please don't reach for another book just yet.
There are Discussion Points on the next page followed by
Prologue Previews of the first two books in the Colorado Trilogy.

Giant in the Valley
&
Wings on the Mountain

I would love to hear your comments about this Colorado Trilogy.
You can reach me at: lfaulknercorzine@gmail.com

Or please visit my website at: lfaulknercorzine.com

DISCUSSION POINTS

1. **Tess Grainger, T. Barrett Tulane and Tanner McKenna were all raised in Christian homes. Why were they so different?**

   So often we desire for our children to experience none of our hardships but all of our blessings. Can they really learn appreciation without knowing hardships or want? Do you think Barrett Tulane would have turned out better if he'd been raised peeling onions in a Missouri Café or was he truly just a bad seed? Is it possible that some people are born bad? Discuss the possibilities.

2. **The importance of God's word!**

   They say train up a child in the way they should go. How did having memory verses help Tess? Is the Bible still as useful now as it was centuries ago in giving us direction and knowledge from God?

3. **Is immorality still a sin?**

   If something has become acceptable to society does that mean it has also become acceptable to God? Does God's code of morality change with each generation? What does He expect from us?

4. **What do you think about seeking God's will for your life partner?**

   Is there someone out there just for you? What do you think about fasting from dating and allowing God to bring the right person into your circle?

5. **Have you ever experienced God turning something bad into something good?**

   Discuss times when a hardship was turned into a blessing. Do you think God might have been teaching you an important lesson during these difficult times? What things have you learned while living through a season of hardships?

   I would love to hear your comments and suggestions.
   Please e-mail me at: lfaulknercorzine@gmail.com

PROLOGUE PREVIEWS

COLORADO TRILOGY – BOOK ONE
GIANT IN THE VALLEY

PROLOGUE
Colorado–1865

"God helps the righteous and delivers them from the plots of evil men." Psalm 37:40

Her golden eyes reflected in the window glass as she watched and waited in the dark. Finally, she saw it: the quick strike of a match, a bare wink of flame, and then it was gone. Quietly, she slipped from the house like a shadow, and made her way to the secluded arbor in her back garden.

The man waiting for her was dirty and saddle weary. Dressed in dark buckskins, he wore a double brace of pistols and his boots bore heavy Mexican spurs with long, sharp rowels. His grizzled face looked even more fierce in the moonlight. Brazenly, she met his cold gray eyes as he glared at her from under the wide brim of his hat.

Taking the thick envelope, she placed in his outstretched hand, he cursed her and grumbled, "I'm callin' it quits—ain't doin' no more jobs fer ya. Done workin' fer a woman!"

His disdain meant nothing to her. Instead, a sly smile played about her rosy lips and her eyes flashed with a look of evil anticipation. Moving closer, her velvety voice became animated as she whispered, "If that's what you want. But remember? You still owe me! You promised you would help me—and then—you would bring her to me—when the timing was right. Well—my sources tell me that he won't be able to protect her much longer. And—if things continue as planned, that worthless little *mistake*...will be delivered right into our hands!"

Then her dark-rimmed, golden eyes sparkled as her countenance turned from malicious to venomous, as she hissed:

"It's going to be…almost…too easy. It's only fitting—after all, she ruined my life, my dreams. And now—I'm going to turn her life—into a nightmare!"

PROLOGUE PREVIEW

COLORADO TRILOGY – BOOK TWO
WINGS ON THE MOUNTAIN

PROLOGUE
Texas -1860

The fog shifted and swirled about Dirk Culley as he walked through the moonlit forest. He waited in the shadows, watching the old gypsy woman, as she sat on a stool and warmed herself beside a crackling fire. She couldn't have known he was there, but suddenly she looked through the fog and with her gnarled hand, beckoned him to come closer. Her face was ancient, but her eyes were fiercely perceptive, dark and keen. They seemed to look right into his soul as they stared up at him.

"Sit down young man, I have been expecting you." Her voice was deep, her words heavily accented. "I have had dreams about you. There are things I must tell you...and warnings I must give."

He paid little attention at first, just an old woman's words for a young man's ears. Easily spoken and more easily forgotten. Then, as the fog and the smoke curled about the old woman's head, her words captured him!

"My first warning is one you must heed. If you trifle with a married woman, it will bring disaster upon you! I say this first, because I have dreamt of two women who will cross your path." She stared off into the forest, her dark eyes a glow in the firelight, as if she could see the days and years to come. "One will have hair the color of sunset and eyes as green as clover. She will lead you to something important! Something—I think of great value. The other woman stands in the light, and in my dreams, she stands so close to you that I cannot see her clearly. All I see is that she wears a band of gold on her left hand, and she is covering a wound. Red blood is bubbling up through her fingers. I do not know if this blood is her blood or yours—and yet I know this wound will cause you great pain. It will also lead to great danger and death, to some who you know well!"

Dirk scowled as he stared into the fire, not knowing what to think of the old woman and her strange words.

Gently touching his arm, she added, "There is one more thing I will tell you. Then you must go—for my people do not trust you. When these women come into your life, they will force you to face a great darkness—a darkness you have feared all your life! The outcome, however, will be of your choosing, for these women will lead you either to your ruination or to your salvation!"

"There before me were two women, with the wind in their wings." Zechariah 5:9